The FOREST where the PHOENIX SLEEPS

BOOK ONE

BROOKE MARLEY JONES

First edition

ISBN: 978-1-7383251-0-8

Cover art by Eeva Nikunen

Formatting by Rae Davennor of Stardust Book Services

For Matthew,
In this story you'll find magic on every page.
And yet, it still falls short of how I feel every day,
with you.

PART ONE

WORLD NEWS

75 Men Die Mysteriously in West Virginia Hospital

Victims Found 'lying bizarrely on the floor, like they fell out of bed and died'

B. Gummer · Real News · Posted: October 30, 2023 8:31 AM EDT | Last Updated: 1 hour ago

CHARLESTON, WEST VIRGINIA - Police say a man was discovered deceased in his room at Memorial Hospital, just after 3 a.m. A second victim was found shortly thereafter, prompting a search of the facility. By 3:30 a.m., all male patients staying in Memorial Hospital were confirmed deceased, at which point, the hospital was evacuated.

"It was scary," said survivor, Calie Ahmed. "All the bodies were lying bizarrely on the floor, like they fell out of bed and died."

An unidentified seven-year-old was the only witness to alleged foul play, having woken when she heard struggling in the adjacent room. "Something came into my room," the seven-year-old said. "But I kept my eyes closed. I couldn't look at it. I knew if I looked at it, it would kill me."

When questioned about the seven-year-old's claims, Chief of Police Steven Brown stated, "The witness was heavily sedated at the time."

Investigations into cause of death are being undertaken. Police attempted to retrieve surveillance footage, which had reportedly been deleted. A data recovery team is on-site.

"I haven't seen anything like it before, but we've got an

experienced team here and we will find out what happened to these men," Brown said in a statement.

Police are asking anyone with information to come forward.

Chapter One

crumble from bed and grumble to the kitchen

Al good things start with coffee.

A lazy Sunday morning.

A date with an old friend.

A book.

I stood in the dim kitchen, rubbing a knuckle at my eye. The clock on the stove read 6:14 a.m. The coffee machine, often filled with a deliciously dark liquid, looked curiously transparent. As if it contained only warm water. My sleep-deprived brain worked through the problem.

I'd forgotten to add grounds the night before.

I stared at the machine.

"You piece of shit," I said out loud.

More to myself than the machine.

I left for work early, locking my apartment and carefully climbing down the janky stairs to the back alley. I lived above a café, and after this morning's debacle, I needed my coffee to-go. Except, instead of going, I'd stay…because I worked there. My boss, Morgan, owned the café and apartment. She gave me a sweet deal on rent and, in return, if she ever needed someone to work last minute, she knew where to find me. And before you ask—no. For me, there is *no* work-life balance.

I'm twenty-six *and* I'm single.

I can't afford to turn down work—not in this economy.

Holding my breath, I hurried down the alley. The historic shops that lined the main street, while beautiful, were built tightly together. That meant I couldn't sneak between buildings to get to work. No, I had to walk behind them, through a trash-laden murder alley.

Reaching the end, I inhaled fresh, garbage-free air.

"Agh!" I recoiled as a gust of wind spewed crunchy leaves in my face. "Pth," I spit, picking bits from my lip. I rounded the corner and doubled back along the main street.

Despite our Niagara location, the town looked as if it were moved stone-by-stone, and brick-by-brick from Europe. In the summertime, tourists flocked to the quaint little boutiques, restaurants, and theatres. I slowed by a white-washed brick building with pink shutters, the word, *Aroma*, printed lavishly above the door. Candles filled the window, all boasting aggressively autumnal scents like *Crisp Fall Nights* and *Harvest Apple Pie*. As the end of October approached, the flower beds that lined the cobbled streets, bursting with marigolds and petunias in the summer months, lay barren. The horse-drawn carriages that sat outside the gingerbread-trimmed hotel were gone.

The town slept.

Perhaps that's why I favoured autumn. I adored the décor in the shop windows, perfect mirrors as the trees changed colour. But I liked the peace and quiet best of all. As I marched to work in silence, not a single tourist stopped me to ask, *"Where is the Lakeside Carousel?"* while standing so close to the Lakeside Carousel that they could touch the Lakeside Carousel.

I passed *Chapeau*, a boutique filled with bright, fanciful hats made of felt and feathers. I'd gone in once, caught sight of a price tag, and fled. During my walks, I admired the hats from this side of the glass. They were accessories for pretty people at weddings and brunches.

But not for me.

Beside *Chapeau* was the café. The sign featured Morgan's surname: *Rousseau's*. I overshot it and peered in the window next door. A display of horror novels beckoned me. Classics with redesigned covers: *The Legend of Sleepy Hollow* and *The Haunting of Hill House*. These were interspersed with newer titles, monopolized by Stephen King. A Joe Hill thrown in for *diversity*. I'd read all of them, save the newest King.

The ending would be terrible.

I'd probably buy it later this week.

Stroking the glass, I whispered, "I'll come back for you."

Trudging back to *Rousseau's*, I unlocked the door and slipped inside. I ducked beneath a giant monstera leaf that threatened to behead those unfamiliar with the café. Morgan had a particular fondness for tropicals. All around, cacti and bright green philodendrons popped against the rustic bricks and white tiles. Though I adored the style, it was a feat I could never achieve myself. Plants often succumbed to neglect in my care. In fact, Morgan specifically forbid me from going anywhere *near* her plants, a few of which still hadn't recovered from an incident we affectionately referred to as the 'Great Drought', which occurred shortly after I was hired.

Weaving through tables, I sidestepped a Chinese evergreen as I rounded the counter. Once I'd prepped and poured myself a coffee, I sat down with a well-read copy of *The Martian*.

Perfect. Everything I need to relax and read.

I set my phone amongst the pages. News out of West Virginia dominated my feed. Apparently, seventy-five men dropped dead in a hospital down there, and no one had any idea what happened.

"I found my patient on his stomach," a nurse said, appearing anxious in an interview. "But uh—his head was twisted all the away around, like it was on backwards." Unease crept upon me as the nurse shook her head helplessly. "I don't know what could have done that."

Could it have anything to do with the other stories?

An erratic burst of laughter echoed from the street. Setting my phone aside, I tucked whatever scrap of garbage I'd used as a bookmark back into *The Martian*. Somehow, even though I'd arrived thirty minutes early, I hadn't managed to get any reading done. I popped an Advil from my bag and took a swig of coffee.

Jangling bells ended my solitude.

Smiling, I braced myself.

"Ahhhh! Nelli!" Sasha screeched. "I was running late and—" Still smiling, I only half-listened. Sasha was my closest friend but…he tended to speak a lot and say very little at the same time. "Then my eyelash fell behind the sink and, you'll never believe this, but I found—" Nodding along, I nudged my phone, checking the time. Normally forty minutes late, Sasha was actually two minutes early today. "And then I couldn't find my good nails, you know, the maroon stiletto ones—" Sasha performed at a drag club outside of town and he never made it home before two in the morning, so, it didn't really bother me that he was always late.

Quiet mornings suited me anyway.

Despite the cool weather, Sasha wore short shorts and a hot-pink, swoop neck top that read, "REALLY QUEEN?" The outfit certainly pushed the boundaries of *appropriate* work wear. As a manager, I'm sure Morgan wouldn't approve, but as his mother…

Sashaying behind me, Sasha spun my chestnut-brown braid in a wide circle. I prepped the dining room while he bounced around the counter and disappeared into the back. Reappearing, Sasha set the cash drawer in the till. While Sasha hadn't been able to convince Morgan that wigs were acceptable work wear for a café, she'd conceded on make-up. Today Sasha flaunted shimmery, cut creased eyes, full lashes, and a powerful fuchsia lip.

Shame gnawed at me as I joined Sasha behind the counter. Beside him, it was easy to feel inadequate. My fault, not his. Sasha did his best to encourage me. He offered beauty advice freely, some helpful, such as using brown shadow to make my hazel eyes pop, and others only slightly insulting, like when he said I had great brow structure, if only I filled them in. Truly, I could put in more effort…

I'm here though, I soothed. Some days, that was enough.

The front bell jingled, and a young girl in an ill-fitted jacket shuffled in. Stringy, unkempt hair jutted from a faded beanie.

"I got it," I said, and waved Sasha away.

Approaching the counter, the girl examined the plants nervously, as if they might strike out and bite her. She mumbled, "Could I have a coffee to-go, please?"

"What's the name for the order?"

"Kristina."

Kristina opened a plastic bag and dumped a pile of change on the counter. The coins clanked and plinked as they struck the marble and bounced. Kristina caught a dime before it tumbled over the edge. Glancing at me, she whispered, "Sorry." One by one, Kristina slid coins across the counter. "Ten, fifteen, twenty-five…"

There weren't enough coins on the counter.

Kristina reached the same conclusion and her cheeks flushed. "Sorry, I—"

"Your order is paid for," I interrupted.

"What?"

"Another customer paid for your order." Kristina peered around the café, looking for whoever meant to play a cruel joke on her. "They paid it forward earlier this morning. It included a baked good as well. What can I get you?"

"Are you sure?" Kristina chewed a chunk of hair.

"Of course." I clacked the tongs. "What would you like?" Kristina scrutinized the display and pointed to a chocolate chip cookie. The cheapest item we sold. "You sure? You can choose anything."

Kristina nodded and scooped coins into her baggy.

"What would you like in the coffee?"

"Just black, please." I handed over the cookie and the coffee. "Thank you so much." Kristina beamed and shuffled out. My eyes tingled and I blinked quickly, reining in any tears. Just finishing up my period, that's all.

I grabbed my wallet and counted out the last of my change.

I dumped it all in the till.

The front bell jingled as I wandered into the back, and I turned to take the order. "Don't worry about it," Sasha said, and waved me away.

I mouthed a, 'Thank you' and slipped my wallet into my bag. I checked my phone. No notifications. No surprise. Sasha was the only one who messaged me.

"My husband has arrived!" Sasha rushed in, flailing so excitedly I dropped my phone. "Come look!" he cried, dragging me out.

The only person in the café, a man, sat in the front, tucked behind Morgan's monstera. "His name is Darragh—like the plant, *Dara*—and

I'm going to marry him," Sasha whispered—well, Sasha whispered as best *Sasha* could. His voice echoed against the tiles, and I winced. Mercifully, Darragh didn't react.

"How do you know his name?" I asked.

"Said I needed it for the cup."

"He's got a glass mug."

"Are you the cup police right now?"

A book lay flat on the table before Darragh. Reading with his hand smushed against his cheek, Darragh's eyes moved hungrily across the pages, slowing only when he brought the mug to his lips. Half of his chocolate-brown hair sat in a knot at the back of his head. The rest tumbled in messy waves around his collarbone. When he turned the page, a few strands of grey caught the light, just behind his temple. A strange contrast against a young face. He couldn't be much older than me.

Did I have grey hair I didn't know about? Note to self: Check for grey hair tonight.

"I *flooded* my basement when he ordered," Sasha swooned.

Wrinkling my nose, I muttered, "Lovely." A drip of water struck my head. I craned, examining the ceiling. Speaking of floods, was there a leak? My apartment was above the café. I didn't *see* any water damage.

"Why do you think he's hiding at the small table?" Sasha asked.

Darragh was a little too big for the table he'd chosen. His knees met the edge, rather than fitting neatly beneath. His back formed a painful "C", like a father attending a child's tea party. There were seven much larger, empty tables scattered around the café. Darragh *chose* the tiny table in the corner. If he was like me, he'd probably selected the small table on purpose, a calculated attempt to dissuade anyone from joining him. The thought made me smile.

I see you, friend.

As if someone called to him, Darragh's hand dropped from his cheek, and he stared straight at us. Our eyes met. Darragh's brows furrowed, and his lips parted in surprise.

Breaking eye contact, I frantically wiped the counter. I sputtered, "I need a clean rag!" and fled. Sasha pursued me while I pretended to look for a rag in a spot where we'd never stored rags.

"D'you know him?" Sasha accused.

"What? No! Why?"

In a tone that suggested I was an idiot, Sasha said, "Girl. He knew you."

"No! He caught us staring. He was obviously uncomfortable."

"No way honey," Sasha replied, matter-of-factly. "He recognized you."

I opened my mouth to argue, but a voice cut me off.

"Excuse me?"

I peered around Sasha. At the counter, Darragh waved. Anxiety pulsed my stomach, but I scurried out. Beneath a well-fitted white T-shirt, Darragh's shoulders were broad, though, overall, he was slim. He looked strong in a lean, wiry way. Now my appearance troubled me even more; I could have at least tried to hide the bags under my eyes, or the old acne scars... I shook my head and focused.

"What can I get you?"

Darragh hesitated, as if he'd forgotten why he'd come up in the first place. "Sorry." He rolled the r's in *sorry*, speaking with a melodic accent I'd never heard. Darragh smiled, his cheek pulled back into a dimple, and crow's feet crinkled around keen, olive eyes. "Could I have some of those"—he paused, searching for the right word—"packets of sweet?"

Unsure what he meant, I repeated it slowly. "Packets of sweet..."

Sasha appeared. Winking at Darragh, he said, "Sugar."

"Oh, right. Sugar." I grabbed three packets from below the counter. Leaning over to Darragh, a faint smokiness struck me. It reminded me of

8

sputtering campfires, and filled me with a cheerful, curious warmth. As I placed the sugar in Darragh's palm, I noticed he wore several intricate rings. Strange. His clothing was so bland—plain white T-shirt, light brown pants. The rings brimmed with character, so unlike everything else about him. Almost as if he'd made every attempt to go unnoticed but refused to remove the jewelry.

"Thank you," Darragh said. Despite Sasha's attempt to insert himself into the interaction, Darragh focused entirely on me. His sudden, intense eye-contact unsettled me, and I broke it. Darragh looked at the sugar packets, as if seeing them for the first time. "Thank you," he murmured, and then wandered back to his table.

Sasha and I exchanged a look.

I put on another pot of coffee, but Sasha, shameless in his desire, leaned on the counter and ogled Darragh. "Do you think he contours his jaw?"

I chuckled. "I do not."

"I'm such a sucker for a good jawline," Sasha said. Darragh glanced over. Sasha gave him a sultry pout and waved. "I'm going to see if I can figure out what—or *who*—he's into." Sasha pulled a cookie from the display and sauntered over to Darragh's table.

I fully intended to eavesdrop on the conversation, but a customer entered and foiled my plan. She left, and when Sasha returned, I asked, "What did you learn?" I jutted my chin at Darragh. "What's he fancy?"

"I can't tell." Sasha crossed his arms and pouted. He grabbed another cookie and said, "You go talk to him."

"Hard pass," I said. Just *looking* at Darragh made my palms sweaty.

Sasha stomped his foot. "Come on!" He leaned on the counter and resumed staring.

"If this were a documentary about the unsolved murders of a bunch of women, I'd take one look at that guy and say, 'He did it. He killed all

9

those women.'"

Sasha's head whipped around. "Damn girl." Blinking several times, he looked me up and down. "Who hurt you?"

"All I'm saying is, no one looks like *that* and doesn't have something to hide."

Sasha rolled his eyes. "You need to watch something that isn't about serial killers for, like, five minutes, okay?"

"I'm telling you," I said and nodded at Darragh, "he's got bodies in his freezer."

"I'd love to be a body in his freezer," Sasha said longingly.

"Sasha!"

"What?" Sasha rounded on me. "I'm sorry, *that's* inappropriate?"

I counted fingers and replied, "You're gay. You're black, *and* you're a drag queen. If people start getting murdered around here, you'll be the first to go."

"At least I'd be dead and not working here anymore." Sasha pushed away from the counter and wandered out to clean tables.

Across the café, Darragh leaned over and parted the strings of pearls dangling down the window. He peered up and down the street, looking for something.

Or someone.

What are you hiding?

Unfortunately, my somber curiosity was short-lived. A man wearing a pink-collared shirt appeared in the front window, prompting my entire body to groan in silent agony. The bell jingled, and flip-flops slapped against the tile as the man entered. I'm sure he'd tell me he wore them because he was, 'On his way to the gym.' The man passed Sasha, and his upper lip curled in disgust. Reaching the counter, the man smiled, and his nose crinkled, more sneer-like than anything else. He jack-knifed his thumb in Sasha's direction and laughed. "He does realize he's a dude, right?" He waited for me to laugh with him.

I didn't.

"What can I get you, Turner?"

"You look nice today. Natural. I like girls who don't put all that crap on their face."

Be nice! You've got bills to pay.

"Thanks. Coffee?"

"I'll have a coffee. Put five creams and five sugars in it." Turner babbled while I worked. "Yeah, I'm just on the way to the gym." I smiled but said nothing. Turner continued, "Hey—has anyone ever told you that you could be a model?"

While performing my finest customer service laugh, a fleeting, isolated melancholy nagged me. When was the last time I laughed for myself? When was the last time I laughed because I found something funny, and not to make someone else comfortable? Placing Turner's to-go cup on the counter, I muttered, "That's four-fifty."

Turner chucked down a folded five-dollar bill. Reluctantly, I picked it up and unfurled it. To speed up the transaction, I slammed the button on the drawer and made change manually.

"Wow, you're pretty good at math for a girl."

In an itemized list of my weaknesses, math was at the tippy-top. Back in university, it was the only course I'd nearly failed. However, even *I* could manage fifty cents.

Pretending not to see Turner's outstretched hand, I set a quarter on the counter. "Is that everything?"

"Are you busy tonight?" Turner leaned on the counter, and I stepped back.

"Oh!" My cheeks flushed. "Um—" I struggled to lie, but my mind emptied. "I, uh—"

"Excuse me?" Darragh joined us, standing so uncomfortably close to Turner that he straightened and stepped back. Pointing to his table, Darragh said, "I spilled my drink. Do you have a towel I can clean it up with?"

Grabbing a cloth, I shouted, "I can do it!"

At Darragh's table, I knelt to mop up coffee while he organized a teetering pile of books. Suddenly, a rough, gravelled voice whispered, "Do you want me to get rid of him?"

I flinched with an unattractive, "Guh!" and knocked the underside of the table. I steadied it and found Darragh kneeling beside me, alert and serious. His eyes, sharp with intent, darted to Turner and back.

"Oh! Oh no. No, it's okay," I said. "Thank you, though." Darragh grimaced, respecting my decision, even if he thought it was wrong. When I finished cleaning, I pulled myself up and nodded toward Turner. "This is nothing." I chuckled. "I've been spit on before."

Darragh didn't seem to think that was very funny.

"Why are you still here?" I heard Sasha ask Turner.

I took my time heading back to the front, wiping down a few clean tables on my way. When Turner finally left, I jumped behind the counter and made a fresh latte, to which I added pumpkin syrup, a dollop of whipped cream, and cinnamon. Coincidentally, the cinnamon formed a perfect heart. I hesitated, and then dumped more cinnamon on top, turning the heart into a splotch. I brought the latte to Darragh's table and set it down. Wearing the scowl of an interrupted reader, Darragh glanced up from his book.

"On me," I said.

Darragh looked between me and the latte. The lines on his face softened and he smiled. My stomach somersaulted, and I looked at my feet. "It's a special. The pumpkin spiced latte."

"Thank you," Darragh said, his voice soft once more.

"Enjoy!" All flustered, I bumped a table on my way back to the counter. Did Darragh notice?

I glanced over my shoulder and caught him smiling after me. Hoping my cheeks weren't as red as they felt, I joined Sasha. He looked me up and down.

"What?" I asked, unable to hide my smile.

"You're gonna be real cold in that freezer, babe."

I stuck up my nose and flung my towel over my shoulder. Sasha and I watched Darragh take a sip, then he quickly went back for another. Grinning beneath a whipped cream moustache, Darragh gave me a thumbs up. I laughed and pointed to my lip. Darragh didn't seem to understand at first, but he quickly dragged the back of his hand across his mouth, removing the whipped cream.

Sasha glared at me enviously.

Unconcerned with the world around him, Darragh remained at his table well into the afternoon, devouring books and coffee. In fact, he consumed so much coffee that, after an eleventh top-up, Sasha asked if we had a responsibility to stop serving him.

"I'm worried about him," Sasha said. Across the café, Darragh swallowed the dregs of another coffee then examined the empty mug sadly. "I think he might die," Sasha whispered.

"Keep an eye on him. I'm going to pee before we close."

I finished and returned my bag to the back, where Sasha cornered me. "Something's weird with ye boy. I suggested decaf, and then I had to explain what caffeine was." Sasha put a concerned hand on his chest. "Should I like, call an ambulance?"

Ugh. Phone calls.

I peered out. "Oh. He's gone."

"What!" Sasha leapt out. "Dang."

Before he left, Darragh had placed his dishes neatly on the counter. Three unopened sugar packets sat on the saucer. Darragh hadn't used them. I started, "Hey look at this—"

"Why don't you come out with me and Lawrence tonight?"

"Can't. I have plans." I tossed the sugar away and washed the dishes.

Sasha cocked his head. "No, you don't."

"I do." I didn't meet his gaze. "Next time, I promise."

After clean-up, we closed and went our separate ways. The antique lampposts cast the old shops in an eerie, subdued light. I loved October, but I didn't care for the dark walk home. I jogged down murder-alley and up the stairs to my apartment. Once inside, my orange tabby, Watney, brushed my leg. He wanted attention—and food. I patted him and filled his bowl. The edges of my vision darkened when I stood up. I steadied myself while the faintness passed.

I'm starving.

In the fridge, I found condiments, pickles, and a miserable bag of spinach that, despite promising myself I would eat it this time, I hadn't.

I should throw that out.

The empty fridge emphasized the sticky stains on the glass shelves.

I should clean those.

I closed the door, hoping the freezer was more lucrative. A half-empty bag of fruit, probably expired, definitely freezer burnt. One frozen dinner: macaroni and cheese. I snatched it, tore up the corner, and tossed it in the microwave. After setting the timer, I shuffled to my bedroom. I pulled off my shirt, smelled it, and recoiled. It bypassed the semi-clean pile of laundry on my chair, straight into the overflowing clothes basket.

I should do laundry.

My bra and pants joined the semi-clean pile. I picked up a crumpled *Foo Fighters* T-shirt and pulled it on over some sweatpants.

Back in the kitchen, I grabbed the macaroni and tossed the paper lid in the garbage. It bounced off an empty dinner tray and fell to the ground. Wandering to the living room, I found my laptop and navigated to an old episode of *Kitchen Nightmares*.

The macaroni was still cold in the middle. I ate it anyway.

After scooping the last few noodles into my mouth, I stacked the empty tray into yesterday's tray, which still sat on the coffee table. I turned over a half-finished cross-stitch that sat beside me. Quietly stitching used to bring me joy. Lately, I hadn't had the time or energy for even the smallest things. I glanced out the window that overlooked the main street. A brittle, brown plant sat neglected on the sill.

I should get rid of that.

My phone screen lit, and a message from Sasha said, "*Have fun with your big plans tonight* 😬 " I turned off the screen and tossed my phone. I'm driven by three things in life: My next coffee, my next book, and my crippling desire to avoid all humankind. So yes, I lied when Sasha asked me to go out.

Laughter rose from the street as drunken, happy people stumbled by. Their joy stoked my guilt, fanning the flames until shame consumed me.

Should I have gone out with Sasha?

I loved my alone time, but every so often…it did get a bit…lonely. It was easier to forget during the day, when the bustle of work kept those thoughts away, but when night came…

I pounced on my phone. Scrolling social media, a headline caught my eye.

Recovered Surveillance Videos Reveal Deadly Miggs Rampage in West Virginia Hospital

I clicked it.

CHARLESTON, West Virginia—Recovered surveillance from

Memorial Hospital shows Miggs attack that claimed the lives of 76 individuals. The following footage was released with a statement this morning. Warning, the footage contains graphic content that might disturb some viewers.

I hit play.

It took me a minute to realize what I was seeing through the black and white grain. A hospital hallway, but the video seemed frozen. Maybe it wasn't loading properly? Before I scrolled away, a figure appeared in the darkness. I brought my phone closer and squinted, as if that might add more pixels and clear up the footage. A person wrapped in bandages walked down the hall. The camera's point of view switched to a patient's room, where a man slept.

The bandaged person walked jerkily into the frame and stood over the man. As the time stamp in the corner rolled over to 3:01, the intruder raised their hand. The sleeping man's arm shot to his throat. At first, it looked like he was sitting up, but he kept rising, until he floated away from the bed. The blankets fell away, and he rose so that only his flailing legs were visible to the camera.

Before long, the thrashing weakened.

The person left, but the invisible rope hanging the man remained.

Limp legs swung gently back and forth.

The camera POV jumped, following the bandaged individual through the hospital. A nurse turned a corner and nearly ran into them, but, as if sensing the nurse, the bandaged person ducked inside a room. Here, another man lay sleeping. Just like the first victim, this patient was hung. The video cut away, and a text overlay said this occurred seventy-three more times.

The camera jumped to the hospital roof, where the individual exited and climbed on the railing. In the distance, lights flashed to-and-fro. At

3:40 a.m., the individual leapt. The camera switched to a hospital room. As if broken from a spell, a body crashed to the floor. Another shot showed a double room, where two men hung. At 3:40 a.m., they both crashed to the ground, and the video ended.

I scrolled to the statement.

The woman in the video is Ellie Bailey, admitted to the hospital Thursday evening after a reported domestic dispute. Bailey's abilities were unknown at admittance. Bailey's body was found on the north side of the hospital, deceased.

Preliminary autopsy reports indicate cause of death for all victims was strangulation. Multiple victims sustained post-mortem injuries, including broken ankles, arms, neck and back.

An employee at Memorial Hospital has been taken into custody after tampering with the original footage. At this time, no further details have been given.

"Our thoughts are with the families who've lost fathers, brothers, and sons," said Chief of Police, Steven Brown.

The investigation is ongoing. Please call if you have any information.

Against my better judgement, I checked the comment section.

these goddamn freaks

they should all be shot

the US will have to bring back the noose

Setting my phone aside, I sat quietly, processing. Stories like this were popping up all over the world, but this was by far the deadliest.

It all started last year, when security footage from London captured an attack in a Tesco parking lot. In the video, a group of men approached a woman loading bags into her car. One of the men grabbed her wrist, and a bright light turned the screen white. As the video cleared, the man was nowhere to be seen. The remaining men clustered together; one drew a knife.

But the woman didn't run, instead, her gaze found the security camera. I still remember the dread I felt when her eyes met mine, as if she was looking straight at me.

The woman circled the men and backed away.

Trying to draw them from the camera.

Eventually, the men backed off, and that was it for the footage.

But it wasn't the end of the story. Police found the four men dead— sort of. Enough pieces were recovered to indicate they weren't alive. The mangled remains were discovered at various distances away. Suggesting that, at some point, the woman chased them.

People still debate whether the video was faked.

The woman in the video, identified as Moira Miggs, was never found. I recalled the headline that broke the internet: *Miggs, Magic?*

That headline provided a label for the phenomenon.

Magic.

The name Miggs stuck too, becoming a nickname for people seemingly possessing magical abilities. It was still less controversial than some other…less savoury names. As you might imagine, the masses didn't react kindly to stories like this. And I mean, I just watched a woman kill 75 people without lifting a finger.

Watney rubbed my calf, pulling me back to reality. After dishing out a healthy belly rub, I double-checked that the door was locked and headed to the bathroom. I caught sight of myself in the mirror. Hair jutted from the confines of my braid, giving me a disheveled, exhausted look.

"Ugh."

I faced the wall while I brushed my teeth.

In bed, I set my laptop next to me and put on a *3 Scary Games*. Halfway through the video, I closed my eyes and tried to relax. I tried not to think about lying to Sasha. I tried not to think about all the horrible news. I tried not to think at all.

Far away, the video ended. Five minutes passed, and the first of the tears fell. Frustrated but not surprised, I propped myself up. Snatching a bottle from the nightstand, I dry swallowed three pills and lay back down.

Deep breaths in.

Deep breaths out.

Did I put grounds in the machine?

Chapter Two

pour yourself a li'l mug of depression

I barely slept, and nightmares ravaged what sleep I did get. Most were promptly forgotten when I woke up, but one remained. At work, Sasha knocked a bunch of canisters off the counter, and I caught them all with a serving tray. Dream Sasha wasn't impressed; he was horrified. He'd cried, "Freak!" and grabbed a paring knife. With help from the customers, Sasha tackled me and slipped a rope around my neck. From his table in the corner, Darragh watched on as I suffocated.

Sasha was busy with a customer when I arrived for my shift at noon. Wearing icy blue contacts, he was exceptionally striking today. He pulsed his brows once in greeting as I snuck behind him into the back.

I threw my bag down and tied on an apron. Finished with his customer, Sasha leaned on the doorframe and said, "Hey sis." He smoothed his tight black pants, some leather substitute, and adjusted the sleeve of his fishnet turtleneck.

"Nice eyes," I said.

"Oh, these old things?" Sasha boasted. He winced and prodded his lower lid. "Good, cause these girls are thick. Everything is blurry as shit." Sasha blinked and refocused on me. To mask my exhaustion, I'd gone overboard with makeup this morning. Now, standing in front of Sasha, I felt silly. He was about to roast me harder than the coffee—

"You're looking fierce today." Sasha made a gooseneck grabbing motion. "Trying to impress someone?"

Oh.

I shrugged. "I just wanted to look nice."

"Could it have anything to do with the stunning boy out front?"

I dropped my voice to a whisper. "He's here again?"

Darragh had *not* been here when I walked in—I mean, I didn't look for him, if that's what you're thinking.

Sasha pursed his bold, red lips. "Yes, ma'am." Pushing by Sasha, I peered into the dining room. Sure enough, Darragh occupied the same spot, obscured amongst monstera leaves. There was hardly room for coffee amongst the piles of books he'd already stacked on the table. Catching sight of me peering out, Darragh made his way to the counter. Instinctively, I backed away, hoping Sasha would take the lead.

Two hands shoved me—*hard*—and momentum sent me stumbling forward. Grabbing the counter, I steadied myself and shot Sasha a dirty look. He busied himself, furiously organizing nothing, and mouthed the words, '*You're welcome.*'

Darragh approached cautiously, eyes darting between me and the back room. Wearing his hair down today, perfect brown waves framed Darragh's face.

"Hey!" I shouted, too cheerfully.

"How are you?"

"I'm—"

Darragh's gaze pinned me with an unsettling intensity. All at once I realized he wasn't asking, 'How are you?' with the expectation of a lie and some quip about the weather, but rather, he was asking, 'Are you okay?'

My heart raced as I considered responses.

No, I'm not okay.

I'm drowning. I cry all the time. I can't stand the sight of myself. I'm alone. And I'm tired.

Darragh's curious eyes lingered on me, as if *searching* for those answers I was so unwilling to give. I felt bare under his gaze, like I was underdressed, and he could see every part of me. Suddenly fearful, my desire for connection was swiftly executed at the prospect of admitting vulnerability before a stranger.

I lied when I said, "I'm good."

Unsatisfied, Darragh's lips compressed.

Feeling as if I'd just failed a test, I asked, "What can I get you?"

"I'd like the pumpkin latte."

"Yeah?"

Darragh nodded. He waited while I made his drink, watching the process intently. When I finished, I slid the mug over. Darragh snatched it without hesitation.

"Careful! It's hot." A flurry of lawsuits flashed before me as Darragh tipped the mug against his lips and chugged. There was no screaming, no burning or recoiling. When Darragh finished drinking, he looked refreshed.

"Thank you," Darragh said, and then headed back to his table.

Sasha caught my eye from the back. Eyes wide, he mouthed, '*What the fuck?*'

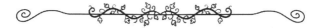

During a break, I checked my phone, only to find more news about the slayings in West Virginia. A post from our Prime Minister, urging people with magical abilities to come forward, said: *We need to study this phenomenon—we need to save lives.* The comment section was a warzone.

If any of those freaks comes near me or my kids, I'll kill them

This is why we need guns

freaks

If I was magic, I wouldn't come forward either.

I joined Sasha out front. We'd entered the afternoon lull, and the café was empty except for Darragh. My phone still open to the post, I slid it over to Sasha. "What do you think of all this?"

"All what?" Sasha read the headline. "The stuff about the freaks?"

'Freaks' was far from politically correct. Hearing it out loud, I winced. "I think we're saying *people with magical abilities* now."

Crossing his arms, Sasha said, "That's just more words to say freak." I didn't respond, and Sasha continued. "I think it's a hoax."

"You *what?*"

"Not the deaths," Sasha clarified. "But Nell, come on." He looked around and lowered his voice. "*Magic?* How old are we?"

It seemed silly when he put it that way.

"I don't know." I shrugged. "There are so many things we don't understand. Maybe this is one of them?"

Sasha narrowed his eyes and nudged me playfully. "Is there something you aren't telling me, Nelli? Hm? Any extraordinary secrets?"

My tone was strict and humourless when I said, "No." Even the thought made my stomach clench so tightly it hurt.

Across the café, Darragh cleared his throat and slid back his chair.

Sasha and I pasted on smiles as he approached the counter. After he ordered another coffee, Darragh lingered. He looked at me like he wanted to say something but wasn't sure how. Sasha, my best friend and unofficial matchmaker, stepped in.

"Okay, there is obviously some sort of"—he waved between me and Darragh—"*energy* going on here." Squeezing my shoulders, Sasha added, "Why don't you give my girl your number, and y'all can chat later?"

Mortification flushed my cheeks.

"No."

I cringed, and Sasha recoiled as if Darragh had reached over and slapped him.

"I don't have one," Darragh quickly continued. Come to think of it, he'd never had a phone or laptop with him. Only books.

Sasha crossed his arms. "Who doesn't have a phone in this country—"

Clattering metal erupted behind us. Frothy milk spewed everywhere as a milk canister rolled across the tiles. "Shoot!" Sasha scooped up the canister while I rushed to find a mop. We finished cleaning the mess, and I glanced across the café.

Darragh was gone.

The shops on main street stayed open late on Halloween. Delighted shrieks pierced the windows as children scurried about, trick-or-treating. As the night came to an end, I happily handed out the last of our candy to a witch and a tiny Ruth Bader Ginsburg. On her way out, Ruth bonked the witch with her gavel, and I laughed.

The laugh died as my favourite customer walked in.

"You know," Turner said, approaching the counter, "you should smile at people when they come in."

Fixing Turner with a heated stare, Sasha threw a towel over his shoulder and crossed his arms. I gave Sasha a look that said, '*If you love me, you'll kill me.*'

Once I'd made Turner's drink, I slid it across the counter, hoping he'd take it and go.

He did not. Instead, he said, "You look tired."

Thanks.

"I didn't sleep well."

Turner scoffed. "I only get two hours of sleep a night, and I don't look tired." When I didn't respond, he asked, "Big plans tonight?"

"Yes, actually. I'm going to my friend's show." I nodded at Sasha. Turner mulled for a moment, perhaps waiting for an invitation that wouldn't come. I pretended to clean the espresso machine until he left.

"You know, you could actually come," Sasha said. Before I could say no, Sasha continued. "You love the Halloween show!"

"I'm tired," I replied. "I'm just gonna go home to bed."

"Come on, Nelli!" Sasha stamped his foot. "All you do is work and sleep."

"Yet I have no money, and I'm always tired."

Sasha's disappointment was palpable, but he didn't push. He did say, "How are you ever going to meet anyone?"

Heat tinged my cheeks. *I could meet them here, if only you didn't scare them away!* Sasha already felt terrible about the incident with Darragh. He'd gone out of his way to be extra nice, which was uncharacteristic, and undoubtedly guilt driven. So, I bit my tongue.

"If it's fate, I'm sure I'll meet them on my way home from work, or even better, in my own kitchen."

Sasha pursed his lips. "Coming from the person who dials 9-1- on her way home just in case? You'd die if you ran into anyone in that alley."

I wish.

"Speaking of which—I brought you this." Sasha pulled a sachet from his pocket. The swirling scent of lavender filled the air as he handed it to me. "It'll protect you from the spirits tonight."

I slipped the sachet in my pocket. *You don't believe in magic, but you believe in this bullshit?*

"Thanks."

Sasha's apron buzzed and he disappeared into the back to take a call. When he returned, he approached me with a sickly-sweet smile.

"Stop," I said. "What? What do you want now?"

Sasha dragged his finger along my arm. "They want performers to check-in early tonight."

"No. You can't leave me here alone."

"You know I gotta beat this mug." Sasha leaned on my shoulder, fluttering his lashes.

"Your skin is flawless." I looked anywhere but Sasha's pleading face.

"It is, isn't it?" He straightened and framed his face proudly. "Fifteen minutes?" he begged.

I didn't budge. I hated closing alone. The task itself was easy enough, but it was a serious health and safety no-no. If Morgan found out, she'd be furious. Sasha pouted, then his eyes widened as a brilliant thought occurred to him. "If you let me go early, I'll take Turner's order for a week." Raising one perfect brow, Sasha smirked.

It was a good deal.

I considered the offer. Sasha *would* leave fifteen minutes early tonight. He knew it. I knew it. I might as well get something in return. Crossing my arms, I muttered, "Two weeks." Sasha let out a triumphant laugh and gave me a spine-crunching hug. He scrambled to gather his things. "While you're taking Turner's orders, can you also turn on the charm and get him interested in you instead?"

"Nuh-uh, can't fix poor taste, honey." Sasha walked out of the back and dodged a moist milk rag. He feigned a look of dismay and tapped the play button on his phone. Tina Turner's *The Best* played from the speaker. Sasha stalked forward with exaggerated strides.

"Please don't," I said.

Sasha held my arms and spun me while he lip-synched to Tina. Twirling around the counter, Sasha rolled across each table on his way out. Before exiting, Sasha pointed at me and said, "You know what you are, Nelli!"

He left, and continued dancing down the street.

My smile faded with the music.

The absence of noise and movement left the café feeling antiseptic and wrong. I locked the front door and flicked the lights off. Once I double-checked that Sasha had cleaned everything he promised he would, I counted the cash and put it safely in Morgan's office. I slipped on my jacket, grabbed my bag, and checked my phone. A message from Sasha popped up:

LOVE YOU BITCH.

'Wait until Turner tells you about his gym routine,' I replied. Guided by muscle memory, my fingers opened the phone app to type 9-1-. Sasha's teasing replayed in my head. I closed the app and tucked my phone away. I unlocked the front door so I could escape, and quickly re-locked it behind me. "Oh!"

A tiny child dressed as Satan bumped me.

"Sorry!" Satan apologized. Three more children scampered by, vanishing down the street. Their laughter disappeared into the night, leaving an eerie silence in its wake. Clutching my coat tighter at my throat, I took off for home.

Footsteps echoed behind me.

Were they mine?

No—the steps sounded after mine. Tucking my hair behind my ear, I glanced behind me. A shadow ducked into a shop doorway. My heart pounded and I walked faster. I jogged as I rounded the corner where I could dip into the alley. Despite the darkness, I could see two people standing beside the dumpster. Turner's blonde hair was immediately recognizable, his stupid pink collar visible under his beige jacket.

Ugh. Not this asshole.

Turner noticed me and gestured to the girl behind him. "I just caught her going through the trash." I recognized the girl; she'd come into the café yesterday. I think her name was...Kristina?

Kristina didn't look up as Turner continued berating her.

"Okay," I interrupted. "That's enough. I'm sure she was just leaving."

Kristina met my eyes and smiled weakly. Eager for an escape, she made her way out of the alley. As she passed Turner, he pointed and snickered. "She's literally got garbage stuck—"

Crunch!

Each of Turner's fingers splayed backward and broke. "Agh!" Turner's cry echoed across the bricks. Trembling, he cradled his hand against his chest.

Kristina turned back, her expression horrified. "I didn't mean to!" she whimpered. Garbage crunched beneath her sneakers as she backed away.

Turner blew out a frantic breath and screamed, "You fucking freak!" He lunged after Kristina.

"Hey!" I grabbed Turner's jacket, but it slipped through my fingers.

Using his left hand, Turner uppercut Kristina. The blow landed beneath her chin, and Kristina, who couldn't have weighed more than a hundred pounds, was thrown backward. Stumbling, she tried to catch herself, tried to stop her head from smashing into the steel dumpster—

BANG!

THE FOREST WHERE THE PHOENIX SLEEPS

The noise tore down the alley like a gunshot and Kristina hit the ground. She did not get back up.

Turner's obnoxious breathing was the only sound to interrupt the electric silence that descended upon us.

Shoving by Turner, I knelt by Kristina's tiny, still body. Crimson blood flowed heavy from a gash through her eyebrow…but it was the angle of her neck against the pavement that turned my stomach. Afraid to touch her, I whispered, "What did you do?"

"You saw it!" Turner shouted. "She tried to kill me!"

"No, she didn't! She was trying to leave!" My vision clouded and my breath hitched. "I—I think she's dead."

"Good!" Turner screamed. "She was one of *those* people! One of those freaks! She would have killed me!"

A fleeting memory of Kristina, timidly sliding coins across the counter, replayed in my mind. I saw her beaming smile as she thanked me, coffee and cookie clutched against her chest. Now she lay discarded like the garbage around her.

"She was scared," I murmured.

Sticking out of Kristina's pocket, I recognized one of *Rousseau's* pastry bags. Half of a chocolate chip cookie had fallen out and lay in crumbs. A sickening leap of sympathy hammered my chest. Whenever I ate something *really* good, I'd save half and stash it in the fridge. That way, I always had one good thing to look forward to. When times get dark, it's always important to have one good thing to look forward to. Even if it's only a stale cookie.

Snatching bits of cookie from the ground, hot rage filled my belly as I rounded on Turner.

"Look at my hand!" Turner cried. "It was me or her!"

That's what he'd tell people, that it was him or the *freak*.

And they would believe him.

I hurled crumbs at Turner. An absurd look crossed his face as he shielded it from the remains of Kristina's joy.

My cheeks flared hot.

"What the fu—" Turner coughed, and a tiny puff of smoke sputtered from his lips. Clutching his throat, Turner cried, "You're one of them too?" His words came out ragged and breathy, as if he couldn't get enough oxygen. Turner slid a hand into his pocket and withdrew something that glinted in the dim light. A *thwick* noise sounded just as Turner cried, "You freak bitch!" and lunged. Pressure stuck my side—I ignored it and shoved Turner away.

I wanted more than to defend myself; I wanted justice for the little girl who lay dead at Turner's feet. My entire body was alive with fury now. Sweat drenched my palms, and I dragged them along my thighs. I wanted Turner to scream, and I wanted to watch his body writhe on the filthy pavement.

In that moment, I wanted him dead.

"Agh!" Turner took a jerky step back and fell, sending a metal garbage bin clanking down the alley. Like someone trying to douse a flame, Turner pawed at his eyes. When his hands fell away, lazy, grey steam trickled from his empty, charred eye sockets.

White goo poured down Turner's cheeks like tears.

A blistery gust of wind swept down the alley, and Turner's face erupted into a crackling flame. Like delicate paper brought to a candle, Turner's skin darkened and curled. He finally screamed—a horrifying, shrill cry—and wildfire consumed his body as he writhed on the asphalt.

All at once, the writhing and screaming ceased. The fire didn't mind that Turner was dead, it continued smoldering. Shock held me in place. One hand covered my mouth, the other cradled my side.

I'd killed him.

But how?! How could I have—

Turner was right. I'm one of *those* people. People with magical abilities. Freak bitch.

A wave of dread rooted in my belly. Fast-moving footsteps sounded against pavement, but I couldn't look away from Turner's crackling corpse. A hand touched my arm. I followed it and blinked stupidly at the person beside me. Darragh. Glancing rapidly between me and Turner, he asked, "Are you alright?"

"I…I think I killed him."

Darragh's brows furrowed, and he opened his mouth, but a distant police siren bleated, cutting him off. Someone must have heard screams and called 9-1-1. Darragh straightened and asked, "What's that noise?"

"The police. They'll be…"—I gulped, finding it difficult to speak—"coming for me."

Darragh held my gaze. His eyebrows scrunched together, like he was trying to solve a complex math problem. A siren bleated again, closer. Darragh scooped up my bag and shoved it against my chest. Pushing me, his voice was urgent when he said, "Go. Now."

I resisted, instead reaching for Kristina. "I'm not leaving her—"

"I'll take care of it." Darragh half pushed, half carried me up the stairs to my apartment. I don't remember unlocking the door, but Darragh grabbed the knob and shoved me inside. "Stay inside. No matter what you hear—do *not* come out." The door slammed behind me. Leaning against it, I slid until I hit the floor. My fingers were slippery as I pulled them away from my side.

Blood? Was it mine? More blood oozed through my coat and a flaring pain shot into my ribs. Definitely mine.

"Ugh." Sickness swelled in my throat, and I rested my head against the door. Within five minutes, I'd witnessed a murder, been stabbed, and killed someone. So, why wasn't I crying? I felt...nothing. Sitting inside my messy apartment, I didn't care what happened next. I reached for my phone, needing to message Sasha. Right about now, he'd be sliding into a sequin dress—sequinsed dress, in his words—and laughing with the other queens. I couldn't take that from him. Who else could I talk to? I exhausted the list quickly. There was no one else. I turned to the last person I should have.

Myself.

The police would be here soon. Two people were dead, and there was probably a blood trail leading to my apartment. Would I go to jail? What would they do to me when they found out I was one of *those* people?

Turner's voice replayed over and over. *Freak bitch!*

My lip trembled and tears blurred my vision. The loneliness, the stress, the fury—all at once, everything pressed in with suffocating clarity.

It's too much.

My breath caught, and all the pain spilled down my cheeks. With great difficulty, I withdrew a pen and an old, tattered receipt from my purse. Fighting the urge to close my eyes, I scribbled a note to Sasha, asking him to take care of Watney. I checked the knob above my head, making sure it was unlocked so the police could get in. As blood and tears poured out of me, I only had one thought:

I don't want to be here anymore.

Chapter Three

stretch and groan

The gentle crackle of fire roused me. Smoke tickled my nose, and I squinted into the flames. The campfire burned bright, a stark contrast against the night sky. My back ached as I sat up. Pain flared up my side. I froze.

A man watched me through the flames.

"Darragh?"

Across the fire, Darragh sat, leaning rigidly against a fallen tree. At the sound of my voice, his shoulders relaxed. Crossing his arms, Darragh turned his gaze to the flickering flames. He didn't look at me when he said, "How do you feel?"

"My side hurts," I rasped. "A lot." Darragh pursed his lips and raised a brow but remained silent. I studied the darkness around us. "What… what are we doing here?" My night vision returned, and thick tree trunks appeared. How did we get here?

I couldn't remember anything.

I gulped a shallow breath and rubbed my chest. What was the last thing I remembered? The café. Working. Sasha left early, and I closed on my own. After that, my memory faded. I ground the heel of my palm into my forehead. Turner's face popped into my mind—

Turner's dead body.

"Hhh!" I covered my mouth. Turner's lifeless, smoking corpse. Followed by Darragh, his face close to mine as he pushed me and told me to go—and then here. My memory was blank between Turner's mangled body and here.

Darragh watched me through the haze from the fire. This wasn't the man who'd ordered coffee from me. The gentle smile was gone; Darragh's lips formed a thin, serious line. It reminded me of the way Sasha looked at me when he was pissed.

What happened?

What had I done?

And why was Darragh so angry with me?

"You're safe here," Darragh said. "Sleep while you can."

"I just woke up in the woods with a stranger. I'm not going to sleep."

"Afraid you might end up in my freezer?"

My mouth dropped. Darragh *heard* that? What else did he hear? My legs shook, but I stood and said, "Take me home." Darragh blinked twice, surprised by the command. Truthfully, I'd surprised myself.

"Only danger awaits you there. In good conscience, I cannot take you back."

I examined the surrounding trees. *Can I outrun him?*

"Are you thirsty?" Darragh asked, interrupting my escape plan. I was glad. Sort of. The firelight did nothing to penetrate the darkness beyond the first line of trees. Darragh offered me a worn, terra cotta mug. Suspicious of the contents, I just stared at it. The awkward tension of Darragh's outstretched hand became unbearable, and I took it. I knew better than to accept a drink from a stranger, but I was *so* thirsty. I looked at the mug, back to Darragh, and back to the mug. It gave off a spicy, cinnamon scent. I drank deeply.

The moment the mug left my lips, exhaustion settled on me like a soft blanket. With my last ounce of strength, I threw the mug at Darragh. He leaned, dodging it easily. I slurred, "You piece of shi—" before my eyes closed and my legs buckled beneath me.

I blinked against the sunshine poking through the canopy and struggled to sit up. "Ugh." I stretched and cracked my neck. Oblivious to my waking, Darragh rushed around the campsite, packing. He wore a loose flannel shirt, the sleeves shoved roughly to his elbows, and fitted brown pants. Darragh moved silently, padding around in high boots of walnut-coloured leather. He bent and picked up a knife, which he tucked into a sheath that wound around his thigh. There was a strange…old-timey-ness about it all.

Still unaware I'd woken, Darragh shoved a cast-iron pan into his satchel. As quiet as I could, I got to my feet. Careful not to step on anything crunchy, I backed into the trees. I turned from the campsite and—

"Where are you going?" Darragh's face was inches from mine.

"OH FUC—" I raised my fist.

"Sorry!" Darragh thrust both hands toward me, like I was some frightened animal.

"What did you do to me?" I shouted.

My voice rang through the wood and Darragh's eyes darted nervously around. He waited for something to happen. Nothing did. Brows raised in disbelief, Darragh's voice was nearly a whisper when he said, "What did *I* do to you?"

"Yes. Why am I here?"

"You were"—Darragh paused, choosing his words carefully—"You were injured. I brought you here."

"Where's here?"

"This is where I live."

Annoyed by Darragh's deliberate attempts to misunderstand me, I took a deep, calming breath. "Where do you live, Darragh?" I enunciated every word, hoping clarity would get me answers.

Darragh stared at me as if mulling over what to say. The silence stretched on. It was uncomfortable, and I struggled not to break it. Darragh ran a hand through his hair, and his shoulders sagged. "You wouldn't have survived…had I left you on Earth."

"What?" I spit the word and then wiped my lips. "What does that even *mean*?"

"You needed magic—"

"What happened last night?" I'd never experienced anything like this before. Even the rare occasion I overdid it with Sasha, I'd never had memory lapses. I patted down my pockets. "Where's my phone?" Fear crushed my chest and I cried, "Where's my cat?"

"Your phone is in your apartment where you left it. It's useless here. Sasha is watching your small friend."

"Right." Vaguely, I recalled asking Sasha to take care of Watney— but why? Why did I do that? My brain loaded, and I heard what Darragh said a few minutes ago. "Did you say *magic*?"

"Nell, time is against us. You must trust me."

"Why would I trust you?!" Darragh recoiled from the shrillness in my tone as if it were a rock I'd picked up and thrown at him.

"Stop shrieking like a banshee!" he whispered. "You'll bring every creature in the woods upon us—"

Knock.

Knock.

Knock.

The slow, deliberate rapping carried through the trees. The lively morning chatter of birds quieted, and an eerie hush permeated the wood. "What was that?" I whispered. It sounded like someone striking a trunk with a rock.

Darragh inched closer, and when he spoke, I could barely hear him. "You will die if you don't come with me right now. That's the truth." Darragh searched my face for something that didn't exist.

Trust.

"Am I your captive?" I asked.

"What?" Darragh's eyes bulged. "No!"

"So, I can just…leave?"

"Yes!" Darragh exclaimed. He scowled, regretful of the answer he'd given so quickly. "You *will* die though."

I crossed my arms. "So, I *can't* leave?"

Darragh's jaw slackened, at a loss for words.

"If the alternative to staying with you is death, it kinda sounds like I'm your captive."

Darragh blew out a loud, frustrated breath. "I should let you wander off," he growled. "See what awaits you in those woods." He ran both hands through his hair and closed his eyes.

Three, slow knocks sounded again.

Closer this time.

Darragh headed back to camp and said, "Follow me—if you're so inclined." His mock politeness was snider than I cared for, but I did as he said.

Next to the firepit, Darragh pulled on a lengthy forest green jacket, well-worn and thin at the elbows. If he held still, I half expected to lose him in the trees. Next, he rolled up the mat I'd slept on, and shoved it in his bag. The mat, though much larger than the satchel, disappeared neatly inside. Pulling a length of cord from his wrist, Darragh tied his hair in a half ponytail. "I can *show* you why we must leave." He walked away, pausing to glance at me. "Unless, of course, you'd like to save us the trouble and trust me?"

"I'd love to see for myself."

Darragh's response was a squinty eyed smile that said, '*Of course you would.*'

I followed Darragh to a break in the trees. A brown flatland, interspersed with dull shrubs and large grey rocks, stretched before us. Against the far-off sky, white tipped mountains jutted from the horizon. The view was spectacular, but—mountains?

I'd never seen a mountain range in my life.

Where am I?

In the middle of the plain, grew a grove of trees. Eerily green, the grove looked nothing like the brown shrubland around it. It reminded me of those old *Scooby Doo* cartoons, where the book that stood out on the shelf was always the key to a secret passageway.

"What am I looking at?" I asked.

Darragh pointed to the grove.

"Is it behind the trees?"

"No, it's not *behind* the trees," Darragh replied hotly. "Give it a moment."

Nothing happened.

Darragh stiffened, his impatience palpable. Cupping his hands around his mouth, he shouted, "Hey!" My body tensed against the sudden shout. Still, nothing happened.

Then, as if woken from a slumber, a ripple passed through the trees. At first, I might have dismissed it as a breeze, but one by one, the trees came to life. Dirt erupted as roots tore free from the ground. Slowly, the trees dragged themselves in our direction.

"We should leave." Darragh tugged my arm. "Hastily."

"I don't understand." I resisted. "The trees are…walking?"

"They're not trees," Darragh said, pulling me away. The trees quickened; the entire grove scuttled forward like a giant centipede. As the distance between us lessened, I gave in to Darragh's insistence. Without letting go of my arm, he pulled me into a run. We headed back into the wood, dodging trunks as we ran. From behind, Darragh's voice shouted, "Hey!" again. I tried to look, but Darragh yanked me ahead. "It's mimicry. Do *not* stop running."

If I were to construct a list entitled, *One hundred things Eleanor Noll is good at*, you wouldn't find cardio on it. If I were to construct another list entitled, *One thousand things Eleanor Noll is good at…* No. You still wouldn't see cardio. If Darragh hadn't dragged me along after him, I surely would have fallen behind to be eaten. We hurtled through the wood, ducking under branches and avoiding thick trunks. Darragh halted. A wide stream flowed at our feet.

Booming crashes erupted as trees snapped and fell behind us.

Yanking me close, Darragh scooped my legs and swung my arm around his neck. He ran and leapt across mossy stones scattered throughout the stream. How he did it without falling, I'll never understand. We landed safely on the bank; Darragh put me down and backed away. He started to apologize, but several loud thuds, like heavy logs hitting the dirt, snapped our attention back to the other side of the stream. The sparse riverbank was now dense with massive trees, which hadn't been there moments before. They stood on the bank like sentinels.

I swore there were faces in the knots of their bark.

"They won't cross the stream," Darragh said, and walked into the golden plains that stretched before us. Struggling to catch my breath, I hurried after him.

"Uh, won't? Or can't?"

"Let's not find out."

We walked in silence until the stream was nearly out of sight. While Darragh seemed content to continue that way, I couldn't contain my curiosity any longer.

"Where are we?"

"Hiraeth." Now free of danger, Darragh resumed a cold, grumpy demeanor. He spoke in short sentences and one-word answers.

"Where's that?" I prodded.

"Far away."

"How far?"

"Far."

"Like, Europe?"

"No."

"Farther than Europe?"

"Yes."

Were the veins behind Darragh's temples always so prominent?

Where on Earth could we be? I thought to myself. A raindrop struck me. Odd, there wasn't a cloud in sight. I touched my hair. Dry.

"We're not on Earth," Darragh replied.

"What does that mean?!"

"We're just not on Earth!"

I scrutinized Darragh. After ten seconds of silence, I continued. "Why did you bring me here?"

Wherever *here* is.

Rather than answer, Darragh asked, "What do you remember from last night?" I scrunched my nose. I hated when people answered a question with a question. I tried to remember, but everything was fragmented and foggy. Had someone put something in my drink? Is this what roofies felt like?

"I remember leaving the café…" Turner's face appeared again. This time, I recalled an intense, stabbing pain in my side. "Did Turner hurt me?"

The muscle in Darragh's jaw clenched. "He did." I remembered Turner lunging at me, and a furious, burning rage. I wanted to hurt him. I wanted to…a sickening weight settled in my chest.

"Did I kill him?"

Perhaps reluctant to upset me, Darragh grimaced. "He wasn't alive when we left." I looked away. My sniffles broke the silence. "Hey," Darragh started. "That man attacked you. He's lucky he was allowed to die so quickly. Do not grieve him."

"I don't remember anything else," I muttered. I groaned and massaged my temples. "So, it's true. I'm one of *those* people. The ones on the news." The words quivered as they left my mouth, and I bit my lip, refusing to cry again.

"Would that be so horrible?" Darragh watched me for an answer.

I didn't give one.

"What do you have against people with magic?"

"I'm not prejudiced, I just…"

Why was the thought of possessing magic so frightening? "What if I hurt someone—" I caught myself, realizing I'd already done so. My side ached, and I rubbed it. *Freak bitch:* that's what Turner had called me. I thought of all the articles I'd seen about people with magic, the horrible names and death threats left beneath them. "And what if someone hurts me?"

Darragh remained silent.

"I'm just—I'm so tired. I just want to be left alone with my cat. I'm not strong enough to handle anything else."

Why was Darragh being so defensive, anyway?

Oh.

I thought myself idiotic for not figuring it out sooner. "You're one of those people, too?" A disheartened chuckle escaped Darragh's lips. He raised his hand and a ball of flame kindled to life in his palm. "Why didn't you tell me that earlier?"

Clenching his fist, Darragh extinguished the flame. "You would have fled."

He was probably right.

I kept that to myself.

"Well, what else can you do?"

Perhaps anticipating an entirely different reaction, Darragh seemed taken by my enthusiasm. The corner of his lip turned up in a tiny, crooked smile. For a moment, the charming man I'd met at the café returned. "Lots of things," Darragh replied. "Like everyone else on Hiraeth."

"You're all...magic?"

"Most of us. To some degree."

"And it's magic, like, actual magic?"

"It looks like magic to you but, it's just energy we convert into power."

"How?"

"I don't know." Darragh shrugged. "We're born that way."

Unconvinced, I repeated, "You're all magic?"

"Yeah. The amount varies from person to person, but yeah. We're all magic."

"So, what—you just pop out of the womb, and can do all this powerful stuff?"

Realizing this would not be a quiet walk, Darragh heaved a great sigh. "When we're born, our parents train us in the basics. Pulling." Darragh's hand shot out. A large, dead log that lay next to the path lifted and flew toward him. My hands shot up to protect my face, but the log stopped in front of us, suspended in midair. Darragh continued. "Pushing." The log arced away and crashed on the ground. "Stuff like that."

"And what about the…not basics?" I nodded at his hands. "Can everyone do the fire thing?"

Darragh's face clouded. "They cannot." I watched him expectantly and he sighed. "Most of us are good at a few specific things. We inherit it from our parents."

"And then what?"

"Children are trained based on whatever magic they excel at. If a child has a propensity for healing, they'll train with a healer. It's just like Earth, if you're good at something, and you have the means, you can make a career of it."

"Is it hard to learn?"

"Magic is powerful, and sometimes unpredictable." Darragh's voice was bitter when he added, "Learning to control it can be difficult. But it's necessary to avoid outbursts."

"Can you teach me?"

"Teach you what?"

"Magic. How to control it."

Darragh grimaced and scratched his nose. "I don't think I'm the right person to do that."

"Why not?"

Darragh rubbed the back of his neck. "I wouldn't know where to start. You're an adult; it'll be a lot more difficult. You could kill someone."

I winced.

"Sorry."

"So, what do you do?" I asked.

"Hm?"

"What sort of a career does a fire-starter have?"

It seemed an obvious question, yet Darragh seemed surprised. His jaw tightened, and he lowered his gaze. "Don't call me that again." An uncomfortable tension settled between us. Darragh was done talking.

On one hand, I really wanted to know more about his magic, but...

I'm worlds away from home.

I'm trapped here with him.

The first day we'd met in the café, Darragh looked at Turner and said, '*Do you want me to get rid of him?*'

A shadow of unease crept into my bones.

I didn't ask any more questions.

For now, I followed the strange magical man into the wild. Over my shoulder, both the stream and the tree monsters were nearly out of sight. As my feet carried me farther and farther away, I wondered:

How am I ever going to get home?

Chapter Four

try to stay alive

The wood before us was ashen, like worn fence posts. Gnarled limbs ignored the border; they grew out, reaching. At the roots, a thick miasma of fog oozed between trunks, obscuring the ground. What manner of things hid beneath that murky blanket? From deep within the wood, a faint cry rang out—followed by a frenzy of yips and snarls.

Some poor creature was being eaten alive.

I'm not going in there.

Darragh plunged into the fog.

Ugh.

I braced myself and trailed him, half expecting my shoes to sink in a soggy puddle. Thankfully, they struck solid ground—a vision exploded in my mind.

No longer in the wood with Darragh, I stood in a medieval village. All around, an uncontrollable fire burned. Flames flickered high on the thatched roofs, and even higher still, a fiery bird screeched in the sky.

Over the roaring fire, screams came from a nearby building. I started toward it. The thatched roof collapsed, sending soot billowing out in a dark cloud. I covered my face. Smoke burned my lungs and someone bumped me, their agonized wails pounding in my ears. I reached out and tried not to recoil from the burnt and misshapen face that met me—as quickly as the vision came, it vanished.

"What was that?" I steadied myself against a trunk.

Darragh stiffened and looked around. "What was what?"

"You didn't see that?!"

Darragh relaxed. "Fire?"

I stared at him incredulously. "Uh, yeah! The fire!" A thought occurred to me. "Was that a prophecy? Did I just see the future?"

"It's not a vision of the future," Darragh said. "It's a warning from the past." He climbed over a fallen tree and turned to help me. "Everyone sees it the first time they enter the wood." Pondering that uncomfortable sentence, I followed Darragh's wake through the fog.

"Where are we—" Before I could finish my question about where we were going, Darragh turned and placed a finger to his lips. No ambiguity in the gesture. *Shush.* The urgency in Darragh's features alarmed me and I stilled. Realizing he'd frightened me, Darragh softened. He gave my arm an encouraging squeeze and nodded in the direction we'd been walking.

*Well, yes. I know we're going **that way**, but that doesn't tell me **where** we're going.* I thought, annoyed.

Darragh rolled his eyes and continued walking.

Why'd he roll his eyes?

A positively horrifying thought occurred to me.

Can you hear me?

While Darragh gave no indication he'd heard anything, I was once again met with the peculiar sensation of water droplets trickling on my scalp. Ignoring the droplets, I glared at Darragh's back.

Can you hear my thoughts?

Nothing.

Earlier in our hike, Darragh had removed his coat and shoved it in his satchel. Both mist and sweat had rendered his cream shirt semitransparent. The fabric clung to the rippling muscles in his back. What might it be like to trace my fingers along them?

Darragh peered over his shoulder. A curious, but playful smile tugged at his cheek. My mouth dropped open. Heat blossomed up my neck and I covered my face. Inside my head I screamed, '*We will talk about this later!*'

The faint exhale of a chuckle carried through the trees.

I didn't have time to go through every thought I'd had since we met. A blood-curdling screech erupted from the fog to our left, a shrill, high-pitched wail that grew so loud, I slammed my hands over my ears. Darragh held still, and so did I. A second, third, and fourth call answered from our right.

The first call sounded again from the left.

Angry screeches called out from the right.

Closer this time.

They were searching.

Hunting.

Darragh faced me, his expression calm. This was, I admit, rather frustrating. I might cry. Or pee. Or both at the same time. Darragh made a flat surface with his left hand and used his right to make a running motion with his fingers. Taking my hand, Darragh gave it a reassuring squeeze. He mimed taking a deep breath, and I took one too.

Darragh nearly took my arm off as he leapt into a sprint.

A chorus of hungry screeches erupted. I fought the urge to cover my ears. If I let go of Darragh now, I would surely die. Underbrush crashed behind us as we hurtled around thick tree trunks. Darragh held so tight, and moved so quickly, I considered the very real possibility he might pull my arm from the socket. Though, I'd happily lose a limb if it saved me from whatever snarled at our backs.

All around, the fog swirled with movement. Beside us, I glimpsed grey fur as a creature closed in. It had four hooved feet and antlers, like a deer. The thing opened its mouth—its jaw didn't stop where it should. A slit opened to the creature's shoulders, exposing a row of jagged teeth. Gobs of foamy white saliva stretched across the gaping maw like some disgusting, stringy grilled cheese.

If I'd had any breath to spare, I'd have screamed.

Another blood-curdling shriek erupted from the thing's throat. It rattled my eardrums, disorienting me so much, I struggled to run straight. Darragh stopped, and I pummelled into his back. He didn't react to the weight of my body slamming into his, and for a moment, I thought I'd run into a tree.

"Don't open your eyes." Darragh pushed me to the ground. I got up to run, but something slithered around my legs, and they snapped together. Arms cartwheeling, I crashed forward. I struggled to see in the fog, but it thickened, cocooning me. My misty world turned black.

I was blind.

The cool fog changed into a warm, swirling wind. It grew hot, like a fire burning all around, but I couldn't see a thing and—

The screaming started.

I covered my ears. It did little to hide the unending, agonized shrieks that battered me from all sides. The acrid stench of smoke grew thick; it burned my lungs as I tried to draw breath. I choked and trapped myself in a coughing fit. Just when I thought I might lose consciousness, the screams weakened.

Gasping, I sucked in fresh air.

Silence filled the wood.

Minutes passed; I don't know how many. The binding on my legs loosened and the darkness ebbed from my vision. Standing a few feet away, Darragh's face was covered in ash, and dark liquid coated his clothing. I struggled to stand, got a whiff of burned flesh, and gagged. A hooved leg lay beside me. It ended in a bloody, singed stump.

I threw up.

Dragging my hand unceremoniously across my lips, I asked, "What happened?"

Darragh brushed ash from his chest. "They ran away." I scoffed and waited for the real answer. Instead, Darragh apologized for using magic to bind my legs. "I was worried you'd run off, and they'd find you before I could." He paused, perhaps waiting for a thank-you that wouldn't come. "Did I hurt you? Can you walk?"

"I'm fine." I jutted my chin at his boot. "You've got red on you." Darragh looked down, a hunk of furry flesh sat on the toe of his boot. He kicked a few times to dislodge it. He resumed walking and I followed. I didn't ask why he'd blinded me. If Darragh could read my mind, he knew I was thinking it. He chose not to acknowledge it. If he could sense my growing distrust in him, he chose not to acknowledge that either.

We walked in silence for ten minutes.

Fifteen minutes.

Thirty minutes.

Gradually, the fog gave way to a living, green canopy. Birds sung happily in the branches, and with each step, my boots kicked up the musty scent of old leaves and pine. Up ahead, sunbeams interrupted the darkness as the trees opened into a clearing.

Darragh slowed so I might catch up.

A well-worn path began at Darragh's feet, sloping down like a ribbon through patches of pink and white wildflowers. Farther still, it wound through shrubs and countless gardens fenced with chopped branches. The path ended when it met a small stone cottage, stained green with moss and shrouded in overgrown droopy purple flowers. It was so much like a painting; I wanted to crawl inside and be lost as a brushstroke forever.

Darragh gazed upon the cottage with the relief of someone coming home after a very long day. "It's breathtaking," I said. While I meant it as a compliment, Darragh seemed unsure of what to do with it. He nodded awkwardly and set off down the path. I followed, but my boot caught a vine and I stumbled. I flailed for branches, but only succeeded in scratching myself as I plummeted. A tangle of vines cushioned my fall but pain splintered through my veins like electricity.

WHAT'S HAPPENING?

My hands and legs were fire. Darragh yelled, but I didn't hear what he said. I brushed my arms to remove the invisible fire, my hands only burned hotter. The surrounding trees spun, and hot vomit touched the back of my throat. As if I were nothing more than a bundle of firewood, Darragh hauled me into his arms. Where his body touched mine, the burning cooled, just a bit. Trying to manage the pain, I focused desperately on my breathing.

I'd burned myself badly once, leaned into an oven for mac and cheese. On the way out my forearms grazed the inside. The metal seared my arms, and when I recoiled, some of my skin stuck to the oven. I remember the pain as my flesh burned and tore… This felt like that. But no matter how I recoiled now, there was no relief.

Darragh moved quickly, speaking while he ran. I have no idea what he said. It was a blessing when I passed out.

I woke, shivering violently, in a pool of water. I tried to scramble out. Two hands gripped my shoulders and pushed me deeper into the water. Only my head remained above.

"You've been burned," Darragh said from behind me. "Your magic has healed you for now, but you must cool down."

Feeling like a cat in a bathtub, I hissed, "Let me out."

"No. You're not cold enough."

"You get in here"—my teeth chattered—"and tell me I'm not cold enough!" I wriggled against Darragh, ready to throw knuckles. Without releasing his hold, Darragh slid into the water. Still clothed, he swung around to face me. Back in the wood, just before those carnivorous deer meant to devour us, Darragh's expression had been annoyingly calm. But now, deep lines creased his forehead, and his irises darted around my face, scanning me.

Now, he was afraid.

I inhaled deeply and focused on Darragh. On his high cheekbones and slightly sunken cheeks. Necklaces dangled around his throat, bits of carved wood and metal hung from thin straps of leather. I closed my eyes and took another deep breath. In through the nose. Out through the mouth. Hold. Forget the cold. What do you hear?

Trickling water.

Chirping birds.

A gentle breeze in the canopy.

With an even voice, I asked, "What happened?"

"Fire nettle—or wildfire. Keeps unwanted visitors at bay."

"At bay?" I laughed. "Do you mean dead?"

Darragh didn't answer. I opened my eyes to find he'd waded to the far side of the pool. Far away from me. He splashed water on his face, washing away ash and grime. No longer worried I might drop dead, Darragh crossed his arms over his chest.

"You need to be more careful," he scolded.

Be more careful?!

"Maybe—as a *responsible* homeowner—you need to put a sign on plants that'll kill your guests!"

"That would defeat the purpose then, wouldn't it?" Darragh snarled. He climbed from the pool, muttering under his breath. Steam billowed from Darragh's shoulders as the water on his skin evaporated. After a quick survey of the surrounding trees, Darragh craned his neck to the setting sun. He offered a hand to help me out.

"We need to go inside before it gets dark."

Chapter Five

the cottage in the woods

The inside of the cottage was inviting and unpretentious. Candles sputtered to life as Darragh rounded the wooden counter that separated the small den from the kitchen. At least, I assumed it was the kitchen. The appliances that typified a kitchen on Earth were absent. Darragh dodged the many low-hanging iron pots and unpacked a handful of jars from his satchel. Pushing aside glass bottles, Darragh added the full jars to the open shelves that ran the length of the wall. He dumped the rest in a wash basin set into the counter. Heading to the den, he paused beside me to hang his coat by the door.

Outside, the sun was setting. The final trickles of light poured through a large, west-facing window. Shadows cast by trees danced to-and-fro on a stone fireplace, which sat facing a plain sofa and rug. Darragh scaled a ladder that led up to a loft. All over the cottage, dried flowers and branches hung from exposed beams, filling the space with the aroma of herbs and spices. The cottage possessed a pleasant, lived-in atmosphere that made me feel at home. I longed to warm my toes by the fireplace, while a crackling fire burned in the hearth.

Speaking of which, the fireplace remained unlit, yet the cottage was strangely toasty.

"How do you keep it warm while you're away?" I called.

"The house is enchanted. It holds a temperature I find comfortable," Darragh's muffled voice replied. He climbed down the ladder and added, "Actually, it's warmer than I'd like. I wonder if it's switched to accommodate you."

It was quite cozy.

"That's a shame. I love a good fire—"

Flames burst to life in the hearth, bringing with them an intoxicating smokiness. I calmed my heart, relaxing only when the eager flames died back to a reasonable size. "Was that the cottage accommodating me, or you?" Darragh didn't have to answer. The way he smirked and looked away was enough. My cheeks warmed...from the fire.

Definitely from the fire.

Now, with us both safe in his cottage, Darragh appeared decidedly less icy. He moved with a comfortable ease, and even smiled when he handed me a pile of dry clothes. I examined the pants and flowy white shirt. Darragh directed me to a door at the back of the cottage. "There's a washing basin if you'd like to clean up."

"And, um, what if I needed to, uhhh…" I trailed off. Unaware of the direction I was going, Darragh looked at me vacantly. I sighed. "Where may I use the bathroom?"

"Oh!" Darragh clasped his hands together and his gaze dropped. "Uh-right-yes." Colour crept up his neck and stained his cheeks. "There's a—what would you call it? A pot? A chamber pot? There's one in there. Don't worry about, uh, emptying it or anything. It'll...take care of itself." We stood awkwardly. Darragh managed to continue, "No need to flush or—"

"I'll be right out," I interrupted and fled. Behind the kitchen, through a small door, sat a glass conservatory. In the fading light, the surrounding trees were just visible through the glass panes.

The bathroom was small, but lovely. A big copper tub sat amongst plants of all shapes and sizes. The remnants of the setting sun shone through a skylight and dust motes danced in the sunbeams. What a pleasant way to spend an evening, soaking in the tub and watching the stars sparkle to life.

The clothes Darragh gave me were *laughably* big, but comfortable. They smelled of campfires. Just like Darragh. Inhaling deeply, I suddenly realized that I was smelling Darragh's clothing. And *enjoying* smelling Darragh's clothing. I dropped the fabric. I rinsed my face using a pitcher of water and—rather awkwardly—saw to my other needs. There weren't any mirrors in the room. I hoped I looked okay. The ends of my hair curled from being submerged earlier, and I felt like a pirate in my big white shirt.

I rejoined Darragh, who sat on the sofa before the fire. The sun now fully set, the only light emanated from the fireplace, and a few candles scattered here and there. Darragh gestured to a sweater that lay next to him and murmured, "In case you get cold." I acknowledged the sweater but didn't put it on as I sat on the rug next to the fire.

"Oh!" While the rug appeared scratchy and coarse, the fabric was soft and…happy? It's hard to explain but, the moment I sat down, I felt it. It was warm, like a hug from someone cherished. I leaned, taking a closer look. "This is beautiful," I murmured. Woven into the fabric, a boat listed in the water beneath a starry sky. On the deck, two people embraced in a passionate kiss. Bright threads came together to create a tangle of red hair that billowed out from one of the two. "Are you sure it should be on the floor?"

Darragh half-smiled. "Someone in my family used to make them." He pointed above the fireplace, where a similar textile hung like a tapestry: a garden scene featuring a thatched wooden house, bordered by all sorts of flowers. Lilac and hyacinth teased my nose, bringing back memories of spring I didn't know I had. "They were traded out of the family for years. I've been trying to get them back."

"Just beautiful," I muttered. A snarl erupted outside. "What was that?" I cried, my body alert.

Darragh hadn't reacted. "You get used to it." He shrugged. "Focus on the fire." It burned with renewed vigor, snapping and crackling loudly. I appreciated Darragh's attempt to comfort me, even if I could still hear the occasional growl.

"Does it take a lot of effort to keep the fire going?" I glanced at Darragh and caught him staring. He looked away.

"Uh…" His brows furrowed, like I'd caught him deep in thought. "Not really. A little initially, to light it."

I stretched my legs toward the fire. A flame playfully licked my toes. "Ah!" I snatched my feet away and glared at Darragh. He suppressed a mischievous grin and stood, heading to the kitchen. He returned with two terracotta mugs, handed me one, and resumed his spot on the sofa.

"Did you drug this?" I swirled the contents, which smelled of chamomile and mint. Darragh sighed and took the mug. He held eye contact with me while he took a large gulp. After wiping froth from his lip, he gave it back. "What if you've built up a tolerance to whatever drug is in this?" I scrutinized the liquid.

"Okay, give it back." Darragh grabbed for the mug. I shielded it with my body and laughed. I sipped the warm liquid and settled in.

"So," I began sharply, "about the mind reading."

Darragh tensed. "How did you know?"

"I can feel it."

"You shouldn't." Darragh leaned in, touched with concern. "Does it hurt?"

"No. It just feels like rain, or trickling water."

"It's undetectable by most Hiraethans."

"Cool. How long have you been reading *my* mind?"

Darragh rubbed his neck. "Since we got here." I stared, awaiting more confessions. Redness crept into his cheeks. "And a few times before that."

"Did you see anything you liked in there?"

Darragh fidgeted and pushed a strand of hair behind his ear. "It's not like that. I can't *really* read your mind, just, passing thoughts as they move through—and I haven't been poking around. I've been translating."

"Translating what? We're speaking English."

Darragh shook his head. "No, we aren't. I'm translating for you. In here." He tapped his temple.

"But you can speak English. Why would we need translating?"

"I don't want to draw attention to us, if anyone heard us speaking English…" Darragh grimaced. "It's just easier this way. Trust me."

He used that word again. Trust. I had no reason to trust him. In fact, I had several reasons *not* to trust him, but…he'd saved my life. Twice that I knew of. Thrice if I believed his story about bringing me here to help me. He *felt* trustworthy, even if I believed he wasn't being entirely honest. The light from the fire danced on his skin, it bounced off the delicate curls that touched his collarbone. Was he trustworthy—or just good-looking?

Darragh shifted uncomfortably on the sofa.

"Can you all read minds?"

"No, only the most powerful of us can—and even then, it's not a perfect art." Darragh sipped his drink. "If you have secrets, try not to think about them too loudly."

Alright. Whatever that meant.

"Okay, well, can you not read mine?"

"I'll try not to."

We sat in silence, and I glanced around the cottage. Several pots filled with lush, healthy plants lined the windowsills. There wasn't much else to look at. One sofa, and one rustic stool made of sticks near the kitchen. Quite the solitary existence out here in the woods. How did Darragh keep busy? My hand itched for my phone. The threat of boredom pressed in already.

"What do you do out here at night? Do you have any books?"

"No books."

"Really? You always had books at the café."

"I leave them on Earth. There aren't any books on Hiraeth."

"But, how? Why?"

"We just don't have them yet." Darragh paused. "While we're at it, there isn't any coffee either."

"What?!" I stared at him. "Why would you bring me here?!" I climbed dramatically to my feet and stomped to the door. When I peeked back at Darragh, he just smiled sadly. I padded back and sat beside him. He inched toward the arm of the sofa, away from me. His fingers spun one of his many rings nervously. The sweater he'd laid out for me was soft and heavy; I slipped it on. "Why aren't there any books?"

"May I take your hand?" Darragh asked, offering me his. Unsure, I hesitated. I stared at his outstretched hand, at the veins that snaked their way up his forearm...

"It will be brief," Darragh promised. I took his hand.

Darragh disappeared and the cottage fell away.

The familiar brick and tile work of Rousseau's greeted me. I struggled to orient myself. I wasn't behind the counter, instead, I sat at a table near the front window. Across the café, Sasha put the coffee pot back in the machine. I recognized the top he wore. Hot pink, reading, 'REALLY QUEEN'. Once finished, Sasha hurried into the back.

*This was Darragh's first time at Rousseau's, the day we met. But this wasn't just a memory; it was like I was **there**, experiencing it through Darragh. The sunshine poured through the window and kissed my skin. The bitterness of coffee lingered on my tongue. The familiar, comforting pages of a book pressed my fingertips. Darragh heard Sasha return but didn't look up. It wasn't until Darragh heard the word, "Friend," whispered in my mind, that he glanced away from his book.*

There I stood.

Looking at myself through Darragh, I felt less repulsed. I didn't recoil as if I'd looked in a mirror. From here, I couldn't see all my flaws.

Intrusive warmth filled my chest.

It's strange. I identified my own thoughts and feelings during Darragh's memory. For example, the pants I wore were disgustingly ill-fitting. I'd throw them in the trash if I ever made it home, but I also felt an entirely separate set of feelings and emotions. The way Darragh felt in that moment. When Darragh saw me, he was surprised, but there was also an overwhelming sense of...familiarity.

Sasha had said, "He recognized you."

Sasha was right.

When we made eye contact, Darragh reacted like he'd caught sight of a familiar face in a crowd. A flush of excitement coursed through him. His stomach tightened, and all the other faces faded. Darragh lingered on me as I avoided eye contact. His gaze travelled down my body, and slowly, the exhilaration turned to—

The cottage reappeared.

Darragh's hand slipped from mine.

Fear.

Darragh was excited to see me, but afraid. I started to ask why. "That's why we don't have books," Darragh explained. "We've no need. We communicate through touch with visions and emotions like that."

"How do you pass on information?"

"We imbue objects with memories. Where your children read books, ours learn from objects."

"What about stories? Fantasy and make-believe things?"

Darragh shrugged.

"What do you tell your children when they're babies to put them to sleep?" The fire went out with a gentle *whoosh*. "What happened?" The sudden darkness made me uneasy. A soft yellow light shimmered in the fireplace. It grew bigger and brighter until it resembled a crouched bird. It leapt from the hearth and onto the ceiling, crackling and trailing embers around the room. The bird grew, oranges and reds blurred together. It exploded in a silent firework until the entire roof was a living phoenix. Green lights shimmered at the edges of the floor. They grew like trees and spread out and up to greet the flames on the ceiling. Flowers made of light flashed around me, in pink, purple, and yellow. They swirled and circled, moving toward the ceiling.

Then the light disappeared.

A fire burned in the hearth, illuminating the cottage as normal. Darragh watched me for a reaction. He raised an eyebrow, silently asking, '*Something wrong?*'

Smiling, I said, "Well, there weren't any dragons." Darragh raised his other eyebrow. "I'm just saying, I'm partial to a dragon in my stories." I met his eyes in the firelight. "But I wouldn't mind falling asleep to that every night."

Darragh shifted. "Speaking of sleeping"—he stood—"you're probably tired."

"Not really."

Darragh was already up and checking the front door. He placed his palm against the wood and muttered under his breath. He did the same to each of the windows on the main floor. When he finished, he walked by the front door again and paused, as if trying to remember something. He put his palm on the door and repeated the same incantation he'd uttered two minutes ago.

Was he locking something out, or someone in?

Darragh caught me staring. "It opens from the inside. You can get out if you need to."

"I thought I asked you not to read my mind."

"I didn't have to read your mind," Darragh mumbled as he walked away.

"Do you blame me?"

"I suppose not." Darragh pointed to the loft. "After you."

I scaled the ladder and Darragh followed with extra blankets. Once I climbed into his bed—just a simple mattress on the floor—Darragh asked, "Are you comfortable?"

"Yes, thank you."

"Are you hungry?"

"No."

"Are you cold?"

"No."

"Do you need anything?"

"No."

"Would you tell me if you needed anything, or would you suffer without it?"

"No, and yes."

Darragh gave me a fussy look before he pointed to a hatch-style window over my head. "Same as the others. If anything happens and you need to abandon the cottage, you can get out here." He unlatched the window to show me. "Anything. An emergency. An intruder. A fire. You run."

"Are you the fire safety warden here?" I joked.

Darragh didn't laugh. He closed the hatch and stepped down the ladder.

"Where will you sleep?"

"Sofa," he grunted.

"Are you sure? I don't mind—"

"Goodnight, Nell." Darragh disappeared.

I hadn't been tired earlier, but now, curled in warm blankets on a soft mattress, I yawned. Worry for my cat, Watney, needled me. What if Sasha didn't close the door properly, and Watney slipped out? What if a car hit him? What if he was taken by coyotes? Did we have coyotes? *Sh, sh, sh.* I quieted my spiraling thoughts. Sasha knew how much Watney meant to me, he would take care of him.

I snuggled deeper into Darragh's bed.

Comforted by the gentle crackle from the fire, I fell asleep easily.

I couldn't remember the last time I fell asleep easily.

I woke in the night, reaching for my phone to check the time. When I couldn't find it, I sat up in a panic. I realized it was far, far away. I relaxed and lay back.

I have to pee. Can I wait to pee?

I rubbed my legs like a cricket beneath the warm blankets. My bladder pulsed.

No. No, I cannot wait to pee.

I tossed the blankets and slid out of bed. The ladder creaked as I tiptoed down. I snuck a peek at Darragh, asleep on the sofa. Illuminated by the moonlight, he slept on his back, his hair unbound. A thin blanket half-covered his bare chest. Darragh's right leg jutted up at an angle, while his left leg hung over the side of the sofa. A twang of guilt nagged me. He must be desperately uncomfortable.

A shadow in the window caught my eye. A silhouette that wasn't there before. I squinted, and the object came into focus. "What the shit!?" I stumbled into the counter. Several canisters and glass jars jostled and crashed to the floor.

Darragh leapt up and crossed the room. There wasn't a trace of drowsiness about him as he asked, "What's wrong?" I pointed to the thing in the window. Darragh shoved me roughly behind his back and oriented himself toward the threat. The moonlight shone behind the creature, creating only a vague silhouette. Darragh took a half step closer, keeping me an arm's length back. His body relaxed. "It's just a nightstalker".

"A what?"

"It must have followed us home. They're harmless, as long as we keep everything locked." Darragh looked at me. "Which I do." The fire kindled to life as Darragh took another step forward.

I wish it hadn't.

Slender and tall, the creature looked almost human, though it possessed bat-like and leathery skin that blended into the night. On its face sat two prominent, unblinking eyes, stretched so very wide open.

Better to see you with.

Two tall, rabbit-like ears sat on its head.

Better to hear you with.

Hundreds of teeth jutted from a grotesque grin that stretched from ear to ear.

Better to eat you with.

Though Darragh walked in front of the creature, its unwavering gaze never left me.

"Why's it looking at me?" I whispered.

"You smell unlike anything in our world. They know better than to follow me, but this one probably got a whiff of you and wanted to have a taste." The nightstalker tilted its head. Its nostrils flared, and hot breath fogged the glass.

"What do we do?"

"Nothing for now. They're more dangerous at night, and its screams will attract others. I'll take care of it in the morning, or he'll just keep coming back every night until we slip up."

"He won't like, go away?"

"No. Once they've scented you, they're on you for life. Horrible things. They'll wait until you get caught out at night or forget to lock a door or window," Darragh continued, oblivious to my rapidly growing discomfort. "They're quite a nuisance. We'll have to be more careful." The nightstalker dragged a thick, dark tongue along the glass. Gobs of drool dripped from its curved, dagger-like teeth.

A fearful squeak left my lips. Darragh glanced back at me. My shoulders were so tense they nearly touched my ears.

"Oh."

Moving between the nightstalker and I, Darragh placed his hands on my shoulders. "You're safe. It can't get in, and even if it could, I'd take care of it." He let out a low, rumbling chuckle. "You probably wouldn't even wake up."

I didn't feel better.

Darragh smiled and rubbed my arms. "I brought you here—and I will protect you with my life, Nell. I swear it." Maybe it was the confidence in his eyes, or the strength of his hands on my shoulders but...I felt a bit better.

Chapter Six

Prima (Bella) Donna

A pained screech rang out in the early hours of the morning. Only one. I listened, but no more came. I dismissed it as a nightmare and went back to sleep.

A skillet jostled.

Dishware clinked together.

Darragh's husky voice, no louder than a whisper, hissed, "Shhhh!"

Sunshine trickled through the window above me. I stretched and climbed down from the loft. In the kitchen, delicate cream curtains wafted on a breeze that carried the gentle scent of roses. Pots and pans littered the counter, and a smear of white powder covered Darragh's forehead. He draped a towel over his shoulder and said, "Sorry about the noise."

"Don't apologize. Were you talking to someone?"

Darragh gestured at the surrounding cottage.

"You…talk to your house?" I asked.

"Of course," Darragh defended.

"Does the house ever answer?"

Snap!

I leapt aside as a bundle of herbs crashed to the floor. I picked up the herbs, and examined the roof where they came loose.

Darragh reached for the bundle and replied, "In its own way."

Recalling the night before, I looked out the window. "The nightstalker—"

"I took care of it."

"Oh. Thank you."

Darragh's response was a grim, fleeting smile.

"Can I help with anything?" I asked, gesturing at the food.

"No."

I sat on the stool across from Darragh. He brushed his hands on the towel and used a length of cord to tie his hair in a messy knot. Before I woke, he'd taken the time to apply dark make-up around his eyes. When he glanced at me, my stomach fluttered. I found myself staring at Darragh's hands, rather than his face, while he worked. After chopping a small, purple fruit, Darragh set his knife next to a vase filled with flowers.

"What are those?" I asked, jutting my chin at the flowers.

Without looking up, Darragh said, "We call them rubies." They reminded me of dahlias, except the petals looked, well, they looked like rubies. Blood-red and faceted, the petals reflected the light, just like a gemstone. I reached over and touched one. It squished, like one of those detergent packets you put in your dishwasher or laundry.

I felt a strange compulsion to pluck off a petal and bite it.

A forbidden Gusher.

I didn't though.

Darragh gave me a curious look and resumed chopping. "They're amazing," I said quickly. Darragh shrugged in a *yeah, I guess* sort of way, but a smile curled his cheek. Even if he pretended not to be, Darragh was pleased I liked them.

I excused myself to use the bathroom, where a twig and a bar of soap sat on a pile of clean, neatly folded clothes. The twig smelled strongly of mint. I used it to brush my teeth, whether that was its intended purpose or not. I pulled on the flowing cream shirt and tucked it into brown trousers. A similar outfit to Darragh's, though when I put the items on, I found they were exactly my size.

"Are you sure I can't help?" I asked as I left the bathroom.

"No," Darragh repeated and then pointed toward the den. I raised my hands in defeat and retired to the sofa.

Darragh dropped his knife and stood straight, like he'd heard something.

"What?" I leapt up.

Darragh placed a finger to his lips, politely shushing me. He leaned close to the window, listening. His eyes widened and he said, "Prepare yourself—"

The front door burst open.

A giant of a man, clothed from head to toe in a flowing, scarlet robe, stooped and entered. Righting himself, he shook out a monstrous mane of black hair. Delicate braids, woven with strands of gold, caught the light and glinted. The man brushed aside a bundle of hanging herbs. Darragh was tall, at least a foot taller than me. This man was at least a head taller than him. Wider too. Broad chested, with thick, strong biceps. He bent to set a satchel down and the seams of his robe looked like they might burst.

"I have to say, Darragh, every time I make this journey, I'm reminded how preposterously *dull* your rural life must be—" The man paused.

He and Darragh stared at each other.

The man stroked his tidy, pointed beard. An old scar jutted through his exquisitely manicured eyebrow, offering a peculiar contrast against his affluent appearance. Like Darragh, dark make-up surrounded the man's eyes. Though, the application was cleaner, more practiced.

Finally, the man pursed his lips and said, "Are you wearing make-up?"

"What of it?" Darragh replied.

"Who are you dressed up for?" The man surveyed the cottage, and his charming brown eyes found me. He yelped, "Oh my!" and covered his mouth. Overcoming the shock, excitement lit the man's face. He clapped his hands and cried, "What delicious little tryst have I happened upon?" He looked at Darragh, who's face conveyed something quite contrary to excitement. Actually, he looked a bit ill. The man plucked a sparkling ruby from the vase and murmured, "My, oh my." He looked me up and down with renewed interest. "Whoever is the auspicious young woman?"

"Bowyn, this is N-Nell," Darragh stammered. "Nell, this is Bowyn."

Was Darragh nervous?

Bowyn sensed it too; he rounded on Darragh like a snake. His eyes narrowed, and he turned to me. To look at Bowyn was an embrace. Though he stood a room away, I felt Bowyn's hands on the small of my back, guiding me forward. His perfume, a burst of fresh florals and citrus, overwhelmed my senses, and dizzying warmth spread through me. When Bowyn smiled, I couldn't help but smile drunkenly back. In my mind, a seductive voice whispered, "*My love. Come to me.*"

The command broke the spell. I shook my head, clearing out Bowyn's voice. "No. Thank you."

Horror contorted Bowyn's face.

Darragh exhaled loudly, and his shoulders sagged. His relief was short-lived. Bowyn bellowed, "Darragh!" and slammed his fist on the counter. Dishes and food bounced several inches into the air. "Darragh. Sorin. Mitalrrythin!" Bowyn pointed at me. "What is she?!" Before Darragh could reply, Bowyn hissed, "Tell me you didn't."

"Don't start with me," Darragh snapped. "Would you like a drink, Nell?"

"You, *of all people*, should know the consequences of what you've done!" Bowyn cried. "I can't believe you'd be so reckless, so stupid—"

"She was going to die!" Darragh shouted.

Stoked by Darragh's outburst, the fire burned uncontrollably in the hearth. I scooched away from the furious flames. "I panicked!" Darragh yelled, glaring at Bowyn. "Would you have me leave her to die?"

"Yes!" A look of incredulity smeared Bowyn's face, as if the answer was obvious. "Yes, that's exactly what I'd have you do!" A gob of spit flew from Bowyn's mouth. Darragh drew a hand across his cheek, disgusted.

I glanced at the door; would they notice if I left? There could be another nightstalker outside though… I looked at Bowyn, hulking in the kitchen.

I stepped toward the door.

Bowyn threw up his arms. He gave me a final, hateful glare and stormed out. The door slammed with such force, the windows shook, and several glass bottles fell off a shelf. Darragh waved, and the bottles put themselves neatly back where they belonged. He did so without looking, and with such complacency that I wondered if this sort of thing happened often.

I waited for the flames to die back considerably before I said, "Is he a…friend?"

There was a bitter note in Darragh's voice when he said, "My only friend."

"Ah." I sat down. "He's kind of a bitch, eh?"

The corners of Darragh's mouth turned up as he suppressed a laugh. "He'll come back. He does this." Darragh walked over and placed a drink in my hand. "Also, he left his favourite bag." Darragh pointed to the satchel nestled by the door.

"It is a nice bag."

"I made it."

"Really?" I raised my eyebrows. "That's impressive."

69

"Thanks."

"So why does Bowyn want me dead?"

"He doesn't want you dead, it's just…it's complicated."

I waited for an explanation.

Darragh groaned and pushed a hand through his hair. "I'm not the only one who can travel to your world. For hundreds of years, my people have made the journey. Not many—it's not an easy trip—but enough. Occasionally, people from Hiraeth would"—Darragh chewed his lip, searching for the right word—"breed with people from Earth."

"I wondered if we were compatible," I said.

Darragh choked on his drink.

"Not you and I," I backtracked. "I meant people from Earth and people from Hiraeth in general." Darragh massaged his throat and gave me a funny look. "I think it's natural to wonder," I defended.

"Anyway," Darragh continued, "Hiraethians introduced magic into a world where it doesn't belong. That magic travels through bloodlines and crops up at unpredictable times. Often with devastating consequences."

"The stuff in the news, the outbursts of magic? Is that what happened to me?"

Darragh nodded and sipped his drink. "It's been happening for centuries. Accidents that people dismiss as miracles, or unknown compelling forces. In the last few years, the outbursts are happening more frequently and more… obviously. Technology on Earth has made it difficult to hide."

"How do we fix it?"

"Travel between Hiraeth and Earth must cease. If an individual was born on Hiraeth, we expect them to return. That's my job. I find those who do not come back willingly. Over time, the magic blood will dilute, and the outbursts will stop."

"What about the kids? People who weren't born on Hiraeth, but still have magic?"

People like me.

Darragh drained his drink. "Nothing. Most never find out they carry the trait. That's the best-case scenario. Magic wasn't meant for your world, and those who have it don't thrive. If a person with magic is discovered…well, your people are so quick to kill anything different from themselves, aren't they?"

Freak bitch. Turner's cry when he attacked me.

Darragh continued. "Those who realize what they are, and avoid detection, tend to live lonely, isolated lives." Darragh examined his empty cup. "Too often cut short by their own hand."

"Why don't you bring them here?"

"Hiraeth is dangerous. We've evolved magic for a reason. If we start bringing people from Earth, even if they have magic, there's a risk their offspring won't. That's a death sentence. Even the most basic Hiraethians have enough magic to scrape by."

"So, Bowyn's mad you might get in trouble?"

Darragh nodded. "I'm not sure what will happen if the wrong person finds out I brought you here."

Bowyn did indeed come back.

There wasn't a trace of residual anger about him. In fact, he possessed such charm that I wondered if the original Bowyn walked into the woods, only to be replaced by a twin. Darragh headed back to the kitchen. As he passed Bowyn, he asked, "Are you finished?"

"I'm not entirely sure what you're talking about, my darling." Bowyn smiled sweetly. Darragh only rolled his eyes and continued into the kitchen. "You're lucky I'm here at all. Do you know how many people would love to have me around?" Bowyn made his way to the sofa and sat beside me.

"Can't imagine why," Darragh muttered.

"Because I'm big! And spicy! And foreign!" Bowyn shouted. He turned to me. "But then again, no one is more foreign than you are. Isn't that right, my love?" My throat suddenly dry, I swallowed. While I sat facing the fire, Bowyn had placed himself so that he faced me. His large knees brushed my thigh.

"Hmm?" Bowyn tilted his chin.

"Yes. I'm from—"

Our eyes met.

Weren't Bowyn's eyes brown? They were silver now. A stunning contrast against his skin. His lips called to me, thick and supple… I shook my head, frustrated. "Sorry. I forgot what I was saying."

Bowyn took my hand. His skin was buttery soft, his touch delicate. "That's alright my love. We've got all day." Unable to look away, I nodded slowly. Dizzying warmth crept into my cheeks again—

A crash erupted from the kitchen. Bowyn tensed and dropped my hand. Darragh knelt to clean up the shards of a plate, which appeared to have *fallen* from the counter. As Darragh stood, he shot Bowyn a stern look. A thought seemed to pass silently between them, and Bowyn grinned. He wore the smile of a child caught doing something he knew he shouldn't be. The silver ebbed from Bowyn's eyes, and he said, "Let's not trouble ourselves with the work of men, my dearest Nell." The sofa groaned as he shifted and stood. "Come. Let's have a walk while Darragh works his magic in the kitchen." Bowyn offered to help me up. I glanced at Darragh and Bowyn hissed, "You're a woman; you don't need his permission."

Bowyn had a point. I took his arm.

The muscle in Darragh's jaw twitched. Without looking up he said,

"Don't go far."

"Look at me." Bowyn flexed. "I'll keep her safe."

"Your strength means nothing here. Don't leave the nettle and stay where I can see you."

Bowyn ushered me out but hesitated himself, shouting, "My dearest, I'm a giant dressed in scarlet! You can always see me!"

Bowyn walked in a swishy way that reminded me of Sasha. A pang of homesickness swept through me. Was I *really* homesick for a dingy apartment and a minimum wage job?

Yes.

I missed Sasha, and Watney. I missed being alone and feeling safe in my apartment, even if it was a little dingy. Now that the choice was taken away, I was struck with the uncontrollable urge to tidy and organize all my things. Once I got home, I'd start right away. I'd do the dishes, and—Bowyn tugged my arm, bringing me back to Hiraeth.

If.

If I got home.

"Nell—that's an interesting name," Bowyn began.

"Short for Eleanor."

"Well, I owe you an apology, Eleanor. I'm dreadfully ashamed of my behaviour."

"It's okay." I shrugged. "Darragh explained it. You're just looking out for your friend."

Bowyn shouted, "Exactly!" and I flinched. With a huff, Bowyn regained his composure. "*However*, I shouldn't have said what I said. Darragh shouldn't have left you to die—and I'm pleased he didn't." Patting my arm, Bowyn added, "I'm thrilled you're alive, especially for his sake."

"Oh. Thank you."

What did Bowyn mean, for *his* sake?

73

Bowyn abruptly changed direction. I clung to his bicep, nearly falling into one of Darragh's gardens. Bowyn didn't notice. He led us to a rustic bench made of branches, nestled beneath a large droopy tree. Bowyn motioned for me sit, and when I did, he sat beside me. Leaning back, Bowyn placed his arm along the bench. He stroked my shoulder absently. "What do you do back home, Eleanor?"

I hated that question.

"I just serve people drinks."

"What do you mean *just*?"

"I don't know. It's not an important job."

"If it's not important, why is there a need for it?" I opened my mouth to respond but closed it when I couldn't think of an answer. "What sort of magic can you do?" I asked instead.

Bowyn let out a disgruntled cough. "It's frowned upon to ask people about their magic."

"I'm sorry," I backpedaled. "I didn't know." I couldn't help myself from asking, "Why?"

"Some have more than others."

"Oh. I'm sorry," I repeated.

Bowyn squeezed my shoulder. "It's alright, my love. I've always said, it's not how much you have, it's how you use it that counts." Bowyn gazed out over the gardens. "I don't mean to be sensitive; I grew up comparing myself to Darragh. He's surprisingly powerful for a man."

"For a man?"

"The weaker sex."

"What do you mean?"

"We men generally aren't as powerful as women."

"Huh," I muttered, wondering if that was true.

Now that I had someone who wanted to talk about magic, question after question raced through my mind. "If you all have *some* magic, why can't you *learn* how to do everything?

"Even if I know *how* to do something, I might not have the capacity." Bowyn pointed to a small stone. "See that rock?"

"Yes."

"Well, you know you're strong enough to lift it, just by looking at it." He pointed to a much larger rock. "You know you can't pick that up. You don't even have to try. You're not strong enough." He saw me eye the large rock. "Don't try. You'll only hurt yourself. Anyway, that's what it's like with our magic. Even if we know how something should be done, some of us just aren't strong enough to do it."

To hear Bowyn say he wasn't strong enough baffled me.

"If I got a crane or a pulley, I could use leverage to move it."

Bowyn looked over his shoulder. I don't know what he was looking for; the only other person around was Darragh. "People on Hiraeth can be a bit...persnickety about technology and sciency things. It's all very controversial. Try not to talk about it."

"Why not?"

"They don't trust it. As far as most people are concerned, science is just something men with little magic do at home when they're bored."

"Do you believe in science then?"

Bowyn pursed his lips and bopped my nose with one gigantic finger. "Cheeky."

"So, what do you do here?"

"I help people who've lost their magic."

"Can that happen?"

"It can. And believe me, Hiraeth is no place for someone without magic."

"How does someone lose their magic?"

"Trauma, sadness. Lots of things can take magic away. I work with

75

people to get it back."

"How?"

"This." Bowyn brushed my arm. "We have conversations, make plans and goals. Mostly I just listen. You'd be surprised how many people find their magic once they feel they've been heard."

"So, could you help me figure out my magic?"

Bowyn's eyebrows furrowed. "Well—"

"Time to eat," Darragh interrupted. I jumped, and Bowyn yanked his arm away. The way Darragh glared at Bowyn, I half expected Bowyn might burst into flames right there on the bench. Even more surprising, Bowyn's playful smile had vanished.

Stroking his beard, Bowyn mumbled, "Uh, splendid. We're right behind you."

Darragh grunted and left.

Bowyn lumbered to his feet and offered me his arm. When I took it, he leaned in close and said, "I'll help you."

After breakfast, Bowyn withdrew several empty bottles from his satchel and set them next to the washing basin. Next, he pulled out a wheel of cheese and a handful of jars packed with seeds. One-by-one, Darragh placed colourful bottles onto the counter, and Bowyn tucked them into his satchel. The soft clinking of glass followed Bowyn as he rounded the counter and grasped my hands. "Lovely to meet you, my dearest, Eleanor." He brought my hands to his lips and kissed both. "I simply cannot contain the anticipation of our next endeavor." To Darragh, he said, "Goodbye, my friend." Darragh simply waved him off. Bowyn snatched a bundle of herbs from a rafter and, after slipping it in his satchel, he left.

"What's all this?" I asked, pointing to the items Bowyn had left on the counter.

"Saves me the trip to town." Darragh unstoppered the empty bottles and placed them in a large wooden basin. The basin filled with water.

"I didn't know you could control water too."

"I can't." Darragh's lips compressed into a hard line. "The cottage does it."

I sat on the stool watching Darragh scrub bottles. "I didn't realize it was rude to ask people about their magic."

Darragh snorted. "Did Bowyn say that?"

Who else would have said it?

"Yes."

"He would say that."

"Because he doesn't have much?" I asked.

Darragh nodded. "Bowyn enchants people. He makes them feel good, and they're drawn to him." Bowyn had made me feel good, like that sweet, happy spot after a few drinks, where my cheeks ached from laughing, and I loved everyone and everything. Darragh continued. "He's a master at getting what he wants, but otherwise, he has very little in the way of magic." Darragh set a sparkling bottle upside down to dry. "*Mostly,* Bowyn uses his magic for good. People feel comfortable around him, and they discuss things they might not otherwise talk about. In his own way, he helps those who are struggling." Darragh shrugged and rinsed a bottle. "When he's not too busy bedding them, of course."

If I was under Bowyn's enchantment long enough, I might very well have offered him the boots off my feet. An uncomfortable thought pitted my stomach. "Bowyn wouldn't use his magic to make people sleep with him though, would he?"

Darragh scoffed and said, "Magic has nothing to do with it." He set the next bottle down so forcefully, I was surprised it didn't shatter.

Chapter Seven

ignis tofana

Darragh wandered into the conservatory, where he made rounds watering plants.

"Magic can't do that?" I asked.

"It can. When I'm away, the cottage cares for them, like an extension of me." Darragh tipped his copper watering can over the lip of a pot. "When I'm here, I prefer to do it myself." He set the can down. "I have some things I need to do outside."

"Can I help?"

"Uh…" Darragh blinked back surprise. "Of course."

We worked quietly in Darragh's gardens. All the plants were unrecognizable, and I did my best to follow his lead. I yanked anything that looked similar to those he'd already discarded. Occasionally, I'd pull a plant and Darragh would hiss like he'd been stabbed. He never complained though, he simply offered a pained smile before he tossed the dead plant with the discarded weeds. I made some efforts at small

talk, none of which got me anywhere. Darragh just didn't say much…
until I pointed to a tall stalked blue flower with red thorns and asked,
"What's this?"

"Queensfoil." Darragh crouched next to me and the plant. "You
make it into a paste. It helps with poisons and wound healing." He
touched a thorn. "You can also brew a tea, calms the nerves."

"Neat." I pointed to a large, succulent-looking plant. "What
about that one?"

"Veria." Darragh broke off a leaf and clear gel oozed out. "Good for
the skin. May I?" Darragh reached for my hand, and I let him have it. His
hands, callused and strong, were hot. Darragh squeezed out more gel. I
couldn't ignore the tremble of his fingers as they moved in wide circles,
massaging me. Such an innocent act that made my cheeks burn. Darragh
pulled away, looking at the ground.

"How's that?"

I felt my hand with the other. It was baby soft. "Can you even it
out?" I offered my unmassaged hand. Darragh repeated the gesture. This
time, instead of pulling away, he lingered. Our eyes met and I felt each
heartbeat as Darragh held my gaze.

He let go and climbed to his feet. "I should get back to work—"

"Wait," I blurted and pointed at another plant. "What about that
one?" Darragh focused on the flower, his shoulders drooped as he
relaxed. I didn't hear what it was called, but I was happy to hear him talk
about it. Slowly, Darragh's tense, jerky movements gave way to fluid,
comfortable actions. We abandoned the work and walked from garden to
garden. I pointed, and Darragh told me everything he knew.

I was particularly taken by a massive patch of flowers Darragh
called *false water*. "It treats burns. When you cook it down," he said.
Sapphire blooms danced in the wind; I dragged my hand along them—

they were ice on my fingertips. In a neighbouring garden, a fragrant flower with a deep, u-shaped bloom caught my eye. When I asked about it, Darragh turned a lovely shade of pink. "Awakens the passion," he muttered, stooping to pull a weed.

Heading to the last garden, I noticed the fence was taller than the rest. Spiked, deadly plants of all shapes and sizes filled the beds. One plant, with deep-purple flowers, dripped a thick, oozing sap. A sickly-sweet smell wafted out, and I pinched my nose.

"Tell me about these ones."

It seemed Darragh had deliberately avoided this garden. He grimaced and said, "Those… Those ones aren't very nice."

I put one foot on the bottom rail of the fence.

"Nell, what are you—" Darragh started. I made to swing my other leg up and over the fence. "Nell, stop!" Darragh rushed after me.

"Why?"

"Because it's dangerous!" Darragh eased me back to the ground. "And I said so!"

All the neat, dangerous plants called to me. I looked back enviously. Darragh shook his head. "I'm going to work on dinner. Stay where I can see you." He left for the cottage, muttering as he went.

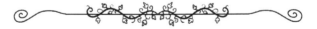

I waited until I was hungry to head back inside. It didn't take long. We'd skipped lunch during our plant tour, and my stomach grumbled. When I returned, I found Darragh had rearranged the living room. A long wooden table replaced the sofa by the fireplace. The table overflowed with more food than two people could eat in a week, let alone one meal. Piles of pillowy breads and thick slices of cheese, plates filled with stuffed mushrooms and roasted vegetables. Darragh carried more food from the kitchen, and I took my seat. He sat at the opposite end.

Eying a wooden bowl heaped with what I hoped was similar to mashed potatoes, I said, "How very *Beauty and the Beast*."

"I don't know what that means, but I have a feeling I know which one I am."

"A beast captures a man and keeps him locked away in his castle. The man's daughter trades her life for her fathers and goes to live with the beast as his captive." I scooped maybe-potatoes onto my plate. "I think that's the gist of it." I left out the bit where the heroine falls in love with the beast.

Darragh shook his head while he ate. "You're not my captive."

"Okay, well, as nice as this is,"—I gestured to the spread—"I am going to have to go home. I have a life. People will miss me."

"Who? Your coworker?"

Okay, wow. Rude.

"And my cat," I grumbled, taking a bite of maybe-potatoes. Not potatoes. Parsnipy in flavour. With a scowl, I heaped some vegetables on my plate and tore a piece of bread.

"It's not safe for you on Earth anymore," Darragh said.

"No offense, but I haven't really felt safe here either."

Darragh frowned.

"Maybe if I knew how to control my magic, I'd feel a little better."

Darragh didn't say anything; instead, he shoveled more food into his mouth.

"Could you at least try to teach me?"

"It's risky." Darragh pushed a mushroom around his plate. "I'm not the one to do it."

"I just think I'd feel safer if I knew how to protect myself."

"I can protect you."

"You can't always be around to watch over me, I'm not a toddler.

I'd like to learn it myself. Or else I may as well go back and take my chances on Earth."

Darragh covered his mouth while he mulled it over. He met my eyes, the lines on his forehead deepened, obviously conflicted.

"Please," I urged and smiled.

Darragh took a long drag from a wooden goblet. His fingers drummed the table while he thought. Finally, he pointed to a small bowl of nuts. "Focus on that bowl."

"Then what?"

"Move it."

Yeah right.

I focused all my effort on the bowl. Everything disappeared as I concentrated on it, on the little crack that snaked from the rim. On the small, yellowed nuts that sat inside. "Picture the movement in your mind," Darragh said.

A slight tremor shook the bowl.

"Hhh!" I gasped. "I did it!"

"That's enough for now." Darragh waved and the plates picked themselves up from the table. Dishes floated after him as he walked to the kitchen. He brought back two bowls filled with bright pink berries. A third bowl appeared, heaped with fluffy white topping. Darragh piled so much into the bowls that the berries disappeared.

"Thank you."

"Mhm," Darragh mumbled.

When we finished, Darragh put the living room back together. He'd barely sat back down when a timid knock came at the door. Darragh rose and cracked it. A hushed exchange of whispers was followed by silence. The door creaked as Darragh opened it wide. "Bring him in." Three people, each dressed in dark travelling cloaks, shuffled in. Two of the individuals withdrew their hoods, a woman and a man. The third individual hung limply between them, his arms strung around their necks for support. The woman saw me and hesitated. "We can trust her," Darragh reassured. The woman didn't move. "On my life, we can trust her." He pointed to the sofa. "Please. Your son doesn't have much time." The man gave the woman an icy glare and dragged his son to the sofa. They laid him down, and the man knelt. He rocked back on the balls of his feet and sobbed. The woman remained stoic, but she rubbed the man's back.

Darragh knelt and withdrew the hood, revealing a young man of maybe twenty. Though unconscious, he wore an uncomfortable scowl. "This is my friend, Nell." Darragh nodded to me. "Why don't you wait in the kitchen while I see what's wrong with Fyn." The woman eased the man to his feet. They both reluctantly followed me into the kitchen.

I struggled with the silence. "Would you like something to drink?"

The woman gave a curt shake of her head.

The man smiled and said, "Thank you, my dear, but no." I nodded, and he continued. "My name is Calyn. You can call me Cal. This is my melaethien, Breda."

Breda hissed in Cal's direction. "He said we can trust her!" Cal whispered.

"Yes, but can we trust him?" Breda snapped.

"We're here, aren't we?" Cal smiled apologetically, his eyes puffy and red. He turned back to his son. I seized the opportunity to focus on the ceiling. People crying made me cry. I blinked a few times to banish the tears. In the den, Darragh crouched over Fyn. "She's gone too far this time," Cal whispered. He looked at Breda for a reply. None came.

"Can you wake up for me?" Darragh asked. Fyn didn't respond. Darragh placed his hands on either side of Fyn's face. Silence filled the cottage; interrupted by the hitching of Cal's breathing while he wept. Darragh repositioned himself closer to Fyn. His brows furrowed. "Fyn, please wake up. Your parents are here." This time, Fyn's eyes fluttered open. A sob shuddered through Cal.

"Agh!" Fyn struck out, clawing Darragh. Cal and Breda rushed forward and grabbed Fyn's arms.

"Aghhh!" Fyn struggled—Darragh fought him, cupping his cheeks. As Darragh held on, the screaming and thrashing weakened. Gradually, as if falling asleep, Fyn stopped resisting. His eyes closed, and his head fell back with a *thunk*. Cal knelt beside his son, brushing sweat-soaked hair from his forehead. The scowl gone, Fyn's face was peaceful in rest. Darragh, who's throat bore three nasty scratches, locked eyes with Breda and nodded to the kitchen. Breda gave Cal and Fyn one last look before she followed. Darragh opened a drawer, two glass vials filled with a milky red liquid clinked together. He plucked one out and handed it to Breda.

"When he wakes up. For the pain." Breda placed the vial in her pocket. Darragh pulled open another drawer. It was empty. He waved and a pile of bottles and vials appeared. Darragh pushed several bottles out of the way and extracted a tiny vial containing a clear liquid. He held it between his thumb and forefinger. Lowering his voice, Darragh said, "Do not mix these two up." Breda's eyes darted between the vial and Darragh. Darragh offered the vial, but pulled his hand away before Breda could take it. "Do not get caught with this. Do you understand?"

Breda nodded once.

Darragh handed over the vial, which Breda slipped in her other pocket. She returned to her son and husband. "Come."

Cal stood, then rounded the sofa and embraced Darragh. "Thank you!" Fresh tears spilled down his cheeks. Darragh, rigid in the embrace, only offered a brief smile when Cal pulled away. Breda stooped and pulled Fyn's arm around her neck. Cal grabbed the other arm and, together, they shuffled to the door. Darragh opened it for them, and they disappeared into the night.

Darragh collapsed on the sofa. Closing his eyes, he sighed. He rolled his neck from side to side and opened his eyes wide—desperately trying to stay awake. I hoped for an explanation, but Darragh sat quietly, content not to discuss anything that just happened.

"You can heal people?"

"I can."

I needn't ask if Darragh could heal himself. Of the three scratches down his throat, only one remained—and even that was shrinking.

"Do these people give you anything for helping them?" I asked.

Darragh shook his head no.

"Why help them?"

Darragh's brows furrowed while he thought. "I don't know."

"Cal introduced Breda as his...melatonin?"

"Melaethien," Darragh corrected.

"Yeah, that. Does it mean like—"

"Their beloved, their partner."

"Like, marriage?"

"Sort of...but it's deeper than that. Our magic, or the energy—it knots us together. I don't know. But after you've chosen someone, that's it."

"What if one of you dies?"

A muscle twitched in Darragh's jaw. "Then the bond will help you find them in the next life." Darragh glanced longingly at the arm of the sofa, like it was the most comfortable thing he'd ever seen.

"What happens on Hiraeth when people decide to get married, or whatever it is they do?"

"Someone proposes, same as Earth." Darragh yawned and rubbed his eyes. "It used to involve an act of bravery, the retrieval of some trinket or jewel from a haunted barrow, or some other ridiculous venture.

Over the years, it's become more of a symbolic gesture; we've kept the jewels and ridded the dragons."

"Tell me about one."

"I don't really know any—"

"Yes, you do."

"It's late," Darragh protested.

"I'm not tired yet." I smiled at Darragh. His eyes, though clouded with exhaustion, softened. He took a deep breath and propped his head up with an elbow.

"Our queen's proposal to the king is the most noteworthy I know."

"Oh good, let's start there." I cozied myself by the fire.

"Leadership on Hiraeth isn't chosen by birth; it's chosen by power. The queen chooses a successor, and the people must come together and approve the decision. As it happens, powerful queens tend to have powerful heirs, so a single family could lead a kingdom for generations."

"What happens if the people don't approve of the choice?"

"An alternate must be provided, and they must prove themselves stronger than the queen's chosen successor." Darragh waited to see that I was done asking questions. "Our current queen was born the daughter of a butcher. Beautiful and tenacious, the townspeople nicknamed her Briar the butcher. Briar caught the fancy of a young man named Erabus, an affection she happily returned. Unfortunately, Erabus was the son of then Queen Aithen. Worse still, Erabus was basic, practically powerless by Hiraethian standards. If Aithen wanted her family to stay in power, she needed Erabus to wed a woman strong enough that the people would accept her as their next queen, and Erabus as king."

Darragh glanced at me, perhaps to see if I was still awake. I blinked back, still very awake. Darragh continued. "Briar was powerful, but not powerful enough to run a kingdom. Certainly not strong enough to gain Aithen, or the people's favour. The day finally came when Erabus told Briar that he would wed a woman from across the sea. Briar was distraught, but she had an idea." Darragh yawned. "West of here, there's a burrow. Trapped inside that burrow is a terrible, powerful creature named Jorgen. Legends said that he wore a ring which possessed the power of a thousand women. For years, people entered the cave hoping to kill Jorgen and take his ring. None left the cave alive. Briar knew this was her only chance to be with Erabus. If she could get Jorgen's ring, she would possess such power that no one could stop her from taking the kingdom." Darragh yawned. "Three nights before Erabus was to wed, Briar entered the burrow."

"And?"

Darragh shrugged. "Briar herself objected during the wedding ceremony. A shiny new ring on her finger."

"Oh, snap!"

"Aithen and the people chose her. Briar and Erabus were wed that evening. Briar became *the Queen*." Darragh uttered the title with equal parts reverie and disdain, as if this queen was wholly different than those before her.

"How did Queen Briar—"

"Not Queen Briar," Darragh corrected. "Just *the Queen*."

"Oh…okay. How did she do it?"

"Only the Queen knows." Darragh's brows knitted. "And Jorgen I suppose."

"Hm." I gazed into the fire. "What happened to Jorgen?"

"He's still there, waiting for the right person to wander in and free him from his cage." Darragh glanced outside; he straightened, drowsy eyes suddenly alert. "It's late." My eyelids began drooping near the end of Darragh's story, so I didn't argue when he suggested we go to sleep.

I cleaned up and headed to the loft, but paused as a question I meant to ask earlier came back to me. "What was that second vial for? The one you gave Breda for Fyn?"

Darragh didn't look at me when he said, "It wasn't for Fyn."

Lying in bed, that thought kept me awake. I'd nearly nodded off when the door to the cottage opened and closed. I propped myself up and peeked through the window. Darragh walked down the path that led to the wood.

Where was he going?

Chapter Eight

the daughter of the queen

Elwyn

The candles did little to illuminate the food on the table. Rivulets of water dripped down the cavern wall and splashed in the puddles on the rock floor. We did not speak. Only the echo of the droplets broke the silence. A man sat across from me. He piled a spoonful of food into a mouth surrounded by a sharp, grey beard. His cheeks looked like small, round apples, tinged red from the drink in his hand.

They often were these days.

His warm, comforting eyes met mine. They made the silence a little more bearable.

My father. My king.

A cadaverous woman sat at the head of the table. Her skin fell, withered and leathery, from her bones. Years of dwelling inside the mountain had robbed it of any colour. Vibrant blue veins snaked across any part of her body that remained bare. Her once blonde hair, now completely white, circled her head in a wiry, unbrushed crown of tangles.

No longer able to sit upright, she slouched heavily against the chair. Her pale hands rested in her lap. A ring, a golden and crimson jeweled monstrosity, adorned one of her twig-like fingers. Her lips parted as an invisible hand carried a spoonful of food to her mouth.

The Queen.

Fur brushed my leg. Careful not to turn my head, I glanced below the table. A small brown critter stood on his hind legs. Tiny paws grabbed the edge of my dress.

Leshy.

He pointed to the table, and then to his mouth. I picked a bit of meat from my plate and snuck it to him. My eyes darted to the Queen, making sure she hadn't noticed. My father winked. When enough time passed, I pushed away my plate, still piled high with food. "Ahem." I coughed in my father's direction. I tilted my head toward the door. He nodded, dabbing his lips with a napkin.

"I think that's quite enough for me." He patted his stomach. "I believe a little walk is in order. Is that alright?" The Queen responded with a guttural noise. Whether that meant yes or no, I wasn't sure. Father leaned over, and my body tensed as his hand touched hers. His voice was warm as he said, "Thank you."

My father followed me into the dimly lit hall. We walked arm in arm through the paths carved into the mountain. "Why do you get close to her like that?" I snapped. "What if she hurts you again?"

Father, supported by a thick wooden cane, hobbled beside me. The cane appeared shortly after an argument with the Queen. Though he'd never admit it, I knew she'd hurt him. Father dismissed me. "The Queen loves me. She won't hurt me."

His stupidity was infuriating. "She will!" We rounded a dark corner. A man bumped my father. I cried, "Watch where you're going—oh!"

My cheeks flushed. "Darragh!"

Darragh kept his head bowed, gaze trained on the floor as he addressed us. "Daughter of the queen, my king."

"Why don't you use my name?" I stooped, trying to meet Darragh's eyes. "Why don't you call me Elwyn?" It upset me when he called me by my title. It was unfamiliar and emphasized the distance between us. Neither of which I wanted to encourage. Darragh smiled but said nothing.

Father raised a knowing brow. "Why don't we postpone our walk for tonight, Elle?" He embraced me and then hobbled down the rocky hall.

Darragh tucked a lock of hair behind his ear. He was so grown from the boy I used to play with—though, playing *with* was a generous insinuation. He was at least ten years my senior, and most of my childhood involved chasing him and Bowyn about, hoping to be included.

Overjoyed it was now just us, I asked, "How are you?"

"Darragh!" the Queen's commanding voice boomed behind us.

"Goodbye, Elwyn." Darragh walked around me. My fists clenched as I watched Darragh walk away from me, toward her. The Queen put a decrepit hand on Darragh's back and ushered him into her chamber. Her feet several inches from the floor, the Queen drifted silently toward me.

"Stay away from him," the Queen croaked.

"Why?" I lowered my voice. "Why can't you even consider him a match for me? He's powerful. He—"

"Tsk," the Queen spit. "The people would never see you as a queen with him beside you."

"What does it matter what the people say? Together, we'd be strong enough to destroy anyone who stood against us." An invisible hand struck me. The force sent me sprawling against the cold passage wall.

"I will not consider it," the Queen hissed. I pushed off the rock and stood straight. A bruise blossomed on my cheek. "Stay away from him," the Queen repeated. With that, she drifted away.

I ran through the stone hallways. In a dark passage, I bumped into a slender woman. Clothed head to toe in a flowing black dress, she was one of the Queen's many guardians. She examined the lump on my cheek. "Are you alright?"

"Get out of my way!"

I made it back to my room, wrenching the door open and storming inside. The door closed with a furious *bang!* I collapsed in bed, buried my head in the blankets, and wept.

Knock-knock-knock-knock-knock-knock-knock.

I fanned tears away and opened the door. Leshy's arms pumped with determination as he scurried into the room. Doubling over, he struggled to catch his breath. He straightened and stretched his paw to give me something. A tiny shard of ice. I laughed and dislodged a fresh set of tears from my chin. The ice melted before I pressed it to my bruise, but I continued with the motion anyway. I sat down and focused all my energy on the purple stain spreading across my cheek. I pulled at the bruise and, slowly, it healed. As the bruise faded, so did the terror in Leshy's eyes. He struggled onto my bed and placed his paws where the bruise had been.

"Gotcha!" I scooped Leshy up and tickled his belly. His delightful squeals filled the room as he squirmed away. "Oh, no you don't!" I pulled him into a tight hug. Leshy was a gift from Darragh, six years ago, on my twelfth birthday. His words lived affectionately in my memory: '*A friend to keep you company in this lonely mountain.*'

Knock. Knock. Knock.

The door edged open and my father peeked in. Leshy scrambled under the bed. Crossing my arms, I looked away, refusing to acknowledge my father. Beside me, the bed bowed under his weight.

"The Queen told me what happened."

My teeth ground each other.

"I brought you a gift." Father placed a parcel tied with fragile paper and ribbon on the bed. I tore it open and found an intricate dress of cream and mauve. I tossed it aside.

I had six just like it.

Father pulled another tiny gift from his robes and held it over the edge of the bed. After a pause, two paws took the parcel, retreating with it under the bed and out of sight. Paper tore and Leshy squealed. Pulling on a tiny red vest and hat, Leshy scrambled to the floor-length mirror across the room. He stood on two legs, admiring himself. He cooed at every new angle the mirror revealed.

Despite the obvious bribes, I hadn't forgotten about the Queen.

"I hate her."

My father glanced at the door, and the creases around his mouth deepened. "Be mindful of what you say, Elle." He fumbled with the head of his cane, an intricate griffin. "She wasn't always like this." He withdrew a lacy white glove from his robe and handed it to me. "Remember her how she used to be."

The glove tingled, and I embraced the memory it held. I saw the Queen through my father's eyes. A breathtaking young woman, with long, cream-coloured curls and lavender eyes. The corners of her eyes crinkled as she smiled a contagious, perfect smile. He loved this version of the Queen so much. The way she looked back at my father, I knew she loved him too.

This woman was not the Queen I knew.

What happened? How could this wonderful young woman, so vibrant and full of life, have turned into the monster that held my father and I captive? Not wanting to see more, I tossed the glove down.

My father held my cheek. "You look so much like her—when she was young."

"Why do we stay?" I shoved his hand away.

The king paused before he said, "I love her."

"You love the person in this memory. That's not her anymore."

"Maybe one day she'll—"

"And what about this?" I thrust my hand in his face. An ugly silver ring wrapped my index finger. For as long as I could remember, the Queen forced me to wear it. She told me I'd had an accident when I was a child and nearly killed us all. To protect me, she forced me to wear the ring. It made me weak, limiting my power to the basics. Every year, she promised me the next year, I could remove it. I had hoped on my eighteenth birthday, it would come off, but the day came and went several months ago. Furious, I'd tried to remove it myself. It electrified my entire body, and I'd spent three weeks in bed, unable to move. After that, the ring remained untouched.

My father groaned as he stood. We'd had this argument many times before, and it always ended the same. "The Queen is protecting you. She knows what's best for us." My father closed the door and left me alone. I snatched the glove and dug my fingers into the delicate lace. The glove tore, and I tossed the scraps aside. I grabbed the vase on my dresser, another gift from my father, and hurled it against the wall. It shattered, sending bits of porcelain and dust billowing out.

A brawny guardian opened the door and examined the carnage. "Clean it up!" I screamed and stormed across my room. I tore open the shuttered window and breathed in fresh air. Leaning on the windowsill, I wrung my hands. The silver ring felt bigger than ever.

I'm powerful—I feel it. Bubbling beneath my skin when I'm angry, or scared, begging me to let it out. I looked out over the woods and the plains that led to the far-off town. One day I'd leave this place. I'd take my father and Darragh with me.

No woman, no matter how powerful, would stand in my way.

Chapter Nine

a talisman just for you

The early rays of dawn lit the cottage as I crawled down from the loft the next morning. Still in his clothes from the day before, Darragh lay fast asleep on the sofa. A board creaked beneath my foot and Darragh stirred.

I waved. "Did you have a good sleep?"

Darragh reacquainted himself with his surroundings and glanced groggily down at his clothes. His eyes widened and darted to me. "I had to run into the village." He pushed his hair behind his ear and looked at his feet. His voice cracked as he said, "Complications with Fyn."

Liar.

Where was he last night? What right do I have to ask?

I waited for the truth. Darragh refused to look at me. I might not have a right to ask where he was, but I had a right to walk away when someone lied. Crossing my arms, I said, "I want to go home."

Darragh propped himself up. "It's not safe for you on Earth."

"I don't care!" I shouted. "It's not safe for me here! Everything wants to kill me. I can't control my magic. I'm lost, and useless. I'm relying entirely on you to keep me alive. It's like I'm trapped in the middle of the ocean, and the only thing keeping me from drowning is this tiny little raft—"

"A raft?" Darragh interrupted. "I'm more of a ship."

"Ships sink!" I shouted. "And then I'm dead."

Darragh inhaled, preparing to argue, but instead he just frowned, then glanced at the ceiling, contemplating. I was right. If anything happened to him…

"I have an idea." Darragh swung his legs off the sofa and sat up. He untied a necklace, from which hung a carved wooden bird. Cradling the necklace, lines creased Darragh's forehead while he concentrated.

The bird started to glow.

"Oh," I said, startled.

The bird burned brighter and brighter, until I had to look away. Darragh grunted as if struck, and the light died. "There," he said, rather proud of himself. He handed it to me. It was an unassuming wooden bird once more.

"It looks the same."

"So ungrateful!" Darragh crossed his arms. "It's a talisman imbued with my magic—a piece of me to carry with you."

I recoiled. "Like, something an evil wizard might make?" I meant it as a joke. Darragh looked confused, and more than a little hurt. "What's it do?" I asked quickly.

"It's a one-off burst of my magic. If you get in trouble, this will help. It might make you feel a little safer until you can control your own."

"Oh, okay." I examined the little bird. "Can I have, like, ten of these?"

"I'm hoping you don't even need that one." Darragh laughed. "It takes a piece of my magic with it. I'll be weaker until it's used up." He lowered his eyes. "And it's quite painful."

I'm terrible at receiving gifts. Unsure how to respond to a gift so meaningful, I shifted and tried to think of what to say. I should have said thank you. Instead, I lowered the necklace over my head and said, "Happy bird-day to me."

Darragh reached out, turning the bird so it sat straight on the leather. His fingers brushed my skin; he frowned and pulled away.

"Do you truly wish to return to Earth?"

Homesickness rose within me. Watney, Sasha, a cup of coffee—all the things I missed flashed through my mind. Mulling the decision, I glanced out the window, to the trees looming at the end of the path. That wood was filled with terrible monsters, all manner of creatures that would have me dead if I wasn't careful.

"Yes." I shivered. "Yes, I do."

Darragh cleared his throat and nodded. "I'll take you back." Blinking quickly, he turned and headed for the door. As Darragh walked away, an inexplicable wave of panic spiked my adrenaline. Before I could speak, the door closed behind him.

Through the window, I watched Darragh walk a few paces and pause. He rubbed his neck and stared at the ground. His reaction puzzled me. We'd only just met. And yet, the way Darragh's gaze rose and lingered on the pale pink sunrise, one might think he was preparing to say goodbye to a very old friend.

Stranger still, while I wanted to go home, a small part of me, growing louder every moment, was disappointed that I didn't join Darragh before the rising sun.

Darragh returned shortly thereafter, wearing a stony, absent expression. I didn't even manage a greeting before he said, "There are a few things

I have to get for our journey to Earth."

"Okay."

"I'll return in a few days."

"Wait—what?" I rounded on Darragh so quickly, he flinched and dropped his bag. "You're leaving me here?"

Pointing at the floor, Darragh said, "You're safe here."

"What if something happens to you? No one knows I'm out here."

"Bowyn knows you're here."

Ugh. I still wasn't so sure about Bowyn.

"I'll only be gone a few days," Darragh reasoned.

I didn't want to stay here, alone, for a few days. I wanted to argue, but there's a level of familiarity in arguing, and I wasn't there yet. It was easier just to say, "Fine." Darragh went to the kitchen, where he unpacked jars and herbs from his bag. They floated away, finding spots on shelves and in cupboards. I crossed my arms and sat sullenly on the sofa. When I realized Darragh had nothing more to say on the topic, I stood up. "I'm going for a walk." Darragh started to respond, but I slammed the door.

I stumbled down the path, and before I knew it, I'd entered the wood. I paced at the edge of the trees, pouting. Fifty feet into the wood, a shadow dipped behind a tree, and I stilled. I squinted, hyper focused on the trunk. A hand with three fingers wrapped around the bark. Slowly, it slid away and out of sight. I backed up the way I'd come, into the sunshine of the meadow.

Darragh's right. I'll be safer in the cottage.

"Ugh," I grumbled at the reasonable thoughts. I looked back down the path. Darragh was sitting, arms crossed, out on the bench where he could see me. I picked my way through the gardens. I brushed aside a droopy branch and sat beside him.

"Are you hungry?" Darragh asked.

I kicked the dirt and muttered, "Yes."

"Let's go eat." Rather than head inside, Darragh walked into the wood. The trees grew thick here, the leaves knit so tight, hardly any light filtered through. Darragh skirted a massive, red-barked tree. I circled the tree—lights flickered above. Glass jars filled with twinkling lights hung from the branches. Beneath them, amongst the soft moss and rocks, lay a blanket and basket filled with food.

I smiled. "Is this how you eat most of your meals?"

Darragh shrugged, a sudden bashfulness about him. "I saw it in a *Home & Garden* magazine." He brushed the bottom of a lantern as he walked by, side-eying me. "Do you like it?"

"I do."

Darragh waited for me to sit. I knelt, and he sat down across from me. I picked up a piece of smoked cheese and popped it in my mouth. A small box sat amongst the food.

"What's that?"

"A peace offering," Darragh said. I met his eyes and his lips tugged into a hopeful smile. I cradled the box in my lap and lifted the wooden lid. It was filled with a curious assortment of trinkets. An ivory fang, a wooden dragon, broken and missing a wing, several stones, a piece of scarlet fabric. I picked up a glimmering, purple stone. Sparks of energy travelled down my fingertips.

"They're enchanted. I thought it might help you pass the time while I'm gone."

"How do I use them?"

Darragh took my hand in his and closed it around the stone. "Close your eyes and open your mind." I did as Darragh said, concentrating on the tingling in my fingers. My surroundings fell away...

A shallow creek flowed at the tip of Darragh's boots. The same stone

I held lay at the bottom of the creek bed. Darragh wanted it. A splash rang out from the other side of the creek as a young red-headed girl placed her feet in the water. She waved at Darragh, and he blushed. Glancing back at the stone, Darragh raised his hand to pull it out—a great force pummelled him from behind. Darragh flew forward, and a shock of cold swept through me as he plunged into the water. Scrambling to his feet, Darragh rounded on his attacker.

"Ha ha ha!" A boy stood on the shore laughing riotously. Though younger and beardless, it was unmistakably Bowyn. Darragh glanced at the girl on the bank, and Bowyn blew her a kiss. She scrunched her nose, slipped her feet from the water, and left. Bowyn, still laughing, put his hand out to help Darragh. A curious shadow loomed over Bowyn. He retracted his hand and pivoted, only to be met with a terrifying creature. Darragh's thoughts supplied the name: manticore. A woman's face glowered down from the body of a giant lion. Features contorted in fury, the manticore swung at Bowyn with a massive, scorpion-tail. Bowyn dodged and scrabbled away, running to the nearest tree. He climbed it, manticore swinging and champing at his heels.

"Do something!" Bowyn shrieked, a pitch so high even the manticore cringed. Darragh laughed as he climbed out of the creek and continued laughing as he walked away.

Bowyn's cries rang out as the memory faded and the trees reappeared. Knowing Bowyn survived the predicament, I chuckled at his misfortune. Darragh's cheeks curled up in a tiny smile. For a brief moment, his keen eyes flicked to my lips and back. It was such a subtle movement, but it silenced my laughter and sent my heart fluttering—

An agonized screech erupted in the distance. Darragh leapt to his feet, and I dropped the stone.

"I'm going to go see what that was," Darragh said. "Stay here."

"I'll come with you." I set the box down.

"Nell. Please." Darragh frowned. "I'll be right back. Stay put for two minutes."

"Fine."

Darragh's back disappeared into the trees.

I rifled through the box. At the very bottom, I found a small wooden doll. I'd seen similar carvings back home, usually sold in a set or "family". Blackened and charred, the doll looked like it had survived a fire. While the other objects felt cheerful, this one felt like...terror and regret. I wanted to drop it, but it was too late. The edges of my vision darkened as the trees fell away.

Burning heat erupted around me. Lying in bed, flames climbed the walls of my bedroom. Screams carried through the house—the door to the bedroom flew open. I could hardly make out the figures through the inferno that consumed me. A man, who looked like Darragh, but slighter, tried desperately to get into the room. The screams that came from him were inhuman—so filled with desperation they sent chills through me. He reached out, but someone yanked him back. I struggled to see the figure in the flames... A woman? With superhuman strength, she ripped the man away. I caught a flash of long, red hair as she slammed the bedroom door. Leaving me alone to burn.

"I'm not sure how that got in there." Darragh, having returned from scouting, took the doll.

Being torn from the memory left me whiplashed. Sweat poured down my forehead as I steadied myself. I choked out, "I don't feel so good."

"Yeah." Darragh crossed his arms and watched as I tried not to be sick. "Let's get inside."

I splashed cold water on my neck and returned to the main room. "Would you like to talk about that?" I pointed at the doll, which now sat on the highest shelf in the kitchen.

Darragh stiffened. "No."

"Okay." I sat on the stool across from him. "If you ever want to, I'm here to listen."

Darragh's shoulders raised.

"Or not," I clarified. "I just wanted to offer."

Darragh relaxed, and he smiled appreciatively. "Would you like a drink?"

"I'm okay. Thank you."

The door opened and Bowyn waltzed in. Darragh raised an eyebrow in my direction and repeated, "Drink?"

"A strong one," I amended.

Darragh puttered around the kitchen. Bowyn set two meaty hands on the counter and squinted at him. "Are you humming?" Darragh's brows furrowed, as if he wasn't sure of the answer himself.

I smiled.

He had been.

Bowyn clapped loudly beside my ear, and I tensed. "I'm not sure if anyone is aware, but there's a man in the garden."

"What?" Darragh peered out the window. "Oh."

I leaned so I could see. Cal waited patiently outside. "I'll be right back," Darragh announced. As he passed Bowyn, he growled, "Be nice." Bowyn feigned a look of offense as Darragh left.

Bowyn went to the kitchen to make himself a drink. "Another satisfied customer, I see."

"Yeah." I scooted off the stool and moved to the sofa. How long would Darragh be with Cal? I peeked out the window again. Arm in arm, Cal and Darragh strolled away.

"He'll be back before you know it, my love," Bowyn whispered. I jumped. He was sitting comfortably next to me, wearing a sly smile.

"Your drink?" He handed me a cup.

"Uh, thanks." I set the cup on the table next to the sofa. Bowyn watched the cup as it sat, untouched. An unbearable, awkward silence ensued. "I'm going to go to the bathroom—"

"He's keen on you, you know."

I snorted. "I don't think so.

"Why do you say that?"

"I don't know. Anytime I get near him he…shrinks away." Whenever I got close to Darragh, he found an excuse to move and change the subject. He did his best to put as much distance between us as possible. I recalled something Sasha had said, that he wasn't sure whether Darragh was interested in men or women. "I just—I can't help but think he might be more interested in *you* than me."

Bowyn threw his head back and laughed. "And how could you blame him?" My cheeks flushed and I looked away. Bowyn placed his hand on mine. "I apologize, my love, but that was *too* easy." He took a long drink and continued. "Once upon a time, I might have agreed with you, but that time has long passed. I promise." Bowyn patted my hand, and then pointed to the rubies. "See those flowers he brings you?"

"He didn't bring those for me—"

Bowyn fixed me with a dead eyed gaze which suggested I was perhaps the stupidest person on the planet. "You should ask Darragh where he gets them. It's no simple task."

"Yeah, maybe," I lied.

"Darragh informed me he's leaving in the morning to acquire certain ingredients for your trip to Earth. By the way, I hope my little outburst didn't influence your decision?"

"No. It's the right decision. I want to go home."

"Well, I suppose you must do what's best for you." Bowyn took another long sip. "Anyway, my point is, Darragh needs more of those flowers—well, the petals. Perhaps you could go with him?"

"I wasn't invited," I replied bitterly.

I sipped my drink.

Bowyn smiled.

"Well, Darragh has tasked me with keeping two of my exquisite eyes on you while he traipses around the country on his little treasure hunt." Bowyn fitted me with a pointed stare. "It would be a terrible shame if I came to call on you, and you weren't here."

"I don't know. Darragh seemed pretty serious about me staying here."

"Darragh would be *thrilled* if you joined him." Bowyn waved animatedly. "It would be a wonderful escapade filled with bonding and adventure and just good fun!"

That sure sounded better than sitting in this cottage for three days.

"He'll be positively jubilant you chose to join him, my love. I promise."

The door opened and Darragh slipped inside. Bowyn tilted his head and lowered his voice. "He'll be heading north, leaving at dawn. I know we must get our beauty sleep but, try not to sleep too late." Bowyn pointed at my cup. "Bottoms up."

The next morning, I awoke in darkness with such an urgency to pee that I leapt from the bed. My leg swung over the ladder as the door to the cottage quietly closed.

Darragh just left!

I had to decide now.

Follow him or stay behind.

Ignoring the remaining rungs on the ladder, I jumped down. In the bathroom, I peed for an eternity. What was in that drink Bowyn gave me? After I finished, I washed my hands and tore across the cottage. My clothes lay discarded on the floor of the loft, and I wriggled into them.

As I ran outside, Darragh disappeared into the trees at the top of the path. I hustled after him, wary of the nettle at the edge of the meadow. Careful not to get too close, I kept Darragh in my sight. I'd never met anyone who created so little noise when they moved, and every time he passed behind a tree or shrub, I thought I'd lost him.

Finally, we came to the river that Darragh had carried me over. The banks were less cluttered; the trees that pursued us must have cleared off. Just like before, Darragh hopped across the rocks with a graceful ease. I waited for him to get a good head start and crept to the edge of the river. My crossing was far less dignified. On the last stone, I slipped, and my feet splashed into the water.

I froze.

Had Darragh heard me?

When he didn't reappear, I hauled myself onto the riverbank. In the distance, Darragh bobbed and weaved through the trees. I jogged to catch up and came to a break in the wood. The white-tipped mountains loomed in the distance. I scanned the rocky landscape for Darragh, and my heart plummeted. The grove of *trees* which chased us had re-rooted back to the middle of the plain.

Darragh walked directly toward them.

"Please don't go in. Please don't go in," I mumbled.

Darragh walked straight into the trees and disappeared within.

"Damnit!" Not wanting to lose him, I trotted across the plain. I paused at the border of the grove; I really *really* didn't want to go in.

This is a stupid idea.

I should walk around, and when he comes out the other side, I'll just tell him what happened.

A gentle wail carried from deep within the grove. At first, I had trouble identifying it. I didn't *want* to identify it.

Screaming.

I strained to hear it more clearly.

"Help!"

Darragh.

"No, no, no, no, no, no," I whispered.

The wailing continued and a tightness spread through my chest. I flexed my fingers and wiped my palms against my pants. I rested my hands on my knees and peered into the dark. An ebbing breeze carried a foul stench from within.

"Is someone there?" Darragh cried. A whimper and an agonizing moan followed.

"Ugh!" I put one foot in the grove, and then the other. The light dimmed, and my skin prickled. The gnarled trees edged closer, I was sure of it. I stalked Darragh's pained moans, tiptoeing over giant roots that lay across the ground like pythons.

CRUNCH.

I yanked my foot away.

What was that?

A white mass writhed below my boot. My eyes adjusted to the dark—I stifled a scream. I'd stepped through a partially eaten rib cage. Wide holes had rotted through the decayed flesh. They wriggled and writhed as if alive, and I squealed as a wave of maggots crawled up my legs. Brushing them off, I backed away, and bumped into something moist.

Bits of rotten flesh dangled from the *nearly* picked-clean bones of a skeleton. Covering my mouth, my eyes darted around. What I'd thought were branches brushing my arms were corpses. Jagged remains of torsos and limbs protruded from the trees. Streaks of blood smattered my hands; I turned to run—

"Please!" Darragh's voice called.

So much fainter than before.

Stifling a cry, I wiped the blood on my pants. I took a shaky step in Darragh's direction.

Focus on Darragh. Don't look at the bodies. At least they aren't spiders.

Darragh would surely be dead if that were the case.

An eerie red glow loomed ahead. I aimed for it, and peered around a tree before stumbling in. "What?" The strange light radiated from a patch of flowers. The rubies. Darragh knelt, picking them, and putting them in his bag. He was perfectly fine.

But if Darragh was fine, who'd screamed?

Something wet *drip-dripped* on my shoulder. "Ah-AH!" I wiped it away. A shadow behind me moved and I froze. Drool dripped from the snarling mouth of a monster I'd mistaken for a tree. Behind it, more tree monsters inched forward. Eyes and gaping mouths, black and depthless like skulls, appeared in the gnarled bark. I stepped back into the clearing with Darragh. Branches tipped with fingernails of thorns reached out, and thick brown vines snaked along the grove floor. I needed to alert Darragh, but I couldn't speak. If I made a noise, the tree monsters would leap on me and tear me to shreds—

A hand grasped mine.

Darragh.

Eyes locked on the trees, Darragh pulled me behind him. All around us, the tree monsters pressed in, shrinking our circle. Darragh held out his hand, a film of blue flame sprung to life. A wave of hisses travelled through the trees, and they stopped creeping. Darragh stepped forward, pulling me with him. One of the trees let out a low snarl, its gaping mouth furious. Darragh pulsed the flame and the tree shrank away. We walked like this, slow and cautious, until the edge of the grove appeared.

My claustrophobia got the better of me. I wanted to run, to be out in the fresh air. My breathing quickened, and I struggled to suck in laboured breaths. The trees sensed the change in me… The weakness.

A vine slipped around my leg and ripped me from Darragh. My feet flew out and I slammed against the ground with a painful, "Oof!" Rolling onto my back, I tugged at the vines. Darragh's arms wrapped around my midsection, and he heaved, trying to free me. Pain shot up my legs, and I was sure they'd be torn from their sockets. With Darragh's fire extinguished, the trees were no longer frightened. Thorns and branches tore at me from all directions. Blood oozed through scratches in my pants.

Darragh muttered an incantation and curled around me. A sudden iciness chilled my skin as an explosion of fire erupted around us. Snapping my eyes shut, I tried not to choke on the smoke. My legs and palms scraped underbrush as Darragh dragged me through the flames.

The crackling fire ceased, and the cold ebbed from my flesh.

When I opened my eyes, we were outside the grove. Well, what was left of it. As far as I could see, scorched trees smoldered. As I examined the carnage, my gaze fell on Darragh. Smeared with dark soot, tendrils of smoke wafted from his shoulders. He crossed his arms, and his outraged eyes said, *explain yourself.*

"Uh, well, Bowyn said—"

"Bowyn said?" Darragh's arms fell to his sides, where his fists clenched.

I gulped. "Bowyn maybe *implied* you'd be happy if I joined you…"

Positively jubilant, I believe, were Bowyn's exact words. Darragh's nostrils flared. Black soot coated the inside of his nose.

Positively pissed was more like it.

I avoided Darragh's eyes when I said, "Honestly, I didn't think it would take you so long to notice me following you. I figured you'd have sent me back by now."

"I knew you were there."

"And you let me follow you into that deathtrap?!"

"I was keeping an eye on you. Did you learn your lesson?"

"What lesson? Not to follow you when I think you need help? Don't worry, I won't be doing that again."

"Firstly, not to disobey me. You should have stayed at the cottage. Secondly, and most importantly, *never* do what Bowyn says."

Disobey?!

"Who do you think you are?"

Darragh raised his voice. "I'm the experienced one! I'm the one trying to keep you alive long enough to get you home!"

"But—"

He was right.

Darragh pointed at the smoldering trees. "They didn't need to die!"

"I'm sorry." My voice cracked.

Darragh pressed a white-knuckled fist to his lips, stopping himself from saying more. He walked into the burned trees and rifled through debris for his bag. After several exaggerated steps out of the rubble, he swept his arm dramatically in front of us. "Shall we continue north, then?"

"Pardon?"

"We're behind. I don't want to camp out in the open. We need to move *now*."

"You're not taking me back?"

"Oh, no." Darragh gave me a too-sweet, sarcastic, smile. "Let's get you back to Earth as soon as possible." He stormed ahead. I took one last look at the devastated grove. I'd come awfully close to witnessing that tree scene from the Evil Dead firsthand.

I shuddered.

Chapter Ten

a riddle in the darkness

"We'll stay here for the night." Having left the plains, we'd trudged through a forested area until we came to a small clearing. The ground was bare, the shrubbery trampled from overuse, and the remains of an old firepit sat in the centre. Darragh pointed to the canopy, where a treehouse was nestled in the branches. I never would have seen it on my own. Darragh tossed his bag down and I collapsed. We'd walked for hours, and I'd dreamed about this moment the entire time.

Darragh remained standing. "We need to check the area."

"For what?" I gestured at the unassuming trees.

"We need to make sure it's secure."

"Do I *have* to?"

"I'd prefer if you stayed where I can see you."

Wasting what scant energy I had left, I sighed, with extra vigor, and dragged myself up.

"Stay close," Darragh muttered.

"Stay close," I mimicked.

Darragh walked silently through the forest, disturbing as little foliage as possible. I stomped loudly after him. A vine dangling next to the path brushed my arm—it wriggled against my skin. "Ah-ah!" I slapped the vine, and it swung away. As it arced back, it came to life and lunged at me. "Oh, shit!"

Fangs gnashed in my face, and I tumbled backward. The thing struck again, and I braced for the bite.

It didn't come.

The creature struck an invisible wall. It slid down the barrier until it reached the underbrush. The snake-vine-nightmare-thing hissed, displaying bright blue fangs, and then slithered away.

Darragh couldn't have looked more unimpressed if he tried.

"That was close, eh?" Smiling at Darragh, I *saw* him bite his tongue. I brushed leaves off my shins and stood. Following more closely, I picked my way through the bushes. Soon, the trees grew sparse, and the ground sloped down to where the forest continued below. The setting sun skimmed the treetops.

Darragh cleared his throat. "I'm sorry about what I said earlier."

"About what?"

"Getting you back to Earth as soon as possible."

"Oh." I shrugged. "It's okay. I deserved it."

"No, you didn't." Darragh faced me. "I shouldn't have said it—I didn't mean it." He shifted and pushed a hand through his hair. Redness crept into Darragh's cheeks; it tinged his ears bright pink.

"What's up?"

"I just… I'm happy you're here." Darragh chewed his lip and looked back to the sunset. "Even if it is for a short time."

A million questions tumbled through my mind, and before I could ask even one, Darragh turned and walked sullenly back to camp.

After a quiet campfire and supper, we climbed into the treehouse. Darragh cast a small orb of light onto the ceiling, illuminating a single room. He laid down a bedroll while I glanced out the open window.

Boots sounded on the ladder.

"Where are you going?" I asked.

"I'll sleep on the ground," Darragh replied. "You stay up here where it's safe."

"Are you sure? I can sleep on this side"—I pointed to the far side of the treehouse—"and you can sleep over there."

Darragh's gaze darted over the wooden boards. "I'll stay on the ground," he repeated. Worry nagged at me; Darragh wouldn't have made the treehouse if it was safe on the ground.

He's wrong; tell him so.

But I don't want to make a fuss…

"Okay."

Darragh disappeared. Then reappeared. "Uh, goodnight."

"Goodnight."

Gentle *thuds* sounded from Darragh's boots as he climbed down the ladder. Each step reinforced my disappointment like a hammer.

The creak of old wood and a sweet smell beckoned me from unconsciousness. Darragh sat neatly in the treehouse, with several plates of food laid before him. I pushed myself up and stretched. "You should have woken me up to help." I yawned. "Or at least eaten without me. You didn't have to wait."

"I kept it warm for us." Darragh piled pancakes onto a plate and handed it over. He slid a jar filled with thick purple syrup across the boards. "It's good with this." I poured the syrup over my food and a lovely, floral aroma filled the treehouse.

Darragh waited, eyes wide and rigid in anticipation. "How is it?"

Swallowing my first bite, I mumbled, "It's lovely. Thank you." I wondered if Darragh thought I was just being kind. He didn't dig into his own breakfast until I was onto my fourth and fifth bite.

"I can make more if you'd like."

There were twelve pancakes left on my plate.

"I think I might be full after this, but thank you."

We set out after breakfast, heading back to the slope where we'd watched the sun set the night before. Darragh and I picked our way down the rocky incline and walked along the base of the cliff.

"So, what are we looking for?" I asked.

"A stone."

"How will a stone get us back to Earth?"

"We trade it for passage. There's a man, Senan, who helps me cross. It's not exactly legal, but he'll look the other way for the right price."

"And this stone is the right price?"

Darragh nodded. "He's like—what do you call them on Earth? They like shiny trinkets and things."

"A magpie?" I guessed.

"Yes. Senan is a magpie."

"He's a bird?" I joked.

"What do you mean?"

"A magpie is a bird."

"No! It's a *person* who collects shiny bits. I read about it in one of your books."

"Yes, you call someone a magpie, based on their likeness to the bird.

The bird famously collects shiny objects."

Darragh looked confused.

"It's a metaphor, I think."

"What's a metaphor?" Darragh scratched his cheek.

I delved deep, searching for English classes. "I think it's when you draw comparisons between two things." I made a mental note to Google it when I got home—if I got home. "I'm sure you do it all the time without realizing. If I were to say, 'Bowyn is a tree,' that's a metaphor. I'm comparing Bowyn's height to a tree, so you know he's tall. I guess learning metaphors would be a nightmare on a different planet. How could you know a magpie was a bird?"

Darragh rubbed his chin, looking shaken. "What's another metaphor?"

"Uhhh." My mind emptied. "There's a famous play about two lovers, *Romeo & Juliet*. In the play, Romeo says 'Juliet is the sun.' I'm pretty sure that's a metaphor." I shrugged. "I don't know. Shakespeare was tough for me."

Darragh looked more confused than ever, but he pointed to a tiny crevice in the rock wall. "We're here."

I looked at the crevice, then Darragh, then rapidly back to the crevice. "We have to squeeze in *there*?"

Darragh nodded.

I swallowed and glanced around the forest. Maybe I could just wait out here…

Darragh, anticipating what I'd say next, said, "You'll be safer in there with me." He pursed his lips. "Actually, you'd be safer back at the cottage, but—"

"Let's get this over with."

Standing tall, Darragh sucked in his chest and slid into the crevice. I slipped in after him, hating the way the light disappeared behind us. The farther we inched, the tighter the walls squeezed, crushing my lungs.

What if I get stuck?

Cut it out!

What if the rocks collapse and I can't get out?

AHHHHHH!

My breathing hitched and I sucked in shallow gulps. A wave of panic started in my belly. My gasps echoed against the rock, so close, it brushed my nose. The terror crested, threatening to take over—Darragh reached back. The rock prevented him from looking at me, but he fumbled around until he found my hand. He gave me a firm, reassuring squeeze.

"It opens up soon," Darragh called. "You're almost there." Gripping Darragh like a vice, I focused on the warmth of his fingers, and the contrast of his cool, metal rings.

The crevice opened up, and Darragh helped pull me out. I doubled over and sucked in air. It was moist and tasted of mold.

"Are you okay?"

I nodded, but Darragh couldn't see; it was pitch black. "I'm fine."

"Close your eyes," Darragh warned. I did, and a bright light flashed through my lids. When I opened them again, a small creature of flame fluttered away from Darragh. It flitted about like a tiny canary, trailing smoke wherever it went. It took off down a dark path that stretched ahead. As we followed, Darragh caught me watching the fiery canary. "I can make it go away if it bothers you." He snapped his fingers, and the light returned to his hand.

"I thought it was cute," I admitted.

Darragh relit the fire creature. It burned brighter the second time. "Ash. That's what Bowyn used to call it," Darragh recalled. He touched my arm. "Don't look directly at it. Bowyn lost his sight for three days after I learned to conjure it."

I made a note to keep Ash in my peripheral. "How long have you known Bowyn?"

Darragh exhaled and scratched his chin. "Since I was six."

"It's nice that you're still friends." Darragh's only response was a non-committal grunt. I noticed Darragh's willingness to chat declined as soon as the conversation turned to his childhood.

The path gave way to a vast, dark cavern. I stayed close to Ash, reluctant to discover what lurked in the shadows. Ash flitted around our feet, and Darragh stooped to pick up a smooth stone, roughly the size of his palm. "We're looking for stones like this."

"Alright," I said, scouring the floor.

"Don't even think about touching anything that's not exactly like this, okay?" Darragh showed me the stone again.

"Yessir," I mocked.

Unsuccessful in my hunt, I wandered farther away. As I reached the perimeter of Ash's light, Darragh called, "I've got one." I headed back. Something red glinted on the rock wall. In the dim light, I glimpsed an ancient painting. It depicted a stick figure, held from all directions by thick chains. I admired the still-vibrant paint on the smooth stone. What would it feel like to drag my hand along it? A *click* echoed through the cavern, followed by a slithering sound. Before I could react, Darragh slammed into me, sending me crashing into the wall.

"What the—" I blurted.

A glowing green chain circled Darragh's legs. I reached out, but the chain yanked Darragh's feet from under him. It flipped him upside down and pulled him high into the air. I braced myself to be dragged up next. Another chain did not come.

"Are you okay?" I called.

Darragh's arms hung toward the cavern floor, his feet tied and held fast to the ceiling. "I've been better," Darragh called. Then more icily,

"You just couldn't resist, could you?"

"I didn't touch anything!"

Darragh crossed his arms. "You thought about it."

"You didn't tell me not to think about it!"

"I did," he replied crossly.

"Ugh!" I looked around. "How do I get you down?" I squinted at the chain. It adhered to the ceiling but came down somewhere in the cave. "Hold tight. I think I see the other end."

"Be careful," Darragh shouted.

"Come on," I beckoned Ash, who zoomed after me.

"I don't mean to be an alarmist," Darragh called, "but this chain is draining the life out of me. Haste is appreciated."

Ash's light bounced off the shallow puddles. I carefully picked my way across the slick ground. We located the chain where it met the far wall. Although it didn't really *meet* the wall, it passed right through it. Beneath the chain, several doors lined the rock. They blended seamlessly into the wall; I couldn't open them. I touched a door and a haunting melody filled the cavern. I tried to locate the source, but it came from everywhere all at once. An ethereal, airy voice joined the melody.

In a quiet meadow across the stream,

A young girl, only seven, picks a wild rose,

For each powerful queen this land has seen.

But nightfall approaches, make haste! She knows

At night, wicked creatures haunt the meadow.

She clutches her basket filled with flowers,

But as she wades across the stream, a shadow

Casts itself across the water, over her it towers.

A bathori! And behind, more wait.

Clever girl knows the creatures cannot cross a rose.

They screech and cry, eyes filled with hate.

On her way she goes,

Back home to her mother.

The creatures must devour another.

I wandered back to stand under Darragh. "Did you hear that?"

"It's a riddle," Darragh's voice was strained; I struggled to hear him. "Including our current queen, we've had thirteen. Bathori always travel in groups of seven, always. Thirteen minus seven is—"

"I can do the math," I called, heading back. I found the first door and counted. When I reached number five, I pushed. Stone ground stone, and the door fell away. I peered into the darkness.

A low, guttural growl echoed from within.

The tiny hairs on my arms stood up. Ash froze mid-flight. He emitted a blinding light and grew until he was the size of a horse. Heat poured from him like lava, and I cringed away. Ash ruffled his feathers of flame and let out an anxious, "Caw!"

With Ash's extra illumination, Darragh could see us. "Which door did you pick?" He squinted and pointed. "Did you pick that door?"

"Yeah, the fifth door—"

"Thirteen minus seven isn't five!"

I stared at the doors. My face pulled back into a deep cringe. "Ohhhh no…" Another growl echoed from the doorway.

Darragh's voice rose an octave. "Pick the door beside it!"

"Left or right?!"

"RIGHT!"

"My right or your right?!"

"WE'RE LOOKING THE SAME WAY! WE HAVE THE SAME RIGHT!"

"You're sure it's this one?" I gestured toward the door to the right of the one I'd chosen, terrified to get it wrong again.

"IT'S NOT MAGIC! IT'S JUST MATH!"

Too late.

Two spindly, black hands reached around the doorway. I zeroed in on the dark opening and shrunk away. A curved, elongated skull entered Ash's ring of light. The creature hissed, a breathy noise that sent drool oozing between silver teeth. It stalked out on four thin, vertebrate like legs.

It looked deadly...and fast.

A long, flexible tail flicked back and forth, cat-like, behind the creature.

Too terrified to scream, I thought as loud as I could: *Darragh, what do I do?* No reply came. I risked a glance over my shoulder. Darragh hung limply from the ceiling, unconscious. A quick-moving, shuffling sound closed in.

Teeth gnashed, and claws ripped my shirt just as bright light and fire exploded in my face. I careened back into a frigid, mucky puddle. I blinked in the dark, regaining my night vision. Like rabid dogs, Ash and the creature fought. High pitched squeals rang out as teeth and fire sought to dominate each other. Ash's bright talons sunk into flesh. The quick-moving tail lashed out and wrapped Ash's throat. The creature swung Ash to the ground.

"No!"

Ash squirmed and screeched as the wet rock ground against him. The creature lifted Ash into the air and slammed him onto the rock again.

And again.

Ash cried weakly.

In the dying light, I saw Darragh, still hanging helpless from the ceiling. Ash's light sputtered and went out, plunging the cave into darkness once more.

Keep the monster away from Darragh.

I sprinted in the direction we'd entered, and loud splashes echoed after me. Without Ash, I was blind, and the ground was uneven and slick. My feet hit a shallow patch of water; I slipped and lurched forward.

Whoosh!

The creature's tail whipped over me. I'd fallen just in time. Unable to see, I felt gangly limbs clawing for me. Scrambling to my feet, I ran back the way I'd come, toward the doors. I pumped my arms but slipped again, hydroplaning. "Oof!" I smashed into a boulder and pushed myself away—the creature's tail connected with my legs. The force propelled me into the cavern wall and knocked me to the ground. Sharp pain exploded up my shin and white stars prickled my vision. Adrenaline and fear kept my body moving. I turtle'd onto my hands and knees but didn't know which way to run. I'd become so disoriented; I had no idea where I was.

An ear-splitting screech rang out, and a searing light flared in the dark. I peered through my fingers; Ash was alive. He attacked mercilessly, swooping and tearing, until the puddles below the creature ran red. The tail swung frantically—a swing went wild, connecting with a hanging stalactite. A splintering crack exploded through the cavern as the stalactite fell. It struck the creature's spine and pinned it. More stalactites and boulders crashed down. I watched in horror and relief as debris flattened my attacker.

The cave quieted.

Ash rushed to me, bathing the area in light. Pushing myself up, I put weight on my good leg. I stepped and steadied myself with the injured one—*snap*! I collapsed and bit back a scream as red-hot pain radiated up my shin. The sweet, syrupy taste of breakfast filled my mouth and I vomited. I couldn't bring myself to look at my leg. Shaking, I crawled across the damp floor. Ash shrunk to his normal size and hopped beside me. Every time I stopped to catch my breath, he made an encouraging *cooing* sound. When I finally reached the sixth door, my clothes were soaked in sweat and dank cave water. I brushed the door with my fingertips. The grounding noise sounded, and the door fell away. Directly inside, the chain was attached to the wall. I hauled myself over, but couldn't reach it from the ground.

"Aghhh!" I pulled myself up. The moment I touched the chain, it unravelled. Across the cavern, Darragh plummeted. Ash beat his wings and streaked toward him. Before he crashed into Darragh, Ash burst into a ball of light. Darragh absorbed the light and awoke mid-fall. Thrusting his hands out, Darragh stopped himself from colliding with the ground. He stood quickly and looked around.

"Nell?" Darragh called, a tremor in his voice.

"I'm here," I croaked. Darragh threw a ball of fire into the air and followed my voice. I saw my leg. Just below my knee, a bloody white lump protruded from my skin. My stomach somersaulted. It was a bone poking through my flesh. I gagged and leaned against the wall.

Darragh knelt, cupping my cheeks. "Are you okay?"

"Uh, mostly." I sniffled. "I think there's something wrong with my leg." I pointed down. Darragh inhaled sharply. He passed his hand over the bone. The pain lessened—just a bit.

Another growl rang out in the distance.

"Is that another one?!" I cried.

"Hey Nell, Nelli, it's okay. Look at me." Darragh smiled. "I'm gonna pick you up, okay? We're going to get out of here." I rubbed away my tears and nodded. Darragh slipped one arm behind my back and the other beneath my legs before lifting me.

"Agh!" I winced. Fresh tears blurred my vision.

"I've got you," Darragh whispered, breaking into a jog. "I know it hurts, but we're going to have to be quiet until we get out of here, okay?" I sobbed quietly. "Close your eyes. I'll help you relax."

I don't remember the pain or our journey out. The faint, quickened beat of Darragh's heart gave way to rustling leaves and gurgling water. In my mind, I was somewhere far away from the depths of the cave.

When the fantasy faded away, the wood boards of the treehouse came into view. I nodded in and out of sleep, unsure if I was awake or dreaming. I think I recalled Darragh kneeling over my leg, working through the night.

The next morning, I managed to climb down the tree on my own. Whatever Darragh did hadn't mended my leg completely, but it was still pretty good, considering there was a bone poking out a few hours ago. Though painful, I hobbled around on my own. Darragh mentioned hot springs nearby, and suggested the soak would be good for me.

"Are they hot?" I looked at the pools. "I like my water hot."

"I can warm it up if you'd like." Darragh pulled off his shirt and tossed it aside.

I bet you could.

Darragh undid his pants but stopped when he caught me staring. "Oh, sorry," I said, then turned away while he climbed in. Darragh moved to the far side of the pool, and kept his back turned so I could slip in. "Ah!" I hissed when my toe hit the water.

Darragh laughed. "I can cool it down if you'd like?"

"Just hang on. Don't turn around." I forced my foot back in. After a moment to adjust, I found I could tolerate the heat. Luxurious warmth hugged me like a blanket as I slid in. Resting my head against the edge, I closed my eyes. "So, what's next?"

"There's a mushroom we need. They grow near home; it won't be a long detour. I hoped to leave the second we got the stone, but I don't really want you walking on that leg right away. We'll see how you feel tomorrow."

"Trying to keep me here longer?" I teased.

"It would be a shame if something happened to your other leg."

My eyes snapped open. "Pardon me?" Darragh's response was a sly smile. I laughed. "Was that a joke? I didn't know you could do that." Darragh gave me a bashful grin as he leaned over the edge of the pool and rummaged in his bag. He handed me a little puck that smelled like flowers.

"For your hair."

"Yes!" I dipped under the water and rubbed the bar against my scalp. I handed the bar back to Darragh, and he did the same.

Darragh waited for me to look away before he left the water.

As we readied to return to camp, there was an air of apprehension about Darragh. He stooped to pack his satchel, which was already neatly packed—by him—and then stood and cracked his knuckles.

When he knelt to re-check his satchel a fourth time, I asked, "What are you doing?"

Darragh exhaled, as if readying for battle. He stood and approached me. Sweat beaded his temple, and Darragh didn't meet my eyes as he said, "May I take your hand?"

"Oh, no." I laughed. "What are you going to show me this time?"

"I"—Darragh fidgeted with a belt loop—"I wasn't going to show you anything."

"Oh."

I hate myself.

I offered my hand, and Darragh took it. My skin sizzled where it touched his. "Ah!" I yelped and yanked it away. Darragh's eyes bulged, and he stumbled back. Whorls of smoke swirled from my hand. I hid it behind my back.

Darragh's throat tightened like he might be sick. Head down, he wouldn't look at me. "We should go back."

"It's okay." I reached out, but Darragh dodged and crossed his arms.

A muscle in Darragh's jaw clenched. He repeated, "We should go back," and turned to leave. I didn't follow. I thought about the nettle I'd fallen in outside his cottage. I summoned memories of the pain, and unleashed a scream so convincing, even I believed it. I'd barely hit the ground before Darragh was on me, his hands cool as they scanned my body for injury.

"Where does it hurt?!" Darragh's frantic eyes danced over me. "Is it your leg?!"

I stopped mid-scream.

"Heh." I chuckled. Darragh's eyes widened, and he froze. The bewildered look on his face gave way to understanding. A seriousness set on him as he climbed to his feet.

"Will you help me up?" I asked, feigning innocence.

"I shouldn't." He eyed me warily. "You trickster." I reached for the hand he hadn't offered. A moment passed before he pulled me up. His touch was warm, but my distraction worked—he didn't burn me a second time. Darragh relaxed his hold, but I held fast.

"Shall we go back?" I asked. Darragh fixed me with one of those stares—a lingering look that saw everything and left me feeling bare. Instead of wriggling away, I smiled.

Darragh did something unexpected.

He smiled back.

A broad, genuine smile that crinkled the tiny crow's feet around his eyes. I blushed and broke eye contact. We walked in companionable silence back to the camp. Darragh's shoulders sagged a little less as we strolled hand in hand. Where my fingertips met his skin, they tingled. I couldn't stop thinking about the way he'd looked at me. The curious expression that tugged at his cheeks. I couldn't be sure but...

I think it was hope.

Later that evening, while Darragh busied himself with dinner preparations, I sat down beside the charred campfire spot. "So how do you make it...you know"—I wiggled my fingers at the scorched ground—"burn?"

"I don't know. I just do."

"Can you teach me?"

Darragh ran a hand through his hair and grimaced. "I don't think it's a good idea."

"Why not?"

"I'm not a teacher." He waved at the surrounding trees. "You could burn this whole place down." Before I could argue, Darragh said, "I'll be right back," and wandered out of sight. I concentrated on the cold campfire. I just needed one spark.

Nothing happened.

Propping myself up with an elbow, I sighed.

I suppose I don't belong here.

My thoughts wandered to Darragh. To his reluctant smiles and his curious eyes. '*He's keen on you,*' Bowyn had said.

I tried again.

Focusing on the campfire, I raised my hands and blocked out everything, willing flames to life. My heart leapt as a tiny tendril of smoke blossomed in the dead campfire. I focused harder. A flame sputtered and lit. "A-Ha!" I laughed. "Look what I've created!" I threw my arms up and boasted to an imaginary audience. "I have made fire!"

Darragh stood at the edge of the clearing, watching me. I pointed at the hungry flames. "Did you see?"

Darragh gave me a lopsided smile as he walked over. "I saw." He placed a basket of fruits down. "I'll take it from here, if you don't mind." The flames erupted into a blaze so hot, I scooched away.

After dinner, Darragh and I relaxed by the fire. Darragh held up the unassuming stone he'd found. "I was expecting more," I said. Darragh slid one boot from his foot and pulled his sock off. He slipped the stone inside. I jumped as he slammed it against the ground. He pulled out the stone, now broken in two, and handed me half. Rainbow-coloured veins ran through a delicate, pearlescent cream centre.

"It's quite striking."

"It is, isn't it?" Darragh inspected it.

"How are you going to get the shards out of your sock?"

Darragh looked up at me, and down at his sock. He furrowed his brows and tucked the sock beside him. Leaning against a tree stump, Darragh pointed up above the fire, to the night sky. "Do you see that star? The brightest one at the top of the sky?"

I followed his finger. "I think so."

"We use it for navigation, like your North Star back on Earth. For thousands of years, people gazed upon it, yearning for home, longing for loved ones." Darragh paused. "In my language, the name means, *the way home*."

I cocked my head. "And what name is that?"

Darragh set his keen eyes on me. "Melaethien."

"Oh! That's what you call each other."

Darragh smiled and turned back to the sky. "Yes," he whispered. "That's what we call each other."

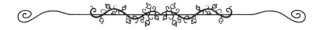

We spent the next two days doing nothing much at all. Darragh brought me food and forced me to relax. I lounged by the fire while Darragh trailed the rays of sunshine on the wood floor, sunbathing. Both were activities I enjoyed immensely. While he lay with his eyes closed, soaking up the sunlight, Darragh and I exchanged stories. We quickly realized that many of our stories on Earth were brought over by Hiraethans.

THE FOREST WHERE THE PHOENIX SLEEPS

On Hiraeth, there's a horrible little creature they call a bone fairy. Bone fairies have a nasty habit of sneaking into the bedrooms of small children and gobbling them up. Fathers took to leaving piles of bones in their children's rooms while they slept, to distract the bone fairy. Hopefully, when the father woke to the crunching of bones, they'd find the fairy had fallen for the distraction, and not the alternative. Something to consider the next time your child slips a tooth beneath their pillow for the tooth fairy.

At night, Darragh massaged my leg and assessed my recovery. To ease the awkward, silent tension of his hands pressed on my skin, I'd made a game of asking him about unsolved mysteries back on Earth. Darragh often researched enigmas as part of his work, trying to determine if they had a touch of magic about them.

"Jack the Ripper?" I asked.

"Magic."

"The Zodiac Killer?"

"No, actually. That one was shoddy police work."

"No shit, eh?" Darragh nodded. His palm passed over the sorest spot on my leg. The coolness in his hand numbed what pain remained. "How do you cool it down?" I asked.

"I don't know if I cool it down, so much as draw the heat out." While his hands moved over my leg, I tried to think of more mysteries.

"Dyatlov pass?"

"I don't know. Which one was that?" Darragh replied distractedly.

"The hikers in Russia. All dead, missing eyes and tongues."

"Oh, yeah. Magic."

My jaw dropped. "What happened?"

"One of the girls, Lyudmila, she—hold on. I need to focus. This might hurt. There's a shard of bone I need to fuse—" *POP.*

"Hhhh!" I gasped and nearly fell over.

"Sorry." Darragh grimaced. "That was the last piece. You'll heal on your own now, as long as we take it easy."

I blinked back tears as Darragh finished inspecting my leg. Rather than draw away, his hand remained. Without thinking, Darragh stroked my skin. Responding to his touch, a wave of goosebumps prickled down my leg. Darragh tensed and leaned back. "I need to go get uh…" He floundered and stood. "I uh—I heard a noise." He wandered into the night.

I fell asleep by the fire, waiting for Darragh to come back.

The next morning, I awoke to the clattering of metal. Somehow, I'd gotten into the treehouse, though I had no recollection of it. I climbed down the ladder and found Darragh hurriedly packing.

Apparently, it was time to leave.

Chapter Eleven

the man with death on his lips

Elwyn

The Queen floated through the stone hallways of the mountain. I trailed her, several paces behind.

"My Queen, why must we do this?"

The Queen shook her head. I couldn't see, but I knew she rolled her eyes, as she often did when I spoke. "To find you a suitable companion," she spat.

"But!" I started. "Darragh would be a perfect companion for me! He's powerful, he knows the kingdom…"

I love him.

The Queen heard the words I hadn't said loud and clear. She whirled on me, growing tall, until her head craned against the rocky ceiling. Her eyes darkened and her mouth drooped open, frighteningly enormous. A sudden choking pressure wrapped my throat. "Hhh!" My knees hit the rocky floor.

"You will never *ssspeak* of, or act on, that intention!" the Queen hissed the words, as if some furious serpent had suddenly seized control of her tongue. She cried, "Do you undersssstand me?!"

No!

The Queen did her best to compose herself, but the grip on my throat tightened. "Everything I do is to ensure we"—the Queen paused and considered her words—"*you* stay in power. Everything I do is for you." Looming above, the Queen's eyes bore into me. "Why are you so ungrateful?" The wispy, shredded fabric of her dress swirled in an impossible wind. "Where would you be without me?" Inky shadows reached for me, and I cowered. The pain they imparted on my skin was unbearable—I stopped struggling against the pressure on my throat. Slowly, it lessened. When it disappeared completely, I stood. The Queen's shadows receded, and as they did, she shrunk back into her normal, cadaverous form. She floated away.

"One more thing." The Queen glanced over her shoulder and flicked her wrist. The shadows tore themselves from the floor, taking the form of many hands. They gripped me and pried my mouth open. An invisible cloth slid down my throat. I wretched and tried to throw it up, but the cloth wrapped around something inside me. I coughed and sputtered as a tightness spread through my chest.

I'd never been gagged before. Who would dare gag the daughter of the queen? Though I could still speak, I'd never be able to tell Darragh how I felt about him; I'd choke on the words. The Queen floated down the path to the great hall.

There are only two ways to remove a gag. The person who placed it willingly removes it, or they die, and the gag dies with them.

I wiped tears from my cheeks.

A smile tugged my lip as I followed the Queen.

As bleak as the rest of the mountain, only a handful of torches provided dim light in the great hall, and much of the exquisite architecture was lost. It was just as well, thick layers of dust and cobwebs blanketed the faces of the previous queens, all intricately carved into the stone. The faint light cast their mouths in shadows, leaving them wide open and dark, frozen in permanent screams.

How I longed for our other homes. Growing up, we'd split our time between many places. My favourite, our forest home, was surrounded by rivers and waterfalls. As the Queen fell to paranoia, she forced us to live here, in the dark.

In this prison.

At the far end of the great hall, the Queen ascended the stairs and sat on her throne. She'd built the throne—a showpiece of polished onyx—and in doing so, she'd broken the tradition of queen's sitting amongst the people. I ascended the steps of the platform and took my place, one step behind and to the left of the Queen. Beside me, to the Queen's right, stood another woman. While all the Queen's guardians wore black, the Queen's Truth wore bright, vibrant colours.

An odd choice for a spy.

The Truth wore an enormous hat, with a wide brim and pointy top. A thick leather band surrounded the hat, into which the Truth tucked various feathers and scraps. Her most recent addition was a tuft of white hair, and I was fairly certain it belonged to the Queen. The Truth wiped a speck of dust from her robe; giant beaded necklaces and gaudy bangles clacked together. I despised the jewelry, if only because it reminded me of her. I'd taken many beatings because of the Truth's whispers.

A row of eager suitors lined the wall before us. "Let us begin my daughter's courtship," the Queen began. Invisible fingers pulled my lips into a smile. I resisted the urge to spit when they let go. "Whoever I choose as my daughter's companion will help her rule the kingdom. In ruling a kingdom, you will garner power and respect. But to rule a kingdom is to put yourself in danger every day." The Queen pointed to the first suitor. "You!"

A stunning, raven-haired woman draped in yards of flowing white fabric and golden chains stepped forward. My gaze lingered on her bare midriff, an uncommon style in this region.

It wouldn't be the first time two queens reigned. Before Queen Ever could take the throne, the people offered their own choice, a powerful woman named Yve. They did not duel—no, they did something the people did not expect.

They fell in love.

Ever and Yve offered the people a compromise: two queens. Successful rulers, they cleared the Aeonian Woods and expanded our territory to the east. After Yve and Ever's tremendous accomplishments, it wasn't uncommon for queens to share the title.

When the woman and I made eye contact, her lip drew up in a confident smirk. My cheeks heated, and I looked away.

A quiet part of me hoped she performed well.

The woman said, "My name is Lyra—"

"I don't care," the Queen snapped. "Show me what you can do." The large doors to the hall swung open. Audra, a sweet but less useful guardian entered. Looking uncharacteristically solemn in her flowing black gown, Audra ushered in a young girl. The girl's boots scuffed the floor as she walked timidly to the centre of the room and stood beside Lyra.

"How far will you go to protect my daughter?" the Queen questioned the room. "How far will you go to protect the kingdom?"

What's going on?

Usually, suitors displayed their power before the Queen, and she excused them. The Queen pointed one frail finger at the little girl. "The person before you is a *criminal*." She growled the word, relishing it on her tongue. "They've broken into your bedchamber during the night.

They're trying to kill *my* daughter. React accordingly."

The girl bolted, and Lyra threw her arms up. A mist of ice sprayed from her fingertips, surrounding the girls' feet. Ice travelled up her legs and froze her to the ground mid-step.

Lyra bowed.

"That's it?" the Queen snarled. "This creature has snuck into your bedchamber to *kill* you and your beloved."

Lyra examined the girl. "Please, I didn't do anything," she begged. Tears streaked her face as she clawed at her frozen shackles.

Understanding dawned on Lyra's face.

"Yes, there it is," the Queen snapped. "Kill her!"

Lyra's nose scrunched, and her lips formed a tight, straight line. She bowed and rejoined the line of suitors, where she crossed her arms and scowled. Fear needled my stomach. The Queen punished suitors for lesser offenses than that. Perhaps excited for the approaching bloodshed, the Queen was in a gracious mood. She left Lyra unharmed…for now.

"Will none of you protect my daughter?" the Queen shouted.

A man, three suitors in, stepped forward. He looked ordinary enough. Strawberry-blonde hair, and a child's face. I wouldn't have thought much of him…except I'd heard whispers, rumours of his powers. Perhaps the gossip was false. If he possessed what people said, it was a rare and terrible power.

The Queen couldn't resist it.

The man approached the girl and she struggled, her feet still frozen in place. He held her cheeks in a calming, paternal gesture.

"Sh, sh, sh," the man soothed.

The girl relaxed.

Sssnap!

Her head twisted round in the man's hands. Her lips contorted into a painful, 'O!' as her neck broke. She fell back and two more snaps, like the sound of breaking wood, rang out as her legs broke against the ice.

The Queen gave a bored nod.

The man muttered, "Get up." The girl's lifeless body twitched. A spasm rippled through her, and she squirmed like a beetle caught on its back. With a snarl and a hiss, the corpse pulled itself upright.

Don't run. I told myself. *Don't look weak.*

Out of the corner of my eye, the Queen smiled.

The corpse screeched and tried to run, its feet still rooted. Goosebumps prickled my flesh as its nails scraped ice. Arms swinging frantically, it fell again. Sinew and flesh stretched and ripped as the corpse tore itself from its own frozen feet. Shouts rose from the suitors as the corpse crawled toward them. It went straight for Lyra. Without hesitation, she sent forth a sharp spray of ice. The corpse froze, and Lyra swung her leg, connecting with its head. Ice shards exploded across the hall like fluffy, white snow.

Lyra looked the man up and down, her chest heaving. He grinned and gave her a finger-wiggling wave.

The Queen rose and clapped.

Each booming clap pierced me like an arrow.

"A necromancer! Lovely. Just lovely!"

Bile rose in my throat.

It wasn't always rare, necromancy. A thousand years ago there were many. But the ability to control the dead was…unnatural. Fearing necromancers, we'd hunted them to extinction.

We missed one.

"What's your name?" the Queen asked.

With a bow, the man said, "Ophyr."

"Magnificent," the Queen muttered. "Just wonderful." She waved at the remaining suitors. "We're done. Get out."

Ophyr met my eyes. He grinned, and his lips pouted into a kiss. My stomach turned.

After scouring the mountain for my father, I finally found him talking with a healer. Father laughed obnoxiously, a large goblet in hand. It wasn't the first time I'd found him here, chatting with *that* healer. A young, blonde woman whose name I hadn't bothered learning. "Yes, dinner tonight was delicious," Father blubbered. I didn't acknowledge the healer as I grabbed my father's elbow.

"I won't have him, Father."

"Elle, my dear, what are you talking about?"

"The necromancer."

"Ohhhh." Father took a long sip. Outraged, I knocked the goblet from his grasp. Only mildly inconvenienced, he waved, and the goblet froze in mid-air. He beckoned, and the goblet floated lazily back, gathering burgundy droplets from the air as it did. He continued, "Maybe the Queen won't choose him."

The Queen's delighted voice replayed in my mind, *'A necromancer! Lovely. Just lovely!'* I lowered my voice. "We need to leave."

My father threw up his hands in an exaggerated, drunken gesture. "I can't leave her."

"Please," I begged. "I'm afraid of him, and I'm afraid of her. I know you are too."

"And where would we go?" My father spoke with a severity I'd never heard before. "What makes you think she wouldn't find us?"

I was taken aback; never had my father voiced his concerns about leaving the Queen. "We'll figure it out—" I stopped. The echoes of our voices sounded different as they bounced off the walls. I peered around my father; a shadow lurked at the end of the hall.

"Who's there?"

Brightly coloured robes crept from the shadows. The Truth glanced between me and my father.

Her smile faded as she slunk into the dark.

Chapter Twelve

here there be monsters

We set out for Darragh's cottage. The longer we walked, the more my leg hurt. When I woke up, it was a dull ache, but the farther we travelled, the more I gritted my teeth every time my foot hit the ground. Even with Darragh's slowed pace, I dripped with sweat. Darragh stepped over a fallen log. I followed and gasped when my foot touched down.

Darragh gave me a piteous look. "Would you like me to carry you?"

"I'm not Frodo," I muttered.

Darragh shrugged. "I didn't finish *The Two Towers*."

"Ugh." I didn't *want* to be carried. I rested my hands on my knees, catching my breath. "Can't you just like…magic us there?"

"That's not one of my strengths," Darragh said, rubbing his neck.

"But it's possible?"

"It's possible but"—Darragh gazed into the middle distance—"The last time I tried, I dropped Bowyn and myself into a basilisk den."

Desperate to get back as quickly as possible, I continued

brainstorming. "It can't be that hard, right? Picture yourself someplace else, throw in a bit of magic, and boom—we're there. No more walking." Darragh shot me an exasperated look. "It can't hurt to try?" I whined.

"Yes, it can! Bowyn nearly lost his *eyes* in the den, and any magical ability he possessed along with them." Darragh pointed to his eyebrow. "That's how he got that scar. His wounds were so great, even *I* couldn't mend them completely." He grabbed for me. "Let me carry you."

"It's fine." I pushed past him. Darragh didn't follow me, and after a few steps, I turned to see why not. Arms crossed and eyes closed, lines creased Darragh's forehead as he concentrated. I didn't *really* expect it to work. So, you can imagine my surprise when he vanished. "Oh," I said out loud to no one. I stared at the space Darragh had occupied.

He didn't reappear.

In the distance, a bird cawed. The surrounding trees seemed thicker than they were a moment ago. They cast long shadows as the afternoon sun began its descent.

"Oh shit," I said to myself.

What are you supposed to do when you get lost in the woods? With Darragh, there was an obvious path. Alone now, the path was gone. Everything looked the same. The compulsion to choose a direction and run was overwhelming. You're supposed to stand still, right? Find a tree, and just stay put… But no one was looking for me. Darragh was the only person who knew I was out here, and he was long gone. Wait—what was that?

I straightened and listened. The wood was silent. No birds, no insects. Nothing. But I swore—*knock-knock-knock.* There it was again! Three knocks rang out in the distance. I'd heard them before, with Darragh. I remembered the anxious look on his face… I pointed myself away from the knocking and stumbled onward.

The afternoon light gave way to dusk, and I realized I didn't have anything to start a fire. Why would I? I had Darragh. I could try to start one on my own but, even if I could get a fire going, what would it attract?

Something moved in the trees. I stilled—

It was only a bundle of sticks. Hanging from a low branch, it swung lazily in the breeze. Now that I was aware, I noticed similar bundles everywhere, dangling from the trees like ornaments. Bits of fabric stuck out of the bundle, all wrapped up and hung with rough twine.

What's in there?

One by one, the sticks fell away. A decaying rot filled the air, and blood dribbled—I backed away. "Ugh!" I covered my mouth.

A human face stared at me.

Well, sort of. It was the skin from a face. Rough twine ran through the eye sockets, and up into the trees.

The skin whispered, "I'm coming to get you."

"Nope!" I ran. "Nope, nope, nope." I hurtled through the trees. I only slowed when the wafting smell of a campfire carried through the wood. Had I imagined it? I scanned treetops. There! A tendril of smoke snaked its way into the clouds. I headed toward it, and it wasn't long before faint laughter carried on the wind. As I approached, I made out words and conversation.

"We need to kill him."

My stomach tightened. *Don't like that.* I took cover behind an ancient, mossy tree. Just beyond, a handful of women occupied a small clearing. Two stood near, and three sat farther back, around a campfire.

Oh no.

On the far side of the fire, two wooden stakes, lashed together and driven into the ground, formed a large T. Mounted on the structure like a scarecrow, was Darragh. His head hung limply, and dried blood smeared his face. It dripped in long, crimson stains down his chest.

"We need to kill him right now," the first voice repeated. The speaker was a short, dark-haired woman. "Geneth, if we don't kill him now, and he escapes, he *will* burn us alive."

Geneth, a much taller blonde woman, rounded on the first. "I've thought about this moment every night since he took my mother to the Queen! When I've decided he's suffered enough, I will kill him. Not before."

The dark-haired woman shook her head. "It was a miracle we bound him the first time. We shouldn't risk it."

"You're not in charge, Ruatha," Geneth snapped. "We will kill him when the time comes. In the meantime, I think we could *all* use a bit of fun." Geneth raised her brow seductively and laughed. A beautiful, horrible sound. "You can join us, or you can sit here and pout." With that, she headed back to the campfire.

Back to Darragh.

I closed my eyes and searched—searched for any magic hidden within me.

Nothing.

Not a scrap.

Laughter rose from the camp. A voice said, "Perhaps we should build a fire around his feet when we're finished? Give him a taste of his own medicine? I'd love to see him burn."

Burn—

"Oh!" Darragh *had* given me something to make fire! I reached for the necklace. "Ah!" The bird carving burned my fingertips, and I snatched my hand away. It must have gotten trapped in my layers of shirts, and I hadn't noticed it growing hot. The pain in my leg forgotten, I sprinted until I found what I was looking for: a dry and decayed tree.

Sliding to my knees, I swept brittle leaves up against the trunk. I yanked the necklace off and dropped it into the pile of kindling. I domed my hands over the necklace and blew.

Nothing happened.

I rubbed my palms on my pants to remove the sweat. Maybe the necklace wasn't hot enough? I tried again. Gentle, controlled breaths. This time, the edges of the papery leaves glowed orange.

A small flame sputtered to life.

"Yes!" The crunchy leaves caught. "Yes! Yes! Yes!" The hungry flames climbed the rotten trunk. I snatched a nearby dead branch and plunged it into the fire which engulfed the tree. I pulled it out and dragged it along the trees and shrubs that led back to the camp. Shouts rang out from the clearing. I tossed the stick into the woods on my left and veered right. Careful to stay hidden behind the outer ring of trees, I crouched when Darragh came into view. My plan worked…sort of. One woman remained to guard Darragh.

Closer now, I saw the damage. Darragh's shirt was torn open, his chest flayed, caked thick with dried blood and dirt. My cheeks flushed, and I searched for anything that could be used as a weapon. With shaky hands, I picked up a large rock. Archaic, but it would work. When the woman looked away, I crept forward. The encroaching roar from the fire covered my footsteps.

Twenty feet away.

Ten feet away.

Five feet... She turned and I swung. The rock made a sickening *thunk* as it connected with her temple. The woman's legs buckled, and she dropped. I tightened my grip on the rock, readying for a second blow. The woman's eyes lulled and she groaned. She wasn't getting up anytime soon. I tossed the rock aside and scrambled over to Darragh.

He stared at me with lifeless eyes. I reached for his arms but…he wasn't tied to anything. How was I supposed to free him? Darragh was just standing against a stick, apparently of his own free will.

"Agh!" I shouted in Darragh's face.

What do I do?

Screams rang out from the direction of the fire. Somehow, the woman I'd brained must have alerted the others. I pulled Darragh from the sticks and he slid to the ground. I jumped behind him and hooked my arms beneath his elbows.

Have you ever tried to drag a body? It's like, really hard. Sweat beaded on my forehead as I dragged Darragh into the trees. Displaced sticks and leaves left a wake that made us easy to follow. I tried not to think about all the furious people coming after us—or the fire I'd set. Wouldn't it be funny if we burned to death in a fire I'd set as a distraction to save us?

"How do I untie you?!" I huffed, knowing Darragh couldn't answer me.

That woman, Ruatha—what had she said? That it took *two* of them to bind Darragh. There were two people keeping him bound. I'd already taken out one with my rock, but there had to be another.

"Where do you think you're going?" An invisible force squeezed my throat and I choked. Ruatha stalked from the trees, palm outstretched. Just like Darragh, my body was frozen. The pressure on my neck increased and my vision blurred.

I tested my fingers. Though stiff, they moved freely. I scraped them along the ground, collecting as much dirt as I could. Through the chokehold I gasped, "Jokes on you. I like this sort of thing."

Ruatha's face twisted in disgust. She gave me a *what is wrong with you?* look and loosened her grip. Particles slipped through my fingers as I hurled the dirt in Ruatha's face. She covered her eyes, and I grabbed the knife from Darragh's belt. Without hesitating, I plunged the knife into Ruatha's thigh.

"AGH!" Ruatha tore the blade free and lunged. I landed on my ass and scrambled away. Ruatha grabbed for me and cried, "I'm going to watch the life leave your eyes—"

Ruatha froze. Her eyes fixed on something behind me, and the rage contorting her face slipped away. A sudden warmth grazed my back. Terrified the fire had wrapped around us, I risked a glance over my shoulder, and squinted against the heat.

It wasn't the fire I'd set.

Flames flickered over every inch of Darragh's body. On his feet now, I shielded my eyes and craned up at him. An uncaring, apathetic look settled on Darragh's face. He raised his arm.

"No. Please no," Ruatha begged.

Darragh raised his other hand and a cooling sensation swept over me. I didn't realize what he was doing until it was too late.

"Darragh, no—"

I curled into a ball as flames exploded around the barrier Darragh had created to protect me. Ruatha ran, slowed by the stab wound in her thigh. The fire overtook her—flames travelled along her skin, turning it to ash. She didn't even have time to scream.

In a moment, Ruatha was gone.

The swell of fire died. I stared at the space Ruatha had occupied in stunned silence. Seconds ago, she was alive and breathing. Now she was gone. Just like that. Dead.

Darragh had killed her.

My hands shook as I stood. When I rounded on Darragh, there were no flames. The wounds were gone from his chest; he did what he could to rebutton his shirt.

"You didn't have to kill her," I whispered.

Darragh bent and retrieved his knife. "She would have killed you," he replied coldly.

"She was running away!"

Darragh pointed in the direction of the others. "She was running *toward* help, so she could come back and butcher us!"

"They were right to be afraid of you!" I screamed. "I wouldn't have helped you if I knew you were going to burn them alive!" My voice cracked, and I cursed the coming tears. "I didn't know you'd throw flames at their backs while they crawled away from you!"

Darragh stood in shocked silence, looking as if I'd struck him. He raised his voice and jabbed his chest. "I saved you, and you're looking at me like I'm a monster."

"I saved you! And I did it without killing anyone! Maybe you are a monster!"

"I know I am!" Darragh bellowed. For just a moment, Darragh's features weren't his. Elongated and wrong—his teeth were knives, and his eyes were fire. But it was over so quickly. Had I imagined it? I shut my mouth and shrunk away. My turn to pause in stunned silence. This was the first time I'd seen Darragh angry. I stood my ground, but I trembled.

Darragh's eyes darted to my crossed arms. Realizing what he'd done, he looked down. "I know I am," he repeated. "I just... I didn't want you to see me as one."

I saw it then. When we think of ourselves, there's always that one thing we can't stand. That one thing we'd change, if we could. We tell ourselves that no one else sees it, or that people don't care, all so we can be brave enough to leave the house. Darragh wore the face of someone who'd just discovered that not only does everyone see what he sees, but they think less of him for it. It made me sick to think I'd thrown someone's flaw in their face.

But I mean, it was a pretty big flaw. He just fucking killed someone. In what world was that okay?

Shouts echoed in the distance.

Darragh composed himself. "Like it or not, this is how it is here. If you don't want me to kill again, we need to move now. They won't extend us the same courtesy." I started to hobble away from the shouts. As the adrenaline faded, the pain in my leg returned and I nearly collapsed. Darragh reached to help, but I dodged him. "Fine," Darragh hissed, "but when they catch us, and they *will*, I will give everything I have, my power and my body, to protect you." Grinding my teeth, I continued hobbling. "I won't let you die, Nell." Darragh walked patiently beside me. "That means most of them will."

I stopped shambling and muttered a quick, "Balls."

I reached to Darragh for help.

"Can I walk now?" I wanted to stand on my own for the next conversation. It felt wrong to yell at Darragh while he carried me.

I wonder if he knew it, because his response was a curt, "No."

"There's no one behind us. Couldn't I just—"

"You've been running non-stop on a broken leg. It will *not* heal."

I pursed my lips. *I ran on it while saving you.*

"If you have something to say, say it." Darragh snapped. "I've seen Bowyn make that face enough times to know there's something you need to get out and the longer you stew on it, the worse it'll be for me."

"You can't just go around killing people!" Passion punctuated my words—unresolved guilt for what I'd done to Turner.

Darragh's arms tensed around me. "Sometimes you must take a life to survive."

"Back on Earth, we'd call you a murderer and send you to prison."

"Back on Earth, you'd call me a soldier, and you'd treat me like a hero."

"I—"

I didn't know what to say that.

It was a quiet, frosty walk home. We paused only so Darragh could forage the mushrooms we needed.

We arrived at Darragh's cottage late in the evening. Bowyn was asleep on the sofa in front of a low fire, with one arm propped behind his head. A pile of cookies lay forgotten on his chest. Darragh slammed the door so forcefully I jumped, and Bowyn jerked awake. Cookies tumbled everywhere as Bowyn leapt to his feet.

"You!" Darragh snarled.

"Me?" Bowyn cried, wiping crumbs from his robe and beard. Darragh watched every crumb fall onto his floor. Bowyn kept the sofa between himself and Darragh, as if that might save him.

"What were you thinking? Sending her after me? You knew where I was going!"

"Eleanor"—Bowyn emphasized my name—"is a grown woman. She makes her own decisions. I just gave her a little push out the door. And look! She's fine."

Darragh pointed at me. "She broke her leg!" Bowyn winced, but Darragh kept going. "She nearly died!"

"But she didn't." Bowyn shrugged, palms up. Glancing at Darragh, I considered the very real possibility he might strangle Bowyn. He opened his mouth to speak, thought better of it, and turned to leave. "Come now," Bowyn ridiculed. "Use your words."

Darragh inhaled sharply. His hands balled into fists as he rounded on Bowyn. Moments ticked by as they held one another's gaze. Finally, Darragh said, "I think you're a capricious, impudent little brat!" He tossed his bag and stormed out of the cottage.

If Bowyn had pearls, he'd clutch them. He muttered, "Capricious?" under his breath, and shook his head. "I don't really understand where that little tantrum came from." Stroking his beard, Bowyn shrugged. "I'm sorry you had to see that, my dear Eleanor." I picked nervously at my lip, while Bowyn brushed more crumbs onto the floor. "Did you have fun at least?"

Emotions warred within me, but it was a smile, not a frown, that answered Bowyn's question.

"Come! Come, tell me all about it." Bowyn dragged me to the kitchen. "Did you rescue Darragh on any of your little exploits?"

I stuck my chin out. "Twice."

"That's my girl." Bowyn winked. He fixed a drink. "Did you… you know."

I didn't understand. "Did I what?"

"Did you and Darragh…" Bowyn paused, letting the silence speak for itself. "You know."

"Oh!"

Sex. He means sex.

"No!"

"And why not?"

"I don't know." I cleared my throat and hoped that answer was sufficient for Bowyn. It wasn't. I thought of how Darragh refused to share the treehouse with me. How he caressed my leg so affectionately, but quickly ran away. "It's like he's scared to be near me."

Darragh dripping in flames. Burning Ruatha alive.

Perhaps I'm scared to be near him too. I didn't admit that to Bowyn.

"Plus, he's hot," I said.

Bowyn laughed. "Well, yes, but you aren't so bad looking yourself, you shouldn't let that frighten you."

"No, I mean, he's literally hot." I raised my hand. "He burned me."

"Oh, his poor nerves." Bowyn chuckled. "He'll get over that. We all get hot and bothered when we're infatuated. Especially when we've found our—"

The door crashed open and Darragh charged in. Glaring at Bowyn, he shouted, "Are you still here?" There was no doubting Darragh and Bowyn's lifelong friendship. With one look, they exchanged an entire, silent conversation. I only knew it was over when Bowyn sighed and put down his cup.

"I'm sorry Eleanor, my love, but it appears I'm needed in town." Bowyn rounded the counter, he eyed Darragh as he took my hand and brought it to his mouth. He kissed it and said, "Until we meet again."

Darragh slammed the door behind Bowyn. He crossed his arms and addressed me. "I'm sorry—" Darragh paused, lowering his voice. "I'm sorry I yelled at you."

The sudden apology surprised me. "I, uh, I'm sorry I asked you to do something you weren't comfortable with." We wouldn't have gotten into trouble today if I hadn't pushed Darragh to move us with magic. I'd nearly gotten us both killed.

Darragh waited, expecting more.

I did not apologize for calling him a monster.

When I didn't say more, Darragh continued, "I promise, wherever feasible"—he looked at the ceiling, as if the idea of what he was about to say next was absolutely ludicrous—"I will not kill anyone else." I didn't know what to say. It seemed like an odd thing, to thank someone for not killing people. Should I congratulate him? Or was that passive aggressive? *Hey, man, congrats on not killing anyone today!*

"I have things I need to do," Darragh said. "I'll be back later."

"It's the middle of the night—"

"There are things I need to do," Darragh interrupted. "We're leaving tomorrow."

"Good!" I snapped.

Darragh left.

All alone, I couldn't help but wonder…is it though?

Chapter Thirteen

dates, drinks, & dead things

Elwyn

"You look rather dashing this evening, Erebus." The Queen complimented my father over dinner. Father pushed his shoulders back and stuck his chin up, a warm smile rounded his cheeks. I scrutinized the Queen.

What's she up to?

"Elwyn, I've arranged for you to meet with Ophyr after supper," the Queen said. "You will get to know each other better."

I looked at my father, pleading. He choked down a bite of food and thumped his chest. "My Queen, perhaps—"

"Shut up, Erebus." The Queen's façade of kindness slipped. She swished her hand, and a pitcher floated down the table. "Have another drink, my darling." Father watched the burgundy liquid pour into his goblet. "Elwyn, you will go straight to the mountain top and meet Ophyr."

"Just me?" I gulped. "Shouldn't we be supervised?" I didn't want to be one-on-one with Ophyr anywhere, let alone on top of the mountain.

"She should have a chaperone," my father said. "Perhaps I could escort her?"

The Queen's lip curled and she glared at my father. "Fine! Take Audra." My heart sank. Audra's only strength was poison detection and identification, and she could only tell if something was poisoned by tasting it. She had no healing propensity whatsoever, and she spent most of her time in the care of the Queen's healers. Audra was lovely, but stupid. Intolerably stupid. I'd once heard the Queen say she kept Audra around because her 'utter uselessness' amused her and that if she 'ever needs to kill someone to set an example, it would be Audra.' My father shrugged and gave me a look that said, *it's better than nothing*. I stayed at the table longer than usual, knowing what awaited me. The Queen wasn't fooled by my delays. My plate vanished and she pointed a frail finger at the door.

My chair scraped the rock as I stood. Father dabbed his lips with a napkin. "I think I'll escort Elle to Audra. Is that alright, my Queen?" She waved dismissively. Father grabbed his goblet and we left. He took my arm in his, humming while we walked. My father might be fooled by the Queen's fake niceties, but I wasn't.

"Something's wrong," I snapped. Father's tired eyes focused on me, as if he'd been lost in a daydream.

"How do you mean?"

"She's scheming."

"Oh, nonsense." Father waved his goblet and liquid sloshed over the side. "Whoopsie." He chuckled.

"We need to leave."

"Ohhh, don't start that again."

The door to Audra's room loomed at the end of the hall. "Please," I begged. "We can go some place safe, where she can't find us. Somewhere with sunshine, where we aren't walking on eggshells every moment of our lives… Somewhere we don't have to marry monsters. Please, Father. For me."

My father considered it. I saw it in his eyes, etched in the weary lines of his face. A guardian passed us, interrupting my father's thoughts. Sipping his drink, he said, "I'll leave you here, my *Besom*."

I crinkled my nose. "Don't call me that."

"You're too old for that?"

"Far too old."

"Well, as long as I'm alive, you'll be my little *Besom*." Before he left, I hugged him tight. I watched him stumble away.

My poor, sweet father.

I had to get him out of here.

For now, I dragged myself toward Audra's room. A door opened into the hallway. I'd recognize the flowing white fabrics anywhere, so different from the dark gowns the guardians wore. Barefoot, Lyra stood a head taller than me. The corner of her cheek tugged up when our eyes met. Her dark eyes sparkled in a mischievous way that sent my stomach tumbling. She beckoned, and several silk bags floated from the room behind her.

"Are you leaving?"

Lyra bobbed her chin, yes. "I know when my time is wasted." My gaze lingered on Lyra's bare stomach, on the jewel in her belly button. She tilted her head, drawing my gaze up to hers. "Unless…my time is not wasted?" She bit her lip and raised an eyebrow.

"I… What…" I stumbled over my words. Suddenly anxious, I tucked a strand of hair behind my ear.

"Come with me," Lyra whispered.

"What—"

Lyra closed the distance between us, carrying with her a floral scent, like blossoming trees in springtime. Lyra's hair brushed my shoulder;

it tickled, and I shivered. She stroked my hand and whispered, "I could teach you so many things. Things you cannot learn here, hidden away in this mountain." I blushed and looked down. Lyra brought her fingers to rest under my chin, drawing my eyes back to hers. Her irises danced as they scoured my face. "Come with me and I'll show you all the wonders of this world." Lyra's lips shone, moist and supple.

Footsteps sounded down the hall. Inhaling sharply, I backed away. My racing pulse only quickened when I saw who it was.

"Darragh?" He bowed his head but continued walking. Abandoning Lyra, I chased after Darragh. "I'm leaving tonight," I whispered. "I'm taking my father and going. Come with us."

Darragh's jaw slackened, and he slowed. "You're what?"

"The Queen is acting strange; I'm worried for my father."

"She will find you," Darragh said. "To leave is to die."

I stuck up my nose. "I'm not afraid of her."

Darragh leaned in so close I felt his breath on my cheek. "You should be," he growled. I crossed my arms. Darragh's footsteps echoed down the corridor toward the Queen's chamber.

When I turned around, Lyra had gone.

Audra and I stepped out onto the mountain top. Wind whipped my hair. It stuck to my lips, and I shoved it out of my face. I hated it up here. Clouds obscured the landscapes below. It was a white, nothing place. At the edge of the platform carved into the mountain, Ophyr stood, his back to me and Audra.

At the sound of our footsteps, Ophyr spun on his heels. "Elle!"

Only my father called me Elle.

"I'm so happy you joined me."

I nearly muttered that I didn't have a choice, but I bit my tongue.

"Isn't this lovely?" Ophyr waved at the clouds.

No.

"Come, have a look with me." Reluctantly, I joined Ophyr. I stood several feet away, but he scooched close. His hand found mine. "Oh my, what's this?" He examined the ring that had been forced on me by the Queen.

"How dare you?" I pulled away. Behind us, Audra stepped forward.

"The Queen's restrained you?" Ophyr frowned.

"That's none of your business."

"I think it is."

"I'm leaving," I snapped, heading toward the stairs.

"I can help you take it off."

I paused.

"I can free you," Ophyr said. And then more quietly, "I can free your father."

I pivoted and glared. "How?"

Ophyr jutted his chin at Audra, his eyes darted to the stairs. Turning to Audra, I said, "I'd like a moment." She nodded but made no move to leave. "Go away, Audra."

"Oh. Yes, of course."

"Don't go far."

As if she could do anything to protect me if the occasion called for it.

Once Audra was gone, Ophyr stepped closer. I could see the light freckles on his cheeks. "I hate to see such a beautiful, powerful creature trapped like this. Hidden away in a mountain to rot." He smiled, tilting his head in a friendly, gentle way. "I can help get that thing off you."

"How?" I repeated.

He raised his palms and smiled, as if the answer was obvious. "We remove the cause—the Queen."

I glanced at the stairs and lowered my voice. "That's treason."

"Don't tell me you care for her."

"I hate her," I spit.

"Think of it; you'd be free. Your father would be safe and out of harm's way." I let myself picture it. A world without the Queen. A dinner with my father. Free of drink and laughing despite it. Darragh beside me—

"All I ask is that you promise yourself to me," Ophyr finished. I recoiled and looked Ophyr up and down.

Who did he think he was?

"I'd rather die," I snarled.

Ophyr's nose twitched, and his nostrils flared. He gave me a tight-lipped smile and flourished his hand. From the white clouds, a tray with a pitcher and goblets appeared. Ophyr poured amber liquid into a goblet and gave it to me.

"Audra!" I shouted.

Audra reappeared and I handed her the drink. Ophyr watched the glass transfer hands curiously but said nothing. He poured and handed me another drink. Audra took a sip. She swirled the liquid in her cheeks; her lips parted in shock. Lunging forward, Audra slapped the goblet from my hand. It flew into the air, where it was eaten by the clouds. Audra coughed and grabbed her throat. She wheezed, "Help," and collapsed.

I fell to her side. The magic inside me tried to burst forth.

Help her! it screamed.

Power bottlenecked in my hands, absorbed by the ring. Audra clasped her throat and fell back. The whites of her eyes reddened, and the corners bled. Kneeling beside her, I was helpless. Frothy saliva foamed from Audra's mouth as she choked out a weak, "I'm sorry." I clutched her hand.

I couldn't save her, but she wouldn't be alone.

Audra stopped choking. It was over so quickly. Hardly even a moment.

The world spun as I stood. I inched toward the stairs, refusing to turn my back on Ophyr. "Stay away from me."

"Stop," Ophyr commanded. He snapped his fingers and pointed to the ground where he stood. "Come back here."

"You can't tell me what to do."

Ophyr laughed and stalked forward, pausing when his face nearly touched mine. He grabbed my hair and yanked my head sideways. His lips brushed my ear as he whispered, "Not while you're alive." Pulling away, Ophyr snapped his fingers.

A low, guttural growl rose behind him. Audra's back arched and her bones cracked. Ophyr approached her and pointed to his boot. Audra rolled onto her knees, and drool dripped from her snarling mouth. Kneeling forward, she kissed Ophyr's boot. "Come," Ophyr ordered. He tapped his lips. Audra rose and kissed Ophyr. He slid his hand behind her head, pulling her close. His tongue slipped between her dead lips—

I looked away.

"Hey!" Ophyr snapped. "Look at her." He wrenched Audra's head around. Blood stained her cheeks like tears. Audra was gone. This puppet looked at me through milky eyes of death. "Do you see?" Ophyr said. "We can do it the easy way"—he stroked Audra's hair—"or, in my opinion, the even easier way. It's up to you, really."

I fled.

Taking the stairs three at a time, I bounded away from Ophyr.

"What happened to you?" a voice called. Perhaps the only voice in the world I would have stopped for. I struggled to even my breathing as Darragh approached. His hair hung scraggly around his face, and dried blood coated his lip.

"What happened to you?" I deflected.

Darragh ignored the question and shoved past me. "The Queen knows about your plan."

"Wh—what do you mean?" I chased him.

"She knows you're going to attempt an escape."

I grabbed Darragh. "I need your help."

Darragh tore himself free. "I'm going away for a few days. Find someone else."

"I don't have anyone else!" I cried. "Please, don't go!"

"Elwyn. I can't do this anymore. I must go."

"But—"

"Be careful. Don't underestimate the Queen."

I watched his back as he left.

Chapter Fourteen

the house at the end of the bog

Whispers woke me.

"Eleanor."

"Nhhh." I rolled over in bed.

"Wake up, my love."

Bowyn? I blinked groggily around the loft.

"Eleanor."

There it was again! It *was* Bowyn; I was sure of it. I dragged myself up, so I could look through the window. In the garden below, Bowyn and Darragh circled each other. Like a ravenous bear, Bowyn's hulking frame lunged at Darragh. Quick and lithe, Darragh dodged easily.

Had Darragh just come home?

For a brief moment, I heard a high-pitched whine, like a cicada in summertime. I wriggled a finger in my ear. Even though the window was shut tight, I could hear Darragh and Bowyn talking, as if I was right next to them.

"She's not a pet you can leave and come back to!" Bowyn shouted.

"Tell her the truth and send her home! You're both going to get hurt. Every moment you delay increases your suffering ten-fold!"

"Are you bitter you can't bed her like the rest of your patients?" Darragh kept a deadly focus on Bowyn's movements. If magic was involved, Darragh would best Bowyn with little effort but...I had a feeling Darragh wouldn't use magic against his friend.

"Maybe that's what Eleanor wants?" Bowyn's eyes travelled up and down Darragh. He sneered. "She certainly isn't getting it from you."

Darragh cracked his knuckles.

"She's an adult," Bowyn spit. "She can make her own choices. Quit protecting her."

"If I want guidance, I'll ask for it."

Bowyn hurled himself at Darragh and they slammed into the ground. Bowyn came out on top; his flesh sizzled and smoked where he held Darragh's arms. Bowyn didn't notice. He glared at Darragh laying motionless beneath him. Darragh remained unbothered. If anything, he looked dreadfully bored as he watched tendrils of smoke waft away. Bowyn smashed the ground beside Darragh's head. Darragh didn't flinch.

Bowyn climbed off and cried, "I'm just trying to help you!" Brushing down his robes, Bowyn pointed at Darragh and said, "Tell her the truth, or I will." With that, Bowyn stalked down the path and disappeared into the trees.

Darragh turned and saw me in the window. My waking moment turned back into a hazy dream, the conversation forgotten the moment my eyes closed.

Breakfast with Darragh was a quiet endeavor. It gave me time to think. What would I do first when I got home? Ugh, I should probably do the dishes—

"Wait," I said. Darragh looked up from his breakfast. "I can't go back."

Darragh wiped his mouth, his brows rising hopefully. "Why not?"

"Turner. If I go back, I'll be charged with murder."

Darragh's shoulders slumped. "You won't," he said absent-mindedly.

"What do you mean? Why not?"

"I took care of it. There's no evidence. No one will ever know what happened."

"But *I* know—"

"As far as your police are concerned, he's missing. Better people go missing every second on Earth."

I shifted on my stool. "I just…I don't know if I can forgive myself for killing—"

Darragh slammed his palm on the table. "What do you think he was going to do, Nell?" Darragh tapped his temple angrily; it made a loud *tap-tap* noise. "I *know* what he was going to do to you! If you didn't defend yourself, you'd be dead!"

Darragh's sudden brutality shocked me. I sat in stunned silence. Darragh rose from the table and muttered, "He got what he deserved," before slamming the door behind him.

I wiped my eyes.

Darragh and I walked so far, I didn't recognize the woods anymore. A mood hung over us, and I hadn't felt like talking. It was only out of sheer boredom that I asked, "How do we get back to Earth?"

Darragh, perhaps regretful of his outburst but unsure how to initiate conversation, jumped at the opportunity to talk. "A long time ago, a Hiraethian named Madelena found a way to Earth." I opened my mouth, but Darragh, now familiar with my incessant curiosity, spoke quickly, "I don't know how." When he was sure that I didn't mean to ask more questions, he continued. "Madelena bestowed the knowledge of her discoveries in a handful of objects. If you find one of her relics, and you're strong enough, you can make the journey."

"What if I'm not strong enough?"

"You're stronger than you think," Darragh replied. "Once cloud walking was made illegal, Madelena's relics were sought out, and most were destroyed."

"But this guy, Senan, he has one?"

"Senan has one."

"Even though it's illegal?"

"Even if it's a crime, there's a market for it. One which Senan is happy to exploit." Gradually, the trees gave way to a grey, misty marsh. In the distance, a small, rocky island jutted from the mist. I trod onward but Darragh snatched my arm. He swung his leg in front of us, dispersing the mist. It revealed dark, murky water. "I can't stress this enough. Follow me *very* closely." I nodded, unable to look away from the placid water. Darragh chose his steps with great care as he navigated a path. All around, unseen creatures swam, swirling the mist.

"What are those?"

"Marsh elver," Darragh said. "Horrible things. If you're lucky, you'll drown before they eat you."

"Huh." I gulped. "Neat."

"Just don't disturb the water."

What if I fall in?

My mind spun images of treading the dark water, while unknown creatures circled my legs. Helpless, anticipating the bite of sharp teeth… My mouth suddenly dry, I said, "For the record, I hate this."

"Senan's a bit of a recluse."

To hear Darragh label someone a recluse amused me.

Darragh reached the rocky shore and hauled himself up. Crouching, he pulled me up after him. "We're here." Darragh jutted his chin at a wooden hut nestled high in the trees. Janky beams, bent at awkward angles, supported the hut. They bore an uncanny resemblance to chicken legs.

"You should call this place *Bog End*," I said.

Darragh gave me an inquisitive look.

"Just a thought."

Darragh said, "The last time I saw Senan…we didn't part on good terms." He paused as if he meant to explain but chose otherwise. Instead, he yelled, "Senan!"

We waited.

Nothing happened.

"Senan, let me up!"

Still, nothing happened. Pinching the bridge of his nose, Darragh waited. This was a game he'd played before. Five minutes passed, and Darragh blew out a loud breath. "I've brought someone to meet you, Moss. You're being terribly rude!" After another long pause, a clattering noise rang out above. Step by step, a staircase formed and descended. It slammed the ground and I jumped.

"I'll go first, if you don't mind." Darragh climbed the stairs. When he reached the top, he opened the front door without knocking.

"Oof," I mumbled.

Darragh was right to compare Senan to a magpie. Shiny amethysts, tall candles, baubles and delicate metal instruments filled shelves on every wall. Skeletons of different animals hung from the ceiling, bones bleached white. I wasn't sure where to put my feet; wooden crates packed with more items covered the floor, stacked one on top of the other. They teetered so precariously, it *had* to be magic keeping them upright. Darragh led me past an imposing spiral staircase that jutted from the middle of the room. It carried up so many stories, I couldn't see the top. We shuffled along a goat path, stopping at a fireplace.

Darragh spoke, "Senan."

"That's how you introduce me? Are you so embarrassed?" I did a double take. A small potato of a man sat in front of the fire. He was so immersed in the things around him, I hadn't realized he was a person until he spoke.

Darragh tried the introduction again. "This is Senan "*Moss*" Mitalrrythin."

"Oh!"

"My grandfather, yes."

Looking remarkably like a little gnome, Senan sat in a red, high-backed chair. Rosy cheeks and a big nose poked out from a lengthy, snow-white beard. He wore a green housecoat; the mottled fabric reminded me of a little mossy pebble. Senan laid his keen eyes on me. Olive, like Darragh's, though they possessed a joyful twinkle.

"You're the first person he's brought to me, Nelli." Senan gave Darragh a sidelong glance. Darragh brushed dust from the mantel, avoiding Senan's gaze.

How'd he know my name?

Senan slipped from the chair and toddled off. When he returned, he placed a pot of water in the fire, and a cookie-filled plate on the table. Senan waved and two chairs appeared, one of which bumped a tall stack of crates. Directly above me, the top crate wobbled, and fell. Darragh yanked me against his chest and caught the crate.

Glaring at Senan, Darragh said, "We seek passage to Earth."

"Is that why you're here?" Senan muttered, looking into the fire. "I should have known. You only visit when you need something."

"I'm busy," Darragh snapped. "And I want no part of your illicit activities."

Senan rolled his eyes, a gesture that earned a huff from Darragh.

Senan patted my hand. "My dear, why are you leaving us so soon?"

A flurry of monsters speckled my mind. Nighstalkers, carnivorous deer, trees that only pretended to be trees. I shifted nervously under Senan's gaze. My leg still ached from being broken, and I'd developed a nasty rash from the nettle.

The real question was, why hadn't I left sooner?

"I'd like to go home," I replied. "I don't think I belong here."

Senan offered a forlorn smile. "We live in a harsh but magical place." He relaxed into his armchair. "I'll consider your request." Darragh pulled sachets of mushrooms and ruby petals from his bag. He placed them on the table, followed by a handcrafted mug. The opal we'd retrieved was set nicely into the mug's side. Darragh slid over the offering. The firelight glinted off the opal and Senan's eyes narrowed.

"We need to go back. I have work to do, and Nell feels unsafe here."

"Is Nell safe on Earth?" Senan asked, his lips pursing.

The muscle in Darragh's jaw twitched, the same way it did when Bowyn struck a nerve. He didn't rise to Senan's challenge, whatever it was. "Please," Darragh said. Senan glanced at the mug and his gaze softened. He plucked it from the table and Darragh smiled. Senan hadn't *said* he would help us, but it seemed Darragh knew he'd accepted the offer.

Without prying his eyes from the opal, Senan asked, "Will you stay the night, or must you leave now?"

"It's better for us to arrive in the cover of darkness. I'm sorry, but we need to leave as soon as possible."

Senan placed a small, clear orb on the table. "Tea first?"

Darragh started to protest, but his shoulders sagged. "One, then we must go."

Senan clapped his little hands together and two more mugs appeared. He placed his newest acquisition on a shelf with several shiny goblets and grabbed an old, weathered mug for himself. Stained brown from years of use, it seemed so out of character from the trinkets that lined the shelves. Senan placed a sachet in his old mug, and then mine. But not Darragh's.

I looked at Darragh, a silent question.

"I need to...*drive*, so to speak," Darragh answered. "But you should drink."

Senan beamed, filling my mug with steaming water. With a wink, he filled his own. Darragh pulled his satchel around and rooted through it. He withdrew a bunch of loose leaves and crumbled them into his cup. He dumped boiling water in. Once everyone sat comfortably with tea, Senan set on Darragh.

"My child, when are you going to find a companion?"

Darragh's head fell back. He ran a hand through his hair and muttered, "I knew it."

"I'd hate to see you a spinster!"

"Moss, please." Darragh rubbed his temple.

"I just want you to be happy!" Senan placed a chunky hand on my arm. "He's not so hard to look at, right? He has a pleasant face, and quite an agreeable stature?"

My cheeks burned. "He's alright," I joked.

Darragh's eyes found mine. A voice in my head whispered, '*My Nell, it's not like you to be dishonest.*' Darragh raised a brow, and a smile tugged his cheek.

My stomach somersaulted.

"He's very easy to look at," I amended, sipping my tea.

"Right. There you have it." Senan laughed, taking a big gulp himself. He raised one meaty hand and counted fingers. "He can cook, he can sew, he can keep house. Sure, he can be disagreeable at times—he gets that from his mother..."

Senan lapsed into silence. Sipping his tea, his nose crinkled.

Senan collected himself and said, "He'd certainly give you powerful daughters." Darragh covered his face. His hands didn't quite hide the cherry-red shade of his neck. "He'd make a lovely companion, right, Nell?" Senan elbowed me.

There was something in the tea. Warmth and a slight nausea swelled in my belly. The fire turned hazy. My mug blurred in and out of focus. Far away, Senan said, "Oh, drat. There she goes."

Dizzying darkness filled the room.

Chapter Fifteen

a passing shadow

Elwyn

The rich aroma of roasted meat struck me as I entered the dining chamber. My stomach growled, and I cursed the saliva that swelled around my tongue. I sat across from my father; a drink was already perched in his hand. It was a relief to sit down. I'd felt lightheaded and foggy all day. I gazed longingly at the apples on the table. I'd never really noticed the fruit before. I thought it was just decoration. Now I couldn't stop thinking about biting into the crisp, juicy flesh…

I hadn't eaten since my visit with Ophyr.

Audra's death replayed in my head, over and over. I looked at the food, and all I saw was poison.

My father looked upon me, eyes touched with concern. "Are you alright, Elle?" The door to the chamber blew open and the Queen stormed in. Shadows swirled and darkened the room as the Queen took her spot at the head of the table. Once seated, she smiled. My father and I exchanged quick glances.

"How was your evening with Ophyr?" the Queen inquired sweetly.

This table was not made for small talk. It took me a moment to overcome the shock that the Queen had spoken to me. "He killed Audra," I spat.

Like the sudden cacophony of disturbed crows, the Queen threw her head back and cackled. "Oh no! Not Audra!" she cried, voice laden with mock concern. She laughed again, so hard her breath came in short wheezes. Between chuckles, the Queen asked, "How did he do it?"

Sickened by her reaction, I stared at my plate. "He poisoned her—"

"AH, HA, HA!" The Queen slammed her brittle fist on the table. Father and I sat in silence as the Queen's laughter bounced off us. She composed herself, but before she could say anything, she broke into another fit of laughter. Finally, the Queen took a deep breath and wiped away a tear. "Oh, poor Audra." She chuckled. "She'll probably be more useful now." She bit down another laugh. Every few seconds, she smiled and looked as if she might burst into laughter once more.

Knock-knock-knock.

"Oh, splendid." The Queen perked up and curled a finger at the door. It swung inward and Ophyr strode in.

He grinned. "What are we laughing about?"

I rounded on the Queen. "What's he doing here?"

The Queen ignored me. "Elwyn was just recounting an amusing tale." The chair next to the Queen slid out. "Sit, my child." Ophyr bowed and accepted the seat. "We're so glad you could join us this evening," the Queen doted. Invisible hands piled Ophyr's plate high with food.

He touched his chest. "It's my honour."

The Queen sat comfortably back in her chair. "I was just asking Elwyn how your date went?"

"I think it went well." Ophyr tore a piece of meat with his teeth.

The Queen nodded happily; a spoon brought food to her lips.

"You'll have to excuse my excitement. It's not everyday you meet a necromancer. You must tell us more; I find it fascinating." She paused, giddy. "Was everyone in your family so capable?"

"My grandmother had the gift, but she was killed when I was young."

The Queen muttered a shallow, "Such a shame," and continued eating.

"My mother has it as well, and my sister. Though they both pretend they're basic, to avoid detection."

"What a dreadful shame!" the Queen cried.

A grumble carried from my stomach, drawing the Queen's frightening gaze to me. "Elwyn, eat. You're beginning to look like a corpse."

Over the Queen's shoulder, Ophyr winked.

Vomit gurgled in my throat as I pushed food around my plate. "I'm not feeling well. I'd like to be excused." I rose, but invisible hands gripped my shoulders. My knees buckled and I slammed back into my seat.

The Queen's inhuman eyes bore into me, wide and unblinking. "Don't be rude to our guest, Elwyn." My body leaned away, anticipating the pain. A bead of sweat dripped down my father's temple. The rosiness gone from his cheeks, he was a ghost in his seat. He mouthed the word, '*Eat.*' My hands trembled, and the tines of my fork clinked against my plate. I brought a piece of meat to my lips, sniffed it, and took a small bite.

It tasted wrong.

I took another bite.

That tasted wrong too.

My fork clattered to the table as I gagged.

"Elle sweetie, are you okay?" My father's voice echoed from far away. "Perhaps she should be excused?"

"Go!" the Queen shouted. I pushed away from the table and lurched for the door. My father must have tried to follow me because the Queen shouted, "Not you!"

I bounded through the halls to my room, barely making it to the adjoining privy before I threw up. My stomach was empty, and acid scorched my throat. I dry heaved until my sides hurt. Exhausted, I crawled into bed and wrapped myself in blankets. Sweat poured from me, it dampened the sheets and left me feeling colder than before.

A knock sounded on the door. The guardian regularly stationed outside my room popped her head in and asked, "Are you alright?"

"Leave me be!" I pulled the blankets tighter and fought the urge to run to the privy again. Someone had poisoned my food; I was sure of it. But if Ophyr had poisoned me, I'd already be dead.

So…who was it?

High-pitched squeals jarred me awake. I bolted upright and squinted against the sunlight streaming in the window.

I'd slept through the night.

Leshy squealed again, leaping onto the bed. "What? What?" I pushed him away. My stomach ached, and Leshy trodding all over it didn't help. Unphased by my annoyance, Leshy crawled back up. He held something in his arms, something he desperately wanted me to have. "What's this?" I took the item from Leshy's paws. Though scuffed and scratched, I still recognized the familiar, ornately carved griffin. I placed my fingers in the ridges behind the griffin's shoulders. It fit neatly in my grip. The perfect handle for a cane.

My father's cane.

I ran to the privy. My body managed to be sick again. Leshy sat outside the room, his paws covering his face as I wretched. When I finished, I leaned against the cool rock. I ran shaky fingers over the griffin. A sickening energy coursed through it. It pulsed through me too, mirroring my quick, terrified heartbeat. I pressed the griffin against my chest and closed my eyes.

My father knelt on his knees before the Queen. The doors to the great hall creaked open. The Truth entered, followed by the healer who treated my father, the one I often found him chatting with in the late hours of the night.

"Kneel," the Truth spat. The healer knelt beside my father. Tense silence pressed in on the room.

Finally, the Queen asked, "I'm curious, after you abandoned me, where did you plan on going?"

My father's mouth dropped open. "What are you talking about, my Queen?"

"I know of your plan!" The Queen pointed at the healer. "Was she coming with you?"

Father looked on helplessly. "Sloane? No! I have no idea what you're talking about!" Sloane's body slammed forward so suddenly she didn't have time to pull her arms up. Her face smashed against the rock. The Queen lifted her hand, and Sloane pulled back into a kneeling position. Her nose broken, blood dripped down her chest. Sloane smashed against the ground again. This time, her skull cracked. It made the same noise as a piece of wood broken over a knee. Again, the Queen lifted Sloane to her knees. Sloane's eyes fluttered, one eyeball wonky in its socket. The third time Sloane went down, her head exploded like a melon during target practice. Human shrapnel sprayed the room.

"Ugh!" The Truth straightened and picked a tooth from the crook of her crossed arms. She dabbed at the blood stain now marring a yellow stripe of her robe. Her lips pouted, and she turned a scowling gaze back to my father.

Father turned a horrified, blood-spattered face back to the Queen. "What was her crime?!"

"Her crime was the same as yours. Treason."

Father looked to the Queen's Truth. He pointed to his temple and cried, "Surely you can see! Sloane did nothing, and I never meant to leave!"

The Truth looked away.

The Queen flourished a hand and hissed, "Silence!" Shadows crept across the floor. They climbed my father, circling his throat.

My father choked out, "Please, Briar—"

The shadows paused.

Suddenly, one hundred years melted from the Queen's face. Sitting on the throne was my mother. Not a horrible old crone—my mother!

Eyes wide and shocked, my mother stared at her shaking hands. I couldn't help the feeling that she was as helpless a bystander as me. My mother winced and blood seeped from the corners of her mouth.

She'd bitten her tongue.

A cough sputtered from her lips, spraying droplets of blood down her chest. My mother writhed, trying to resist whatever evil consumed her. A cackle exploded from her throat, and the aged, hateful Queen returned. With renewed fury, the Queen's gaze fell on my father. She spit a mouthful of blood beside the throne.

The Truth sneered and yanked her leg away.

Shadowy hands gripped my father's throat. I felt the tightness as they squeezed. Father tried to draw breath.

He couldn't.

Despite the pain and terror, I stayed with him until the end.

As my father stopped struggling, relief shuddered through the memory. His life flashed through his mind. The day he met my mother, so beautiful and kind. Interrupted by the screams of a baby, the day I was born. Finally, my own face, smiling up at him, just the night before.

The room re-appeared around me as the memory faded.

His last thought was of me.

After all that, the last thing my father felt was guilt. Disappointment that he couldn't protect me, that he'd let me down. Leshy rested his head against my leg, quivering. I gathered him in my arms and stroked the back of his neck while silent tears fell from my cheeks.

"I'll kill her," I whispered to Leshy. "I'll choke the life from her eyes."

Chapter Sixteen

home is where my cat is

"Well, wake up. You're home."

Reluctant to give up the peace of sleep, I groaned and blinked awake. Outside my apartment, Darragh held me in his arms. "How'd we get here?" I asked. Darragh set me down. He held up Senan's orb in response.

"Why don't I remember?"

"Tea."

I recalled the tea with Senan and Darragh. I'd laughed and enjoyed myself, until suddenly, I couldn't keep my eyes open. "Don't do that again."

"The journey is difficult. I thought this might be easier—"

"I don't like it."

"I won't do it again," Darragh promised.

Snowflakes drifted from the sky, and I looked longingly at my warm apartment. "What happens now?"

"We part ways."

It was obvious that Darragh and I would part ways. But I'd been so focused on getting home, I hadn't really thought about it. Now, faced with the reality that I might never see Darragh again, my stomach tugged—horrified by the very thought.

"It's freezing," I started. "Why don't you stay with me while you're here?"

Darragh's eyes darted to my apartment. "I don't think that's a good idea."

"You'll be safe." I smiled and nodded at the stairs.

Darragh returned the smile, but shook his head. "Goodbye, Nell." I bit my tongue as Darragh made his way down the alley. I trudged up the stairs and closed the door behind me. I looked over my messy kitchen. This is what I wanted, right? To be safe and comfortable in my home. I kicked off my shoes and leaned on the table. Silence stoked the tension in my belly. The apartment was different, somehow changed while I was gone.

The space didn't feel safe, or comfortable at all.

It felt empty.

My mind wandered to Darragh, lumbering away in the snow. The longer I waited, the farther his feet carried him away from me.

No.

This couldn't be the end.

I yanked the door open. "Darragh—"

Darragh stood on the other side, hand raised, prepared to knock.

In my living room, a table and lamp lay on the carpet. "Someone was here," I said, stepping around glass fragments.

Darragh, who was fixated on the tiles by the door, pulled his gaze away and said, "How can you tell?" He looked around the untidy kitchen, over the dishes, which had sat in the sink for so many days now.

The rest of my apartment was undisturbed. I checked cabinets and closets, but nothing was missing. "They didn't take anything." I pointed at the lamp and the table. "It's just this."

"At least they didn't take anything." Darragh stooped to clean up the glass. It was odd, how quickly he dismissed an intruder. If I was alone, I might have been more concerned. A buzzing sounded in the kitchen. I followed it and snatched my phone from a pile of discarded papers on the counter. "Oof." I clutched it to my breast. "I missed you."

"I hope you don't mind," Darragh said, "but I let everyone know you'd be gone for a bit."

I checked my texts. One to Morgan: "*Have to leave for an emergency, will let you know when I'm back.*" And Darragh had sent the same one to Sasha, with an extra line asking him to check in on Watney.

"I see there weren't many people to tell."

Darragh dumped glass shards in the trash. "I don't think even Bowyn would know I disappeared until the food stopped showing up."

A wall of texts awaited me in Sasha's chat.

"*Are you okay?*"

"*What's going on?*"

"*I took your smelly cat to my place. Your place was a mess. Glass everywhere.*"

"*IF YOU'RE ALIVE YOU ANSWER YOUR PHONE!!!*"

"*NELL???? Should I be worried?*"

Crap.

"*I'm so sorry,*" I texted back. "*My phone died and I forgot the charger. I'm home now. Can you drop Watney off otw to the café in the morning?*" Dots arose as Sasha typed, but I set my phone down. Across the apartment, Darragh pressed his forehead against the window, examining the fire escape.

"What are you doing?" I joined him.

"This is the only one?" Darragh pointed at the escape.

"What?"

"Is this the only fire escape in the building?"

I looked at it, seeing it for the first time. "I don't know. I guess?"

Darragh offered a grim nod and turned away.

"Would you like something to eat?" Thankfully, Darragh replied that he would not. I'm sure any food in the fridge was long rotten. Standing awkwardly in my living room, Darragh possessed a jumpy irritation. He glanced at the couch, as if he were deciding whether to sit down or flee. Hoping to encourage the former, I sat and waved for him to join me. "What will you do now that you're here?"

"There's someone in town I need to escort back to Hiraeth." Darragh sat on the edge of the couch. "I'd nearly had him before I—we had to leave."

"Would I know him?"

"He goes by Marlowe here. James Marlowe."

My jaw dropped. "James Marlowe? As in *Sexiest Person Alive*? That Marlowe?"

Darragh sneered and looked like he might disagree. He paused, considering. "If I weren't convinced of his backstabbing treachery, I might think him handsome."

It had to be him. Marlowe, a famous actor, was in town for a show. Sasha gushed about him non-stop, but even his father, Regé, an actor in the local theatre circuit, couldn't get us tickets. My first real crush, I'd had pictures of James Marlowe plastered over the walls of my childhood bedroom. Even thinking about him brought a fluttery smile to my lips. Darragh didn't have to read my mind to know how I felt. He crossed his arms and frowned.

Changing the subject, I said, "I'm not really tired yet. Do you want to watch a movie before bed?"

"Sure. I've read about movies."

"Yeah, they're…well, they're kind of like your *memories*, but fake." I knelt in front of the shelf beside the TV.

"What sort of movies do you like?" Darragh asked.

"Uh," my mind emptied. I looked at the shelves to remind myself of a single movie I liked. *Army of Darkness, Aliens, Tremors* (one through seven), *Ever After*. "I don't know. I like scary things and fairy tales."

Darragh sat more comfortably on the couch. "What's a fairy tale?"

"A magical story with a happy ending."

"What if there's magic, but no happy ending?"

"That would be a tragedy, and I wouldn't be interested."

I chose one my favourites, *Ever After*. Sometimes when I had trouble sleeping, I put it on. I selected it now for that very reason, but once it started, I quickly learned I wouldn't sleep anytime soon.

Darragh watched.

The.

Entire.

Thing.

I also learned I couldn't talk. Every time I spoke, Darragh asked if we could go back a few seconds in case he missed something. I side eyed him as the movie finished, savouring the way he grinned and wiped a sneaky tear away.

"Did you like it?"

Darragh smiled and nodded bashfully. "Can we watch it again?" I laughed, then realized he was serious. The clock on the stove read 3:38 a.m. I thought about how comfortable my bed would be right about now.

I hit play.

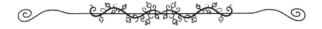

My phone buzzed. Reaching out of bed, I slapped around until I found it. I hadn't missed waking up this way.

Morgan's text read, "*Sasha said you're back. Hope you're okay. Are you free this morning?*"

"*I'll be there,*" I replied.

I dragged myself to the shower. Once cleaned up, I left the bathroom—

"I fixed your plant." Darragh stood on the other side of the door, clutching the plant I'd left to die in my windowsill. The leaves were a shade of green I'd never seen before.

"Nice. How'd you do that?"

"Water. Sunlight. A scrap of attention."

"Sometimes the scraps add up, and plants die." I walked around Darragh to the kitchen. Darragh hugged the plant against his chest and followed. He placed it beside him on the counter, watching me closely while I made coffee.

KNOCK-KNOCK-KNOCK.

"Oh! That's Sasha!" I covered my mouth and looked at Darragh. How could I explain him to Sasha?

Darragh read my fearful expression, and he pushed away from the counter. "I'll be in the bathroom."

I waited for him to leave before I opened the door. "Hey—"

"I'm so late. Mum's gonna kill me!" Sasha shoved Watney's carrier into my arms. Running back down the stairs, he asked, "You comin' in today?"

"I'll be there for nine!" I called.

"Good!" Sasha pointed at me while he ran. "You have a lot of explaining to do!"

Isn't that the truth.

Watney ran straight to Darragh as he exited the bathroom. Darragh obliged, stooping to give him scritches. The coffee wasn't done brewing.

I leaned on the counter, waiting impatiently. Darragh continued to pet Watney, who rolled onto his back, belly displayed for pets. A question I'd meant to ask Darragh a long time ago came to mind.

"How come, on Hiraeth, the magic didn't always work on me?"

"What do you mean?"

"Well, when Ruatha tried to kill us in the wood, she kept you completely immobile, but I could still move. I threw dirt at her. It was her shock that saved us. And Bowyn had trouble using his magic on me too, remember? When he tried to compel me, I said no."

"Well," Darragh started, "you feel different."

"What?" That wasn't the response I expected. "Do I feel *bad*?"

"Wha—no!" Darragh backtracked. "You just feel…different." I crossed my arms and he continued. "As far as I know, you're the only human who's travelled from Earth to Hiraeth. Hiraethians don't know what to do with you." He gave Watney one last belly rub and stood. I poured coffee and slid a mug over the counter. Watney brushed Darragh's leg and screamed.

"Okay!" Darragh whisper-shouted and picked him up. Cradling Watney, Darragh said, "Say Watney bolted for an open door, and you needed to catch him. You know he's furry, you know roughly how much he weighs, you know how to avoid claws…but what if you picked him up, and he was slippery? He looks like a cat, and you should be able to pick him up like any other cat. But you can't. He just slips through your fingers. There's something about him that's different, and you don't really know how to compensate for it." Darragh set Watney down and took a large gulp of scalding coffee. Unphased, he continued. "That's what it's like to use magic on you, on people from your world. You just don't feel the same. It's quite difficult."

"You don't seem to have a problem," I said.

Darragh set his empty mug on the counter. "I've spent a lot of time on Earth. I know how you feel."

"Like a slippery pussycat?" I blew on my coffee, sipping it.

"Yes." He nodded solemnly.

"Noted."

Before I left for work, I pulled Darragh into my bedroom.

Not for that. Calm down.

Wall-to-wall bookshelves lined the room. Kicking laundry aside, I pointed and said, "Help yourself while I'm gone."

Childlike wonder entered Darragh's eyes. "You have a library?"

"Well, I don't really lend them out. But I suppose I can make an exception for you. Just don't dog-ear my pages," I teased. Darragh dragged his hands across the spines. He pulled books out and stacked them in his arms.

"I'm going to work."

Unwilling to pry his eyes from the books, Darragh offered a vague wave. I'd have done the same.

On the way to work, I rehearsed my story for Sasha. Super personal family emergency. Maybe he'd be so happy to have me back, he wouldn't ask too many questions? The door jingled as I entered Rousseau's.

"Where *have* you been?" Sasha screeched. I grimaced and half-smiled at the customers scattered about the café.

"Family emergency." I skirted Sasha and tossed my stuff in the back. He followed me so closely, I smelled his perfume.

"Bullshit," he snapped. "You don't have any family."

"Rude."

"You know what I mean."

"I needed to help a friend."

181

"You don't have any friends either. What's going on?"

"Nothing!" I shouted. "Nothing is going on!"

Sasha shrunk away, stunned.

"I'm sorry," I said, regretting my outburst. "When I can say more, I promise I'll tell you, okay?" I wrapped an apron around my waist.

"Nell," Sasha prodded. "I come to your place, and you're gone and there's glass everywhere. Honestly it looked like a break-in. And with all this magic shit going around—"

"You didn't call the cops though, right?" I asked.

Sasha gave me a stern, sanity-questioning look. "So they could nail me for robbing you? No, ma'am. I got my ass out of there." My shoulders relaxed. Sasha rubbed my arm and said, "You're not in any trouble, right?"

Am I?

"No. I'm not in any trouble," I reassured.

"'kay." Sasha calmed a bit. "I just…I worry about you."

"I know."

We spent the better part of the morning in silence. Sasha pouted around the shop, pissy I wouldn't tell him where I'd been. But come the mid-morning lull, his pouting could only last so long. "Did you see what happened to that poor homeless girl?"

Something tugged at my memory. Did I? I furrowed my brows, trying to remember if I had. A quiet part of my brain supplied the name, "Kristina?"

"Yeah, her!" Sasha jutted his thumb over his shoulder. "She was attacked out back."

My hand slipped on the frother and milk exploded everywhere. The memory of Turner shoving Kristina exploded in my mind. Grief cleaved my chest as I remembered her tiny, lifeless body laying on the ground. I rubbed my chest and caught my breath. "Do the police know what happened?"

"Nah, I bet it was one of *those* people though." Sasha raised his hands and did lazy air quotes. "*People with magical abilities* or whatever we're calling them now."

I steadied myself on the counter. "When, uh, when did that happen?"

Sasha traced his lips and thought. "Actually, you know what? Just before you left. I wanted to talk about it the next morning, but you weren't here." I cleaned up milk in a haze while Sasha carried on. "And you know what else is weird? I haven't seen that bitch Turner since then either. I was looking out for him after I promised I'd take his orders, and nothing."

I killed him.

Waves of grief and guilt coursed through me. I did my best not to cry right there behind the counter. Sasha gave me a funny look and I put on a shaky smile.

"That's good!" I said, with far too much emphasis.

Sasha put a hand on his hip and glared. "Why are you being so weird?"

"You know what? I'm not feeling good. I'll have to grab some drugs when I run upstairs for lunch."

Sasha pursed his lips. "Mhm. Sure."

I tossed my bag on the counter, careful to avoid the plates filled with food. I'm not sure where Darragh found food, but I didn't complain. Lying on the couch reading, Darragh peeked around the cover of his book. "She exploded like the fourth of July." He squinted at the page. "Is that a metaphor?"

I stopped what I was doing to look at Darragh. His curls hung in wet ringlets around his face, fresh out of the shower. "What are you reading?" He waved the cover in my direction. A romance novel even *I* hadn't been able to stomach. "Uh. Yeah, it's a metaphor."

Please don't ask me what it means.

"What does it mean?"

"I'm not sure. Google it and tell me." I tossed my phone over. Darragh clicked around and paused. His cheeks turned pink, and he pulled the book up to cover his face.

"What did you discover?"

"You know what I discovered," he grumbled.

I fiddled with a scrap of paper on the counter. "Can I ask you something?" Darragh closed the book around his thumb. "What happened to Turner's…" I lowered my voice. "What happened to Turner's body?"

"Nell, I told you. I took care of it."

"And what about Kristina's body?" I snapped. "You just…" My breath hitched, and I paused to collect myself. "You just left her in that shitty alley until the police found her?"

Darragh's eyes widened, and he mouthed, '*Body?*'

"Yeah! I remember now! Why didn't you tell me she was there?"

Darragh swung his legs over the side of the couch. "Let's go for a walk."

"A walk? I have to go back to work!" I shouted. "I have to go back to work and pretend like I can live with the consequences of my actions!" I jammed my knuckles beneath my eyes, hoping to stop the tears in their tracks. "A little girl is dead. And I killed a man."

Darragh stood and said, "Nell—"

A knock sounded on the apartment door. It swung open and Sasha peeked in. "Nell, don't worry about—"

Sasha saw Darragh and froze. Sasha looked at me. And back at Darragh. A smile spread across his face. "Nelli, I just wanted to let you know that Mum's come in, and if you're *not feeling well*, you don't need to come back for the afternoon."

"Sasha," I started.

"You and I have *a lot* to talk about," Sasha said. His eyes darted to

Darragh and back. As he closed the door he said, "Feel better soon."

Darragh spoke up. "He thinks we're having sex."

"Yeah, got it. Thanks man," I snapped. "He thinks I'm a liar now too."

Darragh grabbed a slice of cucumber from a plate and nibbled it. He shrugged and said, "Little lies are necessary here and there."

"Excuse me," an orderly dressed in blue scrubs pushed a cart around me in the hospital reception.

"What are we doing here?" I asked Darragh.

Darragh lowered his voice. "Showing you the consequences of your actions." Turning to the nurse behind the desk, Darragh leaned over and smiled. "Hello—"

"One second," the nurse, whose name tag read, ELLEN STRODE, R.N., interrupted. Out of the corner of her eye, she caught sight of Darragh. Ellen abruptly stopped typing, turned, and smiled broadly. "How can I help you, my dear?"

"Hi, my cousin came in a few nights ago. Kristina Byers. Can you tell me where she is?"

I grabbed Darragh's arm.

She's okay?

Darragh smiled.

Nurse Ellen typed and frowned. "Oh yeah, the poor thing. She's on the fourth floor, room 406. She hasn't had anyone in yet. It's nice you've come to see her." Nurse Ellen handed us a clipboard. "Sign-in and you can head up."

Darragh held the pen exactly like someone who'd never held a pen before. I took it and wrote my name down. In a clumsy, childlike script, Darragh tried his best to do the same.

In room 406, Kristina lay in a bed, her head wrapped in a bandage.

I stood awkwardly, but Darragh was natural. He touched Kristina's arm and whispered her name. Kristina's eyes opened and she tensed. She didn't recognize Darragh, though she smiled weakly.

"Sorry to wake you," Darragh whispered and pointed at me. "Someone wanted to make sure you were okay."

Kristina followed Darragh's finger to me, where I stood by the door. Her eyes lit and she pushed herself up. "You saved me from that man," she whispered. A nurse walked by the room and Kristina quieted. When the nurse had gone, Kristina asked, "Are you...are you like me?"

Darragh glanced over his shoulder, and then raised his palm. A tiny flame kindled to life. Kristina's eyes widened and shot to me.

I smiled and sat in the chair next to the bed. "We are."

"Thank you for helping me." Kristina started to cry, and I did my best not to follow suit. "Most people look the other way—pretend they don't see me." Kristina fiddled with the corner of her blanket. "Most people would have kept walking."

Kristina met my eyes when she said, "I'm happy you didn't keep walking."

"Why didn't you tell me?" I asked Darragh on our walk home. He side-eyed my tear-stained face.

"You didn't remember. I didn't want to upset you."

"I'd rather know the truth, even if it upsets me."

Darragh scratched his nose. "Nell, I—"

I clutched Darragh's arm and pointed. "Look!" A rotund, Bernese puppy walked by us on a leash. I watched him waddle out of sight before I said, "I'm so sorry, what were you saying?"

Darragh's irises danced as they examined my face. He smiled and said, "Nothing."

Chapter Seventeen

showman or scoundrel?

I finished in the bathroom and scanned the apartment for Darragh. "Darragh?"

"I'm in here," he called from my bedroom. I found Darragh, examining three dresses he'd laid on my bed. If it were anyone but him who rummaged through my closet, I might be annoyed.

"Looking for something to wear?" I asked.

"I already know what I'm wearing. I'm trying to decide which of these matches."

"Where are we going?"

"I wanted tonight to be a surprise but, I think we've had enough stress today." Without looking at me, Darragh handed over two tickets. I flipped them over—*Alexander Hamilton: A musical about the life of Alexander Hamilton.*

"How?!" I gripped Darragh's arm. "How did you get these?!"

"Don't ask." He pointed to a black dress. "That one."

"What are you gonna wear?" I looked around the room.

"You'll see." Darragh left, but then he peeked back in. "We're leaving at seven."

With my hair curled and make-up done, I slid into the dress Darragh had selected. I picked out a pair of black heels from the bottom of my closet. Though rattier than I'd have liked—scuffed from years of wear—they were the only pair I had. They'd have to do. I bent over and adjusted my bra before heading to the living room.

"I'm good to go."

Darragh stood to greet me, and my breath caught. He wore a well-fitted, black suit. He'd pulled his hair behind his ears and tied it in a tidy knot at the nape of his neck. I shook my head and tried my best to stop staring.

"Do I look okay?" I asked.

Darragh didn't answer. He closed his mouth and blinked. "Sorry—what did you say?"

I smiled. "I asked if I looked okay."

Darragh's gaze travelled down my body and back up, where it rested on my lips. "Yes," he murmured. Desire flickered on Darragh's face, a hungry, insatiable thing. When his eyes met mine, I didn't shy away. To my surprise, I thought that if an opportunity presented itself, I might forget the musical altogether...

Darragh cleared his throat and pointed to the door. "We should go."

Alexander Hamilton posters dangled from the antique lampposts that lined the dimly lit road. Marlowe's face smiled down on us, beckoning me to the theatre. "I can't believe I get to see James. *Sterling*. Marlowe in person." My steps were quick, laced with excitement. It was Darragh's turn to keep up with me.

"I've heard he's quite the showman," Darragh grumbled.

"He's *so* handsome," I swooned. "Hold on a sec." I took a picture of the theatre marquee ahead—careful to get the poster of Marlowe in the shot.

Darragh tried and failed to conceal his disgust. "He's twice your age."

I shrugged unapologetically. "Wait." I grabbed Darragh's wrist. "You're going to wait until the end, right?"

Darragh glanced at my hand, wrapped around his wrist. "Hm?"

"You're going to let him finish the show, right?"

Darragh pulled away and said, "We'll see." He eased through a group of people, who'd stopped to pose with a poster of Marlowe. I shoved through the people, several of whom no longer admired Marlowe; their eyes trailed Darragh instead.

"Darragh. I literally do not care what this man did. I need to see the show."

Darragh nodded politely at a group of women and whispered, "He fathered countless children into a world where their only prospect is loneliness and death."

"Yeah, yeah, yeah." I nodded. "After the show."

"I have to go back to Hiraeth tonight. This is my only shot."

I stopped like I'd hit an invisible wall. "You're going back *tonight*?"

Darragh nodded once, sharply.

"Why?"

"I have somewhere I need to be."

"Where?"

"What concern is it to you?" Darragh asked. "You're back on Earth, where you wanted to be." Darragh continued walking. "You knew I only lingered to get Marlowe. I can't stay."

"I know. I just… I wish you told me sooner." My excitement dulled. I stared at the pavement while I walked.

"I'm sorry."

"It's okay."

It wasn't.

We took our seats near the fire exit. Uninterested in chatting with Darragh, I flipped through the program. Marlowe's headshot was first in the list of cast members, his dark hair cropped short. Marlowe's charming smile was arresting, and…familiar? I'd never noticed it before. The warmth of his eyes… The theatre plunged into darkness. The curtain swept away, and the music that I knew note for note and word for word washed over the theatre.

The crowd drew a collective breath when Marlowe took the stage as Alexander Hamilton. Cheers and hoots erupted from theatregoers when he sang his first line. The more I saw Marlowe move and speak, the more I couldn't ignore the nagging feeling that I recognized him. I told myself it was all the movies I'd seen, but deep down, I knew that wasn't right. I pushed the thought from my mind, determined to enjoy every moment.

The curtains fell for intermission, and I excused myself to use the bathroom. Returning to a sour looking Darragh, I asked, "Do you like it so far?"

"Yes. He's quite the talented fiend."

"He's *so* good." I fanned myself with the program. "He looks great, and you know, I think he has the best voice I've ever heard in person."

"It'll be a shame if I have to kill him."

"Wha—"

The curtains drew for the second half of the show.

I wiped away a steady stream of tears and leapt to my feet. Sniffling, I clapped as the performers bowed. Marlowe left the stage, and the final curtain fell. "Wow," I said. I turned to Darragh and found his seat was empty. All around me, people stood and shuffled out, but he wasn't one of them. Dread pitted my stomach. I followed the crowd, all the while looking for Darragh. My shoulders relaxed when I spotted him leaning on a pillar in the lobby. Arms crossed over his chest, Darragh wore such a foul look, I wondered if I might slip out unnoticed with the crowd.

But then he saw me and perked up.

Damn.

I joined Darragh. The front of his shirt was untucked, and his tie askew. "What happened?"

Darragh's hair was no longer tied at the nape of his neck. Loose strands hung wildly around his face. "Come with me," he growled.

Oh no.

"What did you do?"

We approached a door that read *private*, Darragh looked over his shoulder and ushered me through. We hurried down a hallway and paused before a door labelled, *Marlowe.*

"Avoid his gaze. If you must meet his eyes, do not linger." Darragh looked both ways before we snuck inside.

"Oh no." In the middle of the room, thoroughly tied to a chair, sat Marlowe. Just as disheveled as Darragh, strands of hair jutted from Marlowe's founding father pony. He still wore his Alexander Hamilton costume, with an additional gag shoved in his mouth. I gestured to the bonds. "I see you did it the old-fashioned way."

"The last time I used magic to bind him, he weaseled out of it." Darragh stood before Marlowe. "Seerinth Martell, alias James Sterling Marlowe, once again, you have violated Hiraeth's cloud-walking law, and you've demonstrated a refusal to return. I've been given the order to bring you back, dead or alive."

Marlowe's unamused eyes stared back at Darragh.

Darragh removed the gag.

Marlowe allowed for a pregnant pause before he said, "You know it's pronounced *Sir-inth*, actually." He squinted and smirked. "Sir, for short."

Darragh gritted his teeth and leaned in. "Will you go willingly? Or do you choose the alternative?" Marlowe rolled his eyes and Darragh continued. "Please. Choose the alternative."

Marlowe threw his head back and cried, "Why can't you see what I'm trying to do here? Why can't you see the benefit of uniting our worlds? Their world and ours, science and magic!"

"Magic doesn't belong here!" Darragh snapped. "Your children, your line. Innocent people are dying."

A flame travelled around Darragh's hand.

Marlowe shook his head. "You kill wantonly and condemn me, when my only crime is creating life!"

"You create life and can't be bothered to take any responsibility for it!" Darragh shouted.

Marlowe stuck up his nose and looked away. "You know you prefer it here too." Whether that was true, Darragh didn't waver. Marlowe continued. "If I can't stay here"—his eyes flicked toward me, then back to Darragh—"then you can't either." Marlowe stared at Darragh, waiting for him to say something he might argue with. Darragh didn't oblige. "Surely *you* can see the benefit of uniting our worlds!"

Darragh slammed his hands on either side of the chair. Both Marlowe and I flinched. "Will it be death, then?"

"They worship me here. Did you see that crowd? That was magic." Marlowe stuck out his chin. "I'm not going back." I nearly chuckled. The way Marlowe argued with Darragh reminded me of—

Hold on. I scrutinized Marlowe's thick black hair and brows. Dark chocolatey eyes…

Oh.

Oh no.

"An unfortunate choice, but death it is," Darragh snarled. The flame in his hand pulsed brighter.

"Wait!" I shouted.

"What?" Darragh rounded on me.

"Take him back." I eased between Darragh and Marlowe. "For Bowyn."

Surprise flitted over Darragh's face before he shouted, "Bowyn wants him dead more than I do!"

"No one wants this." I rubbed Darragh's arms. "No one wants their father tied down and executed."

Behind me, Marlowe spoke up. "She's right, you know." I gave him a curt look over my shoulder.

"Please." My eyes searched Darragh's face, begging him to change his mind. "Just take him back."

Darragh opened his mouth to disagree—a knock sounded on the door. A feminine voice called, "Jamie? Are you in there? Are you ready for dinner?"

Darragh pushed me aside and put his face in front of Marlowe's. "Tell whoever that is to leave." Marlowe simply stuck up his nose and looked away. Darragh slammed his hands on the arms of the chair. "Diva!" Darragh cleared his throat, and in a voice that imitated Marlowe he said, "I'm not quite ready yet…darling?"

"I'm coming in," the voice called. A key entered the lock and Darragh pounced on the door.

"Excuse me, my love," Marlowe whispered. Without thinking, I glanced at him. Marlowe had the same dark eyes as Bowyn. Fixed on me now, an intoxicating warmth flooded my body. It reminded me of the day I'd met Bowyn…but Marlowe's power was *euphoric*. Next to

Marlowe, Bowyn was a clumsy little boy. My sore feet and anxious tummy forgotten, happiness and pleasure swept through my chest.

I was weightless, and I wanted more.

Darragh sounded far away and unimportant while shouting for the unknown person to meet him later. Marlowe and I were someplace else, somewhere wonderful. I couldn't resist as Marlowe compelled me to kneel before him.

Why was he tied up? I loosened the knots.

"Nell?! What are you—" Darragh shouted just as Marlowe's warm, brawny arms wrapped around me. Cold metal pressed against my throat. Across the room, Darragh looked frantic.

So what?

No longer interested in Darragh, I could only think about Marlowe's arms. "You're going to help me get out of here, my love," Marlowe whispered. "You'd die for me, right?"

I nodded drunkenly. "Anything for you."

"Move away from the door!" Marlowe shouted. Darragh loomed, unmoving. "Move, or I kill her, and you can watch her bleed to death."

Kill me?

No, Marlowe wouldn't do that. He loved me, and I loved him.

Darragh actually *opened* the door for Marlowe. In a low voice, Darragh murmured, "If you so much as scratch her, I will bring you to the brink of death and keep you there, alive and suffering, for as long as I live."

"Leave me be, and neither of us will have to hurt anyone." Marlowe pushed me into the hall. He shoved through a side door labelled *EXIT* and ran. Like a puppy, I plodded after him. We rounded the side of a building and Marlowe spun me to face him. I recoiled, suddenly sober.

"Where's Darragh?" I wriggled, but Marlowe held fast.

"I'm sure he'll be right behind you." Marlowe peered around the corner. "I'm going to do you a great favour, my love."

"What are you gonna—"

That now-familiar warmth cascaded over me. Marlowe took off, and I trailed him. The lamplight lit our way behind the theatre, where the balconies overlooked the lake. Marlowe left the safety of the light and headed toward the dark water. Pausing at the edge, he pulled an intricate, gilded mirror from his jacket. Marlowe admired his reflection, then reached for me.

"Come, my love."

My heart fluttered as I took Marlowe's hand. He stepped into the water, and I stepped in after him. My heel stuck in the mud, and I cried out, unable to follow. Marlowe waded back, he lifted me and carried me like a bride into the lake.

I murmured, "You're so strong," and twirled his low pony between my fingers.

Marlowe lowered me into the water and said, "Take a deep breath."

I hate the water, yet I did nothing to resist as Marlowe eased my head under. In my mind, Marlowe's voice whispered, *"You're quite beautiful, love."* With one hand, he held the gilded mirror in front of me. *"Gaze upon your reflection."* A quick flash of silver glinted in Marlowe's eyes. Slowly, my infatuation ebbed.

I couldn't breathe.

Marlowe held me down as I struggled to escape. I hammered his arm, but he didn't budge. My lungs screamed for air—water splashed and swirled as I kicked Marlowe's legs. What could I do?! My oxygen starved brain didn't have any answers. My chest was fire, and my lungs were going to explode. Darkness seeped into my vision as Marlowe's voice shouted, *"Look!"* He forced the mirror closer.

I saw my panic reflected in the glass.

I was going to die.

PART TWO

Chapter Eighteen

a room with mirrors on every wall

I scrounged every scrap of energy left within me, prepared to fight for my life. The mirror in Marlowe's hand shimmered, and a glow limned the edges. It shone brighter and brighter, until I snapped my eyes shut.

The sensation of falling ripped through my body.

Wind pummeled me and I flailed, trying to grab hold of something. My hands found only open air. A speck appeared far away, a square of light framed against the darkness. It grew as I hurtled toward it. I tore through the frame.

"Hhh!" I slammed into a wooden floor. Scrambling onto my hands and knees, I coughed, and lake water spewed over the floor.

"Eleanor?" An open-mouthed Bowyn sat across the room. I tried not to slip in the puddle as I stood and smoothed my dress. Despite being fully submerged in water, I was, if slightly windswept, bone dry. Bowyn looked at the puddle below me like it was a rotting carcass I'd dragged in.

"Am I...am I on Hiraeth?" I sputtered.

Bowyn peeled his horrified gaze from the puddle. "Well, I should think that was terribly obvious, my love."

Dragging my hands down my face, I groaned, "Fuuuuuuuuck." I shook my head and glanced around the room. "Where are we?" If Bowyn weren't here, I might have thought I'd fallen into a small parlour of Buckingham Palace. Gilded mirrors plastered every wall, and from where I stood, I could see at least three mirrored tables. The thought of seeing myself from so many angles made me sick.

Bowyn sat amongst his many reflections on a silken, amber sofa. He swept his arm around the room. "This is my home." Bowyn squinted, his eyes set in a suspicious glare. "I thought you went back to Earth."

"I did!"

Bowyn pointed to an ornate, golden mirror on the ceiling. "How did you get in my mirror?"

I motioned to the mirror. "Is that *really* necessary?"

"Where's Darragh?"

"We found your father," I said, while untangling my hair. "He took me hostage, then tried to kill me—well, not really. I guess he was just sending me back here." I rubbed my wind ravaged eyes. I suppose Marlowe hoped Darragh would follow me instead of him.

One of the many gilded mirrors swung inward and Darragh rushed into the room.

Bowyn's mouth fell open. His shock was quickly replaced by a knowing, impish smile. Darragh scanned the room, and his shoulders relaxed when he saw me.

"You found my father?" Bowyn asked. "Did you…?" Darragh shook his head no. I couldn't tell whether Bowyn was disappointed, or relieved.

Darragh addressed me. "Sasha is going to think you're spending a suspicious amount of time out of town."

"Watney?" I asked, rubbing my stomach.

Darragh nodded. "Sasha knows." The look Darragh gave me next bore an uncomfortable resemblance to the look Sasha might give me after he warned me about a spill, which I acknowledged, but slipped on anyway.

"I'm sorry!" I pointed at Bowyn. "Marlowe didn't do the eye thing! How was I supposed to know he was going to compel me?"

"I should have known better. Marlowe's spent a lot of time on Earth. He's practiced, and he knows how to blend in." Darragh exhaled. "It could have been a lot worse." He smiled when he said, "I'm glad you're okay."

Bowyn's eyes moved hungrily between us, his impish grin growing by the second, then he frowned and turned to Darragh. "Did anyone see you come in?" Darragh glared and flicked his hand in Bowyn's direction. A gesture I'd learned meant something along the lines of, *piss off.*

"Nell," Darragh said. "Can you give us a moment?" It was an order, framed as a question. Bowyn pointed to a door behind me, and I reluctantly left. A curtain-draped, four-poster bed told me this was Bowyn's bedroom. Robes, shoes, and undergarments littered every surface. A pair of stockings dangled over a grand vanity, which had no fewer than seven mirrors attached. I leaned against the door, hoping to hear Darragh. A familiar, high-pitched whine teased my ears. Darragh and Bowyn's voices snapped into sharp focus, as if I were right beside them.

Darragh's voice said, "Take care of her. Do not leave her side. If she goes anywhere, you go with her."

"I'm not a babysitter, and she's not a child," Bowyn snapped. "She's more capable than you give her credit for. Take her with you."

"No," Darragh growled. "And if anything happens to me, get her back to Earth."

Arms slid around my waist, and I yelped. A sultry voice whispered, "Don't be frightened." Before I could react, the attacker ripped away from me. He flew across the room and crashed through a post supporting the canopy above Bowyn's bed. The other posts caved in, and the entire canopy collapsed. The door to the bedroom blew open and Darragh burst in. Bowyn followed quickly behind.

"Oh, that's nice!" Bowyn shouted, running to his bed.

"Did he hurt you?" Darragh asked.

Bowyn asked the unknown person the same question.

"I'm fine," I replied.

"There, there, my pet." Bowyn pulled the man from his bed. Wearing only short white braies, he was a very pretty man, slight and delicate next to Bowyn. My eyes lingered on his toned stomach.

Darragh thrust a finger at the mystery man. "Who's this?"

Bowyn stood tall and wrapped a protective arm around the man. "This is Lewy, he's my…" Bowyn looked guiltily at Lewy and then back to Darragh. "Chef?" Lewy crossed his arms, looking very unimpressed. "Lewy, why don't you head home?" Bowyn steered Lewy to the door. "I'll come visit you when I can."

Lewy looked Darragh up and down. He sneered, "How dare you come here."

Darragh reached for Lewy and Bowyn jumped between them. "Alright! Lewy is leaving now!" Bowyn guided Lewy to the front door. Before he opened it, he cupped Lewy's face and his eyes shone silver. "You didn't see them here."

Lewy nodded slowly.

"If you're sore tomorrow, it's because you and I had a little *too* much fun." Bowyn booped Lewy's nose. "Isn't that right?"

Lewy nodded again.

"Stupendous." Bowyn kissed Lewy, then opened the door and shoved him out. Bowyn brushed his hands against one another, as if he'd just cleaned up an arduous mess. "To be quite honest," Bowyn said, and raised his palms apologetically, "I forgot he was here." I stifled a laugh, but furious heat radiated from Darragh.

"I need to leave," Darragh snarled. "Bowyn will escort you to my cottage."

"Can't I go with you?"

"No," Darragh snapped back.

"But I—"

"No," Darragh cut me off. "You *will* go with Bowyn."

Even Bowyn cringed at Darragh's tone. Bowyn raised a finger and started to speak.

"I'll make certain no one witnesses my departure," Darragh said before Bowyn could get a word out. To me, he added, "Go with Bowyn. When I return, we'll work on a plan to get you back to Earth."

Only one word left my lips: "Fine."

Bowyn flinched. He muttered that he'd find me an outfit and disappeared into the bedroom. Darragh and I stood in silence. Bowyn returned with clothing, simple black boots, taupe trousers, and a too-big white shirt.

"I'm sorry I don't have a grand selection of clothing for you, but these are passably fashionable."

In the bedroom, I changed and braided my hair. When I returned, Darragh said, "I'll see you tomorrow."

"Bye."

Bowyn raised his eyebrows hopefully. When he saw that we were altogether finished our lacklustre goodbye, he pointed to the door. "You head downstairs, and I'll be right after you, my love."

On the other side of the door, several sets of steep, covered stairs led down to the street. I reached the landing below Bowyn's just as the door opened for that level. Wearing a silky, purple robe, Lewy leaned on the frame and smiled. Smoke and gentle, satisfied moans wafted from behind him. Tracing a finger along his chest, Lewy asked, "How are you?"

As if summoned, Bowyn's door burst open. He barreled down the stairs, shouting, "Oh no, no, no!" Bowyn grabbed my arm and eased me away from Lewy. "She's with me."

Lewy pursed his lips and pouted. "Perhaps I could see you both?"

"As much as I believe my dear Eleanor is in *desperate* need of your services, I'm afraid we must decline." Bowyn placed another firm kiss on Lewy's lips. "I'll see you later, pet." Lewy responded with a drunken, sultry smirk and went back inside.

"Are you sure we don't have time?" I asked innocently.

Bowyn whirled on me.

A large thud echoed from the floor above, as if someone was listening to us, and dropped a heavy object in surprise. Bowyn's eyes flitted up, and back to me. His lips spread into a fiendish grin. "You're full of surprises." He winked and raised his voice. "When I return, I may not be alone. Miss Eleanor has informed me she'd much love an evening in your company." Bowyn took my arm. "Come quickly, let us flee before I combust!"

I hurried after Bowyn. "You live above a brothel?"

Bowyn put a hand to his chest. "You know Lewy really *is* a marvelous cook, among other things." As we headed down the remaining stairs, Bowyn continued. "You must forgive my sweet Darragh's boorish behavior. He means well but, we can't all be as charming as yours truly." Bowyn's eyebrows performed a seductive wiggle, and silver flashed across his pupils.

We exited onto a cobbled street lined by tidy thatched buildings. The cream-coloured walls crisscrossed with dark wooden beams reminded me of medieval Europe. Though these buildings were much taller; I craned my neck to see the tops. Some of them had to be seven or eight stories high. They teetered at angles that left me cautiously glancing up.

THE FOREST WHERE THE PHOENIX SLEEPS

A bakery sat next to Bowyn's building. A large, stone oven opened onto the street and the aroma of fresh baking filled the air. It left me craving thick butter slathered on warm bread. Bowyn made like a little teapot and motioned for me to take his arm, which I did. People bustled around us, they parted for Bowyn as if he were a rock in a stream. It seemed strange. I'd only seen the wild, uninhabited landscapes of Hiraeth. I hadn't imagined bustling towns. The tidiness of it all surprised me as well. The towns in the Middle Ages were foul-smelling, refuse-littered cesspools, weren't they? I mean, people emptied their chamber pots into the street.

I eyed the windows in the tall buildings and scooched closer to Bowyn.

We'd made it only a few feet before a woman stopped Bowyn. A ravishing strawberry blonde, she grazed Bowyn's free arm. Standing on her toes, the woman whispered in Bowyn's ear. "Oh, my!" Bowyn laughed. "Well, I'm not available this evening, but you'll be the first to know when I'm back in town." The woman trailed her fingers along Bowyn's arm and strolled away. Bowyn shook his head, reorienting himself. "Anyway, pardon the interruption, my love." Bowyn pointed to the cobbled street. "You are currently walking down the main street of Wilbur. It is the last town before Shadow Peak, the Queen's mountain. That's why you see so many inns littered about. I swear there's a new one popping up every week. The Ivy, that's the establishment I live above, is the oldest inn in town. I've lived there for quite some time now, though I have my run-ins with the brothel owner on the sixth story, Mal. Says I distract the boys…" I zoned out, hearing Bowyn, but not hearing Bowyn. We passed a seamstress, where invisible hands stitched a gown in the window. I could have watched it for hours, but Bowyn, who thought it was dreadfully dull, dragged me away. He pointed to an apothecary. "That's where I bring Darragh's flowery bits and bobs."

Three more 'patients' halted Bowyn as we walked. I didn't mind so much; it gave me time to examine all the delightful shops. A glazier, a sweet shop, a potter—Bowyn stopped someone obscured by a cloak. "Shouldn't you be getting ready?" he asked.

The mystery person pulled the cloak away, revealing herself to be a young girl. She tucked perfect white curls behind her ear. "Shouldn't you?" Looking Bowyn up and down, she said, "Surely you're not coming dressed like *that*."

Bowyn's mouth dropped open and he blinked twice.

"Where's Darragh?" the girl asked.

Bowyn examined his fingernails. "Don't know." He stuck his nose up. "If you'll excuse us, apparently I have some getting ready to do." The girl shot Bowyn an ugly glare and stormed away.

"Who was she?" I watched her go.

"The Queen's daughter, Elwyn."

"Oh! Should I have…bowed?"

"No," Bowyn snorted. "Certainly not to her." He pursed his lips and said, "She looked awfully tired, didn't she? It certainly doesn't become her."

I never thought I'd see Bowyn jealous.

"You don't like her?" I asked.

Bowyn looked around to make sure no one could hear us. "I don't dislike her. I'm just not necessarily *fond* of her. I feel about her, how someone might feel about their best friend's baby sister. Growing up, she was always trying to tag along and spoil my and Darragh's fun."

"Why'd she ask about Darragh?"

Bowyn's eyes narrowed mischievously. He elbowed me and asked, "Why do you care?"

"I don't," I replied quickly. I side-eyed Bowyn. "Are they going somewhere tonight?"

"Yes. There's a ball at the mountain."

"Oh." A hideous pang of envy swept through me.

Why didn't Darragh want me to go?

"Elwyn's very pretty," I said.

"*Very* pretty," Bowyn remarked.

The last shop we passed was filled with shiny spyglasses. Bowyn sneered and said, "Astronomer." He quickened his pace as we walked by. The remaining buildings gave way to a charred, burnt section of town.

No one walked here.

"Was there a fire?" I wiped a spot of ash from my boot.

"The Queen lights it periodically."

"Why?"

"A reminder."

"A reminder of what?"

Bowyn's eyes bugged like he'd spoken words he shouldn't have. His face turned as red as his robe while he flipped through excuses in his head.

"Just tell me," I said dryly.

Bowyn exhaled and spoke quickly. "Darragh burned it down."

"What?!"

Ignoring me, Bowyn pointed ahead. "Look, we're almost out of town." His brute strength carried me forward, but I managed to yank my arm away.

"Bowyn! What happened?"

"It's a long story," Bowyn whined.

"We've got a long walk."

Bowyn frowned. He muttered, "Follow me," and headed down a charred side street. We hadn't gone far when Bowyn halted and pointed to a rough set of squares rising only a few inches from the ground.

"Darragh used to live here."

"Really?"

"One night when Darragh was young, while sleeping comfortably, he had a terrible nightmare. The terror consumed him, and he burned while he slept. The fire devoured his home"—Bowyn paused, deciding how truthful he needed to be—"and his parents."

"Oh, no."

Bowyn gave a half-hearted nod. "Someone breached the flames and calmed Darragh, but not before the fire destroyed half the village."

My heart ached as I examined the footprint of the old house, the only remains of Darragh's home.

"The Queen's guardians came for him the next morning. He was six." Bowyn shivered. "The energy here is repugnant; let us talk on our journey." We left the ruins and Bowyn said, "It was obvious Darragh had inherited his mother's gift from the sun, and he didn't really have a choice but to serve the Queen."

"Gift from the sun?"

"We all draw our energy from somewhere. The breeze, running water, the moon and stars." Bowyn put a hand to his chest, indicating himself. "Other people." He continued, "Darragh draws his strength and energy from the sun. Just like his mother, he was born with the ability to summon and control fire. Though it was clear from the start he was considerably more powerful. Being able to control fire; it's a terrifying and destructive power. Darragh hates it, always has. He tried to suppress it, hide it away. After the town fire, well, there was no hiding it anymore, and no one left to help him. The Queen plucked Darragh from his home and perfected those very talents he despised, training him against his will."

"So, the Queen burns down half the town to remind the people?"

"Darragh works for her. The Queen wants them to remember. She wants them to be afraid."

"That's all so sad," I mumbled. "That's why he lives out there all alone?"

"Darragh is not welcome in town." Bowyn sighed. "That's why *I* must trek all the way out to meet him. The townspeople fear him, and deep down, Darragh knows they're right to be afraid. Look what happened the last time."

In my heart, I felt a sudden leap of sympathy for Darragh—for the *outsider*. "He was a child. Surely people can understand that?"

Bowyn shrugged. "If you go too near a fire and burn yourself, you'll think twice before you go near it again."

"I guess." I kicked a stone along the cobble path. "But he also heals people, right?"

"Yes!" Bowyn squeezed my arm. "You're absolutely right. On one hand, Darragh is fire and death, but on the other, he is light and life. The sun nurtures, it sustains, it gives life. Without light, things cannot grow. And Darragh's father, though rather basic, had quite the penchant for healing. Despite the Queen's attempt to crush that part of Darragh, he's continued to practice." Bowyn frowned. "Unfortunately, now that he's grown, that's the gift he has to hide."

A stark contrast to Darragh, there wasn't a moment of silence with Bowyn. "Do you know what they call this place?" Bowyn gestured toward the wood that led to Darragh's cottage.

"No, what?"

"The forest where the phoenix sleeps. Few people will tread here."

I recalled the vision I'd seen when I'd entered the first time. "Did the villagers set that warning up?"

"No." Bowyn chuckled. "My dear Darragh did."

"Back home, we tell stories about witches who live in forests like this."

"What's a witch?"

"Someone with magic, someone powerful."

"Darragh's a sweet witch," Bowyn replied. "What happens to witches back home?"

I hesitated. "We burn them."

We drew near Darragh's cottage, and Bowyn chattered on about the ball. "We used to celebrate out by the Aeonian wood, how enchanting it was! A sound master used to bring *real* birds to sing. And the food." Bowyn put a hand to his chest. "Oh, Nell, the food is exquisite. It's a cheat day for sure. And the dancing!" Bowyn stretched his arms out and spun with an invisible suitor. "We said goodbye to the sunshine and celebrated by the fire, and there were enormous displays of light in the sky. And the gowns! The ladies dress so splendidly, I was always terribly envious." I half-listened to Bowyn, reluctant to learn about a ball I wasn't allowed to attend. To be honest, I looked forward to a warm drink, a snack, and a soak in that big copper tub.

"Of course, you'll see all this tonight."

"Wait—what?" I replayed Bowyn's last sentence. I pointed in front of us. "I'm going back to the cottage."

"Of course." Bowyn laughed. "You have to get ready."

"What do you mean, get ready?" I stared at him. "I'm not going."

"Not—not going?!" Bowyn's left hand clutched his chest, while the other reached for me. "But there will be dancing, and food, and drinks, and such beautiful people!"

"There's food at the cottage." I dodged Bowyn. "And dancing? With people? Bowyn, you don't know me at all."

"You owe it to yourself to go!"

"You only want me to go so Darragh doesn't light you like a candle when he finds out you ditched me to go to some party."

"S—some party," Bowyn stuttered. He stamped his foot and cried.

"The light ball isn't just some party!"

Through the tree trunks, the cottage appeared in the distance. "Where are the mean nettles?" I asked. An utterly panicked Bowyn stopped long enough to examine the ground. He lifted his left leg over an unassuming patch of underbrush, but kept his right leg planted. Straddling the vines, he reached for me. I obliged, and he lifted me and placed me on the other side.

Did this make me feel like a tiny baby? Yes.

Did you get stung by the vines on your way in? No. Don't judge me.

I beelined for the cottage. Bowyn called out, "You're not the only one trying to bed him, you know."

My jaw dropped, and I whirled on Bowyn. "Excuse me?"

Bowyn picked dirt from beneath his nail, a despicable, smug smile on his face. He pursed his lips. "I'm sure Elwyn and Darragh will have a lovely evening together."

Darragh's words echoed in my head. "*Never listen to Bowyn.*"

Just go back to the cottage, I told myself. *Have a nice, relaxing night. Darragh will be back soon enough, and I can focus on getting home.*

My thoughts wandered to Elwyn, and the pang of jealousy when she'd said Darragh's name.

"What would I even wear?"

Chapter Nineteen

you shall go to the ball, whether you like it or not

"Nothing," Bowyn replied.

I stood in Darragh's kitchen. Unsure how to respond, I blinked in disbelief. Bowyn threw his head back and let out a rumbling laugh. Discomfort settled in my stomach as I whispered, "I'll be naked?"

"Are you petrified?" Bowyn teased. I fell silent and leaned on the counter for support. "Oh, don't torture yourself," Bowyn said. "You won't be wearing anything, but you won't be entirely naked either."

Nope. Don't like that.

"So, what will I wear?"

"What do you know of the Queen?"

"Uh, Briar? Was that her nickname? She fell in love with the last queen's son. She had to steal some ring to prove her power or...something?"

"Well, you've robbed the tale of any magic but, yes. Once Briar bested Jorgen and escaped the burrow with his ring, she marched straight to Queen Aithen, who was hosting a wedding for her son Erebus. As you can imagine, Briar didn't posses any fine clothes, or lavish jewelry. Nonetheless, she strode into the court, wearing nothing but her filthy garments. She presented herself to Queen Aithen, and all those gathered in their fancy clothes. Undisturbed by the sneers, Briar smiled before the audience. Darkness filled the great hall, and wild shrieks frightened the contempt from those who judged Briar so quickly. As the darkness ebbed, it revealed a towering beast of shadows. Like a coursing waterfall, the shadows fell away. Briar stood before all, wearing a gown of moonlight." Bowyn stared fondly into the middle distance. "They say she plucked the stars from above and wove them into an ebony gown that shimmered brighter than any celestial body." Bowyn released a lengthy, longing sigh. "We celebrate the light ball every year to commemorate that day."

"I mean, this still sounds like just a party."

Bowyn's eyes bulged and he grabbed my arm. He reminded me of a parent scolding a child as he growled, "It's more than *just* a party." Releasing me, Bowyn continued. "It's a demonstration of power and control. It takes incredible concentration to project magic for an entire evening."

"So, it's like a hologram?"

"What's that?"

"It's a projection of an image. You can see it, but it doesn't exist. If you reached out to touch it, your hand would move through it."

"That's *precisely* what this is," Bowyn replied. "You will create and wear your gown of light. The task requires constant focus, and given that it's a party, there will be many distractions." Bowyn flourished his hand, conjuring a floor-length mirror. He pulled me before it. I cringed, and focused on Bowyn's reflection behind me, rather than my own. "Now, are you ready to forge your dress?"

"What?!" I balked and tried to back away. "I don't know how I can possibly do that. Any magic I've done has just…happened. I have no control over it whatsoever."

"I'll help you." Bowyn placed me squarely before the mirror and squeezed my shoulders. "You'll be the most beautiful person there." He admired himself. "Except for me, of course."

I shook my head but said, "Okay."

"Marvelous." Bowyn clapped. "Now, you must think of light as fabric." He closed his eyes and trailed his hands through the air, painting the scene. "Picture a sunbeam falling through your window. Focus on the motes dancing in the light, make them sparkles in your train." Bowyn trailed his hands over his body. "Think about every fold of fabric, every jewel, every movement." Opening his eyes, Bowyn smiled. "Use your imagination—anything you can dream of." Bowyn covered his eyes so I might undress. "Go on, give it a try."

After a silent pep talk, I stripped. I closed my eyes and conjured images of the things that made me happy, of the things I loved. For some reason, my mind kept trailing back to Darragh. Dress. Darragh. Dress. Darragh. I thought of how much he'd loved *Ever After,* the comfort movie I held so close to my heart.

I had an idea.

I envisioned a white gown. My shoulders bare, the delicate fabric cut low across my chest. Gems twinkled down the long sleeves that ended in neat points over my hands. White and grey layers of sheer light tucked in beneath my breast, and then flowed into a lengthy, trailing skirt. I left my feet bare. Where they touched the ground, white flames crackled around my slender ankles.

Bowyn squeezed my hand.

I opened my eyes, and it was there. I dragged my fingers along my chest. Despite seeing intricate jewels and fabric, I touched skin. Bowyn wore a proud smile. "Resplendent," he murmured. "In a million years, I couldn't have created a gown so breathtaking." He took my braid in his hands. "Do you trust me?"

"No."

Bowyn looked up, hurt. His face softened when he noticed my smile. He gave my braid a playful tug and removed the elastic. Bowyn's large, but dainty fingers brushed my hair. With each stroke, the strands grew darker and longer, until my hair fell in vibrant, effortless curls over my breasts.

"Can you all do that?" I played with a curl.

"Those of us with vision."

While admiring myself in the mirror, I caught sight of Bowyn's proud gaze, and realized I hadn't spoken in quite some time. "What if I lose my concentration and slip up?"

"I suggest you watch how much you drink and if something happens, well, everyone will know this isn't your natural hair colour, won't they?" Bowyn gave me a cheeky smile and withdrew a small glass bottle from his robes. He squished a pump attached to the lip and spritzed me with perfume. I coughed and crinkled my nose. It smelled just like Bowyn, which was fine, though it wasn't my taste. Certainly not something I'd wear if given the choice.

"What are you going to wear?" I asked.

"Ah yes!" Bowyn raised his hands. "That is the real question, isn't it? Stand back, my darling." Bowyn twirled, and the skirts of his robe raised around him. When he stopped spinning, he wore a slightly more intricate version of the red robes he'd worn before. Perhaps a few more tassels of gold here and there. He grinned and clutched his hands together, reminding me of a child who'd just donned a tiara and a princess dress. His outfit was much less grand than I'd anticipated. Beside me, Bowyn actually looked a bit dull.

Still quite handsome though.

"Can I call you Bo?"

Bowyn stroked his beard, considering the request.

"In some places back home, beau means beautiful." I paused, "Or belle, if you prefer the feminine, I suppose."

"Well! Far be it from me to deny you the opportunity!" Bowyn beamed. "Oh! I have one more thing for you." Bowyn shuffled around in a bag he'd thrown on the counter. He withdrew a glittering object and handed it to me. I traced my fingers along the sparkling silver pin. Shaped like a fox, its cunning eyes were inlaid with diamonds. The foxes tail tapered into a sharp, deadly point.

"What's this?" I touched the point. "Ah!" Blood blossomed on my fingertip.

Bowyn held my finger to stop the bleeding and murmured, "A last resort."

"Uh, thanks." I looked at myself in the mirror, covered, yet naked. "Where uh, where do I keep it?"

Bowyn looked down and winked.

"Bowyn!"

Bowyn laughed. He took the pin, drew my hair back, and tucked it amongst the curls. The sly, silver fox sparkled in the light. The pin was gorgeous…though I couldn't help but wonder what I might need it for.

In the mirror, my smile faded.

Elwyn

I'd hardly left my room since my father's death. Today, that would not be permitted. I'd be attending the Queen's light ball, willing or not. Staring at the mirror, I tried to conjure anything to wear. All I could muster was a pathetic, ill-fitted, black gown. It hung from my bones, unflattering and saclike. The colours weren't crisp, the black nearly faded to grey. The Queen would be disgusted.

Good.

An annoying, rhythmic knock sounded on my door. Leshy, napping on my pillow, jerked awake. He rolled off the bed and scurried beneath. "Yes?" I called. Bright colours reflected in the mirror, and I whirled on the Truth. "What do you want?"

The Truth smiled, a sweet, sickening thing. "I come bearing gifts." She laid a brown box on the bed. "Nice dress." She pumped her eyebrows once and said, "See you tonight," before closing the door behind her. The gift reminded me of my father. An ache cleaved my chest, I fought a sob and crumpled onto my bed.

I examined the box, careful not to touch it. The familiarity to my father bled away. Fear seeped from the brown paper like blood through a bandage. Leshy crawled back up, giving the box a wide berth. Taking wary steps, he jabbed the box with a paw.

The box moved.

Leshy squealed and scurried beneath the bed. I picked up the box. It moved again, this time accompanied by a dull *thump thump*. I unwrapped the brown paper. Another *thump thump* sounded as I lifted the lid. Smears of red stained the inside.

Thump thump.

The heart within beat again.

"Guh!" I dropped the box. It tumbled to the floor and the heart spilled out.

Thump thump.

Blood spurted from a valve. It sprayed across the floor and pierced the light of my dress. Warm droplets splashed my ankles.

Thump thump.

The valve pumped once more. This time, an object oozed out. With shaky hands, I picked it up and smeared blood away. It was an intricate bouquet, carved in white bone. A sharp, golden pin backed it.

A broach?

The broach tingled with energy. Before I could resist, the memory of its creation ensnared me.

Ophyr knelt over a man. I recognized him, though I didn't know his name. He'd been in the great hall while the Queen interviewed suitors. Now, the man writhed, and foam spilled from the corners of his mouth.

Just like Audra.

Unlike Audra, Ophyr didn't wait for the poison to finish the job. He plunged a blade deep into the suitor's chest, dragging it down to his navel. The man tried to scream, but only choked, spewing frothy saliva into the air. Bones cracked as Ophyr dug in the man's chest cavity.

"Here we are, almost done." Ophyr made a few quick slices with his blade. Blood dripped from his face as he pulled the heart out. He stood and inspected it. "Perfection." Talking to no one in particular, Ophyr said, "Oh, I almost forgot." He knelt over the corpse and braced it with his foot. He snapped away a piece of the sternum and examined it. "This will do nicely."

The memory fell away.

I ran to the window and hurled the broach out. It arced through the sky and fell out of sight.

I needed to leave.

I needed to leave right now.

I tugged a satchel from under my bed; Leshy came with it. "Get in," I ordered. Leshy scrambled in and moved aside as I shoved in clothes and a jewelry box. After hiding the satchel beneath the layers of light that comprised my dress, I snuck out. Heading toward the kitchens, I walked quickly. I'd grab food and flee. I rounded a corner.

Ophyr strode down the hall. We locked eyes and he waved. I retraced my steps and ducked into the main hall. I'd wanted to avoid it, sticking to the side paths where fewer people would see me.

"Elle!" Ophyr shouted. Footsteps echoed against the rock as he chased me.

I grabbed my satchel and hissed, "Hide!" Leshy leapt out and bounded to a crack in the wall. I tossed the satchel, and he dragged it in after him. Leshy disappeared just as Ophyr rounded the corner.

Ophyr scanned the area. "Who were you talking to?" I didn't respond. Ophyr looked me up and down. "Did you receive my gift?"

"Yes."

"You're not wearing it." Ophyr frowned. "After I put so much thought into romantic presentation." He put a hand to his chest, and another to his forehead. In a dreadfully mocking tone, he said, "My heart, it only beats for you."

I felt sick.

"They don't call me a nec*romancer* for nothing." Ophyr nudged me with an elbow. I stepped away—Ophyr grabbed my arm, gripping it so tight, my hand numbed.

"Release me!" I pulled, but Ophyr held fast.

"Such spirit. I like that."

A familiar, raspy voice uttered, "What are you doing?" Both Ophyr and I tensed. Darragh paused at the entrance to the main hall. He glanced at Ophyr's hand, still clasping my arm. Darragh grabbed Ophyr's forearm and wrenched it off me. Ophyr tried to pull away, but Darragh's arm was granite. He held tight. Looming over Ophyr, Darragh said, "If I catch your hand on her again, it'll be the last thing you touch."

"So strong," Ophyr sneered. "I could really put that strength to good use."

"You'll have to kill me first."

Darragh let go. A bubbling, blistered handprint remained on Ophyr's skin. As Darragh turned to leave, Ophyr shuffled in his pocket. Torchlight glinted on metal—

"Look out!" I screamed.

Darragh didn't flinch.

Ophyr froze, the knife he held still suspended above Darragh's neck. The tip of Ophyr's blade glowed red, and heat waves distorted the air above. Veins corded in Ophyr's throat as he struggled to move.

Darragh held him firm.

The blade began to melt, and liquid metal *drip-dripped* onto the ground. Ophyr's eyes widened as thick, silvery metal oozed down the hilt. The metal hit Ophyr's skin, where it sizzled like a hot skillet. A scream muffled in Ophyr's throat, unable to escape his paralyzed lips.

"It'll go numb any moment. Don't worry." Darragh crossed his arms and leaned on a stone pillar. He watched Ophyr, unbothered by the throaty screams that filled the hall. Ophyr's hand was completely coated in boiling metal now. It reached his wrist and—

Darragh released him. Ophyr collapsed, cradling his arm. I expected him to threaten Darragh, scare him, or promise something terrible.

Ophyr said nothing.

"Best see if the healer can save that hand," Darragh said.

Ophyr kept his gaze trained on the floor. He trembled as he climbed to his feet and slunk away. He didn't turn his back on Darragh until he reached the end of the hall.

"Tell me if he comes near you again." Darragh stalked in the opposite direction.

"She killed my father."

Darragh hesitated. "I'm sorry, Elwyn."

Before I could say anything else, the Queen and the Truth entered

218

the main hall. Darragh ducked behind a pillar, making himself as small as possible. The Queen caught sight of me and snapped, "Is that what you're wearing?" I glanced at the dark, drab gown. When I looked up, Darragh was gone.

"Come now. Erabus wouldn't want you mourning forever." The Queen twirled her fingers and white light crept from the floor. Goosebumps prickled my flesh as it travelled up my legs and smothered me. The light fell away, and a lacy gown of creams and lilacs remained. The Queen flourished her hand and a gleaming train fell down my back. It shone like a white river down the hall. The Queen pointed at the door. "Now, we'll go to the great hall."

"I-I'll be right th-there," I stammered.

"No." The Queen beckoned me. "Now." Invisible hooks tore my skin, forcing me to follow. "And one more thing." My heart fluttered as the Queen extended her hand to me. "I'd like you to wear this." She unfurled her skeletal fingers.

Ophyr's broach sat in her palm.

My fingers trembled, but I took the broach. I glanced at my bare skin, covered only by folds of light.

"Put it on," the Queen hissed.

Nell

"When does this thing start?" I peered at the sun setting over Darragh's cottage. "Won't it take us forever to walk there?"

"Walk?!" Bowyn balked. "Looking like this?" He swept a hand down his body. "No. No, that won't do, my love. I've asked a client to meet us and take us to Shadow Peak. We'll walk a little way from

Darragh's cottage and meet them outside of town."

"How will they get us there?"

"They're a cavort."

"A what?"

"They jump from one spot to another." Bowyn took my arm as we walked. "We've got some time to kill. Would you like some gossip about Darragh?"

"Always."

"Hmmm," Bowyn pondered. "Where to start?"

"What about Darragh's parents? He never mentions them."

"He'll never forgive himself for what happened. To acknowledge his parents is to acknowledge what he did. It's easier for him not to discuss them at all. It's a shame, really." Bowyn placed a hand on his heart. "They've quite the passionate tale, Lin and Ani."

"Can you tell me?"

Bowyn frowned. "It's not the shortest of stories."

"Oh."

"Well, perhaps I can summarize it for you," Bowyn suggested. I gave him a sideways smile. Bowyn squeezed my arm and returned the smile. "Darragh's mother, Linovahle Mitalrrythin, was a guardian to the Queen. Lin wasn't particularly powerful, nor was she high-ranking, but when the Queen began her"—Bowyn paused, as if the next word tasted foul— "gathering missions, Lin was amongst those chosen for the task."

"Is that how you came here?" I interrupted.

Bowyn's mouth fell in surprise. "Yes." Bowyn's tone was laced with an uncharacteristic bitterness. "I was scooped from my family and brought here to be *civilized*."

"I'm sorry," I said. "Is Bowyn your real name?"

"It's the name I was given when I arrived."

"What name did your parents give you?"

Bowyn hesitated. He inhaled deeply and whispered, "Sira."

"That's beautiful."

Bowyn blinked a few times and tugged my arm. "I'm sorry, my love, where was I?"

"Gathering mission," I murmured.

"Ah, yes! During a gathering mission, Lin and her company came upon a small village. They kidnapped many men. Santiana, Darragh's father, was among those men. On the journey home, Lin was charged with guarding the prisoners. Now, Santiana—Ani—wasn't powerful, and I imagine he was taken for his…visual assets." Bowyn wiggled his eyebrows suggestively. "Many of the crew took a fancy to Ani. While Lin was doing her rounds, she caught a crewmate forcing themselves on Ani. Lin, renowned for her *wicked* temper, tore the woman away and tossed her overboard. The captain was outraged, she had Lin tied to the mast for three days without food or water. When Lin came down, the captain had her thrown in the brig with the men. Ani, forever grateful for what Lin did, refused to let her die. With what little power he had, Ani nursed Lin back to health." Bowyn sighed. "I suppose they were smitten with each other after that."

"That's a very sweet story."

"Yes, well, unfortunately it doesn't end there. When the ship landed, Ani was sold."

"What?!"

"The captain was quite jealous of the budding relationship. She made sure Santiana was sold, discreetly. Lin was heartbroken, and she abandoned the Queen. An *exquisitely* risky thing to do." Bowyn raised his brows for emphasis. "Lin spent ten years looking for Ani—"

"Ten?!"

Bowyn nodded solemnly. "One day, while travelling, Lin caught sight of her old captain. Eager for revenge, Lin concealed herself with magic and followed the captain…straight to a brothel. Although it was Linovahle, not the captain, who was about to get a nasty surprise."

"Santiana," I murmured.

"Yes. When Ani undressed, Lin could conceal herself no longer. She exploded in a rage of fire, incinerating the captain. One death was not enough to satiate Lin's fury. She blew through the brothel and burned every client. Her fire was only extinguished when she caught sight of Santiana's horrified face, begging her to stop."

I remembered my argument with Darragh in the forest.

I'd called him a monster.

"Lin stole Ani away. He wept, believing Lin dead, a lie fed to him by the captain. The night Lin and Ani were reunited was filled with such passion—if Darragh was conceived then, it's no wonder he's so powerful," Bowyn said, matter-of-factly. "When Lin and Ani returned, Lin was arrested. News of the brothel slaughtering travelled quickly, and the people demanded justice. Lin was brought before the Queen to be tried, but a remarkable thing happened."

"What?"

"The Queen spared her."

"Why?"

"The Queen sensed the life Lin carried inside her. She claimed Lin's actions were justified, and she would not be tried, but the Queen bade her a warning: 'A life for a life. I will claim my debt one day.'"

Bowyn straightened and scanned the trees.

"You should take greater care out here in the wild," a voice called from behind. Bowyn's shoulders sagged, and he exhaled. His smile didn't meet his eyes as we turned to greet whoever had called out. Spreading his arms wide, Bowyn cried, "Sateen, my love!"

A few steps behind us, a person stood on the path. They were slender, with severe, high cheekbones. The sides of their hair were shaved short, and the top cut at an angle so that one side was slightly elevated. Black whorls and markings covered their arms and neck.

They were tall.

Very tall.

They could easily look Bowyn in the eye.

Speaking in a quiet, sensual voice, they said, "A handsome boy like you knows better than to be out here so unarmed." They looked Bowyn up and down. "And dressed like that?" They made a *tsk* noise and shook their head.

An incredible thing happened then; Bowyn blushed. He gripped my arm tighter. "I've got a powerful young woman here to protect me." Sateen's eyes found me. They were piercing, a dreamy pale blue. It was my turn to blush. Bowyn said, "Sateen, this is Nell. Nell, this is Sateen. They'll be taking us to the mountain."

Sateen gave the tiniest of nods. "Would you give us a moment, my love?" Bowyn released me and strolled over to Sateen. I waited while they exchanged small talk. There was a frightening stillness about Sateen. They did not fidget; the only movement was the occasional shift of their eyes between Bowyn and me. I kept an anxious eye on Sateen, I couldn't shake the uncomfortable sensation that they crept closer every time I blinked.

I didn't want to be alone with them.

Bowyn returned. "Sateen will take you first, and then they'll come back for me." I tried to hide my dismay. Sateen watched me closely.

"Sounds good," I lied.

Sateen grinned. The smile looked so big on their slim face. They approached me with slow, deliberate steps. "May I?" I gulped and nodded. Sateen crouched so they could slip an arm around my waist. Sateen's thinness was misleading. A strong, sinewy arm curled around me. "I suggest you close your eyes; the experience can be rather…

disorienting." The thought of willingly blinding myself around Sateen made me queasy. Though I didn't want to, I shut my eyes.

Whooshing wind pummelled us. My stomach shot up inside me, like a rollercoaster cresting that first drop. "You smell like somewhere far away," Sateen whispered. Before the panic took hold, our feet smashed into the ground, hard. My knees buckled and I tumbled forward. I picked myself up, and—Sateen's face was right in front of mine.

"Agh!" I leapt away. "Can you *not* do that?"

Sateen cocked their head. "Do what?"

I stooped to brush a leaf from my knee. "Get closer when I'm not looking at you." I stood back up. Sateen was an inch from my face.

"Like this?" Sateen leaned down to meet my eyes.

"Hhh!" I stumbled back.

Sateen straightened and chuckled. They faded into thin air, reappearing with Bowyn seconds later.

"Are you coming to the ball?" Bowyn asked.

Sateen's lip curled. "No."

"Why not?" Bowyn stamped his foot. "It'll be fun."

"I have no use for spoiled children," Sateen replied. "Remember that." Before leaving, Sateen met my eyes and smiled. My stomach clenched. Whether the cause was excitement or fear, I wasn't so sure.

Sateen vanished.

Stroking his beard, Bowyn said, "I think they eat people."

"They what now?"

Bowyn made a face of mild inconvenience. "Well, I mean, you met them." He gestured vaguely at the air Sateen had occupied.

I stared at Bowyn, open-mouthed. "What makes you think they eat people? And if they do, why are we traipsing around with them?"

"Well, as far as I can tell, Sateen likes me." Bowyn walked toward the mountain. "And they're *very* useful."

"What makes you think they eat people?" I repeated.

"Oh, just, things that come up in therapy. People that go missing. I hope they have mushroom bread tonight. You're going to love it."

"Aren't you worried they'll eat you?"

"Mind your manners and you'll get along fine."

Chapter Twenty

just breathe

Standing in a doorway that was taller than my entire building back home, I squinted into the great hall. I gave Bowyn a wary glance. This couldn't possibly be the same ball he'd so joyously described. Sparse candles provided little light; they barely illuminated the carved stone pillars running the length of the great hall. All around, ladies dressed in glittering ebony gowns slunk around tables laden with food that looked as inedible as it smelled. The only noise came from the whispers of those brave enough to disturb the silence.

This room felt sick.

As if everything inside died long ago, and rot and decay had taken hold.

This was a ball for corpses.

Bowyn jutted his chin to the far end of the hall. "The Queen." The only individual seated, the Queen's presence imposed on the room like a loaded gun. Her dress wasn't made of light at all, but the absence of it. Darkness clung to her sickly, gaunt body, and charcoal make-up smeared her eyes.

"How old is she?" I whispered.

"Fifty-six."

"No!" My jaw dropped. "Fifty-six!?" I couldn't believe it. If Bowyn told me she was one-hundred-and-fifty-six, I still might not have believed him. From back here, I wasn't even sure she was alive. Behind the Queen, stood a stunning ghost of a girl. Elwyn, the one we'd met in town. White light mimicked delicate folds of lace against her skin. She shone like a pearl in the dark hall. Her shoulders rose and fell as she sighed, staring longingly into the crowd of people. A sweet-looking, baby-faced man stood beside her, uncomfortably close.

"The woman to the Queen's right. That's the Truth. The Queen's spy." Looking like the offspring of a witch and a clown, the Truth wore garish colours and a gigantic pointy hat. "Stay away from her at all costs." Bowyn peered around. "I wonder where the Cage is. Terrifying creature, the Cage. I suppose it's hidden out of sight, trying not to make everyone too uneasy."

I imagined a ghastly monster named the Cage would be right at home here.

My eyes adjusted to the dark, then my breath caught. Darragh leaned against the wall, several steps behind the Queen's throne. He hadn't dressed for the occasion. His clothes were regular, black fabric. He blended into the shadows, keen to remain hidden in the background. Arms crossed, Darragh stared at the ground.

Bowyn stepped into the great hall, but I resisted. "Bowyn, I don't know about this."

Dragging me after him, Bowyn whispered, "Have courage, my love." I glowed like a beacon in the dark, and one by one, people faced us. Whispers rose as we joined the crowd.

"Who is she?"

"Look at her dress."

"He's a serpent, that one."

"I've never seen her before."

Darragh looked up, curious about the commotion. We made eye contact and my heart stopped.

Just breathe.

Darragh's lips parted, and his arms fell to his sides. His eyes travelled from my face to my feet, and back. I wondered if he was reminding himself to breathe too.

The briefest of smiles crossed my lips.

Darragh's eyes darted to the Queen. They widened and shot back to me before settling on Bowyn. There were no words exchanged between the two, but I imagine the silent conversation went something like:

Your death will be slow.

I look forward to it, darling. Isn't she beautiful?

"Let us promenade, Belle." Bowyn paraded me around, ever the proud mother. Surrounded by all the ladies in raven and ebony gowns, Bowyn and I were candles in a sea of darkness.

"I don't think I understood the assignment," I whispered to Bowyn.

"You understood it better than anyone else—"

"What are you doing here?" Darragh snapped. He'd crept through the shadows and appeared unnoticed.

Bowyn scrunched his face, as if the answer were terribly obvious. "We're enjoying the ball."

"No." Darragh grabbed Bowyn's wrist and twisted it behind his back.

"Ow! Come now, that's my dodgy arm! What are you—"

Darragh shoved Bowyn toward the door. "You're leaving. Right now. Take her and go."

Her?

"Excuse me," I said.

"Why don't you and Belle—sorry, Eleanor—have a dance?" Bowyn beamed. I glanced hopefully at Darragh, who looked like his head might explode.

"No," he growled.

My hopes melted away.

"Suit yourself," Bowyn said, and stuck up his chin. People around us stared, and Darragh reluctantly released his friend. Darragh's hand flexed at his side, and a small flame sputtered to life.

"Ah, ah." Bowyn's eyes darted to the Queen. Darragh scowled in silent fury, but the flame died. Without acknowledging me, Darragh left and resumed his spot on the wall. He rubbed his jaw and glanced at the Queen.

"He wouldn't even look at me," I said, more piteously than I meant to.

Bowyn brought a finger to rest under my chin. "Let's give him something to look at."

Across the room, Darragh watched Elwyn, his gaze focused where the baby-faced man's hand rested on her arm. Jealousy warmed my cheeks. "How do we do that?"

"We dance."

I fidgeted, looking around the room. "There's no music."

"Listen, my love."

"I don't hear anything—" Slowly, a melody rose. "Are you doing that?" Bowyn backed away, beckoning me with his finger. I couldn't resist.

My hand found Bowyn's and we embraced. Pressed against him, I was stiffly reminded we were naked. Intoxicating warmth pushed away any thoughts or feelings of worry. All around, people stared as we danced. On any other occasion, I'd have called this a nightmare, but today, I was beautiful. Rather than shrink away, I let them look.

In Bowyn's arms, I couldn't help but laugh and smile. Bowyn twirled and lunged sideways, dipping me low. Slowly, he pulled me back up to him. His warm breath brushed my skin as his lips travelled up my neck, where they nearly met mine—

THUNK!

"Oof!" I slammed into the stone floor. My dress flickered, and for one terrifying moment, I thought I'd lose it. Bowyn rubbed his temple, where a ruby red line of blood trickled. Curiously, it wasn't a look of pain on Bowyn's face…it was satisfaction. He smirked and rubbed the blood between his fingers. The goblet that struck him rolled noisily back and forth on the cobbled floor. Everyone stared at us now, mouths agape.

Across the room, Darragh buried his head in his hands, as if he'd just made a dreadful mistake. In my peripheral, I glimpsed the Queen.

My blood chilled.

Her large, owl-like eyes burned into me. The Queen stood and a gentle murmur rose from the crowd. The Queen raised a frail arm and pointed a bony finger at me. A voice in my head whispered, '*Approach.*'

"Agh!" Tiny tents of skin littered my arms as hundreds of invisible hooks yanked me up and pulled me toward the Queen. I scanned the crowd for Bowyn.

Gone.

An unbearable silence fell upon the great hall. This was the nightmare I'd feared. The voice in my head spoke again, '*Who are you?*' I tried to wipe my mind. The familiar rain drop sensation dribbled on my scalp. It built until a downpour pounded my skull and white stars speckled my vision. I closed my eyes and gripped my head. Inside my skull, the Queen sifted and prodded, searching. Through the hammering, the voice said, '*What are you?*'

Don't think too loud, I screamed the reminder to myself. Darragh had told me that.

Darragh.

The Queen gasped and recoiled. I cracked my eyes and—

"Oof!" Darragh doubled over and clutched his stomach. An unseen hand grabbed the front of his shirt. It dragged Darragh before the Queen, where he fell at her feet.

"What is your relation to this strange young woman?" the Queen hissed. Elwyn, who'd hardly given me a second glance in town, looked like she might scratch my eyes out now.

"I've never seen her before," Darragh said.

He refused to look at me.

The Queen whispered to the woman sitting beside her, the one Bowyn called the Truth. The Truth grinned and pushed a sleeve to her elbow. She raised her hand.

Darragh climbed to his feet and leapt in front of me. An invisible force struck him and he dropped. "Aughhh!" Darragh writhed. His back twisted, as if wrung like a wet towel.

The Queen smirked. "I thought as much." Elwyn covered her mouth, petrified eyes locked on Darragh. "Take him to the Cage," the Queen instructed. The Truth waved at Darragh, who climbed shakily to his feet. Unable to stand straight, his hands gripped his midsection.

"No!" Darragh resisted.

"Silence." The Queen snapped her fingers and Darragh's mouth clamped shut. He fought every step, but gradually, he followed the Truth.

The Queen's wide, unblinking eyes surveyed me. So much scarier up close, she smelled of decay—like rotting meat and sweet, putrid fruit. "Well, well, well. There's something different about you, isn't there?"

'I know where you've come from,' the Queen's voice whispered in my head. *'You can't hide it from me.'* Too frightened to say anything,

I stared at the ground. The Queen cocked her head and said, "I'm not going to kill you."

Based on her tone, I didn't believe that for a second.

She may not kill me…yet.

"I'm going to make you a deal," the Queen said. A painful silence stretched on; the Queen relished the fear. "West of here, there's a burrow—"

A hiss of whispers rose from those gathered. The Queen's eyes darted about the room, hushing the crowd. She continued. "Inside the burrow is something I desire—a necklace, which I carelessly lost during my last visit. I have sent many individuals to retrieve it, each time I have been eternally disappointed. Perhaps a person of your…*upbringing* can acquire it." The Queen stifled a smirk, suggesting she believed quite the opposite. "You, and *only* you, will go into the burrow and get my necklace. If you bring it back, you may leave."

"And Darragh?"

A whisper went through the crowd. Elwyn's hands balled into fists and the Queen snarled, "What about him?"

"If…" I gulped, my mouth drier than ever before. "If I bring it back, I want you to free Darragh."

The candles flickered.

A monster with charred eyes and snarling fangs replaced the Queen. The illusion was over before it started.

"Of course." The Queen smiled. "If you return my necklace, you, and Darragh, will be released."

"Death is a release," my voice quivered. "I want both of us alive when we leave here."

A laugh sputtered from the Queen's decrepit lips. "My goodness, you're a clever thing, aren't you?" She waved. "Fine, retrieve my necklace, and you and Darragh may leave here…alive."

The deal felt wrong—tricksy, like a genie with messed up wishes. My eyes darted between Elwyn and the Queen, both of whom looked ready to eat me alive, if given the chance.

What other choice did I have?

The Queen examined a frail, greying fingernail. Without looking at me, she said, "Do we have a deal?"

"Yes."

"Very well. Escort her out."

I glanced down, surprised to see my dress still shimmering. I'd been so distracted, I thought surely, I'd be naked. A tiny girl, no more than ten, took my hand.

"Best of luck," the Queen's haunting voice called.

Unable to bear all the gawking faces, I watched my feet as we left.

Once out of earshot of the great hall, the young girl introduced herself. "My name's Hazel. What's yours?"

"Nell."

"I like your dress."

"Thanks. It has pockets."

Hazel looked a little confused but smiled anyway.

"Where are we going?"

"I'm going to leave you with the Cage while I get a few things for your trip." My stomach tightened. What had Bowyn called the Cage? A terrifying creature? We walked deeper and deeper into the mountain. I pictured a dank, wet holding cell full of cockroaches and rats. Or worse, people. Hazel paused, and we doubled back down a hallway. "Where is it?" she muttered, while her tiny fingers wrung a stray curl. "I can't go back and ask."

Obviously lost, Hazel chewed her thumb and looked like she might cry. I pointed down a side path and said, "We haven't tried that way yet."

"Oh!" Hazel took off. "Yes!" We came to a wide, dark opening.

Hazel looked down the stairs and stammered, "I—I've brought you someone!" A carpet of fog oozed up the steps, and a noise, more akin to the rattling of chains than vocal cords, wafted from below.

"Send them."

"You"—Hazel pointed—"down there." She was already sprinting away as she called, "I'll join you once I've gathered your things!"

Swirling mist surrounded me as I descended into darkness. I placed my foot on the next stair—there wasn't one. My stomach lurched and my arms flailed as I fell. Before I could scream, my feet connected with soft ground. I blinked, adjusting to the dim light. The surrounding mist dispersed, and I realized I wasn't in the mountain anymore. A creamy white moon illuminated a flat, grassy plain. As far as I could see, knee high grass swayed in the breeze. A figure stood in the distance, his back to me.

"Darragh?"

Turning to my voice, Darragh gave me a weak smile. He waded through the tall grass and stopped several feet away. Darragh gestured to the ground between us. A thin line glowed at his boots, surrounding him in a wide circle. "My feet can't cross the line," Darragh whispered. I crept closer so I could hear him, careful not to step over the line.

"Where are we?" I asked.

"The Cage has us."

The breeze rustled the grass, a rhythmic, peaceful sound. "This isn't what I pictured at all."

"You and I both," Darragh agreed.

The moonlight bathed Darragh in a soft, welcoming glow. With the wind rustling between us, and my dress still alight, I couldn't help but think, had our circumstances been a little less dire, this might have been a perfect moment.

"I owe you a dance." Darragh's voice was wistful, filled with regret.

"And an apology." Anxiously spinning a single ring around his finger, Darragh inched closer, toeing the line. "I couldn't say this before, but…" Darragh coughed, cleared his throat, and continued with some difficulty. "You're breathtaking, and you were so happy. The way you looked with Bowyn…" Darragh's eyes travelled along the folds of my dress. He reached out to touch me, thought better of it, and dropped his hand. "I wished it was me beside you."

Unsure what to say, I blushed and looked at my feet. The dress sparkled, a lantern in the night. "Oh, uh, yes, the dress is lovely, isn't it? I couldn't have done it without Bo."

"Bo?" Darragh placed an upward inflection on the word, lacing it with suspicion.

"Bowyn, sorry."

Darragh took a deep breath and his nose scrunched. His brows rose, and he crossed his arms over his chest.

"What?" I asked.

Oh.

Bowyn's perfume. Before we left the cottage, Bowyn had practically doused me in it. And at the ball, while we danced, Bowyn's lips nearly met mine…

I suddenly felt very foolish.

Darragh's jaw set. He looked at the ground and said, "Beau means boyfriend on Earth, no?"

"What? No! I mean, I don't know, maybe." I shook my head, clearing it. "It's just a nickname! I'm stupid. I shouldn't have trusted him." I pointed to my temple. "Read my mind. Nothing happened between us."

Darragh didn't answer, but the sharp lines on his face softened. He relaxed and his arms fell to his sides. "You're not stupid. Bowyn just…" Darragh shrugged. "He has his agenda, and he has a way with people.

You can't always trust him."

"Yes, well, I won't be making that mistake again…again."

Bowyn brought me here on purpose. He *wanted* the Queen to discover me. He'd wanted me gone the moment he'd met me. "*She doesn't belong here!*" he'd bellowed. I felt a pang of betrayal. "I told you he wanted me dead," I moped.

Darragh shook his head. "He doesn't want you dead. Back on Earth? Probably. Dead? No. I think this all went much further than he intended." Darragh sighed. "Anyway, he'll get his wish. You're going home."

"No. I'm not."

"Nell." Darragh tilted his head. "It's time to go. *Bo* will get you home."

"He seems to have disappeared," I replied bitterly.

Darragh eyed my dress. "He's around here somewhere."

"If I run—if I go home now—the Queen will kill you."

"It's not ideal, no," Darragh said, with a scoff. "Even if you succeed, she'll kill us both. I'm not getting out of this alive." He gave me a reassuring smile. "If this is the end for me, I'm glad I could see you this way."

"Maybe, maybe I *can* get her necklace?"

"No. You're not going in that burrow," Darragh said. "You *will* die."

"I *might* die," I corrected. "But you *will* die if I don't try."

"Nell, please." Darragh closed his eyes and pinched the bridge of his nose. With great difficulty, he remained calm. "For once, do what's best for you. You find Bowyn, and you run."

"I'm not abandoning you here—"

"Forget me and go *home!*"

Darragh's shout exploded like a clap of thunder, shattering the serene plain. The gentle rustle of swaying grass vanished, eclipsed by Darragh's furious breathing.

My pounding heart rose to meet him.

"Why do you get to decide what's best for me?" I snapped. "Have you considered how letting you be executed would make me *feel?*" I tapped my chest. "I can barely sleep at night as it is. If I run, I have your death weighing on my conscience forever!"

"Why are you so willing to throw your life away?" Darragh shouted.

"I think it's time to go," Hazel called. So preoccupied with Darragh, I hadn't heard her enter.

Darragh's panicked eyes searched mine. "What can I do to convince you? Do you want me to beg? Get down on my knees? Anything, I'll do anything—"

"Live!" I shouted.

Darragh's mouth clamped shut, but his chest heaved. I stuck my nose up and whispered, "I'll be back in a few days." I turned away, but Darragh caught my wrist. Careful not to draw my feet over the line, Darragh yanked me to his chest. I sucked in a breath as his lips pressed against mine. Darragh released me and I stumbled back.

I stood still, shocked.

I'd spent a fair amount of time wondering what it might be like to kiss Darragh. He'd kissed me with such fervor, it made my knees weak...but there was no joy in it. No pleasure. It was desperate, and so hurried I barely knew what was happening until it was over.

The wind rustled the grasses.

A painful knot formed in my stomach.

"Hey!" Hazel sent a pulse of energy at Darragh. It struck him in the chest, and he flew across the plain. Hazel stalked forward; hands raised.

I opened my hand. During our kiss, Darragh pressed several trinkets into my palm. They crackled with warm, fiery energy. When Darragh imbued the bird necklace for me, he'd smiled bashfully and said, "*It's quite painful.*" I counted the talismans in my hand.

There were seven.

One was a silver pendant, shaped like a sunflower. Then two earrings, a seed Darragh must have had in his pocket, and three rings. I slipped a ring on my finger.

"What was that?" Hazel snapped.

Shoving my hand behind my back, I said, "What was what?"

Hazel made a grabbing motion, as if I were a puppy with forbidden food in my mouth. "What do you have?" Darragh threw himself at the edge of the foot trap. The moment his feet crossed the line, he bounced across the plain again. "You're just hurting yourself, you idiot!" Hazel shouted. Darragh leapt to his feet. He wiped a dribble of blood from the corner of his mouth and readied to try again.

The soothing whisper of rustling grass ceased. Hazel's shoulders hunched and she cried, "Now look what you've done!" The moonlight dimmed, and a wisp of smoke curled around our feet. Hazel whimpered and the hair on my arms prickled.

A voice resonated all around. It rattled, "You're dismissed." Hazel's head whipped from side to side as she searched for the source. She scanned the plain and turned in a small circle, trying to decide which direction to turn her back on. I blinked.

Hazel disappeared.

"Nell," Darragh beckoned urgently, "come to me." I hurried over. Our toes pressed against our respective sides of the thin, glowing line. A noise crept up from behind, like bits of metal struck upon each other. Darragh offered a brief, reassuring smile, and whispered, "Have courage."

The deafening clanking of chains filled the plain.

We turned to greet whoever approached, and I craned my neck to see them. Cloaked in black, a hooded figure stood so tall, it blocked the moonlight. The thing hunched, its back and neck curved like a scythe as it stalked forward. Each step was disjointed, and accompanied by loud cracks, as if the bones were never meant to bend that way. My legs trembled as the figure slunk closer. I looked to Darragh for reassurance. The softness was gone. A muscle twitched in his jaw, and a deadly focus set in his keen eyes. Darragh's magic might be chained, but a fire burned within.

"I will incinerate you where you stand," Darragh warned, stepping forward.

Darragh threatening this bone-chilling monster, who was at least twice his size, struck me as silly. That thought, coupled with feeling impossibly frightened, forced an awkward chuckle from my throat.

Darragh glared over his shoulder, eyes wide. The figure craned its long neck, turning its gaze from Darragh to me. There was no face beneath the hooded cloak, only darkness. An unending sense of dread washed through me as I looked upon the emptiness. I couldn't find the strength to look away. In that moment, I was alone, and I was sure I would die—

"Look at me!" Darragh snapped his fingers, bringing the attention back to him. Released from the spell, I wiped a tear from my cheek. Determined not to look at the figure again, I stared at Darragh's back. "If she survives the burrow and I get out of here, I will kill you quickly," Darragh threatened. "But if she dies while you have me trapped here, your suffering will be immeasurable. I will—"

The figure laughed, a horrible, wheezing sound. "I suggest you start planning my lengthy torture. She won't leave the burrow alive." Darragh's fists balled at his sides. The figure bent its long, cloaked neck directly before Darragh. "Boy, do you know who *I* am?"

"You're the Cage," Darragh scowled. "The one creature people hate more than me. Disgusting. Foul. *Thing*!"

"Such fortitude," the Cage hissed. Skeletal hands pulled the hood away. Pale, papery skin covered what was more of a skull than a face.

The nose had long rotted away, replaced by two sunken holes. More alarmingly, the top half of the Cage's face was covered in eyes. It blinked, and hundreds of eyes blinked at once. The Cage skirted the edge of the trap, reaching long, spindly fingers for me. Frozen in place, I did nothing to stop the hand curling around my arm. The brittle bones were deceptive, the strength in the Cage's grip was breathtaking, like someone slid a pressure cuff on me and blew it up tight—my arm would surely snap. The Cage dragged me away from Darragh and laughed. "Take one last look at him while you can."

The resolve on Darragh's face vanished, replaced by cold dread. He mouthed the word, "*Run.*" I waved and smiled half-heartedly. Darragh's shoulders sagged.

The last thing I saw was his head hung in defeat.

The same fog that brought me to Darragh took me away. I came out in a stone-walled room. Hazel leaned against the wall, picking her nails. I coughed to announce my arrival and Hazel snapped to attention. When she realized the Cage hadn't followed me, she relaxed.

"I brought you a few things." She handed me a pile of clothing.

"Oh." I took the items in a haze. "Thanks."

"You're naked, by the way."

"Oh, my!" I clutched the clothing, covering everything important. How long ago had my dress faded?!

Hazel turned around and I yanked on pants. I stuffed Darragh's talismans in my pocket, bar the ring I'd already slipped on my finger. I liked the shine and weight of it and—why am I explaining myself? It's just a ring. I pulled a thin flannel shirt over my head, snapped a belt around my waist, and slid on a pair of black boots.

Hazel handed me a satchel. "I've filled this with a few things you might need."

"Thank you." I pulled the strap over my head and nestled the bag at my side. "Why are you helping me?"

"If you succeed, perhaps the Queen will be kinder to us all." Hazel tilted her head sympathetically, seeming so much older than ten.

"What was that thing?" I asked.

Hazel looked behind us before whispering, "The Cage," like that meant something to me.

"Yes but, what *is* it?"

Hazel became increasingly distressed, as if speaking the thing's name out loud three times might summon it. For all I knew, it could. "I don't really know." Hazel lowered her voice. "If you go to the Cage, you don't come back."

"But we just did."

"Darragh's just being *held*. He hasn't been sentenced yet."

"Oh. I see."

Hazel escorted me out. In the hall, the baby-faced man from the ball spoke to a woman in a slinky black dress. He said, "Can his power work in there?"

Did he mean Darragh? I made eye-contact with the man as we passed. Hazel approached a door—

"Please allow me!" the man ran forward and opened the door for us. He smiled, a charming, wide smile filled with perfect white teeth.

Despite my upset, I smiled back. An unfortunate reflex I'd learned over the years. I murmured, "Thank you." One of the man's gloved hands reached out and grabbed hold of me. "What the—"

"Excuse me!" Hazel snapped. Without releasing my arm, the man reached into my pocket.

"What are you doing?" I tried to wriggle away.

"I think that's enough," Hazel commanded, but made no move to

241

pry the man off. He slid his hand out of my pocket and released me.

"Let's go." Hazel tugged my pants. I checked my pocket.

Darragh's enchanted talismans were gone.

The man mouthed a, '*Thank you.*'

He blew me a kiss as Hazel dragged me away.

Chapter Twenty-One

the mother with many faces

I stood, helpless at the foot of the mountain. Shadow Peak loomed above, casting the ground in darkness. I didn't even know which direction to go.

"Hold on!"

A small, paunchy woman ran after me. The two guardians who watched over the touch stone to enter the mountain side-eyed each other. They laughed at the woman when she wasn't looking. Upon catching up, the woman doubled over and sucked in air. Her cheeks flushed with effort, they clashed with her light, mauve-pink buzz-cut. Through laboured breaths, the woman asked, "Are you the foolish girl on the Queen's errand?"

"That's me."

"What's your name, child?"

"Nell."

"I'm coming with you, Nell."

"What?"

"The Queen sent me to escort you." The woman stood tall, as tall as she could, and wiped sweat from her brow. "She wants to make sure you make it to the burrow alive. It would be a right shame if you died before Jorgen had a chance to kill you."

My brows furrowed as I took in the small woman. "I'm sorry, what's your name?"

"Brana. Do you have a hat?"

"I—what?"

"A hat. We've got a long walk." Outfitted for travel, Brana wore a little backpack, and something that, back home, we called a fanny pack. She pulled a large, witchy sunhat from the pack. Handing it to me, she asked, "Do you have protection?"

"What?" I repeated.

Brana pointed at the sun and pulled out a glass bottle. She plucked out the stopper and dumped the contents in my palm. She did the same for herself, then smeared the liquid over her face and arms.

"Ah." Sunscreen.

"Off we go then." Rather than head to town, Brana waddled down a path that led around the mountain.

I trudged after her. "How long will it take us to get there?"

"Three days."

"Three days?!"

"I've got short legs and bad ankles."

My mind raced. I didn't want to leave Darragh trapped here for nearly a week. Brana sensed my trepidation. "If the Queen is going to kill him, she'll wait until you're back to do it."

I shoved my hands in my pockets and muttered, "Groovy."

"I'm surprised she let you live," Brana said. "She executed the last girl Darragh looked at."

"What?"

"Oh sure. I can't remember what happened exactly, but Darragh saved the poor guardian from being killed out in the wood. The Queen had her publicly executed the next morning, said she, 'didn't want someone protecting her who couldn't protect themselves.' But we all know she was sending a message."

"And what was that?"

Brana pursed her lips. "Don't touch my things."

I shook my head. I'd kill Bowyn if I ever got my hands on him. "What about the Cage?" I asked. "Will they hurt Darragh?"

"No. It wouldn't disobey the Queen."

"What is it exactly?"

"No one knows much about the creature. It showed up by the Queen's side in the last few years. Nasty thing."

I thought about what Darragh had said, that people hated it more than they hated him. "I feel bad for it."

"It's a monster!"

"I imagine it's lonely."

"I... I suppose." After a few moments of silence, Brana asked, "Do you have children?"

I shook my head no. "You?"

Brana's face brightened. "A son! Pip." If we were back home, this would be where she'd pull out her phone and show me photos. Instead, she reached for me. "May I?" I offered my hand. An image of a young boy, maybe fifteen, popped into my head.

"He's practically a man," I cooed.

Brana released me, her eyes dewy. "I suppose he is, isn't he?"

I wasn't much for children myself; I didn't really know what else to ask. Thankfully, Brana didn't need prodding. "I almost lost him you know, when he was a baby. Seeing him grow up"—her voice cracked— "I treasure every moment of it." Brana wiped her eye. "Look at me, all sentimental." She shook her head and said, "I'm sorry. Would you like something to eat?" Brana rummaged in her pack. She withdrew a softball sized pastry and gave it to me. It looked like a muffin, with a gooey, liquid centre poking out the top.

"Uh, thanks." I bit down on the soft pastry and uttered an unseemly moan. Brana beamed as she devoured her own pastry. "This is incredible," I mumbled through my second bite.

"Pip made it. He's quite the baker, you know." Pride lit Brana's eyes and curled her cheeks into a warm smile. "Would you like another?"

"I think I'll finish this one first but maybe later, thank you."

"Don't be shy." Brana scarfed down a second muffin and patted her pack. "There's lots."

Walking with Brana was actually…quite nice. She told me stories about Pip and fed me snacks. For a while, I forgot all about the burrow, Jorgen, and the likelihood of my own death.

"Shall we stop for dinner?" Brana wandered off the path and tossed her bags on the ground. "I'll get started here. You grab firewood."

"Wait, you need wood?" I'd never seen Darragh use any.

Brana gave me a funny look and laughed. "Of course we need wood!"

"I just thought…"

"Do you know how much effort it takes to keep a fire going? How much control? What happens if I get distracted while I'm cooking? We'll burn the whole place down!"

"Alright, okay I'm going." I dropped my bag and started toward the trees.

"Be careful!" Brana shouted. "I'll not have the Queen choke me for letting a nightstalker eat you before you get to the burrow!"

"Yes. That would be a shame," I muttered.

While searching for fallen branches, I stooped to pick up a few twigs, but struggled to find anything substantial. I wandered into the trees and scanned the ground. "A-ha!" A sizeable dead log lay across the wood floor. I grabbed a rotting branch, and started to wiggle it free.

Splinters exploded up as a boot slammed onto the branch. I stumbled away and cried, "What the—"

My heart plummeted.

Three women stood before me.

Specifically, the three women I'd forced Darragh to let live after our last predicament in the wood.

What were the chances?

Oh, who am I kidding? With my luck, it's a wonder I hadn't run into them sooner.

"Where's your pretty companion?" Geneth asked. She spun, and I saw a dark blur before her boot met the side of my head. I careened back, sending up a cloud of bark and twigs. Pinpricks of light speckled my vision, and I tried to scream for help. Something coiled around my throat and yanked me to my feet.

Geneth approached with her hand outstretched. The invisible rope tightened against my neck, pulling me backward. My feet struggled to keep up with the momentum, and I tried not to slip on the twigs I'd dropped. "Oof!" I slammed into a tree. The rope curled around my entire body, tying me to the trunk. With every breath I drew, the rope curled tighter.

"You killed our friend," Geneth hissed.

My response was choked and breathy. "Technically, I didn't kill anyone." I made eye contact with a woman behind Geneth. "I did hit you with a rock. Sorry. I'm glad to see you're up and about." She scowled and took a step, but Geneth stopped her.

"You should have watched your man better. You're just as much to blame."

"He's not"—I struggled to speak—"my man."

"Then why not let us kill him?"

I remained silent.

Geneth let out a shrieking laugh. "That's what I thought."

The woman I'd brained with the rock snarled, "Break her neck."

"I'm trying!" Geneth's face contorted with effort, but the coil wouldn't tighten. Like an approaching storm, a shadow fell over the wood. I only realized the dark wasn't the result of my nearness to fainting when Geneth cried, "What are you doing?" She looked over her shoulder and the pressure around my neck lessened. "How are you doing that?!"

I had no idea what was going on, but I certainly wasn't going to tell her that.

Tendrils of smoke oozed from the trees; they snaked toward Geneth. The strange, grey vapor curled around her ankles, and ascended her legs. Geneth batted the smoke like an unwelcome insect. It washed over her hand and continued to climb her body. "Uaah—"

Geneth's scream cut short as smoke slid into her mouth. She clawed at her throat, erupting in violent, dry coughs. Smoke seeped from her nose, and her eyes turned red as the blood vessels burst. Geneth's companions watched helplessly as she drew one final, wheezing breath and collapsed.

She did not get up.

A familiar, gut-wrenching noise permeated the trees.

Rattling chains.

Metal clanking against metal.

Twigs snapped above, and a hooded figure descended from the canopy. Legs of dark smoke stretched from the figure, giving the impression of a giant arachnid approaching its prey. It craned its long neck toward Geneth's companions, and a sickly arm pulled the hood away.

I knew who it was long before I saw myself reflected in the many eyes of the Cage.

It followed me.

The Cage reached forward with one withered hand, and the women at my side vanished. My feet held firmly in place; I couldn't run. I had some movement left in my arms; I grabbed Darragh's ring.

"I wouldn't if I were you," the Cage rasped.

Before I could decide whether to heed the warning or use the ring, the Cage raised its frail arms over its head and stood tall. Wisps of smoke crept up the Cage's body, enveloping it like a cocoon. When it fell away, my jaw dropped.

"Brana?"

"Couldn't stay out of trouble for two minutes, could you?" Brana looked at me in that disappointed, pitying way only a mother can. "I wouldn't waste that." She pointed at the ring. "You're going to need it."

We sat cross-legged beside the campfire. I kept my eyes trained on Brana. Oblivious to my discomfort, she puttered about the fire and said, "Let's put some meat on those bones." Brana handed me an earthy plate heaped high with food. "We'll give you a fighting chance against that Jorgen fellow." She paused, deep in thought. "Or at least give him a hearty meal." Thinking of Jorgen didn't do much to encourage my appetite, but it was hard to resist Brana's cooking. I ate a crisp, golden morsel. It tasted like juicy fried chicken. When I finished, Brana took my plate and gave me a second portion. I finished that too. She motioned to give me thirds.

"Please no," I begged.

Pointing to a pot on the fire, Brana assured, "There's lots."

"I can't."

Brana made a disagreeable face but took my plate. She handed me a mug filled with a warm, sweet drink, before nestling in front of the fire herself.

"So...you're the Cage, eh?" I did my best to keep my tone casual. As if I'd inquired about someone she was dating, not that she was perhaps the most pants-shittingly scary monster I'd ever seen.

Brana exhaled and let her head fall back. When she finally looked at me, she stared with such focus, I had to look away. "I am the Cage, but the Cage isn't me. I'm Brana first. The Cage second."

"So, this is what you look like? You just...turn into the Cage?"

Brana nodded. "You're the only person in the world who knows. Even the Queen doesn't know who I truly am." She stared into the fire. "You were right about the Cage. It's a terribly lonely life." She chugged the contents of her mug. "I worry about Pip. If anyone found out who I was, or who he was to me..." Brana trailed off. "I should kill you right now."

I sipped my drink.

"Unfortunately, with all this nasty Queen business, I can't kill you." Brana shrugged. "Fortunately, you'll probably die in the burrow."

"Thanks," I replied, unappreciatively. "What if I *don't* die in there?"

"Then I guess we'll revisit this once you deliver the Queen her necklace," Brana said, grinning.

"Noted." I thought of Geneth's companions. When Brana snapped her fingers, they'd simply vanished. "Where do people go, when you send them away?"

"Honestly? I don't know. I just sort of, keep them up here." Brana pointed to her forehead. "When the Queen passes, I plan to release them. The innocent ones—which is most of them. I'm just keeping them safe for now."

My pulse quickened. "Do you have Darragh in there?"

Brana frowned. "Before I left, the Queen ordered me to give him to the Truth." She gave me a serious stare. "We should be swift."

Fresh worry for Darragh's safety needled me. *Please, one ridiculous problem at a time*, I thought. *Survive the burrow, then worry about Darragh.*

"The Queen didn't send you to make sure I made it to the burrow alive, did she?" Brana shook her head. "Then why are you helping me?"

Brana leaned over and took my hand. "May I?"

"Go for it—"

The fire slipped away as I tumbled into Brana's memory.

I regretted my decision. A sudden and crushing pressure weighed my chest. I struggled to catch my breath and took in Brana's surroundings. The only window in the room, a tiny opening between the wooden beams and cob, was shuttered. A few candles, burned down so they were only stubs, flickered faintly. Brana stepped forward—

Crunch!

She pulled her foot away and picked up a tiny wooden dragon. Brana approached the small bed nestled against the wall, pausing to place the broken dragon in an overflowing toybox. Her gaze travelled up the bed and settled on the frail child nestled beneath the blanket.

The pain coursing through Brana made itself known.

Grief.

She sat tenderly on the bed, careful not to wake the boy.

Her baby, her entire life.

Brana lay her head on the pillow next to him. Watching his chest rise and fall, she tried not to think about what came next. She needed to focus on this, just to be close to him for a little while longer. The bedroom door opened, and a woman entered. I didn't recognize her, yet I knew she was Brana's mother. The boy who entered the room behind her, I did recognize: Darragh. He was much younger; the hair around his temples hadn't greyed yet. His face, less-weathered, still had the roundness of youth.

Brana leapt up. She put herself between Darragh and Pip. "What's he doing here?"

"Step aside," Brana's mother snapped.

"Did anyone see him come in?" Brana seethed.

"He can help!"

"Get him out of here, now!"

Brana's mother dropped her voice to a whisper. "Pip will be dead by morning if we do nothing." Brana swallowed hard; her mother pointed at Darragh. "He was cursed with death, but he has the gift of life! Please! Let him save my grandson." My stomach tugged as Brana's mother choked on the word 'grandson.'

Brana looked at Pip, grimacing while he slept. A part of her pretended he was smiling—the same smile he wore when she arrived home after a long day. A beautiful gift given to her simply because she was there, because she existed. She thought of the way Pip grabbed her legs and dragged her to the kitchen to show her the dinner he'd made. With Grandmama's help, of course.

How can I come back to this house without him? Brana wondered. How can the world exist without him?

Brana sobbed.

She'd do anything to keep him alive.

Brana stepped aside.

Darragh knelt beside Pip's bed. "He was bitten?"

Brana wiped snot from her nose and nodded. "He was playing outside the village. He told me a big snake bit him. The healer"—Brana hiccupped—"she said there was nothing to be done. Pip doesn't have much magic... She barely even looked at him."

No one cared about a little boy who hardly had enough magic to take care of himself.

But Brana cared.

Brana cared for him more than anything else in this world. All the things he wouldn't experience tumbled through her thoughts. He'd never fall in love or have a family of his own... A fresh surge of tears poured down Brana's cheeks and she moved to the back of the room. Darragh picked up Pip's hand and examined the bite. The wound was putrid and festered, but Darragh didn't recoil. He placed Pip's hand against his cheek. Several tense moments passed before a tear fell from Darragh's eye, dripping onto Pip's wound. Gently, Darragh placed it back on the bed. We waited in silence, watching the rise and fall of Pip's chest. It fell...

...and it did not rise again.

Brana stopped breathing.

Her mother whimpered and reached out. Brana pushed her away and grabbed for Darragh. He dodged and crossed the room. Smoke rose from the floor and crept up Brana's legs. She shrieked, "How could you!"

Brana's mother leapt between her and Darragh. "Please, Brana!"

"You killed him!"

Two thin arms wrapped around Brana's waist. The familiar pressure of a tiny head pressed her belly. "Are you alright, Mama?"

Brana's world froze, and she stilled with it. Slowly, her trembling hand curled in Pip's hair. She had to make sure he was real; she tousled his hair. Pip's laugh filled the room and he cried, "Mama, stop!"

The weight of Brana's body collapsed on the floorboards with a loud thud. She grabbed Pip and held him tighter than she'd ever held anything before. "Oh! Oh, my baby!" Brana wept and kissed Pip's head once, twice. Pip laughed and wiggled away. His laughter was the sweetest noise in the world. Brana looked up, searching for Darragh.

"He's gone," her mother said. "He didn't want to risk us further."

"I have to go after him." Brana rose to her feet. "I owe him my life."

Her mother motioned toward Pip and whispered, "It's not the time."
She refused to meet Brana's eye, as if she harbored guilt of some sort.
Brana knew then, her mother had given Darragh something.

But what?

"I will repay him," Brana murmured, "one day."

"I know." Her mother frowned.

The crackling fire reappeared as Brana let go. I wiped my nose and cheeks on my sleeve. "Darragh saved Pip?" I sniffled. Brana nodded, poking embers with a stick. "So, you're helping me to repay Darragh? Surely the Queen will kill you if she finds out?"

"I owe him my life," Brana echoed the phrase from the memory. "Truthfully, I think the Queen wants you to come back from this journey. If you find her trinket, maybe she'll be lenient with us both." Brana chuckled to herself. "Or at least kill us quickly. Either way, I'd rather have her angry with me than Darragh."

I cringed, giving Brana a look that said, *really?*

"Did you see Darragh's eyes when I ripped you away? If any harm comes to you, he'll make good on his promise—he *will* burn me alive. The Queen will kill me quickly, but Darragh…well, you know how men are."

I cocked my head.

Brana *tsked* and said, "So emotional." I bit back a laugh as Brana poured herself another drink.

"You know, I asked Darragh not to kill those women in the woods."

Brana choked on her drink and thumped her chest. "You *what?*"

"We ran into them before, and he killed one of them. I begged him not to kill the rest. He said they'd come back and butcher us if they had the chance." I gazed into the fire. "He was right."

"It was a mistake to leave them alive," Brana agreed. She smiled, and added, "I won't tell him."

"I'd appreciate that."

We awoke to a crisp morning. "Are you warm enough?" Brana asked, half-pulling a cloak from her pack.

"I'm fine."

Brana handed me the cloak anyway. We didn't bother making a fire. Brana fed me pastries and water, then we set out. As the burrow loomed closer, even Brana's stories about Pip couldn't cheer me up.

Would I die in the burrow?

Would I make it back to the mountain and die there?

So many possibilities.

"Well?" Brana called out.

"Sorry—what?"

Brana gave me a pitying look.

"Sorry. I'm just distracted." I stared at my feet while we walked. "Can you tell me anything about the creature in the burrow?" Brana winced, but I pressed. "Please. I need all the help I can get. What do you know?"

"He was a man once, Jorgen. He was born, oh, over five hundred years ago now—"

"Five hundred?" I repeated breathlessly.

"That'll be the least of the shocks in this story, just listen."

"Sorry."

"Jorgen was born with very little magic. Basic, like my little Pip." Brana spit the word *basic* with scorn. "One day while Jorgen was working in his family's jewel shop, a woman tried to rob him. The stories say he killed her—that it was self-defence, but we never can be sure now, can we?" Brana's brows raised conspiratorially. "Anyway, the moment the woman passed from this world to the next, Jorgen was overcome with power. *Her* power. While he revelled, a customer entered the shop. Jorgen panicked and killed them too. Same as before, when that woman passed on, Jorgen absorbed her magic. He continued this way, killing again and again, absorbing the abilities of the dead. Until one day—he couldn't take on anymore."

"What changed?"

"He was full up."

"So, what did he do?"

Brana shot me a cross look that said, *we'll get there when we get there.* "Sorry."

"Jorgen's family were expert jewellers, and Jorgen, never distracted by magic, was the finest of the lot. He found a way to store excess power inside a ring. As you can imagine, Jorgen's killing spree didn't go unnoticed forever. The townspeople begged the queen at the time, Queen Aeress, to help them. While Queen Aeress couldn't *kill* Jorgen, she was able to ensnare him in a burrow. For hundreds of years, people entered the burrow, hoping to kill Jorgen and take the ring. All of them were killed, and Jorgen grew stronger, and stronger."

"Until the Queen stole it?"

Brana nodded. "She wasn't the same after that, the Queen." A shudder passed through Brana. "She got the ring, but people reckon she brought something else out with her."

We crested a hill above a valley. The landscape below was mostly barren, some craggy rocks here and there. Imposing ruins stood in the middle of the valley. "Those ruins guard the entrance to the burrow. We'll camp here tonight. You'll go in tomorrow."

"You?" I stammered. "As in me? Alone?"

"The Queen chooses her words carefully. You must go alone."

"But how will she know?" I panicked.

"The Queen shares a powerful bond with this place. She will know if I join you." Brana busied herself unpacking. I dropped my bag and set off collecting wood, hoping the monotony might calm me. After several trips back and forth, I plopped down beside Brana.

"Am I stupid?" I asked.

Brana smiled while she prepared supper. "You'll have to be more specific."

"Should I run? Should I just go home and forget all this happened?" I rubbed my temples. "I'm going to die for someone I have a *crush* on. I barely know Darragh. This is ridiculous."

Once I finished venting, Brana handed me a knife and a pile of gigantic green beans. "Trim these." I sawed at the woody ends. Brana cringed at my inaptitude but didn't intervene.

"When I was young, there were people we called matchmakers. Gifted with incredible foresight, a matchmaker peeked into all possible futures before you. They returned with visions, fragments of a beloved— of someone whose magic weaves into the very fibres of your heart." Brana stirred the boiling cauldron. "Matchmakers revealed the one person who might love you so *completely* that you have no choice but to be the best version of yourself, for your sake and theirs." A darkness settled over Brana. "It became a common practice for mothers to bring their daughters and sons to matchmakers. Children wasted less time and energy searching for love if they already knew who their beloved was, whom they might call melaethien."

"And what happened to them, the matchmakers?"

"The practice was outlawed. Too much corruption. Mothers, eager to find their children powerful matches, bribed matchmakers. Instead of showing a child their true love, a matchmaker provided a false prophecy, showing a powerful suitor." Brana dropped the beans in the boiling cauldron. "My mother, Lore, was a matchmaker. I'd like to imagine she never took any bribes but, none of us are infallible, are we?"

"I suppose." I wished Brana would get to the point.

"After matchmaking was outlawed, my mother never used her gift again." Brana waved a hand, stoking the fire. "Until the night Darragh saved Pip." She looked at me to see if I understood.

I didn't.

She rolled her eyes and sighed. "Darragh knows who his beloved is. He knows because my mother showed him."

My jaw slackened, and I stared at Brana.

Hundreds of tiny moments fell into place like delicate puzzle pieces. Sasha's matter-of-fact whispers. *'He recognized you.'* Bowyn's casual allusions, that he was happy I survived, *'for Darragh's sake.'* And Darragh, who looked at me with such enduring conviction, as he offered his power and body to protect me...

Brana continued. "So, if you're asking me if you should run, my answer is this: Darragh might have found his melaethien, but that doesn't mean you've found yours." Brana gave me a pointed look. "The choice is up to you."

I gazed into the fire, mulling Brana's words. If Darragh truly believed I was his beloved, why did he always shrink from my touch? I picked up a blade of grass and began shredding it between my fingers. Perhaps all this time, Darragh was terrified to do or say the wrong thing and scare me away?

Night had fallen while we talked, and I found my gaze drawn to the sky. I felt some comfort when I located the brightest star in the dark expanse. As I looked upon it, I couldn't help but wonder:

How many nights had Darragh held my face in his memory, hoping to find me?

After a deep breath, I tossed the blade of grass into the fire.

I would not—*could not* leave Darragh to die.

"But what can I do?" I said. "What chance do I have against some monster that's killed thousands of people?"

Brana pulled away from cooking. "It does seem awfully hopeless, doesn't it?"

Story of my life.

Brana dragged her bag over and pulled out a small vial. "This past summer, Pip had his first outing with a young woman." Brana fidgeted with the vial. "I bought this to send with him because, well, you know how young girls can be."

"What is it?" I asked apprehensively.

"Do you have any protection at all? A blade? Anything?"

"No—wait!" I tugged out the pin Bowyn had tucked in my hair. The sharp point glinted in the firelight. Brana plucked the stopper from the vial, and, taking the pin, dipped it inside. When she withdrew it, a thick, purple liquid oozed over the blade. I pinched my nose against the sickly-sweet stench. Brana held the pin to the fire, and the liquid dried clear.

"Pierce Jorgen's flesh with this, and it just might buy you enough time to get out." She handed me the pin, pulling away before I could take it. "Don't accidentally nick yourself with this, alright?"

I took the pin. "What do you think I am—oops." I searched for the pin in the grass. "Heh." I picked it up and *very carefully* tucked it back in my hair. Jutting my chin at the vial, I said, "I'd hate to be one of the girls interested in Pip."

Brana chuckled. "Can't be too careful."

"Where'd you get that, by the way?"

Brana tucked the vial away. "Only one person supplies the town with poison."

My mind wandered along the path from Darragh's cottage, through the winding shrubs and flowers, and stopped at the final garden with the tallest fence.

Inside, a deep-purple flower dripped a thick, oozing sap.

Chapter Twenty-Two

a rotten marionette

Elwyn

Sleep refused me the night after the ball. When I tired of pretending, I slid from beneath the covers with a single task on my mind.

"Where's Darragh?" I asked the guardian outside my room. "Is he with the Cage?"

The guardian glanced down the hall before saying, "I believe the Truth has him."

That was much worse. The Cage garnered fear through mystery. Once you were given to the Cage, you were never seen again. No one knew what happened; you simply ceased to be. But with the Truth, you knew.

Darragh was already suffering.

"Where is she keeping him?"

"I don't know. You know how she is."

Unfortunately, I did.

The Truth hated interruptions. It broke her concentration and ruined the theatrics of torture. She regularly changed locations—sometimes even creating rooms to hide her victims. I had to get Darragh out, but I needed to find him first.

"Thanks for nothing," I muttered as I left.

I spent hours scouring the mountain. I checked every door in every room. And then I checked again. The smell of spices and roasted meat told me dinner was served. I didn't attend. I'd suffer the repercussions. Feeling hopeless, my feet carried me along a path my father and I used to walk. I headed to the Hall of Memories; a section of the mountain carved with the faces of our queens, and imbued with their stories. I remembered how father always paused at the final depiction of Queen Aithen, his mother. He would laugh, recalling how he'd told his mother it was closer to a likeness of a bearded wolf than her. Inevitably, his mood darkened. Shortly after my father wed, Aithen went into the woods and never returned. A guardian found her mangled body several weeks later.

Father always missed her terribly.

I rounded the corner to the hall and stopped. At the end, someone admired the carving of Queen Aithen. The slightly stooped stature—and the rich blue robe—was unmistakable. I croaked, "Father?"

I ran.

A foul, rotting stench met my nose. "Father!" I closed the distance between us. Stopping next to him, I whispered, "How did you—"

Teeth gnashed as my father spun around and grabbed for me. "Agh!" I dodged his grasping hands and fell back. I barely recognized this decomposing creature, who wore my father's clothes, but looked at me through glazed eyes and mottled, purple flesh. Falling to his knees, my father skittered along the rock. I scrambled away, but he caught my foot and dragged me back. He clambered on top of me, his teeth snapping ravenously—

Someone caught the collar of my father's robe, halting the attack. Suspended a few inches from my face, my father continued to snarl and hiss. From behind him, Ophyr's smirking face appeared.

"Afternoon!" Ophyr knelt, keeping my father's frantic corpse just far enough away that he couldn't bite me. "Have you seen Darragh?" Ophyr asked. "You know, it's the strangest thing. I swear he was around here somewhere." Ophyr placed an exasperated hand on his cheek. "But I just can't seem to find him."

"I—I—I don't know," my voice chugged.

"Are you lying to me?" Ophyr asked, inching my father's biting corpse closer. "Dishonesty is unbecoming, you know."

"I don't know!" My arms buckled as the weight increased. Snapping teeth brushed my nose and I craned my head sideways. "If I knew where he was, I'd be there!"

Ophyr squinted. "You've got me there." He pulled my father away. "Here." Metal clanked on stone as Ophyr placed a blade beside me.

He released my father.

My arms flattened and I dodged as teeth smashed against the rock. Climbing to my feet, I snatched the dagger. My father ran at me, and I swung the blade, cutting his throat. Still, he did not stop. He pinned me to the wall.

I drove the blade as far as I could into the side of his head.

My father stilled, then fell.

I cowered against the rock as the corpse twitched at my feet. Ophyr clapped and punched a fist in the air. "Fantastic job!" He put a boot on my father's head and dug the blade out. He wiped the blood on the bottom of my dress and tucked the knife away. I wrapped my scratched, bloody arms around myself to keep from shaking.

Ophyr stood before me and made a pouty face. "Aw." The rock pressed against my back, I couldn't escape him. He raised a gloved hand, inches from my face. One by one, Ophyr pulled the glove from his fingers. It fell away, revealing a burned, nearly skeletal hand. Ophyr flexed, and bits of sinew pulled his fingers into a fist. "You know, I can't feel a thing." He dragged the bones along my cheek. "I have your friend to thank for this." Ophyr leaned in, his bones curled around my throat and squeezed. I choked and gasped for air.

Ophyr kissed me, forcing his tongue between my lips. The taste of decay lingered in his mouth. When he pulled away, I gagged.

Ophyr smiled.

"I suggest you find him before I do."

Chapter Twenty-Three

the scariest tea-party I ever was at

We descended upon the stone ruin the next morning. Brana bypassed many of the fallen walls, locating an unassuming wooden door. Inside, we found a passable living space. Two women dressed in black relaxed in a rudimentary den. The first, a slight woman with pin straight black hair, dropped her knitting and greeted us.

Brana started, "We're here to—"

"The Queen said you'd come!" the woman cried.

The second woman, who looked remarkably like the first, albeit not-so-slight, raised her brow suspiciously. "The Queen said only *one* would come." The second woman turned to face us. She wore a roughly fashioned eye patch.

Brana paled. "Well—"

"The poor girl obviously needed a guide," the first woman said. "I'm sorry about my sister. She gets grumpy out here."

"It's a miserable place," her sister groaned.

"I like it. I can stitch in peace." The first woman turned back to us. "I'm sorry, we're being rude. I'm Annwyl, and that's my sister Anval. Now, can I get you anything? Tea? Are you hungry?"

"They're not guests!" Anval cried.

"When someone new arrives, that makes them a guest!"

"She's about to be ripped apart. She doesn't want tea!"

I didn't feel so good.

Annwyl looked at me for confirmation. I hated to side with Anval, but I didn't want anything. "No, thank you."

Annwyl glared at Anval. "Father would be ashamed of you." And to me, "Are you certain I can't get you anything?"

"An Uber home."

"Pardon?"

"Nothing. I'd like to get this over with if you don't mind."

"Very well." Annwyl frowned. "Follow me." She paused, pointing at my clothes. "Is that what you're wearing?"

I looked down. "What else would I wear?"

"You can't wear that. He'll be displeased," Annwyl said, shaking her head. "Here, come with me." Annwyl led me to a bedroom. Stunning handcrafted robes and gowns hung from the rafters. I bumped a table piled high with neatly folded tops and trousers.

"Wow."

Annwyl chewed her nail. "We've found it's best to keep our minds, and our hands, busy." I grazed the soft fabric of a rich burgundy robe. Annwyl continued, "Jorgen's whispers call to us from below… They're not very nice things." She laughed anxiously. "One minute you're fine, and the next thing you know…" She mimed a stabbing motion. "You're jabbing your sister in the eye with a knitting needle."

My stomach turned and I withdrew my hand. "Well, they're beautiful."

Annwyl beamed, pulling down the burgundy robe. "I always loved this one," she said, examining the floral pattern stitched into the trim.

"It's just going to get ruined," Anval called from the doorway. "Let her go with what she's wearing."

"I'd want to look nice if I was going to my death," Annwyl said absent-mindedly. She handed me the robe. "You know what? Hold on." She snatched the garment away and headed to an old wardrobe in the corner. Inside were a handful of outfits. Annwyl dragged her hand along the clothing. "This is my favourite," she said, and withdrew a flowing, pale blue gown. "He loves blue." It looked like the sort of dress a woman might wear as she scoured the halls of her haunted Victorian mansion, candelabra in hand. And I don't mean that in a bad way. It was stunning, if old-fashioned.

"I can't," I protested.

"Please, I have a good feeling about this one," Annwyl urged, handing me the gown. "I have a good feeling about you." The dress was weightless. I ran the skirt through my fingers and found a softness I could never imagine. Let alone afford.

"Perhaps you'll bring it back to me," Annwyl said.

Her smile was hopeful. Her eyes were not.

I changed, and only tripped on the hem of the skirt once as I rejoined the others. I wondered if I'd be able to run if the occasion called for it.

"Don't run," Anval said.

"Wha—"

"Trust me." Anval gave a tight shake of her head. "It excites him."

Feeling a bit woozy, I steadied myself with a chair.

Annwyl led Brana and I into the basement, nothing more than a rough room dug into the dirt. Torches sat on either side of a single wooden door. Annwyl strode forward and gripped the doorhandle. She paused and whispered, "I hate this part." Annwyl turned the knob.

WHOOSH! The door burst open, and Annwyl leapt away as an ear-splitting screech shattered the silence. The door slammed the dirt wall and sent wooden splinters spraying across the room.

Blood and scratches littered the inside of the door.

"Some people almost make it out…" Annwyl's eyes glazed. "Almost."

Anval slunk down the stairs. "If we don't hear from you within the next hour, we'll assume you're dead and alert the Queen of your passing." Annwyl cringed. I opened my mouth to tell Anval that they may as well alert the Queen now, but Brana shot me a dirty look and I refrained.

Annwyl squeezed my arm and gave me a torch. "Just…head down." The flickering light revealed stairs carved into stone. Hot, humid air pulsed from below. My mind conjured the image of a dragon curled over a mountain of gold. As it dozed peacefully, each rotten breath travelled up to meet me.

A whisper crept up the steps, "I can feeeel your ssshaking body."

"I told you," Annwyl murmured. "They're not very nice things."

Ugh.

"Any last-minute advice?" I stalled.

"He hates rudeness," Annwyl started.

"Be polite and hope he kills you quickly," Anval finished.

Brana fidgeted with her sleeve, unable to look at me. "Thanks for getting me here," I said.

Brana's lips compressed, as if she didn't trust herself to speak. When her eyes finally met mine, they were dewy and tinged pink. "Well, off you go then!" she shooed.

I stepped onto the landing. Behind me, the door latched with a gentle *click*. The low rumble of laughter carried from below. No turning back now.

I descended.

Intricate drawings covered the walls. I brought my torch closer, examining them. The first scene depicted a figure rubbed with blue pigment. In one hand, the figure held a pair of legs, in the other, a woman's torso. Whorls of magic floated from the torn body. They swirled into the blue figure's mouth, it's jaw wide and unhinged, like a massive snake. I brushed the wall—

"Aughhhhh!" A high-pitched scream shattered my eardrums. Terror shot through me and I stumbled back. I coddled my hand like a child who'd touched a hot stove. I swung the torch around; the scenes of slaughter continued all the way down. The next sketch showed the figure in blue, victoriously mounted on a pile of limbs and corpses. Red dye pooled at the base of the bodies. I stared at my feet as I climbed down the remaining steps. The visceral scream clung to me like an unwelcome bur.

None of this felt real until that scream, the pitched wail of a woman fighting for her life. The reality of my situation set in with stunning clarity.

I'm going to die here.

Tears stung my eyes as I thought about Sasha, and Watney. It hurt my chest, to think of Watney at home, watching the door that I'd never come through again. Back at Shadow Peak, Darragh would be executed, but not before he learned of my brutal demise—*stop it!*

Pushing the catastrophizing thoughts aside, I stumbled into the dimly lit cavern. These walls were meticulously carved, thousands of depictions of those who came before me. Those who failed. *He may be a monster, but he's certainly talented.* I admired the carvings glumly. *I suppose he's got the time.* A red glow emanated through three doorways in the cavern, a set of stairs behind each. I rubbed my neck. *Red means scary.*

Which stairs do I take?

A chilling voice rose from below. "All pathsss lead to me."

When in doubt, go left. I started down the left-most passage. My boot crushed glass—I yanked it away. Shards of a bottle remained. I lurched over that step and continued. More and more items littered the stairs, overflow from the room below. I carefully avoided a pile of clothing.

Wouldn't want to fall and break my neck.

I shuffled into a grotto, and skirted mounds of objects strewn about the rocky floor. Each pile was filled with similar items: staffs, lanterns, a cluttered heap of boots. As I picked my way around the piles, I realized it was a maniacal filing system. My guts twisted at the thought of seeing my own boots tossed with the rest. I peeked around an enormous stack of hats. At the far end of the grotto, amongst shinier stacks of loot, a figure sat upon a throne. Shrouded in darkness, I could barely make them out.

A pair of eyes snapped open. Two slitted beacons in the dimly lit cavern.

"Approach."

I rounded the pile of hats and shuffled to the throne. What I thought were spokes of wrought iron or metal were actually bones. Femurs and tibias jutted behind the throne in a giant half circle.

"Sssstop."

I paused mid step.

The figure's face entered my torchlight. Jorgen looked like a person, but he also…didn't look like a person. His eyes were far too big, his mouth too broad. He grinned; the corners of his mouth touched his ears. Like Alice and the Cheshire Cat, I looked upon Jorgen timidly. His body remained coiled in the darkness, and I worried he might strike out at any moment.

Slowly, Jorgen rose and stepped into the light. He wore a striking cerulean robe, patterned in woven scallops. Jorgen took another step and his robe shimmered, as if covered in delicate scales. Glancing at Jorgen's feet, my breath caught. Beneath him were several rugs made of skin.

Human skin.

Their mouths open in silent screams, flat, eyeless faces stared up at me. Jorgen followed my gaze as it bounced between the human rugs, and the bone throne. He smiled wickedly, and waved a frail, swishy hand at his throne. "A gem must sssit on a pedestal, and building materials are ssso hard to come by." Jorgen hissed his S's; I imagined a forked tongue hidden behind his teeth. He slunk forward and sniffed. "Fassscinating. I've never sssmelled anything like you before." As he spoke, his head swayed from side to side.

It was quite…hypnotic.

Stay vigilant, I reminded myself.

"I-I'm looking for s-something," I stuttered.

"We're all looking for ssssomething my dear…" Invisible tendrils prodded me as Jorgen explored my mind. "Eleanor?"

I hesitated, but figured I had nothing to lose. "It's Nell."

"You're not a necromancer, are you?" He didn't wait for an answer. "Hm, no. You're not. Disappointing. I've never had one before. Would you like a drink?"

"I—what?" I remembered Anval's warning. *Be polite*. I reached within, coaxing the version of myself who worked at the café. Forcing my biggest, most genuine smile, I said, "I'd love that. Thank you."

The red hue that permeated the grotto ebbed. Jorgen looked more human in this light. "Come! Come!" he insisted. His foot caught on the rug, and he stumbled. "Oh! Be careful!" He waved at the rug. "I must move that. It's so dangerous, but I *adore* the drama when people come down." He chuckled and raised his hands like claws. "Ahhh, rawr. Anyway, libation?" Jorgen flourished his fingers, and a table of bones grew up from the ground. He clapped, and a tablecloth of stitched skins appeared in the air. Jorgen raised his hands and brought them down, and the skin cloth fell neatly on the table. Two chairs appeared, one of which Jorgen pulled out for me.

"Thank you kindly," I murmured, and took a seat. Jorgen sat beside me, scooching his chair enthusiastically to the table. Jorgen clapped and a bone harp appeared behind us. A wave moved across the instrument as an invisible musician plucked the sinewy strings. A tea set made of skulls rose from the table.

Bone china.

I chuckled.

Jorgen's eyes narrowed.

"I've just never seen a table set so gracefully," I quickly explained, then looked down before realizing that might be rude. I forced eye contact with Jorgen.

Jorgen picked up the skull pot. "Isn't it interesting how a tea pot represents the pleasures of company?" Jorgen poured steaming red liquid into the tiny bone teacup before me. "I find it terribly lonely down here, especially during teatime. But then I look at this skull pot—oh dear, what was her name?" Jorgen brought one dainty hand to his lips, searching his memory. "Xaria, that was it. I think of lovely Xaria and I'm reminded that I'm not alone, and that company will come along soon." Jorgen set the pot down. His eager eyes darted between the teacup and my mouth.

I picked up the steaming cup and braced myself. "Uh, cheers?" The coppery liquid burned my throat on the way down. I struggled not to spit it out and coughed. "It's… It's nice."

"It's blood," Jorgen replied, his shoulders bouncing with glee.

"Yeah. Yeah, of course it is." I set the teacup back on the table, far away from me.

Jorgen picked up his cup and saucer, and brought the cup to his mouth. "Mmm!" He smacked his lips in a chef's kiss. "Mmm, ooh, absolutely miraculous." The hissing gone, Jorgen had a lovely, articulated tone of voice. With hand gestures that I, again, found mesmerizing, he leaned in and gushed, "Can you taste the sweetness?"

It tasted like a punch in the mouth. Blood filled the crevices in my teeth, and I tried not to run my tongue along them. "It's kind of...salty?" My stomach lurched. I traced the stitches on the skin tablecloth as a distraction.

Movement above Jorgen caught my eye. A spider rappelled from the ceiling. "Ahh! Hello!" Jorgen stretched out his hand, allowing the spider to land on it. Jorgen brought the spider to his ear. "Mhmm, yes?" He nodded. "I'm so sorry, you're right. That was quite impolite of me." Setting the spider on his shoulder, Jorgen reached into his mouth and yanked a tooth from his gums. He ran his tongue along the empty gap. A new tooth grew and filled it. Jorgen turned the extricated tooth upside down. His fingernail grew long and sharp, and he bore into the bone, hollowing it. Jorgen blew bits of dust away before filling the tooth with a drop of blood from the pot. He gave it to the spider, who ascended. With a dismissive flick of the wrist, Jorgen said, "Just Hank," then picked his saucer up again. "Now, what are you hoping to find down here, Nell?"

"Something that belongs to the Queen."

Unphased, Jorgen nodded and sipped his tea. He already knew why I was here. "And how is our enchanting Queen?" An image of the decrepit, too-old crone popped into my head. Jorgen smiled; he knew exactly how she was. "I suppose you know she stole something from me?"

"Your ring."

"The ring didn't matter!" Jorgen slammed his teacup on the table. It shattered, sending blood and bone everywhere. "The stone mattered!" My body tensed at the outburst. Jorgen calmed himself. "Sorry." He twirled his fingers. Drops of blood seeped back into the teacup as it repaired itself.

"What was so special about the stone?"

Jorgen's eyes flared. "It wasn't just any sssstone," he hissed. "I *made* the Screaming Diamond. I squeezed the blood from thousands of women. I crushed it, heated it. Facet by facet, I *made* the Screaming Diamond."

"Wow." I didn't have to fake the awe in my voice. Jorgen's shoulders twitched with pride. "And you called it the Screaming Diamond because—"

"When you look upon the stone, you can hear them." Jorgen's eyes grew frenzied. "The ghosts of those I flayed in its creation." He looked into the distance and put a hand to his heart. "Oh, dear, I miss it."

The screams of the dead would drive anyone mad.

Jorgen continued. "The Queen came to me, a *thief* in the dark. She was handsome, amiable, and meek, and far cleverer than I gave her credit for. She may have lacked power but oh, she was cunning. I shouldn't have underestimated her." He stared at the steps leading from the cavern. "She's the only person to leave here unscathed." A wicked smile curled Jorgen's cheek. "Well, mostly."

"Until today," I said.

Jorgen pulsed his eyebrows. *We'll see.* He pointed to my cup. "Your blood is getting cold." Ugh. Just pretend it's iced coffee. I downed the remaining liquid, shivering as the lukewarm blood slid down my throat. Jorgen continued. "She may have taken my ring, but I took something from her." Jorgen parted his robe, revealing a necklace. Invisible hands lifted the necklace over his head and placed it on the table. It didn't look like much. A pendent with a pressed mauve flower on a simple silver chain. Certainly not fit for a Queen. Jorgen, still listening to my thoughts, replied, "She wasn't a Queen when she robbed me."

"Did she take all your magic?"

Jorgen's lip curled.

Shit. You can't just ask people about their magic.

Jorgen took his cup, brushing my hand. An electrifying vision of slaughter and screams nearly knocked me off my chair.

"I'm sorry!" My mind raced. "It's just, I've heard so many stories of your magnificence."

Jorgen raised his chin and puffed his chest. "Oh well, you know."

274

Jorgen exploded.

"Hhh!" I cringed as bits of flesh blasted in all directions. Skin and viscera transformed into a swirling mass of bats. They chirped and circled me before flying to the ceiling. All at once, they fell to the floor, each transforming into their own Jorgen. Hundreds of them filled the grotto—sitting on piles of loot and waltzing in the background. With a chorus of maniacal cackles, they all drifted and joined into one Jorgen. He sat proudly next to me, sipping his tea.

My mouth opened in awe. "How'd the Queen out-magic you?"

Jorgen's excitement faded. His face was that of a child who'd received 99% on a test, only to come home and have a parent ask what happened to the other 1%. "Are you looking for ideasss?" he hissed.

I was running out of time.

How far would I get if I grabbed the necklace and ran?

The necklace slid to the far side of the table. Jorgen placed his hand over it.

I pushed a hand through my hair, tugging Bowyn's poison covered pin. Before I could lose my nerve—I leapt up and slammed the pin through Jorgen's hand.

My entire body shook as adrenaline coursed through it.

Unbothered, Jorgen admired the diamond inlaid fox. "Oh my, that's lovely." His eyes narrowed, and he pointed to his hand. "Is this poisoned?" Before I could respond, Jorgen bent forward and slid his wrist between his teeth. Bones crunched and snapped between Jorgen's powerful jaws. When he righted himself, blood dribbled from his lips, and more spurted from the stump at his wrist. Slowly, a new hand grew in its place. Jorgen tore the pin from the dead hand and tossed it aside. The disembodied hand flipped over, and nails *click-clacked* against the table as it crawled away. The hand leapt down and disappeared into a murky pool. Jorgen examined a rip in his skin tablecloth, clearly displeased.

"Now that you've gotten that out of your system," Jorgen purred, "maybe we can come to some sort of arrangement?" Again, he placed his hand next to the necklace, toying with the chain. "You see, I've been down in this tomb for quite a long time. I'd very much like to leave."

I didn't like where this was going.

"I will give you the necklace, out of the sheer *goodness* of my heart. I simply want one, tiny, insignificant thing in return."

"I don't have anything."

Idiot. I cursed myself for giving such a thoughtless answer.

"Mmm, so modest." Jorgen replied. "You have two hands, two feet… two eyes." Jorgen paused; his gaze found the ceiling while he thought. "Well, yes, I suppose after that, you don't have much to offer. Hardly worth killing at all, really. Though…" He pointed to the instrument in the background. "My harp could use new strings. I imagine you've got lovely guts. What's your diet like? Do you often have inflammation?"

I felt inflamed right now. Filled with blood, it clawed at the back of my throat. "What do you want from me?" Jorgen poured himself another cup of warm blood and sipped it, savouring my discomfort.

"I want your tongue." He ran his own tongue along his lips.

"…my tongue?"

"Well, your voice."

What kind of sea witch bullshit is this?

Jorgen held up his hand; the necklace floated above it. "Your voice for the necklace." I opened my mouth to respond. Nothing came out. I just sat, frozen.

How did it come to this?

Was any of this real?

Jorgen twirled his fingers. The necklace spun slowly.

What would happen if I said no?

Jorgen's hungry smile grew wider.

He'd eat me. Strip my bones and feed me to the next fool who came down here.

What was Darragh doing now? Was he okay? I recalled the hopeful way he looked at me, the way he pushed his hair behind his ear when he was nervous. He'd saved me, countless times. Now…it was my turn. If I traded my voice, there was a chance, however small, that I could get back to him. I could save him.

Jorgen stopped twirling the necklace. "What will it be?"

"Take it."

"Oh!" Jorgen's brows raised. "Oh, good. That was easier than I thought." He motioned to shake on it. I scooted one hand out from beneath myself, where I'd been sitting on it. Slowly, I shook his hand.

"Ach!" Jorgen's fingers crushed my knuckles. He yanked me forward, pressing his lips on mine. I squirmed, but his other hand had found the back of my neck. Unable to escape, Jorgen sucked the air from my lungs.

Everything went dark.

Drops of water splashed my cheek and I blinked awake. I focused on the wet, rocky ceiling of the grotto. My back ached as I sat up. Jorgen was still at the table, legs crossed leisurely. I tried to ask about the necklace, but only air came out.

My voice was gone.

"Splendid," Jorgen said in a high, feminine voice.

My voice.

Jorgen touched his throat. "Oooh, ahhh. Why I *do* declare." He coughed, stretching his vocal cords. A bloodcurdling shriek left Jorgen's lips. I slammed my hands over my ears.

What's he doing?!

Jorgen shrieked again, a horrible, agonizing screech. I'd never made these sounds before, I hadn't thought myself possible of such anguish. I tried to ask, "What are you doing?" but a garbled choke came out. Climbing to my feet, I backed away.

Jorgen's arm flew out and my legs seized. Jorgen's neck swivelled and his feverish eyes locked on me. Easing to his feet, he said, "You didn't come alone did you, Eleanor?" I struggled against Jorgen's hold, but my feet wouldn't move.

I came down here alone!

Jorgen gave me a condescending look. "That's not what I meant."

What do you mean?

The clanking of metal chains echoed down the stairs. A familiar, rattling voice called out, "Nell?" With great difficulty, I twisted, peering at the steps that led into the grotto.

Surrounded by a grey cloud of smoke, the Cage stood at the base of the stairs. I'd never been so happy to see anyone in my life—

Jorgen chuckled. Excitement twitched his body as a hungry, victorious smile spread from ear to ear.

The Cage was about to kick Jorgen's ass. But, why did he look like a child about to rip open a present? Jorgen spent hundreds of years in this prison, shouldn't he be terrified of the Cage? A creature who creates and destroys personal prisons like its nothing—the breath left my chest.

Oh.

Oh no.

We'd made a devastating mistake.

Chapter Twenty-Four

a merry world, indeed

Jorgen threw his arm sideways, and an incredible force knocked me against the wall. Tiny stars pricked my vision and I struggled to orient myself.

Snap! Jorgen snapped his fingers, and a cloud of smoke enveloped the Cage. The smoke dissipated, exposing Brana, who's mouth fell open in shock. Jorgen clasped his hand into a tight fist and Brana coughed. Clawing her throat, Brana collapsed against the wall. Jorgen grinned and made a seductive, *come hither*, motion. Brana fought the command, grimacing against Jorgen's magic.

Yes, be strong! I begged Brana.

"Aghhh!" Brana climbed to her feet.

Jorgen danced and hopped about, giddy, like some twisted jester. He mimed pulling an invisible rope and Brana stumbled forward. Jorgen's nostrils flared as he inhaled, and an excited quiver ran through his body. Abandoning my voice, Jorgen slipped back into a snake-like cadence.

"I've heard ssstories of you. What isss it they call you?" Brana couldn't reply. Sweat poured down her reddened face as she resisted. Jorgen stroked his chin as he prodded Brana's mind.

With a sharp hiss, Jorgen's eyes narrowed. In a voice hardly more than a whisper, he said, "The Cage." A sly, too-wide grin parted Jorgen's lips. "I knew a relative of yoursss, many, many yearsss ago."

A soft voice called, "Eleanor." I scanned the grotto, but there was no one else here. I swore I heard someone call my name—

"Eleanor," the voice repeated. Paying attention now, I zoned in on the whispers.

The necklace.

It sat abandoned on the table. With urgency, the voiced shouted, "Eleanor!"

Jorgen seemed to have forgotten I was here, or assumed I posed no threat. Inching closer to Brana, he prepared to devour her. "Sssstop ressssissssting me."

I tiptoed over and snatched the necklace. It was mine, after all. I slipped it over my head and tucked it beneath my shirt. I crept behind a pile of robes.

"I can help you get out of here."

I clutched my chest and fell into the robes. A fair-haired girl stood beside me. "Promise to take me with you," she said.

I opened my mouth to speak, only to let out a garbled choke.

"He's been holding me captive," the girl cried. "Please, I just want to get back to my family—"

A spine-chilling shriek pierced the air. Brana used both hands to keep Jorgen's jaws from snapping down on her. Crimson blood trickled down her arms as Jorgen's teeth tore into her flesh.

I concentrated on the girl and thought as loudly as I could.

Fine! We'll take you with us.

The girl pointed to a hefty wooden staff at her feet. I grabbed the staff, and the girl made a motion of snapping it with her leg. I did. The staff broke in half, leaving me with a sharp, deadly point. "As hard as you can, through the belly," the girl instructed. Across the grotto, Jorgen's mouth widened around Brana's neck.

Okay, I—

The girl vanished. I looked around, but she was gone. Tucking the murder-staff behind me, I picked my way around the pile of robes. Brana's eyes rolled back and Jorgen closed in on her throat. Without thinking, I grabbed the pot from the table and threw it.

Thunk!

The pot connected with Jorgen's head. It tumbled and smashed, sending shards of bone everywhere.

Jorgen stilled.

"Xaria."

Slowly, Jorgen's long, serpent-like neck turned on me. His eyes, reptile slits, harboured the animalistic excitement that accompanied a killing frenzy. "How dare you touch my favourite sssskullpot!" Jorgen dropped Brana, and she crumpled into a bloody pile. Like a crocodile gliding along the water, Jorgen prowled forward. He threw his hand out and my body froze. I tested my fingers, wrapped tightly around the staff behind my back. Jorgen kept one hand trained on me, and one hand trained on Brana. His head swayed on his long, extended neck. I kept my mind blank. Except for the fear. That I let through. I couldn't have contained it if I tried.

Jorgen stepped closer, Brana's blood dripping from his teeth. It dribbled onto the cavern floor, its echo interrupted by Brana's laboured breathing.

Jorgen came closer.

Close enough.

I thrust the jagged staff into his stomach.

"*Huffff*!" Jorgen doubled over and sent me sprawling into a pile of torches. Jorgen tore the staff from his belly and tossed it aside. Chest-heaving and bloody, Jorgen shrunk, until he was roughly the size of my palm, and burst into a hundred miniature versions of himself. Each Jorgen screamed and ran in a different direction. The torches dug painfully into my spine, and I struggled to get up. One mini-Jorgen, brandishing a cloak pin, climbed a torch and leapt at my face.

The pin pierced my cheek and stabbed my tongue.

Sonofabitch! I tore the pin out and grabbed at the mini-Jorgen. He ducked and skittered away, laughing. The coppery taste of blood filled my mouth again, my own this time. I chased furiously after the mini-Jorgens. Every time I stomped on one, they disappeared with a *poof.* Each time, the laughing grew louder.

Where are you?!

The girl stepped from behind a pile of shiny goblets. Eyes wide and terrified, she pointed behind me.

My hair brushed my face as hot breath grazed my neck.

On shaky legs, I spun. A belly of scales met me. I followed the snaking neck up to the roof, where Jorgen's face smiled down. A snake-body coiled behind him, tensed and ready to strike.

"You drank my venom, and sssstill, you feel nothing?" I stepped back. Jorgen's neck arched forward, and he hissed, "That wassss a quesssstion!"

I don't know! I thought. *I feel no worse than normal!* I continued backing away. My foot struck something, and it moved. Jorgen's tail slid around my legs.

"Very curioussss." Jorgen's mouth drew closer. "Alasssss, I'm terribly hungry. I'll be eating you now." Jorgen's head swayed side to side as he unhinged his massive jaw. His neck pulled back, preparing to strike. I cringed, readying for pain.

Brana struck first.

She leapt on Jorgen, and two, thick glowing chains appeared. The metal links rattled as the chains slithered around Jorgen's scaly neck. Brana thrust her arms out and the chains snapped taut. Jorgen's head swung around; a fang glanced off Brana's shoulder. "Agh!" she cried but pulled tighter. Jorgen gasped and shrunk, transforming back into a man. His tail released me, and I wasted no time. Grabbing the other half of the staff, I plunged it into his stomach again. Jorgen stopped fighting. Brana did not stop squeezing. "Aghhhh!" Her face contorted. The chains squeezed tighter and tighter.

Pop!

Warm blood splattered my face.

Our ragged breathing filled the cavern.

Jorgen's head fell from his body.

Brana recoiled as thick blood spurted from Jorgen's neck. His headless figure collapsed with a dull *thud*.

Brana collapsed too.

I slumped beside her. Terror and adrenaline coursed through me, and my hands shook violently. I tucked them beneath myself. In stark contrast, Brana sat stone still, her elbows propped on her knees, her head hung between them.

"Are you okay?" I choked. I felt my throat—my voice was back.

Brana glared at me, her face smeared with sweat and Jorgen's blood. "No! No, I'm not okay!" she screamed, despite my proximity.

I winced at the hysteric tone in her voice. "Okay, I had that one coming." I stared at the ground. "Are you ready to get out of h—"

"Give me a moment!"

I scooted to my feet, giving Brana some space. I looked around the chamber. The girl stood beside the pile of torches.

Oh.

Yeah.

The girl gave me a pleasant smile and said, "Good job." I opened my mouth, but the girl put a finger to her lips. "Shhhh." I looked back at Brana, who stared straight at the girl. Straight *through* her. Brana couldn't see her. When I looked back, the girl was gone.

"Alright." Brana offered a hand, and I hauled her up. She took one step and fell to a knee. "Agh!" She clutched her shoulder. Despite applying pressure, the wound bled around her fingers.

"Here." I wrapped my arm around her and helped her to her feet. I steered her to the stairs, but she hesitated.

"Wait." She pointed at Jorgen's body, and we hobbled over. Brana picked up Jorgen's head and gave it to me.

"Take this."

"Uh, I really don't want it."

"Take it!" Brana forced the head on me. Jorgen's face was frozen in a permanent grin. A vein dangled from his neck and wiggled against my arm.

"Ew!" The jaws contracted and tried to bite me. "Oh!" I thrust the head away.

"He's dead. It's just muscle memory," Brana said breathlessly. Dizziness and nausea swept through me. I bent over and wretched. Only blood spilled out. Brana eyed the pool of blood. "Are you alright?"

"I'm fine. It's not mine." Brana gave me a funny look. "Do I really have to take this?" I held the head an arm's length away.

"Yes." Brana took a step and collapsed again. I heaved her up and wrapped her arm around my neck. I walked slow as Brana limped up the stairs.

"Why did you come?" I asked.

"You know, you remind me so much of Pip. You're both so clever, and inventive, and sweet. I was picturing him coming down here…and then I heard you screaming."

"That was Jorgen."

"I know that now," Brana snapped.

"You didn't have to come in."

You could have let me die.

"I know," Brana responded curtly.

"Thank you," I said.

Her response was a pained grimace.

"I can't believe we did it," I said.

"Everyone wanted the ring and the glory of killing the creature for themselves," Brana said.

"Silly, no one ever thought to bring a friend," I replied. Or two. A vision of the ghostly girl tugged at my thoughts.

Brana gave me a sidelong smile. It faded quickly. "When Jorgen had me…all I could think about was Pip, that I'd never come home for him." Warm tears dripped down my arm. I squeezed Brana tighter. I was faintly aware of a third set of footfalls echoing on the stairs behind us. I glanced around and saw no one.

Still, I couldn't shake the feeling that something, or someone, followed us out.

Annwyl and Anval did not greet us as we exited the blood smeared door. Before I could say anything, Brana snapped, "Don't ask." I was disappointed I couldn't return Annwyl's dress, even if it was covered in blood. We climbed out of the basement, and I found a discarded sack to stuff Jorgen's head in. I tied it around my waist.

"Ewww," I whined.

"What?" Brana asked.

"It's leaking." A black stain seeped through the bottom of the sack.

It dripped down my leg and I gagged. Brana rolled her eyes and checked her wounded shoulder. The skin around the gash had turned black, and it continued bleeding freely. I wrapped a piece of fabric around her arm and fretted as the blood immediately stained it crimson. Waving me away, Brana hobbled to the door. "Are you sure you don't want to rest?"

"We can rest on the way," Brana replied. "I don't want to be here when the looters come. Not in my condition."

We left the ruins quickly, walking until Brana collapsed. Pouring sweat, she rubbed her shoulder and groaned.

"You're right," I said. "I think we should stop for the night." Brana protested and struggled to her feet. "It's getting dark. We can barely see." I guided her back to the ground. "I'll get a fire going." Brana's eyelids lulled, and she lay down. I undid the bandage on her shoulder; blood and yellow pus oozed out. Gagging, I tossed the bandage aside and rifled through Brana's bag for water. I doused the wound before re-wrapping it with fabric I'd stuffed in my pockets. Brana moaned and shivered.

She wouldn't survive a three day walk.

I stayed where I could see her while I gathered wood.

"Alyth."

I jumped and threw my hands up to protect myself. The girl from the grotto stood behind me. Clutching my chest, I waited for my heart to calm down. "Sorry," she apologized. "My name is Alyth."

"Why can't Brana see you?"

"When you get me home, I can tell you everything. Please, I wish you no harm." Tears welled along Alyth's eyelashes, and her voice choked. "I *just* want to go home." With her hands together, begging, Alyth certainly didn't *feel* dangerous.

"Where is home?" I asked.

Her shoulders relaxed. "There's a forest between Wilbur and the mountain. My beloved—he's expecting me. I can show you."

"It's okay, you don't have—"

Too late, Alyth grasped my arm. A young man with a neat beard popped into my head. "I must get back to him!"

"Alright! Okay!" I soothed. "You can come with us."

Alyth murmured, "Thank you." I nodded and stooped to grab a stick. Alyth pointed to a tall stalked blue flower with red thorns and said, "That might benefit your friend."

"Oh!" I pounced on the flower. What had Darragh called it? Queensfoil? I stared stupidly at the flower. It was in the *good* garden, right? I glanced at Brana, who was lying alarmingly still, and then back to the flower.

Well, I mean, she'd die anyway, right?

I crammed the flower, stalk and all, into my mouth. "Blegh." I gagged again. It was bitter, like an orange peel. Scurrying back to Brana, I tore the bandage from her arm and spit the paste out. I slathered the wound and re-wrapped it. "Hopefully, this helps." I swirled some water in my mouth and spit. The bitterness lingered. "Yuck." Once I finished collecting wood, I rummaged in Brana's bag for a firestarter. After a few strikes. The fire sputtered to life, illuminating our immediate surroundings.

I froze.

A creature stood at the edge of the light, watching us. I recognized the brown fur, the hooved feet… It was a carnivorous deer, the same creature that chased Darragh and me through the woods when I'd first come to Hiraeth. Wiping sweaty palms along my thighs, I whispered, "Hey little guy—"

The deer opened its mouth, and a screech pierced the darkness. Twigs snapped as two more deer plodded from the trees.

Brana stirred.

Good! These deer-demons wouldn't stand a chance against Brana. She rubbed a knuckle at her eye and struggled to focus on the deer. Climbing drunkenly to her feet, Brana raised her hand…and fainted.

Oh no.

"Invite me in."

Through the flames, Alyth stood between me and the deer.

"W-what?" I stuttered.

"Invite me into your body," Alyth urged. "I can help you." Invisible claws tugged my skin. As if someone were trying to pull me on, like a pair of snug pants.

"No offense, but that is absolutely the *last* thing I'm going to do."

The deer, though wary of the fire at first, slunk closer.

What could I do?

Beside me now, Alyth whispered, "We can work together. I can show you how to use magic, but you *must* let me in." I ignored her. I wished Darragh was here. He'd made easy work of these deer last time—

Wait. I stared at my hand, at Darragh's ring. I'd completely forgotten about it in Jorgen's burrow.

As the deer crept closer, I slid off the ring.

The first deer opened its mouth and leaned back on its hind legs. Like a jumping spider, it prepared to pounce. I tossed the ring into the air and dropped to shield Brana. Heat exploded above, burning my back. "Agh!" I buried myself in Brana's hair, protecting her from the inferno.

The blast faded, and I pulled away from Brana. The first deer lay dead on the ground, its fur singed, and skin charred. The other two lay at the treeline, also dead.

Alyth was nowhere to be seen.

For now.

Brana awoke, ignorant to the surrounding wreckage. "Hm, is it time to eat, then?" I stared back, smoke wafted away from bits of my burned hair. Her brows furrowed as she surveyed the carnage. "It was just a simple fire, Nelli." Brana climbed to her feet and walked away. Her spirits and health seemed to have improved. She collected sticks and muttered, "If you want something done right, just do it yourself."

Chapter Twenty-Five

broken hearts & broken bargains

Elwyn

The Queen's screams woke the mountain.

I didn't get up to check. I happily fell back asleep. Dreams of a life without the Queen, and visions of Darragh, punctured my rest. A loud cough woke me a second time. I rolled over and found a guardian in my room. I'd ordered her to wake me before the sun rose, and I was glad to see the morning light hadn't come through my window yet.

"You can go."

The guardian slipped out. I dressed and took off down the hall, heading to the kitchens. The Truth refused to let anyone cook for her, and I had a feeling she'd be up early today, excited for her new project. I paused in the shadows outside the kitchens, watching for the bright robes. Any minute now, she'd finish breakfast, and head to see Darragh.

My suspicions correct, it wasn't long before the Truth sauntered out. I slunk deeper into the shadows while she passed, and then followed.

"A terrible thing happened," a sickly voice whispered.

Down a side path, the Queen wandered, lost and listless. Her movement, so often smooth and fluid, was disjointed, like some creature possessed. A guardian approached and headed down the hall, hesitating when they saw the Queen. We exchanged glances as the guardian retraced their steps, avoiding the Queen entirely.

Down the hall, the Truth rounded a corner. Scared to lose her, I took one last glance at the Queen and set off. The Truth walked through the mountain, around twists and turns, before entering a door which hadn't been there the night before. When she didn't come out, I crossed my arms and waited.

Hours passed.

I started to nod off.

Creak.

The Truth crept out and I jolted awake. When her footsteps faded, I rushed the door. The Truth hadn't wasted much effort creating this room. Just a stone hole in the mountain. A few candles flickered on a table, a chair, and—

My breath caught. Lying on a slab in the middle of the room was Darragh. The stone was elevated slightly at one end, so that Darragh was in a semi-inclined position. I hurried to his side. He didn't have any physical wounds, but that meant nothing. The Truth didn't need to touch you.

Darragh woke and struggled to focus on me. "What are you doing here?" he asked, as if it were an accusation.

"We're getting out of here, now." I tugged his arm.

Darragh resisted. "No."

"What?" I spit. "What do you mean, no?"

"If Nell comes back and I'm not here, who will protect her?"

I gestured toward him, lying on the rock. "You think you can protect anyone like this?" Darragh turned away. "How do you even know she's coming back?!"

"I don't. I hope she doesn't." Darragh closed his eyes. "But if she does, I can't risk leaving."

"Darragh, you don't understand. Something happened to the Queen; she's in a *foul* mood. I don't know what she'll do to you. I don't know what she'll do to *me* if she finds me here."

"You should leave while you can. There's nothing left for you here."

I have one thing left, I thought miserably.

"The Truth's coming. I can feel her," Darragh muttered. "Get out of here."

"Come with me," I begged.

Darragh shook his head. His refusal spiked an uncontrollable rage within me. "That girl won't come for you!" I pounded my fist on the stone. "You'll die on this table!"

Darragh said nothing.

"Fine! Rot!" I slammed the door on the way out.

My mind raced as I stormed through the halls. What was so special about this girl? What powers could she possess? Somewhere along the way, my anger disappeared. How had this girl bewitched Darragh so thoroughly that he was going to die for her?

I quickened my pace and hoped no one saw me crying.

For Darragh's sake, I wanted the girl to return. But for mine...I don't know what I'd do if I saw her again...

Nell

Shadow Peak loomed in the distance.

"I want to show you something." Brana veered off the path and examined a tree. Shaking her head, she approached another tree. "Aha! This is it." She scanned the area and knelt by a large rock. "Verata."

Beside the rock, the ground split. The split travelled in a sizeable rectangle and the ground fell away. Dirt stairs led down. "It's a secret cache," Brana explained. "If someone needed to hide something and come back for it later, this would be a good place for it." She fixed me with a pointed stare.

"Got it."

"Do you remember the password?"

"Uhhh." I recalled the last minute. "Verada? Veranda? It was a V-word for sure."

An unimpressed Brana repeated, "Verata."

The cache closed.

"Verata, got it."

The cache opened.

"It's a *secret* so, don't say it out loud unless you must. Think the word with the intention of opening the cache, and it will."

"Okay." Brana headed back to the path. "I should really write that down," I muttered.

"What do you mean?"

"Nothing, never mind. So, what happens now?"

"We part ways."

"You're not coming?"

"No." Brana patted her arm. "I need to get this looked at, discreetly. I'll head to the mountain later."

I nodded and kicked the dirt. "I, uh… I couldn't have done any of this without you—"

Brana embraced me in a hug so tight my spine popped in three places. "I can't guarantee we'll be friends next time we meet. Watch out for yourself."

"Thank you for everything."

"Right, off you go then." Brana wiped her cheek and started walking toward town. She called back, "Don't forget to close up when you're done." When Brana was nearly out of sight, she waved. I smiled and waved back.

Once finished in the cache, I closed it. During my short trek to the mountain, my mind wandered to Darragh. I promised myself he was okay, and that this would work. I daydreamed of a future together; perhaps we could travel? I'd always wanted to travel. Could Darragh get on a plane? Getting him a passport would certainly be an endeavor, perhaps more stressful than freeing him from the Queen. Maybe we could go to New Zealand. I bet Darragh would love New Zealand. From what I'd seen in photos, the rugged terrain and mountains looked so much like Hiraeth…

The great hall didn't look much different now than it had for the light ball. Dark and grim, I wondered how many spiders lived in the cracks and crevices. The Queen sat on her throne, spinning a monstrous red gemmed ring around her finger. The Truth and Elwyn stood on either side. I'm not sure who looked more furious about my return, the Queen, or her daughter. Arms crossed, Elwyn's nostrils flared when our eyes met. All around us, the Queen's guardians filled the hall. So many ladies dressed in dark, flowing gowns. They kept their eyes low, only gazing upon the Queen occasionally.

"Against all odds, you've returned," the Queen spit. I winced, as if her words were a spell meant to strike me. "Well? Where is my necklace?"

"I—I don't have it," I mumbled.

"I can't hear you!"

"I've hidden it!"

The Queen's lips parted, and a ripple of shocked whispers travelled through those gathered. A puddle of shadows oozed from the throne as the Queen asked, "Where is it?" I tried to step back but my feet held firm. I wasn't going anywhere.

"Let me see—"

The Queen slammed her palm against the throne and cried, "Speak up!"

"Let me see Darragh first!"

Behind the Queen, Elwyn trembled. She looked like a beautiful, cursed doll—ready to attack at any moment. The Queen's nails scratched the arm of her throne, and her shadows crept closer to my feet. "I could bring you a piece of him," she growled. "I assure you, it will be a piece you miss. Would that suffice?"

"That depends. I'm sure I could break open the necklace and bring you a petal."

The shadows touched the tips of my boots and froze. The Queen stiffened and her nostrils flared. Slowly, her lips parted into a smile. It was creaky and foreign on her face. "Fine," she snarled, "bring him out." The Queen snapped her fingers and the Truth left. When she returned, five guardians escorted Darragh into the hall.

Disheveled hair hung over Darragh's gaunt, dirty cheeks. He stared at the ground while he walked behind the guardians. I wanted to run to him—to ask if he was okay, if they'd hurt him. All I managed to do was squeak, "Darragh?"

Darragh's eyes met mine and a gasp of relief shuddered through him. He shoved his way through the escort and crossed the space between us. I dropped my bag, instinctively opening my arms to him. Darragh clutched the back of my neck and tugged me into a tight embrace. Pressed against his chest, fevered heartbeats hammered my ear. Darragh's breath carried strands of hair along my cheek as he whispered, "Nell."

In a room surrounded by people who would have me killed, I felt safe.

The guardians scrambled after Darragh, and he rounded on them. Keeping me behind him, he backed toward the main entrance. The Queen looked mildly inconvenienced, but Elwyn… She wrung her hands, strangling an imaginary foe.

The guardians stalked forward.

"While I breathe, you won't lay a hand on her," Darragh seethed.

The guardians exchanged glances. The Queen gagged and muttered, "Surely, that won't be much longer."

Darragh flicked his wrist, and the flame from every candle in the chamber flew to him. Tiny orbs of fire surrounded us. A guardian approached and a fiery ball fell upon her. Flames crept up her dark gown and shrill screeches filled the air.

Darragh pushed me and muttered, "Run." I obeyed as Darragh extinguished the flames, plunging the room into darkness.

In a bored tone, the Queen said, "Leave Jan to put herself out. Retrieve them."

Up ahead, the path split. I had no idea where I was going. "Which way—"

"*Your* left," Darragh grunted. I skidded around the corner and Darragh shouted, "That door, at the end!" We ran inside and Darragh slammed the door behind us. We'd run into a closet sized room, empty except for brooms and buckets. A small window let a trickle of light in. Darragh ran to the window, unlatched it, and looked out. Darragh hooked his hands beneath my arms and sat me on the windowsill. "Do you see that ledge out there?" Under the window, a tiny rock ledge wrapped along the rock.

"Yeah."

"Good. You're going out there."

"I'm what?" My body stiffened.

"Climb down and get to Senan's." Darragh shoved me. "Go home."

I splayed my arms on either side of the window, gripping it tight.

"I'm not going without you!"

"Yes!" Darragh struggled to pry my fingers from the window. "You are!"

"No! I'm trading the necklace for our freedom!"

"It's too late!" Darragh continued shoving. "She knows how much you mean to me. The second she has that necklace, you're dead, if not worse."

The door opened across the room. Darragh let go of me and slammed his weight against the door. "Nell, please!" He pointed out the window. "Go!"

"No!" I jumped down. Darragh flung his hand out and I launched through the window. "Agh!" I scrabbled at the rock as I fell. My fingers grasped the ledge, and I narrowly avoided the deathly plummet. Above me, shuffling and grunts rang out. Green flashes exploded from the window like bright fireworks. I swung my legs sideways, trying to pull myself onto the ledge. They fell woefully short. "Ugh!" I tried again. My legs were even farther this time. My arms shook and my fingers started to slip.

How was I supposed to get out of this?

A guardian peeked out the window. She gave me a sarcastic smile and offered a hand.

I stood before the Queen.

Again.

Darragh was gone.

Elwyn's hands clenched and unclenched. Her chest heaved as she looked upon me. "Speaking of escapes," the Queen began drolly, "how did you escape the burrow? No one escapes the creature."

"You did."

The Queen's brows raised, and she half-smiled. While a small part of me thought she admired my petulance, I was quite certain that if I didn't have her necklace, she'd have killed me right there. The stares the guardians gave me when I spoke to the Queen made me uneasy. Like I was a new student, talking back to a teacher they knew I shouldn't be.

There was a reason no one spoke back to her.

I picked up the bag I'd dropped and struggled with the drawstring. The rank odour hit my nose and I gagged. I flipped the bag upside down and Jorgen's head tumbled out. It landed face down on the floor.

"What's this?" the Queen asked, her tone suggesting I was wasting her time.

"Hold on. Just, uh…" I nudged Jorgen's head with my foot. It rolled, and Jorgen's frozen, grinning face greeted the crowd. The mouth contracted, trying to bite, even in death. A chorus of gasps filled the hall. Shock parted the Queen's lips. All around, the guardians stared, wide-eyed and astonished. Whispers rose amongst them…

"She must be powerful."

"How did she do it?"

The Queen stood and a tremor shook the floor. Shadows grew behind her, and suddenly, she was as tall as the ceiling. The Queen's voice thundered through the mountain, "I didn't instruct you to kill him!"

"I didn't have a choice!" I shrunk away.

"Someone helped you!" Hardly recognizable, a hellish demon of smoke and shadows replaced the Queen's weak, gaunt body. "You couldn't have defeated him alone!"

"You said bring you the necklace! I'll give it to you. Just let me have Darragh!"

"I instructed you to go alone! You didn't. Our bargain no longer holds. Tell me where the necklace is!"

"No!"

The Queen huffed as shadows swirled around the hall. Dust and rocks tumbled from the ceiling, nearly crushing guardians who were too slow to get out of the way. The shadow demon loomed above, but I would not falter.

Gradually, the mountain stopped shaking, and the Queen shrunk back to her frail self. She raised her arm and the Truth rose with it. "Take her," the Queen hissed. And to me: "I will ask you again in a few days."

Eager to leave the Queen, I followed the Truth. She brought me to a...holding cell? Just a room carved into the rock, with a stone slab sat in the middle, and one chair next to it. I thought of escape for the briefest moment while examining my surroundings. It was just a room carved into stone, there was no escaping it. I tried the door; a powerful shock shot down my arm and I yanked my hand away.

I sat down on the slab.

The exhaustion from the day hit me full force.

I lay back and waited.

Elwyn

The moment the Queen left the great hall, I fled. The Truth would be busy with that girl for some time. This was my last chance to get Darragh out. I hurried, walking calmly anytime I crossed paths with a guardian. When I came to the room that held Darragh, I glanced over my shoulder and slipped inside. Darragh stood against the slab, his back to me.

"We need to—"

Darragh whirled around and snarled, "Get away from me!" His face was gaunt, his eyes dark as onyx. I backed away until the cold stone pressed my spine. Black flames surrounded Darragh as he skulked forward. "Why do you insist on affection where there is none? I hold no admiration for you, you're pathetic—"

"Stop!" I cried. "Why are you doing this?"

Crow's feet crinkled around Darragh's dark eyes, and he cackled. The flames rushed across the floor and fire climbed the walls. Darragh's laughter filled the room, and unbearable heat choked me. I ran for the door, but it wouldn't open. As the fire consumed Darragh, he shouted, "You should be afraid of me!" Holes burned through Darragh's cheeks, revealing layers of red sinew and teeth—

"Please stop!" I begged.

The crackling fire died.

Darragh's burned bones hit the floor, sending up a cloud of ash and dust. I fell and scooped up the ash, which spilled between my fingers. A low, feminine laugh echoed through the chamber and the ash pulled back together. It grew taller and taller until it became a person.

The Queen.

I leaned on the wall and pulled myself up. "Where is he?" I stammered. The Queen waved, revealing Darragh, unconscious on the stone slab. The Queen floated over and caressed his cheek with one sickly hand.

"Please, stop this!"

The Queen flicked her wrist, and the door blew open. She swung her arm, and a force sent me tumbling out. I struck the rocky wall in the hallway and the door slammed shut. The wind knocked out of me, I struggled to catch my breath.

A firm grip wrapped around my wrist and pulled me to my feet.

"Afternoon!" Ophyr chirped.

I tore my arm away and screamed, "Don't touch me!"

"Or what?" Ophyr slid his fingers under my chin. I jerked away from his touch. He frowned and pointed at the door. "Is he this way, then?"

"Who?" I blanched.

Ophyr gave me a patronizing look. "Your pretty friend." He placed his hand on the door, "I assure you; he won't be so pretty when I'm done."

"Wait," I started. "Would you like to"—my stomach turned—"go for a walk?"

Ophyr took my hand and pulled me close. "I *would* enjoy that." I shivered and did my best not to recoil. "I look forward to a wonderful evening…" Ophyr leaned in, brushing my nose with his. "As soon as I'm finished here."

He let go and pushed through the door.

"No!"

Ophyr reappeared. "Thank you, by the way. I never would have found him, if it weren't for you." He pulled a handful of trinkets from his pocket, analyzed them, and then disappeared.

I slid down the wall and sat on the floor.

I stayed there even after Darragh's screams started.

Chapter Twenty-Six

a deal with a ghost

"Wake up Nell."

I rubbed my eyes and shifted on the stone. "Darragh?"

Beside the slab, Darragh tilted his head and cooed, "Are you alright?"

"Uh, I'm okay, I guess." Darragh's clothes were awful, a bright yellow robe and a giant witch's hat. Instead of his normal hand carved necklaces and earrings, he wore gaudy beads of mismatching colours. "What are you wearing?"

Ignoring my question, Darragh took my hand and intertwined our fingers. "Where'd you leave the necklace?" He smelled pungent and sweet, like fermenting fruit. Nothing like the smoky campfire smell I'd grown so fond of. "Tell me where the necklace is, and we can get out of here—together." Darragh smiled a beautiful, beaming smile.

Darragh's eyes were wrong. They possessed an uncomfortable ferocity—pride and malice seeped through the pupils like venom.

I leaned away. "Where's Darragh?"

A wave rippled across Darragh's face. The veneer faded into the Truth, who shrugged and said, "I thought I'd try the easy way first."

I tried to slide my legs from the slab; I couldn't.

"I can feel there's something different about you." The Truth rapped her knuckles on my skull. "I've tried prying into that little noggin' of yours, and I can't seem to crack it." She crossed her arms. "I know the little, insignificant details of your pathetic life. I know your name is Eleanor. I know you have a friend named Watney, and I know you're very sad." Her lips pouted in mock sadness. "But anything of substance, anything of use to me... It's the darndest thing. I just can't seem to grasp it." The Truth sighed and stared at me. "Fortunately, I have a few more tricks up my sleeve. They don't call me the *Truth* for nothing." The Truth uncrossed her arms. "Sure, you won't tell *me* where the necklace is..." She faded into Darragh. "But what about a lover? You'd be surprised how often this works." Again, she didn't fully shift into Darragh. It looked like him, but I could tell *something* wasn't right.

Maybe some of the Truth's magic was lost on me?

"You know, mind reading isn't as easy as everyone thinks. I can't just pop in there and get what I want. Minds are massive. I wouldn't know where to look." The Truth rolled her eyes, as if that was so painfully obvious. Pointing at me, she said, "You need to lead me to the answers. And mind reading doesn't equate lie detection. People believe their own lies all the time. I could ask you where the necklace is, and you could picture some random location. Doesn't mean it's there, doesn't mean it's the truth. It's art, a puzzle of pieces you must put together. What you're thinking, what you're telling me, what you're *not* telling me—"

The Truth liked to talk an awful lot.

Catching my wandering eyes, the Truth's next sentence came out sharp. "But my name isn't the Queen's Options, I'm the Queen's Truth, and I will get it. I can't just read thoughts—I can put them there as well. I make people see what I want them to see." A cruel smile twinged her cheek. "I make them feel what I want them to feel. Five minutes with me and I'll have you reliving the worst pain of your life, over and over."

Jokes on you. I relive that every night.

A tingle radiated up my fingers, but nothing more. Truth-Darragh's face contorted with rage. "Why don't you scream? Does it not hurt?"

"Oh! I mean, ah!" I screamed weakly and confusedly. A small glimmer of satisfaction flitted across the Truth's face. I faked another scream, and again, she smiled.

"Where's the necklace?" the Truth snapped.

"Where's Darragh?" I cringed in mock pain.

The Truth's face contorted with effort; I made a spectacle and screamed louder. We continued back and forth for hours. Sweat coated the Truth's upper lip as she focused everything she had on me. It started to hurt…a little. To be honest, I was more bored than anything else.

Should I just tell her so we can stop?

The Truth chattered on, but my attention was spent. I zoned out and a look of satisfaction crossed the Truth's face. Perhaps she thought the pain too much for me to bear. Truthfully, I'd nearly dozed off. My eyes closed as I relaxed against the stone slab.

I wonder if Brana made it back.

"What's this?" I opened my eyes and shifted my gaze lower. Brana sat on the stool beside me. The Truth looked down at her new body. "Hm? *Who's* this?" Her eyes snapped open. "No!" She covered her mouth and turned back into herself.

The Truth's lips mouthed one silent word.

Cage.

The door to the room flew open.

The hulking, black-robed figure of the Cage ducked in. The Truth didn't cower as the Cage's dark shadow eclipsed her. Instead, she smiled into the depthless hood.

"The Queen has summoned you," the Cage rattled.

"Why didn't I feel her call?" the Truth asked, examining her nail.

"Perhaps you were too focused on your task." The Cage waved one boney hand in my direction. "Have you learned anything from the girl?"

"Oh, yes." The Truth rose and grinned. "It seems…" She craned her neck toward the Cage. "That not everyone is who they say they are."

The door closed behind the Truth, and a film of smoke enveloped the Cage. A red-faced Brana rushed over.

"She knows," I blurted.

"I gathered that much, my dear." Brana helped me down. "I've freed Darragh. He's waiting downstairs."

"You did?!"

Brana nodded quickly, then opened the door and looked down the hall. A layer of smoke swept up and cocooned her. "Follow me." The Cage left the room, and I followed as its captive. We hurried through the mountain. More than one guardian gave me a sidelong glance, but they scurried off when the Cage looked their way. "Brace yourself," the Cage rattled. It opened a door and ushered me in.

No bigger than a closet, there was barely room for me and the Cage. My boot kicked something.

Darragh.

He leaned against the wall, eyes closed and resting. One arm wrapped his stomach, his shirt was crusty with blood. I knelt beside Darragh, and nearly cried out. Two fingers were absent from his left hand. Where his pinky and ring finger should have been, only bloody stumps remained.

"The Truth did this?" I hovered over Darragh, scared to touch him.

The Cage transformed into Brana, who followed my gaze to Darragh's hand. "It was someone much more wicked. The boy's lucky to be alive." Brana knelt. "He hasn't seen the sun in many days. He's very weak." I brushed stringy, sweat-soaked hair from Darragh's face. One of his eyes was swollen and charred beyond recognition.

Darragh roused. I don't know how he found the strength, but he smiled when he saw me. "Are you alright?" he croaked.

I choked back an uncomfortable laugh. "I'm perfectly fine. How are you?"

Darragh made a thumbs up with his good hand, and a weak flame erupted from his thumb like a lighter. He grimaced.

The flame died.

"I begged you wouldn't come back." Darragh's eyes fluttered. "Though I hoped you would."

I chewed my lip and shot Brana a wary look.

"If you want him to survive," she whispered, "you need to get him out of here *right* now."

I glanced at Darragh's legs. "Can you walk?" Darragh nodded. I slipped my arm around his back and lifted. Darragh cried out as he straightened his stomach. "I've got you," I murmured, gripping Darragh tighter.

"I can get you out of here," Brana said. "You can't go to his home."

"We'll go to mine," I replied.

The smoke consumed Brana, and she became the Cage one last time. It opened the door and looked both ways before nodding at us to follow. We shuffled quickly through the halls. The Cage covered us with their cloak every time a guardian drew near. After what seemed like an eternity, we entered the chamber that housed the touching stones to escape the mountain. Two guardians stood on duty. One of them opened her mouth—the Cage waved and they both vanished.

"Won't they report you to the Queen?" I asked.

"If they ever were to reappear, they might."

I winced.

"Besides, I imagine the Truth has told the Queen all about me by now."

Darragh and I shuffled to the stones. Wind whipped us as they sparked to life. The Cage remained on the far side of the chamber. "What are you doing?" I called. "Let's go."

"I can't come with you; the Queen will just call me back."

"What about Pip?"

"When I don't come home, my mother will flee."

"No! You can't—"

Footsteps sounded down the hall.

"Get out of here, you fool!" the Cage hissed.

The mountain wall faded, and the Cage blurred. Through the swirling wind, I saw the Truth enter the chamber. As Darragh and I escaped, the Truth's shrill voice screamed, "Traitor!"

Our feet hit the ground at the base of the mountain. The guardians who watched the entrance were gone. Brana must have gotten them too. Above us, the sky was grey, and a light trickle of rain kissed our skin.

"Frig!"

Darragh needed sunlight.

Just ahead, the path wound through a forest. If we survived long enough to get there, we'd have some cover. Darragh's body was heavy against mine, and I struggled to walk straight as he swayed.

We reached the tree line and I looked for the rock Brana had showed me earlier.

There!

Verata!

The ground shifted and molded into a staircase. Darragh and I eased onto the first step when a lighting-crack sounded from the mountain. The Truth and several guardians pursued us. I led Darragh down the remaining stairs and helped him to the ground. I found the satchel I'd hidden, pulled out the Queen's necklace, and yanked it over my head.

Darragh's jaw dropped. He slurred, "You brought that *here*?"

"I'm sorry. I didn't have time to pop over to your cottage on the way back. How's your hand, by the way?" Darragh's mouth snapped shut. The shadows in the cache shifted as Alyth crept forth. I watched Darragh, gaging his reaction.

Nothing.

He couldn't see her either.

I prepared for my next move. Darragh wasn't going to like this bit. I bolted up the stairs and stepped outside. *Verata!* Darragh's shocked eyes met mine as the stairs folded above him.

"Hey!" A guardian shouted, closer than I'd anticipated. Legs and arms pumping, I sprinted from the cache. As I ran, Alyth appeared in the woods beside me every few feet, offering words of encouragement.

"If you plan to outrun them—" Her voice faded as I ran past her. She reappeared ahead. "I've surely underestimated your stupidity."

"What would you have me do?" I dodged trees and leapt over underbrush.

"We can fight them, you and I." Her voice faded.

"How?"

She reappeared. "Open your mind. Trust me."

The distance between trees increased, until they fell away completely. I slowed my pace and skidded to a stop.

Oh no.

A sheer cliff met my feet. I peered over the edge—

"Guhhh." I shivered and stepped away. It was a two-hundred-foot drop to the dry creek bed below.

"There!" a shout rang out behind me, and I faced my pursuers. There were five in total; four guardians, headed by the Truth.

"Invite me in," Alyth whispered urgently.

I didn't have a choice.

I closed my eyes and cleared my mind.

I pictured a clean, white expanse. The white was broken only by the crisp lines of a door.

Knock-knock-knock.

The door swung open, Alyth stood in the frame. Demure and innocent, she waited.

"Please, come in."

Alyth grinned as she crossed the threshold. She offered a soft, delicate hand and asked, "May I?"

"Yes."

Alyth's grip was ironclad as she drew me to her chest. We clashed together—there was a touch of madness behind her eyes as she held my gaze. Alyth threw her head back and laughed.

Regret rooted in my belly as the laughter washed over me.

Alyth faded.

She became a part of me.

I opened my eyes.

Energy pulsed from my chest. It shot down my arms and burned my fingertips. Awestruck, I stared at my hands. I half expected to see tiny sparks leaping between my fingers.

"The shadows." Alyth pointed to the trees. I raised my arms, mimicking what I'd seen Hiraethians do. I could *feel* the shadows, like each one was connected to my fingers by tiny strings. I yanked—the shadows came loose and streaked along the ground. They shot up my legs and surrounded my hands in a swirling cloud of darkness. Alyth said, "Force them back." I packed the shadows until they formed a thick, dark mass. I wound up and tossed the dark orb like a softball. It arced through the air and landed two feet in front of us. Alyth looked on forlornly. "We're doomed."

Our attackers, unsure of what I might do, approached cautiously. I called on more shadows, and Alyth's eyes darted between me and the Truth. "You're casting magic like a boy! You need to mean it." The power shooting through me was exhilarating…and terrifying. My arms shook as I focused on the Truth, willing every ounce of power in her direction. A black disc exploded from me so forcefully it propelled my hand back and I knocked myself in the nose.

"Agh!" I stumbled back, teetering on the edge of the cliff. Blood trickled from my nostril, I smeared it with the back of my hand.

"Stop. Stop. Stop," Alyth repeated. "You're going to lose an eye." She planted her legs beside me and held her hand out. "Hold your hand *away* from your face! Flex your arm, keep it steady, control the power. No short bursts!" Her hand gestures were desperate and animated, like a frantic football coach. "Focus on one person at a time and *push* them back."

Concentrating on the Truth, I planted my feet and locked my elbow. I took a deep breath and envisioned the attack. Shadows shot from my fingertips and surrounded the guardian *beside* the Truth.

Ah well. Close enough, I guess.

It took great effort, like pushing a large cabinet, but the guardian slowed. I braced my arm and continued to push. Her advancing stopped altogether. She struggled, but I kept pushing.

"Agh!" I threw everything I had at the guardian. As if struck by a bus, the guardian flew back into the trees. The remaining guardians and the Truth stared, mouths open. "Ha!" I blurted out a shocked laugh.

They broke into a sprint.

"Oh. Oh no."

"Again!" Alyth cried.

I panicked and sent all the shadows at once. A thin veil spread among the remaining attackers. "Focus on one target!" Alyth shouted, backing away. I ignored her. They were too close now. I didn't have time to choose one target, but the force of everyone pushing against me was too much. My feet slid closer to the cliff. I risked a glance over my shoulder.

The Truth saw her opportunity. She broke through the shadows and yanked the necklace from my throat. "Ah-ha!" she cried. "You're coming with—"

The pendant slid from the chain. I snatched it from the air before it tumbled over the edge. The remaining guardians scrambled for the pendant. One of them bumped into another, who bumped me.

My arms windmilled as I tried to regain my balance.

I fell.

Clouds of shadow cocooned me, they cushioned my impact when I hit the first rocky shelf. I bounced and continued plummeting. The second impact knocked the pendant from my grasp. The shadows disappeared, and I scrabbled at the edge of the rock. My momentum slowed, but I kept sliding. The skin on my forearms tore as I grabbed at branches and twigs jutting from the deposits of soil littering the rock. My legs hit air, and I slipped over one final edge.

I dropped into a small crevice at the base of the ravine. My body slammed into the ground, but I'd slowed myself enough that the fall didn't kill me. I leapt up before the pain and stiffness took hold. My chest heaved as I examined the crevice holding me captive. Only a few meters long, a large opening ran the length of the crevice. Though the edge was only a few feet above my head, years of rainfall had smoothed the walls. I took a few steps back and ran at the edge. I slid back down.

I tried again. This time, I jumped when I started to slide. My palms slapped against the wall, a foot below the rim.

I sat down to rest, leaning against the cool, damp rock. A memory nagged me. Watney caught a mouse one day, and rather than kill it, he'd dropped it in the bathtub. When I pulled the curtain back to shower, I found the poor thing trying to climb the smooth walls. The mouse slid back down. Every *single* time. He had probably been trying to escape for hours. If it weren't for me scooping him up in a box and releasing him, he would have died in there.

The story sank in.

There was no one to help me. No way out. I rested my forehead against my forearms.

I'm going to die here.

I thought about Darragh, alone in the cache where I left him.

Will he suffocate or starve first?

I started to cry. Quiet tears initially, which turned into ugly, heaving sobs. Gravel crunched above and I covered my mouth. Did the Truth follow me down here? I leaned against the rock, making myself small. I begged she wouldn't peer over the edge.

"Nell, where are you?" Darragh's voice croaked. A sob of relief shuddered through me—I froze.

Was it a trap?

"It's not a trap," Darragh called. "Are you hurt?"

"That sounds like something someone would say if it was a trap," I yelled. The crunch of stones quickened and Darragh's dirt smeared face appeared. A combination of a sob and a laugh sputtered out of me.

Darragh's voice was hoarse and breathy. "I'm going to find something to pull you out. Hold on." He disappeared.

Crunching gravel announced Darragh's return. A vine fell beside me. I tested its strength; Darragh grunted, but it held. Tying the vine around my midsection, I leaned back and climbed out. As I crested the ridge, I realized Darragh had nothing to tie the vine to. He'd wrapped it around his midsection too. Fresh blood oozed around the vine where it squeezed his stomach.

"Why'd you do that?" I scolded, running to him. I untied the vine and eased him to the ground. Darragh swayed and struggled to stay upright. "How do we fix you?"

"I need to rest," Darragh replied, with barely enough breath to utter it. A grimy bandage wrapped Darragh's head, covering his eye. Once Darragh caught his breath, he turned one lovely, olive eye on me. I couldn't even imagine how terrible I looked. Dirty, and eyes puffy from bawling. We'd come so close to death just now. I bit my lip and looked away as fresh tears welled again. Darragh struggled to his feet and pulled me tight against his chest. The gentle smokiness washed over me, and I knew.

I knew it was him.

"I'm here now," Darragh whispered. "I've got you."

A small rock tumbled down the cliff face. It clanked all the way to the bottom of the ravine. "We need to move." Darragh pointed ahead. "The cliff curves around over there. There's a path. That's how I got down." I kept Darragh's arm around me as we trudged out. I told him it was comforting. But really, I think we both knew I was supporting more than my own weight.

"How'd you get out of the cache?"

Darragh raised his good hand. "Dug."

"I thought some sort of enchantment would prevent that."

"Whoever built the cache wanted to keep people out, not in. They were smugglers." Darragh glared. "Not psychopaths."

"We don't have to talk about it now," I said quickly. Darragh grunted in response. Tendrils of sunshine peeked through the clouds, and an object twinkled in the dirt ahead.

The pendant!

"Ah-ha!" I cried, scooping it up as we walked by.

"You *lost* it?" Darragh gasped.

"I *dropped* it, when I was pushed off a *cliff*." I slid the pendant in my pocket.

We came to the path, but Darragh hesitated and whispered, "We're being followed."

"What?" I straightened and scanned the area.

"Keep walking," Darragh grimaced. "There's a waterfall ahead. If we're quick, we can hide and hope they pass." We began our ascent, heading toward the sound of crashing water.

Every few steps, I glanced behind. "I don't see anyone."

"I can feel her."

We arrived at the waterfall; the rushing water cut down the right side of the path and down the ravine. While the main path continued up and out, a smaller one branched off to a ledge that ran behind the waterfall. I stepped onto the ledge, but Darragh pulled me back. "I'll go first." He checked behind us again. When he was sure it was clear, he disappeared through the veil of water. After a moment, his hand appeared. I took it and held my breath as freezing water cascaded over me. I hit air and gasped, already shivering. The ledge was only a foot wide; it was a snug fit in here. Darragh pulled me in front of him so that I faced the rock. His body shielded me from behind.

Is he protecting me from the water, or whatever's following us?

The waterfall was deafening. I rested my forehead against the cold rock and shivered. Darragh pressed against my back, warming me and the surrounding rock. Intoxicating smokiness filled the small space. I struggled to focus on anything but Darragh's body—tried to ignore the gentle breath that brushed my ear and sent shivers through me... The water crashing around us quieted. I glanced up, confirming it still flowed. I looked over my shoulder, up at Darragh.

"Is this one of your tricks?"

Darragh tugged my arm, and I carefully faced him. He looked down at me, his face grave. "What you did back there was idiotic."

"You couldn't outrun them." I gulped. "I could."

"It was very brave."

I ignored him. "Look what they did to you. What would they have done if they caught you again?" I stopped talking. "Did you say I was brave?"

Darragh unwrapped the bandage covering his eye. It was dirty...but healed. The cascading water washed away most of the grime, sweat and blood. Darragh's hair fell in dark, wet ringlets around his face, and stray droplets streamed down his throat. "Thank you," Darragh murmured. His gaze dropped to my lips and my pulse quickened. He brought his hand to rest under my chin and tilted my head. "May I?"

I blinked quickly and nodded. Darragh closed his eyes and softly pressed his lips to mine. His heart hammered his chest; I felt every beat as if it were my own. When he pulled away, I nearly cried out.

Don't go.

Darragh rested his forehead against mine. Eyes still closed, he whispered, "Thank you," again. Despite the freezing water, an exhilarating warmth coursed through me.

Happiness.

My wonderful, obnoxious smile faded when I glimpsed the blood stain on Darragh's shirt. A stark reminder of our situation. Worry curbed the warmth in my belly. "What do we do about that?" Darragh lifted his shirt. An angry red burn marred his stomach. Even as I watched, the burn slowly shrunk.

"I'm working on it." Darragh dropped his shirt back into place. "I'll be vulnerable until it's healed." He held up his hand, wiggling the bloody nubs of his fingers. "These are going to take a while. We'll have to have to be *very* careful for the next few days."

"We need to go back to Earth," I said. "We're not safe here." Darragh didn't say anything. "It doesn't have to be permanent, but it's safer for now."

Darragh deliberated and sighed. "You're right."

"Do they know how you travel back and forth? Do they know about Senan?"

"I don't know. I don't think so."

"How long will it take us to get there?"

"We should reach my cottage by nightfall. If we bypass it and walk through the night, we could be to Senan by mid-morning, given we aren't waylaid."

"That's what we'll do then."

"The risk will be great. The Queen's guardians are looking for us, and even people that aren't looking for us..." Darragh's Adam's apple bobbed. "Nell, if anyone finds out I don't have magic... I've upset many people." Darragh tucked a wet strand behind his ear. "We can avoid the road for most of the journey, stay hidden in the wood, but..." Darragh rubbed his neck. "The wood isn't exactly safe either."

My gaze fell to his lips once more. "We'll be careful."

"Our pursuer has passed." Darragh pulled away. "We should go."

Chapter Twenty-Seven

the price of power

"There's no other way?"

Darragh and I stood amongst the trees, off the main route that led to the village. We stared at the single bridge that serviced the path. A solitary guardian stood in our way. "There's no other way," Darragh replied bitterly. "We must cross."

"Should we wait until it's dark?"

"We can't afford to wait." Darragh squinted at the guardian. "I know her. She'll recognize me." Darragh ran a hand through his hair and paced.

"What if I distracted her and you crossed?" I suggested.

"No."

"Listen, she won't recognize me, right? I'll walk back a bit and make a big ruckus. When she comes to investigate, you sneak over. I'll wait until she leaves, then hop on the path and use the bridge like nothing happened."

Darragh crossed his arms and scrunched his nose.

"We don't have any other options!" Before Darragh could argue, I headed back the way we'd come. "I'll see you on the other side." When the bridge was out of sight, I cupped my hands around my mouth and let out a loud, "CAW!" I walked farther and did it again. Tiptoeing into the wood, I hid behind a tree and waited. Sure enough, the guardian walked up the path. Darragh better not piss away the opportunity. Finding nothing, the guardian gave up. I doubled back even farther and hopped back on the path.

Walk normal, I instructed myself.

Do I have a guilty walk?

The bridge and the guardian came into view.

Don't be weird.

"Howdy!" I shouted. The guardian narrowed her eyes. I waved obnoxiously and pointed at the bridge. "I'm just gonna scooch by."

"Of course."

I took a step—

"Of course, I'll need to ask you some questions first."

Shit.

"What's your name?"

"Uhhh…" All names left my mind. "Underhill?" I asked. The guardian reminded me of border security. I clasped my hands together; they were slippery with sweat. Even when I hadn't done anything wrong, border security made me nervous. The problem was, in this case, depending on who you asked, I *had* done something wrong.

"Well?" she pressed.

Shit.

She'd said something, and I'd missed it entirely. I swallowed hard, my mouth suddenly parched. "Uh, could you say that again?"

"Where are you travelling from?"

My scumbag brain couldn't think of anything, so I told her the truth. "Uh Peak, Shadow Peak, big, uh…big mountain." I pointed over my shoulder.

Why's it so hot?

"Oh?" The guardian cocked her head. "What was your business there?"

I fanned my face. "Uhhhh…"

"Tamsyn?"

Tamsyn whirled and raised her hands. Darragh stood behind her. He'd approached silently, his palms raised in peace. Darragh smiled, a broad, genuine smile that lit his eyes. "We mean you no harm." Darragh's charm was undeniable, and he focused all of it on Tamsyn. It reminded me of the way he'd been when we first met in the café. A surprising, but powerful twang of jealousy forced me to look away.

Tamsyn wasn't fooled. "Don't move Darragh."

Darragh spoke in a calm, soothing voice as he approached. "Tamsyn, please. Let us pass."

Tamsyn stretched her arm out. "I have to take you back."

"Remember when I helped your father?" Darragh continued advancing, hands raised. "I asked for nothing in return."

"She'll kill me if she finds out I helped you."

Getting nowhere, Darragh changed tactics. His arms fell to his sides, and he hooked a thumb in his pocket. "Are you really going to stop me, Tamsyn?" Darragh gave her a lopsided, cocky grin. "I'm much stronger than you."

Tamsyn jutted her chin at Darragh's mangled hand. "Not today you aren't—"

Darragh struck. One quick punch. Tamsyn fell and Darragh scrambled to catch her before she hit the ground. I grabbed her legs. "Nice punch," I said, hauling Tamsyn up.

"It didn't feel nice," Darragh muttered. Together, we dragged Tamsyn into the wood. Darragh knelt beside her. She sported a welt, a precursor to a nasty black eye. Darragh held her cheeks. He grunted, and the redness around her eye faded.

"Do you have the energy for that?" I asked.

"She's a good person," Darragh mumbled. Impatience needled me, and I glanced around. Darragh stood and brushed off his palms. "She'll be fine when she wakes up." As we walked out of the wood, he was almost smug when he said, "Did you see? I didn't kill anyone that time."

"It's almost like you never had to."

Darragh shot me a glare which suggested a reconsideration of his anti-murder oath. We walked right over the bridge. It was easy.

Too easy.

"Don't you think it's weird that they only posted one person?" I asked.

"Maybe they're still regrouping back at the mountain—"

Darragh put his arm in front of me. One by one, ladies dressed in black stepped from the trees ahead. Darragh and I watched, frozen, as twenty guardians gathered on the path. I slid my hand into my pocket, and my fingers curled around the pendant.

"Do you remember where Bowyn lives?" Darragh spoke quickly.

"Yeah, why?"

Darragh threw up his arms and called out, "I'll come with you. Let my companion go and I'll walk back myself." Darragh knelt and put his hands behind his head. To me he said, "Bowyn will help you get back to Earth."

"We both go back, or neither of us go back."

"They'll kill you." Darragh gave me a frustrated sideways glance.

Like a ghost, Alyth crept from the wood and stood beside me. "They can try."

A guardian stepped to the front of the pack. A black robe slit to her waist showed thigh high black boots. "Darragh Mitalrrythin, you have been accused of ferrying an individual from Earth. You will be tried before the Queen." Her robes caught in the wind and billowed behind her as she raised her arms. She grimaced, perhaps rejecting the foul words about to leave her mouth. "All those who accompany you shall be executed—on-site."

"No!" Darragh pushed to his feet.

He wasn't quick enough.

The guardian swung her arm and a dagger of ice hurtled at me. I didn't have time to think, but Alyth was ready. My shadow peeled itself from the ground and leapt in front of me. The dagger exploded inches from my nose and shards of ice blew out like snow. They floated lazily to the ground in front of twenty bewildered guardians.

"I don't want to kill anyone," I whispered.

Darragh's face turned from jaw-dropped shock to suspicion.

"That makes two of us," Alyth replied. "Call to the shadows. They will help you." All around us, long shadows stained the ground. I closed my eyes and imagined the shadows tearing themselves free. In my mind, they grew into demons, with bent legs and upside-down heads. I opened my eyes—and they were there. Skittering between trunks, the demons rushed forward like a wave of spiders. Screams erupted as the shadows surrounded the guardians. A pulse of energy flared from a tiny woman, pushing the demons back.

It did not stop them.

They surged and overtook the guardians.

Chaos broke out as guardians used all manner of magic to fend off the assault. The demons dodged attacks like insects avoiding a boot. They scurried about and pounced on the women, concealing them in dark cocoons.

"I admire your creativity," Alyth said, watching a demon grow wings and drag a woman into the sky. "I never could have pulled this off on my own."

Magic shrapnel flew by me, grazing my face. "Agh!" I touched my cheek and my fingers came back bloody.

321

"You should run," Alyth suggested.

Right.

I reached for Darragh—

A guardian held him by the throat. Using his body as a shield, the guardian pressed a shard of ice to Darragh's neck. "Call off the attack or he dies," she screamed. I recognized her voice; the lady who'd addressed us. The one who nearly killed me. Darragh winced as the ice dug into his flesh. A drop of blood trickled down his neck.

All around, my shadow demons fell flat. I swung my arm, and the shadows shot across the dirt like lightning, converging on the woman all at once.

CRACK!

The guardian crumpled, dragging Darragh with her. Darragh scrambled to his feet. The guardian did not. Darragh grabbed me and ran, but I was slow to follow.

"Is—is she dead?"

"It's not the time!" Darragh dragged me after him. My focus waned and the shadow demons fell back. A bolt of energy, like a firework, whizzed by us as we retreated. I called to the demons. They flew after us and burst, concealing our departure in darkness.

Confident we'd outrun our pursuers, Darragh and I slowed to a brisk walk. "That's the second person I've killed," I muttered.

"She was still alive," Darragh said. I looked at him, but he wouldn't meet my eyes. She was absolutely *not* still alive. "Besides," Darragh continued, "she would have killed you." I didn't say anything. "She would have killed me." Darragh grazed my hand; an appreciative smile quirked his lip. As quickly as the smile came, it vanished. "How'd you do it?"

"How'd I do what?"

"Nell." Darragh made a *come-on* face. "Magic."

"Oh." Movement in the woods cut me off before I could say more. Alyth stalked amongst the trees, paying close attention to us. Darragh gave no indication of Alyth's presence; he still couldn't see her. "I—"

"Don't!" Alyth interrupted. She walked beside me now, between me and Darragh.

"I—"

"No!" Alyth hissed. "You cannot tell him about me." Irritated, I scowled. Behind Alyth, Darragh squinted.

Why not?

"I'm sorry, but I can't let you tell him. Lie. Say it just happened."

I'm not lying to him!

I opened my mouth. Alyth reached out and grazed my neck. An unseen fabric slid down my throat and choked me. Staring at Alyth incredulously, I tried to tell Darragh, but nothing came out. I doubled over and choked. Unable to breathe, I collapsed and clutched my throat.

"What's happening?!" Darragh knelt and scanned my face.

"I'm sorry." Alyth crossed her arms. "I can't let you tell him."

Shadows seeped from the corners of my mouth as I choked. Darragh froze. "Oh Nell," he whispered, "what did you do?" I coughed again, knocking tears loose. "Okay stop. Sh. Sh. Sh. I know, I know." A crushing understanding came over Darragh. He sat behind me and held me. "It's okay." He squeezed my hand and rocked me back and forth. "Focus on my voice, breathe." He inhaled, and I did the same. "Whatever happened, we'll figure it out. You don't have to tell me right now. Just breathe."

His voice was strong.

But his hand trembled in mine.

Wilbur loomed in the distance. "When we get to town," Darragh started, "you'll go through, stick to the outer roads. I'll go around and meet you on the other side."

"We're not splitting up."

Darragh, surprised by my tone, backtracked. "It's safer for you to go through town."

"You couldn't light a candle right now. It's safer for us *both* to go through town."

"I can't."

"You can't even walk through it?"

Darragh's jaw twitched. "They hold no compassion for me there. I will *not* risk us both."

"Either we both go through, or we both go around. It's your choice, but I'm not splitting up." Darragh stopped walking and stared at me. Hungry and tired, I could do without Darragh's stupid faces. "That's compromise," I snapped. "Maybe you've lived alone in the woods too long, but that's what we call this."

Darragh's mouth fell open in shocked fury. "You know nothing of compromise!"

I resisted the urge to scream back. Yelling at each other in the middle of the street would just draw attention. "My vote is we go through town. You keep your head down, and we avoid the main street." I started walking again. "Maybe we'll get lucky."

"Look at me!" Darragh threw his arms out, his clothes covered in dirt and dried blood. "People will notice!"

"Okay, fine! We go around!"

"That's even worse! Agh!" Darragh tugged his hands through his hair, clasping it in a tight clump at the back of his head. He stared at the ground with his brows furrowed.

"I can't read your mind. Think out loud, please."

"If we go around, I can't protect us from the creatures in the woods. If we go through the town, most people will *probably* avoid me." Darragh rubbed his palms against his face. "If they find out I'm powerless, we're dead."

I wanted to go through town, so I didn't point out that I could protect us from anything in the woods. "Going through town is the safer option," I said.

Darragh dropped his arms, defeated. "Fine."

As dusk fell, the sun peeked through the clouds, shining through the grain and grasses that surrounded Wilbur. The grains swayed in the breeze, a golden wave around us. Up ahead, the tall, crooked buildings of Wilbur loomed. Since our decision to go through town, Darragh was awfully quiet. This wasn't out of the ordinary—he wasn't a talker—but usually, when I asked questions, Darragh gave me thorough answers, or answers that at least indicated he'd listened. But now, any attempt I made at conversation was met with a grunt, or a non-committal answer that didn't really make any sense.

"The sun feels nice," I said.

"Mhm."

"Are you feeling any better?"

"I should have brought my veria seedlings in."

"What?"

Darragh lowered his voice and babbled some nonsense I couldn't hear.

His physical demeanor changed too. Out in the wild, Darragh was sure of his movement; he walked with a graceful ease. Each step he took was confident, purposeful. But now, he kept tripping. Every time he stumbled, his head snapped back to see what he'd tripped on, in a sort of furious surprise. Despite looking straight at the rocks strewn about the path, Darragh didn't see them.

His mind was far away.

We passed the first row of buildings. Darragh and I pointed to a cobbled road on our right…the direction that avoided Darragh's burned home. We hadn't gone far before Darragh slowed. In the street, two girls and a small boy tossed a ball back and forth. One of the girls waved, and the ball went where she commanded. The boy chased the ball and grabbed it. He wound up and threw it back. Darragh stopped walking. He looked around timidly, like a dog expecting a kick.

"Come on," I urged, pulling Darragh behind me. We passed the children and I smiled. The tallest of the girls waved and sent the ball flying. The little boy leapt to catch it, but the ball soared over his head. It arced through the air, straight to Darragh, who caught it. He stilled as the little boy ran up to him.

"Nice catch. I have to use my hands too." The little boy flailed his arms around. "I'm not good like Wynnie and Marn." Darragh handed over the ball. "Thanks!"

"Bhaltair!"

Bhaltair jumped and dropped the ball. "Wyn! Marn! Get in here!" The children scampered over to a man standing in a doorway. They gathered around the man, who knelt and whispered to them.

Darragh nudged me on. "Let's go."

The man wrapped his arms around his children, who all wore frowns. Bhaltair's hateful scowl followed us as we walked on. An elderly woman headed in our direction, and Darragh stepped behind me so we could walk single file. As the woman approached, she gave me a warm smile.

"Hello, my child."

"Hello." I returned the smile. Her milky eyes travelled from me to Darragh. She spat and quickened her pace. I chased her. "Hey now!"

"Don't." Darragh grabbed my arm.

I pushed my sleeves up. "No! I'm going to—"

"Let's go." Darragh pulled me away.

The old woman stood in front of a house, whispering to another woman. As they glowered after us, I shook my head in disgust. Darragh walked quickly now, and I was thankful to see the edge of town ahead.

A tall, lanky figure slunk from the shadows and approached Darragh. *Please, just leave him alone.*

"If you had a bath, I imagine you'd be quite pretty."

I recognized the voice. "Sateen?"

Sateen's gaze shot from Darragh to me. "I'm sorry, I didn't realize he was with you…" Sateen paused and scrutinized me. "You're Bowyn's friend."

"Yes."

Sateen examined Darragh, peering through the grime. "You're that man. The one who burns things." Darragh didn't say anything, but a muscle corded in his neck. Sateen approached me and lowered their voice. "Do you need my help?"

"We're fine," Darragh snapped.

Sateen's eyes narrowed. They smiled like they'd just found an interesting—and potentially useful—piece of information. "You're together?"

"No. We're not *together*," Darragh snarled. He grabbed my arm and yanked me roughly away.

"Guh!" I cried out in surprise.

Sateen's eyes lingered on Darragh's white-knuckled fingers squeezing my arm. Their nose flared. To me, they said, "If you need my help—"

Darragh advanced on Sateen, challenging them. "Try to take her from me!" Sateen didn't move. Darragh's eyes moved up and down Sateen. "I thought as much," he mocked. Turning away, Darragh wrenched me after him.

"How did you know them?" Darragh asked.

"They're Bowyn's friend. He had Sateen ferry us to the mountain for the ball."

"Never trust them—*ever*." Darragh looked over his shoulder to make sure no one followed before he let go of me.

"Okay, that was super rude." I massaged my arm.

"I'm sorry. They can't know we're"—Darragh hesitated, looking for the right word—"friends."

Ouch.

"Trust me, it's better if they think I'm holding you against your will. If anything happens, you may need Bowyn's help. I don't want them to think you're associating with me willingly."

"Mhm." I walked ahead and kicked a loose stone. It arced into the wood and bounced off a tree.

Darragh watched the rock roll along the ground. He brushed a strand of hair behind his ear. "I'm sorry—"

"It's fine," I snapped. "I'm the one who should be sorry. I shouldn't have made us go through town."

"That wasn't so bad actually," Darragh shrugged. "Did you know tarring and feathering isn't specific to Earth?"

Chapter Twenty-Eight

no small sacrifice

We reached the shore beneath Senan's hut by noon the following day. Darragh walked around back, stopping in front of an ancient tree. He pulled a piece of bark away, revealing a hollowed section. "For the necklace," he said.

"Will it be safe?" My fingers curled around the pendant, reluctant to part with it.

"We can't take it to Earth."

Withdrawing the pendant, I rubbed the little flower between my thumb and forefinger. A fleeting, furious anger toward Darragh rose within me.

Why should I give it up?

Darragh's eye furrowed at my hesitation. I quelled the rage. Though it was difficult, I set the pendent in the trunk. Darragh slid the bark back and headed to the hut.

We found Senan in his usual spot by the fire. Without turning to greet us, he said, "Oh my. Two visits? In one week? What's the special occasion?" Darragh, who normally reserved a special sarcasm for Senan, responded with an unamused grunt. Senan glanced over. His eyes widened as he took in Darragh's dirty, bloodied clothing. "Oh, dear." He wiggled to his feet and hobbled over. "Are you hurt?" Senan poked and prodded Darragh. He hissed when he saw Darragh's hand.

"It's fine," Darragh muttered, shooing Senan away. "I'm working on it." He showed his hand. Indeed, his ring finger had grown back entirely.

"Tsk! Give me those!" Senan pointed at Darragh's bloodied clothing. Darragh stripped off his shirt, revealing the red burns along his belly. Senan cupped his cheeks. "Oh my. What trouble are you in this time?"

"You're one to talk," Darragh sniped.

Senan motioned toward Darragh's pants. "Those too." Darragh unbuttoned his pants, pausing to look at me. "Oh—hold on." Senan threw his hands down and rolled his eyes. "I'll find you some clothes." He scuttled off between his crates and clutter.

Darragh perked up. He reached for me and pulled me close. "She's here."

Senan reappeared and pointed at me. "You. Get in the back." He grabbed for Darragh, but Darragh wriggled out of his reach and backed away.

"She'll kill you," Darragh said. Senan clasped his fingers together, like a duck snapping its beak shut. Darragh's mouth did the same.

"Go." Senan pointed. Darragh's biceps tensed as he resisted the command. "Now!" Senan waddled around Darragh and pushed him. Darragh followed me, his gait rigid and forced. Senan ran in front of us and waved at the floor. The dusty, red rug rolled itself up tight. Senan whispered an incantation and a large, glowing rectangle materialized on the floor. A handle appeared, and Senan stooped to lift it. "Get in." Having no choice in the matter, Darragh crouched beneath the floorboards. Senan turned to me. "I couldn't have bound him if he weren't injured. Thank goodness for that." Senan put a hand to his chest. "If anything happens to me, my bind on Darragh will break. Do not let him come out."

"But—"

"I mean it." Senan's eyes bore into me. "Do not let him come after me."

I nodded.

"Good." Senan handed me a cloth parcel. "Take this." I peeked beneath the cloth; the orb glowed within. "Listen carefully." Senan jabbed a pudgy finger at the orb. "This is your bridge between Earth and Hiraeth."

"Okay."

"As soon as she's gone, take Darragh and get back to Earth. If she finds you before you leave, destroy it."

"Okay."

"As a failsafe, if the relic breaks, it will send the user back to their home location. If you drop this and it shatters, you will return to Earth."

"What about Darragh?"

Senan licked his lips and frowned. "He will remain here."

"But—"

"No buts. Do you understand?" My shoulders sank, but I agreed. Senan took a good look at me. His eyes softened, and he cupped his hands beneath my chin. "I wish I could have known you better." Senan gave me a bittersweet smile. His old eyes twinkled in the firelight. My lips were frozen in a frown. They couldn't say the words I thought.

I wish I could have known you better too.

Senan hugged me and said, "Now hide." He helped me under the boards and beckoned Darragh to his feet. Senan reached up and, placing his hands on Darragh's chest, said, "I know you're quite cross with me." Indeed, Darragh's glare was incendiary. "Perhaps it's for the best that I'm not around when this concludes." Senan chuckled before a cold seriousness came over him. "No matter what happens, you will not come out. If she catches you…" Senan glanced at me, then back to Darragh. "Fingers regrow—but you can't bring back the dead." Senan's face scrunched as he hugged Darragh's midsection and whispered, "Until we meet again."

Once the embrace was broken, Darragh knelt back below the boards. Senan lowered the trapdoor, it closed with a gentle *click*. Thin lines of light trickled through the floorboards above us.

A gust of air whirled as the trap door snapped open. Senan leaned in and pointed at me. "If you break his heart, I'll come back for you."

"I understand," I whispered. Senan pointed to his eyes, and then back to me as he closed the door once more. Senan muttered his enchantment and the door sealed. The rug rolled into place with a *thud* and sprinkling of dust.

Knock. Knock. Knock.

The floorboards creaked as Senan strolled to the door. "Oh my! Darragh!"

Someone who sounded like Darragh, but was certainly not Darragh, replied, "Grandfather."

The Truth.

"Oh, my! Let me put the kettle on." Senan's footsteps pattered across the floor. "I'm surprised you're back so soon!"

"What do you mean?" the Truth asked, mimicking Darragh's voice, *almost* perfectly.

"Well, I just sent you and that girl off to Earth—"

"You what?" Darragh's voice hissed.

"Yes, you left last night, or was it this morning? Oh my! I'm so forgetful these days. Did you bring the orb back—"

Whump!

The floorboards quivered as a heavy weight hit them. Senan's low groan carried through the floorboards.

Darragh's eyes closed.

A tense silence stretched on. It was the Truth's voice, not Darragh's, that spoke next. "For quite some time, the Queen looked the other way while you broke our laws for profit. Darragh might have a pass to travel back and forth, but you've let more than just Darragh cross, haven't you?"

"Well, no. I—"

"You've brought someone back. Someone who doesn't belong here."

Guilt twisted my guts.

The Truth meant me.

"I can't possibly control who comes or goes all the time."

"*You* possess the relic. *You* are responsible for who goes, and who returns."

Silence.

"Where have they gone, and when do they intend to return?"

"How should I know? He's a terrible grandson. He hardly visits, and he certainly doesn't tell me anything."

Footsteps sounded as several sets of boots entered Senan's hut. The Truth began, "Senan, you are charged with the possession of an illegal artifact."

"But I no longer possess the artifact—"

The Truth cut him off, continuing louder. "You are charged with illegal ferrying and aiding an enemy of the Queen. Make this easy on all of us; give me the answers I need. I'm going to get them either way."

"No," Senan huffed. "You won't."

"What are you doing... Stop him!" the Truth shouted. Stomping boots descended on Senan. The boards shook as crates were knocked over, their contents spilled. Bodies shuffled and Senan grunted.

A final, dull thud hammered the floor.

Unbearable stillness filled the hut.

Beside me, Darragh's faint breathing halted.

As if the life had gone from him too.

Free from Senan's enchantment, Darragh's head fell forward. He buried his face in his hands.

"Poison," the Truth snapped. Glass smashed. More crashes vibrated the floor. "Take the body!"

Boots shuffled across the hut...and then they were gone.

Darragh dragged his forearm across his face. "Let's go." He moved from a crouch to a squat, prepared to stand.

"Should we wait a minute?"

Darragh's face scrunched, as if he was listening. "You're right. She's waiting outside."

"Are you okay?" Of course, he wasn't okay. What a stupid question.

"I—" Darragh's voice broke, and he looked away. After a few moments, he murmured, "She's gone."

Darragh repeated Senan's incantation and the secret door unlatched. Darragh climbed out; he turned and pulled me out after him. The boxes and crates that contained Senan's things were toppled everywhere. Darragh stooped to pick up loose objects, placing them gently back in their boxes.

"Shouldn't we hurry?" I whispered.

"He wouldn't want his things to get broken." Darragh picked up Senan's old, worn mug and placed it back on the table. After a pause, he turned the mug to face the empty chair.

We cleaned up Senan's things in silence.

When we finished, I followed Darragh to the water's edge.

"Are you ready?" he asked.

I looked at the water, infested with marsh elver. The suffocating feeling of Marlowe holding me in the lake resurfaced. Darragh put one foot in the water and reached for me. I backed away, fidgeting with my nails. "You know what? You should knock me out."

Darragh furrowed his brows in a *what gives?* sort of way. "But you said—"

"I know what I said."

"Are you sure—"

"I'm sure."

Darragh climbed out of the water. He kicked his leg. Water sizzled and evaporated. "Back inside."

Chapter Twenty-Nine

some happiness, for pities sake

"Why don't you take a shower? I'll find you something to wear." Darragh hadn't thought to grab a shirt from Senan's before we left.

I hadn't reminded him either.

Bare-chested and grimy, Darragh stood in my kitchen. There was a haunted, faraway look in his eyes. He nodded absently and left.

Watney brushed my leg. I scooped him up and, despite his struggling, hugged him tight. "I missed you, buddy." Watney allowed me exactly two seconds of cuddling before wriggling free. He headed to the bathroom door, where he waited for Darragh. I really owed Sasha for looking in on Watney so much. I'd have to check out the cosmetics wish list he'd sent me for his birthday in July.

After his shower, Darragh put on one of my baggy Måneskin T-shirts and oversized sweatpants, which fit him like capris. He fell asleep on the couch, knee bent at an uncomfortable angle to accommodate Watney sleeping in the crook of his leg. I turned off *Ever After* and tiptoed to bed. The horrors of the day still fresh in my mind, I wouldn't sleep anytime soon. I opened my laptop and the screen flickered to life.

"HI EVERYBODY MY NAME IS MARKIPL—"

I slammed the laptop shut. Darragh stood on the other side, illuminated in the doorway. He asked, "What was that?"

"What was what?" I asked, guiltily.

"A loud man." Darragh stooped to see under my bed.

"Oh, get up." I opened my laptop and showed him. "Videos help me sleep."

"May I come in?"

I patted the bed and scooted over. Darragh lay beside me. "How are you doing?" I asked.

"I've killed every person who ever mattered to me."

Oh. So, it was going to be *that* kind of talk.

"The Truth killed Senan," I started.

"I shouldn't have involved him. I put him in danger. It was my fault he…" Darragh couldn't finish his sentence. He knew the word, even if his lips couldn't say it.

Died.

It was my fault he died.

"I killed my parents too. Did Bowyn tell you that?"

"He… He may have mentioned it."

Darragh scrunched his nose. "I figured." I waited to let him speak, hoping the silence encouraged him. "Everyone I've ever cared for is dead because of me."

"What about all the people who lived because of you? Fyn, Pip. If you never saved Pip, Brana wouldn't have helped me. I'd be dead." I pointed between myself and Darragh. "We'd both be dead." I was right, but the look on Darragh's face hadn't changed. I wasn't making him feel better.

"Can you tell me about your parents?"

I expected him to shy away, but this time, he didn't. "My father, he made textiles and loved his garden." Darragh found my hand between the sheets and held it. A vision of a dark-haired man kneeling in the garden danced in my mind. An overwhelming sensation of love warmed my chest. "He taught me how to heal."

"You look just like him."

Darragh blushed, taking it for the compliment it was.

"Did he make all those lovely rugs and blankets in your cottage?"

"Yes." Darragh's eyes twinkled, touched that I remembered. "Nearly everything from our home burned in the…" He swallowed, then continued with some difficulty. "Burned in the fire."

"I'm sorry." I squeezed his fingers. Darragh squeezed back.

"My father sold some and gave others as gifts. I've tried to get them back."

"What about your mother, Linovahle?" Darragh flinched, his smile ebbed. In my mind, I saw a strong, scowling woman. She had a flaming mane of red hair, pulled back in a ponytail filled with braids. Lin yelled a phrase I couldn't understand, but the emotion that coursed through me was unmistakable.

Fear.

"Lin made glass and pottery," Darragh said. "I was a disappointment to her. That I couldn't control what I had." He fidgeted with my pillow. "She was right." Eager to change the subject, Darragh asked, "What about your family?"

"I don't have anyone."

"I'm sorry. How did they die?"

"They aren't dead." I shrugged. "I just don't talk to them."

"Would you like to talk about it?

"Not really."

Darragh didn't press, but his grip tightened around my fingers.

We talked into the night. I don't remember what we said. Nothing important. I just remember the way Darragh's fingers grazed my hand beneath the sheets, and the way I forced myself to stay awake, so I could listen to his voice a little longer.

Buzz.

I rolled over in bed. Darragh was gone. I checked my phone.

"I saw your lights on last night. Are you available today?" Morgan.

"I'll see you soon," I texted back. I crawled out of bed and found Darragh sitting in the window, quietly reading. In one hand, he held *Daughter of the Moon Goddess*. The other hand grazed a leaf on the nearby plant.

"I'm gonna head to the café for a bit." Darragh nodded and continued reading. I hated to leave him like this, but I felt bad missing so much work.

When I arrived later that morning, Sasha wouldn't even look at me. He was my friend, and I wanted to tell him *everything*. But how could I? All I could do was thank him, and apologize for leaving, especially on such short notice. Sasha just waved. After that, he kept busy to avoid me. I was thankful and sad to head up for lunch.

Darragh slid a cup of coffee across the counter. I grabbed for it but misjudged the distance and sent coffee spilling everywhere. My breath hitched. Darragh eyed me while he cleaned the mess.

I started to cry.

Darragh froze. "What's happening?"

"Sasha hates me." I covered my face.

"He doesn't."

"He does!" I rubbed my eyes. "He knows I'm not telling him something. He won't even look at me." Darragh spread his arms, offering a hug. Though his strength was comforting, my heart ached.

"Could you make up something that might satisfy him?" Darragh suggested.

"Sasha's my friend, I won't lie to him."

After a pause, Darragh said, "You should eat before you go back."

"Hmph," I grumbled against his chest.

I talked little while we ate, my brain focused on ways to fix my deteriorating relationship with Sasha. We finished eating and I put my plate in the sink. "I don't want to go back."

It's lonely down there.

Darragh brushed a batch of crumbs from my shirt. "Stay with me."

"I wish." I frowned. "I'll see you later."

I trudged back down. Sasha ignored me when I walked in. I threw my stuff in the back and heard the jingling of the bells as a customer entered. I peeked out to make sure Sasha served them. Darragh sat in his usual spot at the front of the café. When he saw me, he waved.

'What are you doing here?' I mouthed.

Darragh shrugged and got Sasha's attention. I might be getting the silent treatment, but when Darragh smiled, Sasha couldn't jump up fast enough. I missed their conversation as a customer walked in. She wore a wide-brimmed hat over voluptuous blonde curls and a large plaid scarf. Long fingernails tapped her phone. She didn't look at me as she said, "Chai latte with soy milk."

"To go?"

For a moment, she said nothing.

"Hm? Oh yeah," she finally replied.

"What's the name for the order?"

THE FOREST WHERE THE PHOENIX SLEEPS

Another pause.

"Braxlynn," she mumbled. I prepped the latte. Braxlynn continued in an annoyed tone. "And I'm deathly allergic to dairy, so I'll know if it's not soy."

I eyed the cream before I rang up her latte. "That's five-fifty."

"Can I have the lemon-cheesecake bar too?"

I bent to grab the bar and hesitated. "There's milk in the—"

"It's fine," Braxlynn snapped.

Sasha returned and gave Braxlynn a wide berth as she left. "This bitch," he muttered, watching her go. Braxlynn saw Darragh and gawked, nearly crushing her latte between her chest and the door. She continued staring back through the window as she headed down the street.

I mustered up the courage to ask Sasha what he and Darragh were chatting about—the bell jingled *again*. A petite woman with black hair and perfect kinky curls rushed in and scooted behind the counter.

When Sasha performed in drag, he looked just like Morgan except...taller.

"How are you Nelli?" Because she was quite soft-spoken, I often found myself leaning closer to Morgan so I could hear her. I responded to nearly everything she said with a 'Pardon?' or an 'Excuse me?' And even after she repeated herself, half the time I still wasn't sure what she'd said.

This time, I thought I heard her correctly. "I'm okay."

Morgan told Sasha he could head out, and he left without a goodbye. Morgan thought it uncharacteristic and asked, "Is something wrong?" I started to answer but choked when Darragh got up and left. He didn't walk toward home; he followed Sasha.

What's he doing?!

Where's he going?!

Morgan followed my gaze to the front of the shop. "Uh, sorry. I

341

don't know," I replied. "You know how Sasha gets."

Morgan exhaled loudly. "I do." She looked me up and down. "So… any boyfriends yet?"

"No," I replied. "Not yet." I started brewing a fresh pot of coffee, and my mind wandered to Darragh. I thought of his sharp, clever eyes, and pictured the way they always seemed to settle on my lips. As if all Darragh wanted to do was reach out and—

Coffee grounds and steaming water spewed into the coffee pot. I'd forgotten to add a filter. I slammed the off button and glanced at Morgan. Mother and professional lie detector, Morgan fixed me with a pointed stare. My cheeks flushed and I looked away.

"No boys, eh?" Morgan pursed her lips. "Whatever you say, hun."

I bit my lip to keep from smiling.

On break, Sasha didn't respond to any of my texts. I mean, I wasn't surprised. He was mad, right? Probably nothing wrong. Darragh wouldn't do anything…would he?

My stomach knotted.

I ran home after work. Taking the stairs three at a time, I shuffled with my keys. Voices muffled through the door.

"It's stunning!"

Sasha?

I barged in with such force, papers flew from the kitchen counter. Sasha and Darragh sat on the living room floor, legs crossed. Sasha beamed, mascara wand in hand. Darragh smiled, lips painted red, one set of eyelashes done. "Ahhh! Nelli, come look!" Sasha leapt up and raced across the kitchen. Dragging me over to Darragh, he asked, "What do you think?"

When Sasha dragged himself up, he looked like a different person entirely. Darragh still looked…well, he looked like Darragh. With lipstick on.

"His foundation is too dark."

"Hm." Sasha scrunched his nose and crossed his arms. "Yeah, I was afraid of that." He threw his hands up. "Anyway, I gots to get going." Sasha kissed me once on each cheek and whispered, "This one's a keeper," before pulling away. Sasha squeezed Darragh's bicep. "I think you look sickening." Sasha packed up his make-up bag and waved on his way out. "See you hunnies tomorrow."

The door closed and I rounded on Darragh. "What did you tell him?"

"I showed him enough to understand. Nothing more."

"Oh," I paused. "Well, thank you."

"Of course."

Looking at Darragh all done up, I laughed. Darragh's bright red lips parted in a broad smile. I tugged at his shirt. "Should we put you in one of my dresses?"

"If it'll make you smile." Darragh's hand found my waist, pulling me close. He kissed my forehead. As he drew away, his eyes lingered on my lips.

Suddenly Darragh seemed a lot less funny.

"I, uh," Darragh started. "I'm gonna go shower, wash this stuff off." Darragh left, and I rummaged in a cupboard for a box of crackers. As I snacked, I found myself daydreaming.

What's he look like in there? Lathered in soap and water...

Darragh reappeared in the doorway. He pointed behind himself. "Would you join me?"

I choked on wheat shards. After I downed a glass of water, I said, "Uh, yeah. Sure."

I caught the tail end of Darragh climbing into the shower and my mouth dropped. Darragh was always so modest, I almost felt compelled to look away.

Almost.

Darragh rubbed a bar of soap under each arm. Bubbles trickled down his obliques. "Are you coming in?"

"Uh." I shook my head. "Yes." Every stretch mark and blemish begged me to quit undressing. Darragh would see them. See me. I wiggled out of my pants quickly, worried he might see any extra skin bunched around my belly. I wish I'd had the chance to shower *before* my shower with Darragh. I should have shaved. Covering myself as best I could, I jumped in behind him. Darragh turned from the water and pressed against me. He pulled my hands away from my body and kissed them, one after the other.

Don't look down, I told myself.

My eyes shot down.

Oh, shit. I looked down.

My cheeks reddened and Darragh chuckled.

"I'm sorry," I whispered. Unsure where to look.

Darragh's rough fingers caressed my throat, his index finger guided my face back to him. His lips nearly touched mine when he said, "Look at me." Darragh slid one strong arm around my back and kissed me. Soft and warm, I savoured the feeling. He pushed me against the cool tile. I had one moment to wonder how long ago I'd last cleaned the shower before he kissed me again.

This kiss was wholly different than the first.

A firm, starved kiss.

I traced my tongue along Darragh's lower lip, and he moaned against my mouth. Pulling away, he trailed kisses up my neck. His breath flared in my ear and goosebumps tingled along my skin. Darragh slid his hand down my chest and—

"Agh!" Darragh tore himself away. Soapy water splashed out of the tub, and he steadied himself with the shower bar.

"What?" I covered myself. "What happened?" Darragh's lips

moved, but no sound came out. His eyes fixed on something outside the shower. I glanced over my shoulder, afraid of what I might see.

Nothing.

Just my bathroom.

A haunted look crept in and settled on Darragh's face.

He'd seen something.

"I—I'm sorry," Darragh started, his eyes still fixed on some invisible creature behind me. "It's nothing. I just… I thought I saw something."

The hair on the back of my neck prickled. Even if I couldn't see it, I felt it. Something, or someone, lurked over my shoulder. Eager to leave the bathroom, I said, "Let's get cleaned up and go watch a movie." Darragh nodded but refused to look at me. When I tried to touch him, he flinched.

The next morning, I had a few errands to run. Groceries for us, food for Watney. Darragh accompanied me. He held the bags, and my hand whenever the opportunity presented itself. As we walked along the shop windows, our reflections walked with us. We wore joyful grins, obscured by messy hair as the blustery November wind blew at our backs.

I glimpsed a life with Darragh.

All at once, I realized how comfortably his hand nestled in mine and how lovely it felt to smile. A mundane task, suddenly cherished, simply because he existed and shared it with me.

What happiness would come if he existed for a million more?

We stopped at the café. "I want one more pumpkin latte before we roll over to the holiday drinks," I reasoned. We said hi to Sasha and then made our way back to my apartment. After changing into a large, burnt orange sweater, I turned on *Sleepy Hollow*. Darragh joined me on the couch. Curled up with my latte, I stitched beside him.

When I asked what he thought of the movie, Darragh replied that it was, "Okay." He never enjoyed the scary ones. For me, horror films were fiction. They weren't real, and they certainly couldn't hurt me. But for Darragh, growing up on Hiraeth, a lot of them seemed real. I'd learned that the hard way after I'd bugged him to watch *Dead Alive*. The dead coming back to life didn't sit right with him. We'd had to watch *Pride & Prejudice* after that, just to make him feel better. Darragh liked love stories and fairytales best. I hoped he didn't like them for the same reason I liked my horror films.

Sensing the headless horseman was too much for Darragh, I asked if he wanted to play a game. Darragh perked up and agreed. I pulled a box labeled *SEQUENCE* from the shelf beneath the TV. I laid a board covered with pictures of playing cards on the coffee table. "It's like connect four," I said. Darragh's face remained blank. "Ah, right. Basically, you draw seven playing cards. When it's your turn, you play a card and place a chip on a corresponding space on the board." I gave him a bag of green chips. "When you get five in a row, that's a Sequence. If you get two Sequences, you win." I shuffled the cards. "Easy enough, right?"

Darragh furrowed his brows but nodded.

I won the first five games.

Darragh threw his cards down after I uttered, "Sequence," for the tenth time.

"Wine?" I left for the kitchen and returned with two glasses. I pushed a glass across the table and made myself comfortable. Darragh uncrossed his arms to take a sip, his eyes never leaving the board. "Could you like, try to win one?" I joked. Darragh's lids drooped in annoyance. Already feeling brave from the wine, I smiled and said, "I'll make out with you if you win." Darragh fumbled with the chip he held. His eyes set on me, and a muscle flexed in his jaw. He gave me one purposeful nod. I took another sip, hoping to drown each of the butterflies in my stomach. I planned a spot to place my chip. During Darragh's turn, he used a wild card and placed his chip where I'd wanted to go.

Damnit.

I placed my chip somewhere else and prepared my next move. Once again, Darragh used a wild card and placed his chip where I'd planned to go. This happened four more times, before I said, quite frustrated, "You're cheating."

"Never."

Darragh's smirk suggested otherwise.

I planned my next move. Darragh placed his chip on the spot I wanted. "There's no way this is chance." I pointed angrily at the board. "Are you reading my mind?"

"No!"

"Then how'd you know I was going to go there?"

"Because you haven't stopped staring at that space!"

Annoyed, I prepared my move and readied my chip. Once again, Darragh used a wild card and placed his token on the spot I'd planned. "Okay, I'm done! You're cheating!" I threw my cards down, knocking over the discard pile. Despite Darragh discarding several wild cards during his turns, there weren't any in the discard pile. It was all regular cards now, none of which matched the spots he'd played. Somehow, he'd made regular cards look wild.

"You rat," I whispered.

Darragh peeked at me from beneath his lashes. "You wound me." He shuffled the cards. "Let's have another go." I crossed my arms. Darragh continued without looking. "I didn't realize kissing me was such a terrible thing."

I stuck my chin out. "I don't make out with rats." Standing to clean the table, I grabbed a bowl half-filled with popcorn. The bowl didn't move. I pulled harder, but it didn't budge. Had I set it in something sticky? Was my table ruined?

Darragh smirked.

"Will you stop?" I swatted him with a pillow. I grabbed the bowl and heaved. The bowl flew up with ease. Popcorn exploded everywhere, and I slammed into the couch. Darragh sat amongst the popcorn as if nothing had happened.

"I'm not cleaning this up," I snapped. Bits of kernels hung in Darragh's hair, and I looked away to keep from laughing. Darragh finally broke and laughed. Beautiful and infectious, I couldn't resist laughing too. Darragh waved and the popcorn disappeared. "Good." I crossed my arms, like I'd achieved some victory. Darragh's smile faded and his jaw set in a serious manner. His eyes filled with that sort of, hungry desire I'd come to see more and more these days. I fiddled with my sock. "Can I ask you something?"

Darragh's body tensed.

"Have you ever…you know…with anyone?"

"What do you mean?"

"Sex?"

Darragh frowned. "Yes." The silence in the room stretched on. "I've been with two partners." It was his turn to fiddle with a loose piece of thread on his pants.

Only two? That's not ideal.

I hadn't said anything out loud, but Darragh winced.

"Hey!" I swatted his arm. "I *knew* you were reading my mind! You promised you wouldn't do that!"

"I didn't mean to," Darragh growled. "It slipped."

"What if I got you a gift, and I didn't want you to spoil it?"

Darragh crossed his arms. "Yeah, what a lovely surprise. Happy Birthday: I think you're going to be a shit lover."

I bit my lip so I wouldn't laugh.

"We're not our first thoughts," I said. "It's what you choose to say and do that counts." I touched his arm. "It doesn't matter how many people you've been with, and I can be as patient as you need."

Our conversation lapsed into silence.

"Was one of them Bowyn?" I finally asked.

He nodded.

"I knew it."

"Just the once." Darragh tucked hair behind his ear. "I want to be with you, more than I've wanted anything before. But…"

"You can tell me anything."

Darragh's Adam's apple bobbed. "Since we've returned to Earth"—he shifted on the couch and dropped his voice to a whisper—"I can see her."

I squinted around the room. "Who?" Darragh's eyes darted to a corner of the apartment. I followed his gaze and saw nothing, but my skin tingled.

"The Queen." Darragh exhaled. "She's calling me back."

I thought of Alyth. She hadn't appeared since we left Hiraeth. I guessed she couldn't make the journey. I wanted to tell Darragh, but I'd nearly suffocated the last time. The thought of my throat closing like that again… I took another sip of wine. Could Darragh's Queen and my Alyth see each other? I imagined them having a conversation, calmly discussing the weather while Darragh and I spiralled into madness.

Darragh held his stomach and straightened.

"What?" I asked, setting my glass down.

"Agh!" Darragh doubled over and slid from the couch. On his hands and knees, he coughed.

"What! What's wrong?" I knelt beside him. "Are you choking?!" Between coughs, Darragh shook his head, no. He arched his back like a cat and dry heaved. He threw up and heaved again.

What do I do?!

I inched closer but Darragh pushed me away. He heaved and an object fell from his throat. It hit the ground with a sharp *ting*. Drips of spit and blood trickled from Darragh's lips. Dragging his arm across his mouth, Darragh picked up the mysterious shard. His fingers sizzled like a skillet as he rubbed it against his shirt. An ugly, red smear remained on the white fabric. Darragh held the shard to the light.

Glass—no, a mirror. For a fraction of a second, a wisp of red and black reflected in the mirror. Darragh covered his mouth as he looked at the shard. My eyes shifted between Darragh and the shard.

"I don't understand," I said.

"She has Bowyn." Darragh turned the mirror so I could see. An unkempt and beaten Bowyn stared back. Darragh leaned on the couch. He ran a hand through his hair.

The look on Darragh's face frightened me. I responded by doing what I always do in an uncomfortable situation.

"At least it came *up*," I joked.

Darragh didn't laugh.

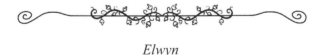

Elwyn

Bowyn's broad chest rose and fell as he slept against the rock wall. Like this, quiet and unanimated, even I admitted his beauty. I swished the goblet in my hand. Liquid sloshed against the edges.

I tossed it on Bowyn.

"What—" Bowyn awoke furiously. He wiped water from his eyes and looked down at his drenched robe. Boots scuffed rock as Bowyn leapt to his feet and loomed over me. Arms raised, he readied to strangle whoever had woken him so unkindly. I glared at him, refusing to cower beneath his hulking presence. As Bowyn recognized me, the rage slipped from his face. Curling his lip, he sneered. "Ugh." He leaned against the wall and slid back down.

"You *will* help me get Darragh back."

Bowyn clasped his face in his hands. "My precious Elwyn, you really are obsessed." His shoulders drooped and his hands fell away. "Can't you just leave Darragh be?"

"I will have him," I seethed.

"Why must everyone place their happiness in others? Why can't you be like me?"

"A narcissist?"

"Content with myself," Bowyn snarled. He brushed dirt from his robe and continued, "Aren't you afraid if he returns, the Queen will kill him?"

"I'd rather be with him in death than live without him."

Bowyn cringed and stared at me piteously. From below, he managed to look down on me. "I hope for both your sakes he never sets foot in this wretched bastille again." I wanted to rip his smug, pitying eyes out. "You can't get everything you want, Elwyn." Bowyn laughed and tapped his chest. "And that's coming from me."

He wasn't going to help me.

I'd never see Darragh again.

I swallowed the anger that swelled in my belly and crouched beside him. "Please! I can get you out of here!"

Bowyn threw his head back and laughed. "Has Darragh not endured enough?" He scoffed. "I will *not* lure him back to die."

"You'll die!"

Bowyn pushed me away. "I've had a grand run. If this is how I go, so be it. At least my body will be young and beautiful."

I stared at his neck, wondering what it would be like to wring it. "We'll see about that."

"What's going on in here?" The Truth entered. Ophyr strode in behind her.

"What's he doing here?" I glared at Ophyr.

The Truth pointed at Bowyn and said, "He wanted to have a go."

I glared at Bowyn.

You will be sorry you didn't help me.

"I want to watch," I said.

The Truth straightened, a smile tugging her cheek. "Very well." She knelt before Bowyn. "I'm sorry, but this won't be pleasant." She brushed a finger down Bowyn's arm. "Darragh must feel you suffer."

Ophyr approached, examining Bowyn.

"His eyes," I said.

Bowyn's beautiful, chocolate eyes fell on me.

I smiled.

Chapter Thirty

a game of snatch

Darragh and I sat on the cozy balcony of a two-story café. We overlooked the glassed-in veranda of a particularly splendid, and exquisitely expensive, restaurant. I'd jumped at the opportunity to go out with Darragh, but now, I saw the real reason we'd come. Marlowe sat on the veranda below, enjoying dinner with an elegant young woman. I scooched closer to the patio heater. The radiating heat did little to warm me against the cool November evening, and I shivered. Without letting Marlowe out of his sight, Darragh's hand found mine. A lovely warmth flowed up my arm.

"How will Marlowe help us rescue Bowyn?"

"The Queen holds a special contempt for Marlowe." Darragh scowled. "His powers of persuasion are unmatched in our time. Every time I've presented him to the Queen, he's managed to escape. He's made a mockery of her and her guardians."

"Why hasn't anyone killed hi—"

Darragh ripped his eyes from Marlowe and glared at me.

Right. I'd stopped Darragh killing Marlowe the last time…right before Marlowe escaped.

Darragh turned back to Marlowe. "Just as well. I'll have more bargaining power if he's alive. I'll lay Marlowe at the Queen's feet in exchange for Bowyn's life." Our waitress returned with two hot chocolates, smothered in whipped cream and caramel. Darragh thanked them before returning a scowling gaze on Marlowe.

"What are his weaknesses?" I asked, licking whipped cream from the mug.

"He has a fondness for flattery and beautiful people." Darragh took a drink, his eyes never leaving Marlowe.

"We could always ask Sasha to do your makeup again."

We sat in silence.

"Actually, you know what…"

"We need your help." I held my phone so Darragh could see Sasha on the screen. "We need you to persuade James Marlowe to come home with you."

Sasha looked around nervously and moved somewhere private. He lowered his voice. "You're really talking to me about kidnapping right now?" He blinked. "You want me to *kidnap* a man?"

"Actually, what you'll be doing is *luring*." I gestured to myself and Darragh. "We're kidnapping."

"The jury won't care," Sasha cried. "They're not gonna convict you, or a good-looking boy like him. They won't even have a trial; they'll send me straight to prison." Sasha shook his head. "No, ma'am."

Darragh took the phone. "Marlowe doesn't belong here. You'll be saving countless lives. Please." Darragh held the phone close, speaking directly to Sasha. "I need your help."

Sasha's face softened. "I don't know." His shoulders bunched. "This is insane…"

"I promise no one will know you had a hand in it."

"What if—"

"I won't let you get hurt," Darragh promised. "I'll keep you safe." I rolled my eyes, but it did the trick. Sasha melted under his gaze.

"Say I help you, what am I getting in return? Other than a go straight to jail card?"

"A date with James Marlowe," I said from behind Darragh.

Sasha started to argue, but snapped his mouth shut. He zoned in on Darragh. "I want a date with that boy you showed me. The one back home."

"Who?" Darragh's brows furrowed. "Oh." He sneered. "Bowyn?"

"I don't know." Sasha shrugged. "The big boy."

I grabbed the phone. "Don't you have a boyfriend?"

Sasha licked his lips and set me with an annoyed stare. "No. If you were around, you'd know that—"

"Okay, I'm handing you back to Darragh now." I shoved the phone back at Darragh.

Darragh bit his lip and smiled. "A date with Bowyn is a curse, and I can't guarantee I can get him here, but if I do, I'll introduce you."

Sasha pursed his lips. "So, when is all this going down?"

"Tomorrow night. The *big boy* is in danger. We need Marlowe as soon as possible."

Sasha rubbed his temples. "I can't believe I'm doing this."

The seductive *click-clack* of heels signaled Sasha's arrival. Darragh let out a breathless, "Wow," as she joined us in my kitchen.

"Yeah." I sighed, not bothering to hide my envy. "I know."

Sasha wore a shimmering copper dress. Slit to her navel, it covered only what was necessary. Her legs shone, reminding me of gorgeous people on billboards and magazines. Sasha tossed a section of sleek, black hair over her shoulder and motioned from her shoes to her head with her clutch.

"I should charge you for all this."

My expression said, *fair enough.*

"Alright, let's go over everything one more time," Darragh began. "We'll sit at the bar. Marlowe will arrive with a date and sit in his usual spot. When his date goes to the bathroom, I'll intercept her. I'll remind her of her *alternative* plans for the evening and introduce her to her oldest friend, Sasha. She'll take Sasha back to Marlowe, apologize for having to leave, but suggest Marlowe and Sasha will get on."

Darragh looked at Sasha expectantly.

A startled expression crossed Sasha's face, like she was called on to give an answer in class. "I do whatever I can to get Marlowe out of the restaurant and away from the crowd?"

Darragh nodded and urged her on.

"I head back to Nelli's—"

"Stop at the corner before the alley," Darragh interrupted. "Three of the shops on that corner have cameras. Nell and I will meet you there and take Marlowe with us. If anyone asks you anything, tell them Marlowe ran into a friend and left with him."

Easy enough.

I gave Sasha a spare key before we left. I'd asked her to watch Watney and my apartment for a few days. "Thank you for everything." I said, as she slipped the key in her clutch.

Sasha wrapped me in a hug. "This is for all those times you covered for me when you didn't have to." She released me. "But if I go to court, I'm telling them this was your idea."

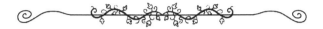

At the bar, Sasha ordered a cocktail for herself and a rye and ginger for me. I'd barely taken a sip before Darragh nudged me. He jutted his chin to the door, where Marlowe and a woman chatted with the host. They followed the host to a table on the veranda.

"Hey isn't that Braeleigh?" Sasha asked.

I squinted, trying to see the woman better. "Who?"

"Braxlee."

I further scrunched my face in misunderstanding.

"Braelyn." I had no idea who Sasha was talking about. "Breighleigh?" Sasha guessed again. The woman turned so I could see her better.

"Oh. Braxlynn," I corrected.

Marlowe and Braxlynn took their seats. It wasn't long before Braxlynn excused herself. Darragh slid from the chair and looked at Sasha. "Ready?"

"Yes, ma'am." Sasha downed her cocktail and checked her breasts in the mirror behind the bar. She kissed each of my cheeks and left. Darragh stopped Braxlynn before the bathroom. His hand lingered on her arm while he introduced Sasha.

I turned to the bartender and held up my glass. "Can I have another?"

Darragh returned as the bartender slid my drink over. Across the restaurant, Braxlynn paraded Sasha in front of Marlowe. Braxlynn excused herself and Sasha took a seat. She peeked at Marlowe demurely from beneath her bangs.

"Let's hope Sasha works her magic," I said.

Darragh watched Sasha's leg brush Marlowe beneath the table. "I don't think we have anything to worry about."

"Would you like a drink?"

Darragh shook his head. "I can't let him get away again. Not this time."

"Suit yourself." I sipped my drink in silence. Darragh's eyes never left Marlowe's reflection in the mirror.

Across the restaurant, Sasha excused herself and headed to the bathroom.

"Can you ask her what's taking so long?" Darragh said.

"Sure." I slid off my seat. "I'll be right back."

In the bathroom, Sasha met my eyes in the mirror, fixing her lipstick. "How's it going?"

"Amazing." Sasha fanned herself. "He is *so* charming."

"Darragh's getting grumpy. Are you having trouble persuading Marlowe to leave?"

"Oh, he was ready to go before the entrée, hunny." Sasha smacked her lips, admiring the lipstick. "I'm just enjoying myself now."

I laughed. "Well, I suppose we owe you that much."

Sasha dropped the lipstick in her clutch. "Alright." Her masculine voice popped back in. "Let's do this, marines."

"You got this." I gave her a thumbs up as she disappeared through the door. I rejoined Darragh, across the restaurant, Marlowe and Sasha rose to leave.

"Let's go," Darragh muttered. We followed Sasha and Marlowe down the main street, giving them a wide berth. When they reached the corner, Darragh sped up and shouted, "Hey, I know you!"

Marlowe apologized to Sasha, "I'm sorry, my love, just another fan." He froze when he saw Darragh. Marlowe's gaze drifted to me. He smirked and said, "Hello, my darling."

I stared at the pavement. Not today, Marlowe. Not today.

While I knew to protect myself, Sasha didn't. With all the prep, we'd forgotten to warn her. Marlowe took Sasha's slender hands and gazed into her eyes. "Do you see these two? If I'm to say, oh I don't know, vanish? I want you to tell anyone and everyone that they've killed me, all right?"

"Uhhh…" Sasha turned two very alarmed blue eyes on me and Darragh.

Sasha's eyes were brown.

She was wearing contacts.

I winked, hoping she understood. Turning back to Marlowe, Sasha said, "Sure thing, baby." Marlowe pressed a firm kiss on Sasha's lips. She giggled and fanned herself, which I didn't believe was acting. The *click-clack* of Sasha's heels rang out as she scurried away. Behind Marlowe's back, she gave me a subtle thumbs-up.

Darragh grabbed Marlowe's arm.

"Careful! This is merino," Marlowe whined. Where Darragh's fingers met the fabric of Marlowe's suit, a tendril of smoke wafted away. "Oh, that's nice!" Marlowe scoffed.

Back in my apartment, Darragh used an old pair of tights to tie Marlowe to a chair. "Do you have anything we can put over his eyes?"

I rummaged through the junk drawer in my kitchen and found a pair of rainbow sunglasses. Gigantic and awful, I'd gotten them at a pride parade with Sasha. Darragh put the sunglasses on Marlowe. He pillaged Marlowe's pockets and pulled out the mirror that sent me back to Hiraeth.

"Excuse me, you brigand! That's mine!"

Darragh shoved the mirror into his own pocket. "From the moment Bowyn was born, you have failed him. You abandoned him, and you've been absent when he's needed you most. He is going to *die* if we don't help him." Putting a hand on either side of Marlowe, Darragh leaned forward so they were eye to eye. "You will come with us, and you *will* offer yourself to the Queen in exchange for your son's life."

"That's an unfortunate turn of events…" Marlowe paused, deep in thought. He sighed heavily, readying to say something very important.

The silence stretched on; Marlowe opened his mouth.

"I'm not going back."

Darragh raised his fist. "You sonofabitch."

I grabbed Darragh's arm and dragged him aside. "What if we get him to help us?" The idea was so abhorrent to Darragh that only a garbled choke came out in response. "You said it yourself; his powers of persuasion are unmatched. An enemy of your enemy is your friend, right?"

Darragh's jaw clenched, and his nostrils flared.

"And what happens to you after you trade him for Bowyn? Hm? You think the Queen's just gonna let us walk free?"

That caught Darragh's attention.

"If he helps us, we don't turn him in, and he rescues his son. Win-win."

Darragh turned to Marlowe. "Did you hear that?"

"I did."

"And what do you say?"

"Eleanor, while I admire your diplomacy—I'd rather die here with my fans than face that tired old hag." Marlowe pursed his lips and nodded once. "Bowyn will understand."

Darragh opened his hand, and a ball of fire flickered to life. I snapped his hand shut, dousing the flame. "Why don't you go cool off for a minute?" Fuming, Darragh stormed out of the apartment. Angry footfalls sounded on the metal stairs.

Marlowe's pride sunglasses sparkled when he said, "My dear, you really can do better."

I lay comfortably on the couch, reading *Stolen Tongues* when Darragh returned. He pointed at Marlowe. "What's all this?" Marlowe, who'd fallen asleep in his chair, now wore a feather boa and a sparkling top hat.

Turning a page, I shrugged. "It matched." Darragh collapsed beside me, and I tucked a thumb between the pages of my book.

THE FOREST WHERE THE PHOENIX SLEEPS

"How can I make Marlowe go back if he doesn't care about anything?" Darragh asked. "Normally when I present someone with death, or returning to Hiraeth, they happily accept the latter. Death doesn't frighten him, and even if it did, we need him *alive* to rescue Bowyn…" Darragh let out a frustrated breath. "And now he knows that."

"How'd you get him to go back the last time? Can't you just force him?"

"If it were only him and me, I could bring him back, willing or not. But I won't be able to focus entirely on him and bring you at the same time. If he struggles during the trip, he might fall out along the journey. Or he might push you out."

"Could you make two trips?"

Darragh frowned. "It's no easy task, especially carrying another person. It could take a day or two for me to gather enough strength for a second journey. I can't leave Bowyn that long." Darragh rubbed the back of his neck. I stared at the cover of my book, mulling over the problem.

"Marlowe cares about how he looks," I said.

Darragh's brows raised, and he met my eyes. He grabbed the front of my shirt and planted an excited kiss on my lips before leaping from the couch. Darragh snapped his fingers in Marlowe's face. He jerked awake and blinked lazily through his big glasses. Darragh sat on the coffee table next to him. He raised his hand, and a thin blue flame travelled around it.

A single drop of sweat formed on Marlowe's brow.

"What are you going to do with that?"

Darragh smiled in a *funny you should ask* sort of way. "I'm going to burn the skin from your face." Marlowe's eyes pinballed between Darragh and the fire. "Don't worry." Darragh laughed. "You won't die." He booped Marlowe on the nose.

Marlowe's flesh sizzled and he squealed, "Not my face!"

"Yes, your face," Darragh responded. "Your face, and then your neck." Darragh trailed a finger down Marlowe's throat, the skin bubbled and blistered. Darragh glanced down. "And anything else I might meet." Darragh retracted his hand, and the azure flame pulsed in his palm. "Ready?"

Marlowe's wide eyes locked on Darragh's hand. "You wouldn't."

"I need you alive. I don't need you pretty." Darragh reached out, inching the flame toward Marlowe's face—

"Alright!" Marlowe wailed. "I've had a change of heart!"

"I thought you might," Darragh growled.

"I'll help you!"

Darragh did not withdraw the flame. "Help us what?"

"I'll help you save my son!"

Darragh shook his hand, dispelling the fire. He leaned in, meeting Marlowe's panicked gaze. "If you struggle while we're travelling, I will cut out your tongue and disfigure you so crudely, no one will ever recognize you. Do you understand?"

Marlowe bobbed his head.

Darragh untied him and we prepared to leave. I slipped on my shoes and gave Watney one last pet.

Since this adventure began, I couldn't wait to get home. And yet, when Darragh had resolved to return to Hiraeth with Marlowe, the question of whether or not I would accompany them never came up. I didn't have to fight to convince Darragh to bring me along, and he gave no indication he would leave me behind. It was as if, somewhere along the journey, our hearts had spoken to one another.

'I'm coming with you.'

'Of course you are.'

Standing before the door, Darragh asked, "Are you ready?"

"I am."

Under the cover of darkness, we headed to the lake.

PART THREE

Chapter Thirty-One

the horrors persist, but so does love

I choked out swamp water and fell on the rocky shore beneath Senan's hut. "Why?" I gagged out more water. "Why do we have to do it that way?"

"I'm sorry," Darragh apologized. "When you're fighting for your life, you divert all your energy to survival. We harness that energy for the trip."

"I hate it," I spit, yanking swamp weed from my hair. Darragh helped me up.

"Excuse me? A hand?" Marlowe shouted from the swamp. A flame enveloped Darragh's hand as he reached to help. Marlowe, unimpressed and wet, glared at Darragh. "How pleasant." He crawled out of the water himself. Wasting no time, I headed to the old tree behind Senan's hut. I tore the bark aside and grabbed the pendant. Tension eased from my shoulders as I clutched it to my chest.

"Do you have a strap I can put this on?" I asked Darragh. He undid his hair and handed me a long piece of leather. I slid the pendant on the strap and tied it around my neck. A tingle of power flowed through me. I shivered.

"Where'd you find him?" Alyth, suddenly at my side, nodded at Marlowe. He stood on the shore, bickering with Darragh. Neither of them noticed Alyth.

"Earth. We brought him back."

Alyth crinkled her nose.

"I'm going to use the bathroom," I called, and pointed at Senan's hut. Darragh stopped arguing long enough to give me a thumbs up. The stairs were permanently down now and I climbed them. Alyth waited below, watching Marlowe.

Despite the overflowing shelves, there was a sense of emptiness in Senan's hut. I skirted a pile of crates and passed a particularly marvelous skull. Ten beautiful antlers crowned the skull—a purple sachet dangled from one.

"Oh!" The sachet of lavender from Sasha. On Halloween, he'd mentioned it would ward off evil spirits, or something?

The same night Turner attacked Kristina, the night I killed him…

"Fat lot of good that did me." I unhooked the sachet, and it tingled with energy. A memory lurked amongst the dried buds. I let it wash over me…

Senan sat before the fire, well-used mug in his lap. With a great crash, the front door blew open and Darragh backed in. He carried something heavy in his arms.

Senan gasped.

Darragh carried a body.

Darragh jerked his chin at the table and all the items, which was a great many items, soared across the room and collided with the wall. Senan rose to his feet. "My teacups!"

"Damn your teacups!" Darragh slammed the body on the table. Senan didn't recognize it, but I did.

It was mine.

Senan bellowed, "What's gotten into you, boy?!"

Darragh pressed his ear to my chest and listened. He sagged against my body, resting his forehead on my chest. He breathed, "She's alive."

Senan took a step back, blinking rapidly. "She's not from here, is she?!" Darragh ignored Senan. He knelt beside my body, poking and prodding my side. Senan said, "If the Queen finds out…"

"You're one to talk, old man."

"I am old! I've lived my life. You've barely started yours and you're going to throw it away." Darragh said nothing, his concentration entirely on me. Senan stroked his beard and sighed. He grabbed a blanket and folded it. "Here, let me help." Scampering over, Senan wadded the blanket beneath my head.

"Thank you," Darragh muttered.

"You'll be the death of me, you know that?"

"Are you ready to go?" Darragh's voice snapped me from the vision. As it bled away, both Darragh and Marlowe came into view.

"I, uh, sorry. I still need to use the bathroom." Darragh's eyes narrowed as I sheepishly went to find the bathroom.

When I rejoined them, Marlowe shouted, "My turn!" and pranced away before Darragh could stop him.

"Touch nothing!" Darragh shouted.

When Marlowe was out of earshot, I rounded on Darragh. "That first night you brought me to Hiraeth…you said Turner hurt me, right?"

Darragh straightened. "He did."

"Nothing else happened?"

Darragh rubbed a hand over his mouth. "No—"

"Much better!" Marlowe waltzed out. Somehow, he'd managed to change his outfit. He tucked a flowing white shirt into tight black pants, and pulled on a knee-length, leathery black jacket. I noticed a gold earing, and a gold medallion tucked into the opening of his shirt.

"Put those back." Darragh pointed behind him.

Marlowe raised his palms. "They're mine."

"No, they're not."

"Listen, Senan may have been your grandfather, but that doesn't mean he wouldn't deal with my ilk." A muscle twitched in Darragh's neck; his hand flexed at his side. "Look!" Marlowe spun and slid his hands down his body. "They fit me like a glove." Marlowe winked as he walked by me.

Darragh gave Marlowe a thorough, prodding look. "He thinks you like the pants," he said bitterly.

"Ah." My eyes lingered on Marlowe's "pants". They did fit him *very* well. Darragh crossed his arms over his chest. "Sorry—were you saying something?" I smiled.

Darragh's face said, *you are unbelievable.*

"He looks even better in leather than I imagined," I teased. Darragh cracked his knuckles as we followed Marlowe down the stairs and out to the edge of the marsh.

"You first." Darragh pointed Marlowe across the water.

"I'd be delighted." Marlowe bowed. "Single file. No pushing now." Marlowe walked with his arms out, as if balancing on a beam in the water. I half expected Darragh would plant one boot on the square of Marlowe's back and send him to the marsh elver. Surprisingly, we all made it to the other side unharmed.

"Ugh, I already miss the lovely ease of pavement under my boot," Marlowe said. A shrill screech rang out in the trees. Marlowe straightened and pranced around to hide behind Darragh. "I've assessed the situation and I do believe I'll let you handle this," Marlowe whispered, close to Darragh's ear.

"Get away from me!" Darragh swatted at Marlowe. "I'll go ahead. Follow me slowly." To Marlowe, he added, "If I catch you looking at her, I'll burn you in those boots. Do you understand?"

Marlowe saluted and Darragh walked on. "Oh, look at him go! Our little *fiery* godmother!" Darragh shook his head and stalked ahead. Marlowe lowered his voice. "You know, I reckon he'll do anything for you, but you really can do better, my dear. Does he ever smile? Just a black cloud all the time—"

I smiled and kept walking. The more I learned of Marlowe's character, the less his allure worked on me. He felt slimy and left me feeling desperately uncomfortable. One-on-one, I was worried what he might say, or what I might admit. As if anything I said could and would be used against me in a court of Marlowe.

Marlowe pointed at my chest. "That's an interesting necklace."

"Thanks."

"How did you come by it?"

"Found it." I picked at my lip.

"And where did you find it?"

I turned on Marlowe. "Why do you want to know?"

"Give it to me," Marlowe urged.

His eyes flashed silver so quickly, I wondered if I imagined it. Alyth appeared at my side, and together we firmly said, "No."

"Hey!" Darragh shouted. He pointed at Marlowe, and then in front of himself. "Where I can see you! Right now!"

Marlowe threw his head back and laughed. "Oh, Eleanor. I'm just kidding!" He punched my arm. "Don't take everything so seriously." Marlowe's eyes lingered over my shoulder. Flashing a broad smile, he trod on. "Is the coast clear, my boy?"

I glanced at Alyth.

Her eyes widened, confirming what I suspected.

He might pretend otherwise but…Marlowe could see her.

"Do not trust him," Alyth whispered.

We had to be getting close. Tired and hot, I stared at my feet while we walked. One foot in front of the other. Up ahead, Marlowe's crashing footfalls ceased. He and Darragh stood on the crest of a hill at the edge of the treeline. We'd made it back to Darragh's cottage. The relief was overwhelming, and I quickened my pace. I searched the ground for nettle as I joined Darragh and Marlowe.

Then my heart stopped.

The clearing, normally abundant with greenery and life, was dark. I batted away a wisp of ash. The sprawling wildflower meadow was gone. Darragh's gardens were charred. Black soot lined the westernmost walls of the cottage.

Burned.

All of Darragh's work. His effort, his escape.

Everything was gone.

Achingly quiet, Darragh's chest rose and fell as he stared at the wreckage—at his home. Marlowe broke the agonized silence. "Bad luck, old chap." He elbowed Darragh. "You really should think about finding a new avenue of employment. You know, you sneer at us *actors,* but you're quite handsome yourself. You would do well—"

Darragh punched Marlowe.

"Oh!" I nearly toppled over as Marlowe dropped between us.

He did not get back up.

Alyth laughed riotously.

Darragh started down the ashy path. An invisible force dragged Marlowe behind him. I caught sight of the nettle and stepped over. Darragh dragged Marlowe *through* it. Curled and dead shrubs lay on either side of the path. Darragh focused on the cottage ahead. Tears welled as my feet crunched on charred twigs, each one belonging to something Darragh had cared for. Darragh took a side path around the cottage, which led to a small shed. He opened the door and Marlowe slid inside. Without a word, Darragh slammed the door and headed back the way he'd come.

Alyth didn't move. "I'm going to stay and watch him."

I mouthed, '*Okay,*' and trudged back around the cottage.

Darragh was crouched by a pile of burned items. He dragged a hand along his face and left the pile, entering the cottage. The big bay window in the den was blown in. Char marks marred the bottom of the loft. "It's not safe for us up there. I'll have to fix it," Darragh said, absently. For the most part, the inside of Darragh's home remained unharmed. The conservatory was untouched completely, as if whoever had pillaged the place was interrupted, or ran out of time. "I'm going to clean up," Darragh said, turning to leave.

"I'll help—"

"No."

"Why not?"

"Whoever did this might still be around."

"I'll be careful. I just want to help—"

"Nell," Darragh said, and pinched the bridge of his nose. "I've lost enough today. Stay inside." Darragh shut the door as he left. For a fraction of a second, I considered following him. I reminded myself that Darragh was hurting more than I could imagine… I bit my tongue and remained inside. Planning to sweep up the glass shards from below the window, I searched for the broom.

Where's the rug?

The rug that covered the floor, the one Darragh's father made, was gone. So was the tapestry that hung above the fireplace. "No." I hurried up the ladder and peered into the loft. The beautiful, handwoven blanket which had adorned the bed was gone.

Whoever was here, they burned them.

That's what the pile out front was—each of Santiana's handwoven pieces turned to ash. I crept down the ladder and peered out the window. Darragh was on his knees at the edge of one destroyed garden, methodically pulling out burned twigs and sticks. For a moment, Darragh held still; he stared at the remains of his sanctuary.

Death smiled back, mocking.

Whether it was the townspeople who burned Darragh's home, or the Truth on the way back from Senan's, I wasn't sure. Either way, there was only one message left amongst the ruins, meant just for Darragh: If you find something to love, just remember…*we can burn things too.*

Darragh's shoulders sagged, and he resumed pulling out dead plants.

In the conservatory, I dragged several large, terra-cotta pots to the corner. I found the broom, which usually swept the house of its own accord. It wouldn't help me, so I swept the floor myself. Once finished, I walked out and examined the scorched, weakened beams of the loft. Definitely shouldn't walk up there. I climbed the ladder and grabbed a corner of the thin mattress. I pulled it over the edge and leapt out of the way as it teetered and fell into the den. After dragging the mattress into the conservatory, I collected candles. I set them up around the conservatory, amongst plants and on shelves—

"What are you doing?" Darragh stood in the doorway. He wore a stony, emotionless expression. No matter how I tried to meet his eyes, Darragh wouldn't oblige. He trained his gaze low—as if that might hide the pain that tinged his nose and eyes red.

"I thought we could stay in here tonight."

Away from the carnage.

Darragh grunted in agreement and left. He returned with an armful of quilts and blankets. As Darragh walked by, candles sputtered to life, a wave of flame in the falling night. He tossed the blankets on the mattress. I arranged the blankets, none of which looked or felt special, while Darragh relocated candles that I'd placed too close to his plants. He moved sullenly, his strides lacklustre and slow. The air of loss was palpable, and I recognized someone about to shatter.

"I know it's not much," I started. "But, I'm here."

"I'm glad you weren't here when they came," Darragh said. "If anything happened to you…" He sighed. "Believe it or not, this was probably the best-case scenario." Despite the painful ache in my chest, my cheeks warmed. Darragh loved his gardens, yet I knew that, if he had to choose everything he had here, or me…he'd choose me. I took his hand.

My heart fluttered as he pulled away.

Darragh's head fell. "Why are you here?"

"I… What do you mean?" I asked.

"Why would you want me?" Darragh turned an angry scowl on me. "I have *nothing*!" He jabbed a finger at his chest. "I have *nothing* to give you!"

"I—I don't understand," I stammered. "Where is this coming from?"

"Look around!" Darragh yelled. "I have nothing to offer but a life filled with loneliness and contempt and scorn!"

"I don't need anything!" I shouted. "I don't need anything but you! I don't care what everyone else thinks!"

Here in the darkness, I see you, and I want every part of you.

Lightning lit the glass conservatory, streaking across the sky like a silent, white river. A clap of thunder rang out, and the glass panes vibrated. The pitter-patter of fat raindrops fell heavy on the glass. I tried to get close to Darragh, but he pushed me away. "No. I won't condemn you to this broken life with me."

"I'm not here to fix you!" I yelled. "I'm here to love you—" My breath hitched, and I caught myself.

Don't cry.

DON'T cry.

My gentle sniffle broke the silence.

I cried.

"No." Darragh scrunched his face. "Don't say that."

Another crack of lightning, followed by a long, low rumble of thunder. Tears spilled down my cheeks, and I threw my arms out. "I don't know what you want me to say."

Darragh took an unwavering step forward. His hand curled behind my neck and guided my face to his. Darragh's lips crashed against mine with such urgency, they knocked the breath from me. At that moment, I didn't want air—I breathed him in. Smokiness tickled my nose, like the brief, catching scent of a campfire on the breeze. Darragh held my face, and his rough, calloused fingers traced circles along my cheeks. "I'm sorry," he murmured. "I'm furious, but not at you." Resting his forehead on mine, Darragh whispered, "Never at you."

Sliding his arms around me, Darragh nodded at the table. Plants and candles slid aside as Darragh picked me up and sat me on the tabletop. Easing between my legs, Darragh's fingers grazed my throat as he kissed me again—a perfect, thorough kiss that curled my toes. My fingers tangled in his hair, found the nape of his neck, and pulled him closer.

It wasn't close enough.

Tugging Darragh's shirt from his pants, I slid my hands around the small of his back. I savoured the warmth of his skin. Darragh shivered and pulled away, so our lips barely touched. His keen eyes met mine. Flickering candlelight danced on Darragh's skin as he searched me. I let him look, dared him to find a fault or lie in any word I'd spoken.

And I saw it.

The decision.

Darragh's throat tightened, and whether he meant to or not, his head nodded. Only a tiny movement, but I saw it. As if, after denying himself for so long, he finally gave himself permission. Whatever battles he fought, I didn't know. But I know that, at that moment, a choice was made.

Darragh chose me.

When he kissed me, everything vanished. The acrid stink of burned land, the pitter-patter of rain pelting glass—it all disappeared. There was only him, and I opened myself to him. In that moment charged with sorrow and loss, with love and desire…I chose him right back. This time when Darragh kissed me, I couldn't contain myself. A low moan escaped my lips.

I needn't ask twice.

Darragh grunted as he tore my shirt open.

"Your shirt!" I blurted against his mouth.

"I can fix it," he growled, his voice muffled as his lips moved down my chest. He slid one breast in his mouth, biting my nipple playfully. I sucked in a quick breath, and he brought his lips back to mine. He pulled me against his chest, and I wrapped my legs around him. Heaving me into his arms, Darragh's heart pounded as he carried me. He laid me on the mattress, and in one fluid movement, the weight of his body pressed on me. He nudged my legs apart, resting his knee between them. Darragh's hands roamed my skin, sending sparks of excitement wherever they touched. I slid a hand down—

"Not yet." Darragh caught my wrist, dragging it back to his chest. "I want to enjoy you as long as I can." Trailing kisses down my throat, Darragh tore the shirt further. I resisted the urge to cover myself. He wouldn't have let me anyway. Darragh's eyes met mine as he unbuckled my pants and slid them away. Darragh dragged his fingers along my thigh as he crept back on top. He kissed me, letting his hand rest between my legs. Two fingers brushed against me. Darragh pulled away, his lips barely touching mine. "I've waited for you," he murmured, "for a very long time."

"What happens, now that you have me?" I reached down again, but Darragh caught my hand.

Sliding my underwear aside, Darragh slipped his fingers in. His eyes held mine as he rubbed lazy circles against me. "I'm going to bring you close," he whispered. "Until you're begging for me." He stroked me harder. "Only then will you have me."

That won't take long.

Darragh kissed me, stroking his fingers back and forth. I moaned and bucked my hips into his hand. Darragh smiled against my lips and pushed a finger into me, then a second. He moved in and out, slowly building pleasure. A soft, satisfied whimper left my throat and Darragh groaned. His fingers slid in and out. I was already so close. I couldn't take it much longer—Darragh's hand found mine, and he nestled it between his legs. He was firm, and ready…and I wanted him.

It took every ounce of self-control, but I pushed Darragh away. Breathing deep, I forced myself to calm down as I crawled out of his reach. Darragh smirked. He yanked his shirt off and tossed it aside. His hair, tousled and unkempt, fell against his chest. Glistening with sweat, it heaved up and down. I prowled forward and pushed him back. Just as he had with mine, I tore his pants off.

Unlike me, Darragh did not wear anything beneath his pants.

And he was *very* excited to see me.

I trailed my fingers in a circle against Darragh's thigh. "Maybe I'll just wait over here, and we'll see who's begging for—"

Darragh pounced. One arm wrapped my midsection and dragged me to the head of the mattress. With a low grunt, Darragh ripped my underwear off and tossed them aside. He slid between my legs and slipped an arm beneath my back.

"Wait-wait-wait," I said. Darragh stiffened, alarmed. "I—I didn't bring any protection… I don't want to get pregnant," I said breathlessly.

"I take something," Darragh replied. "You don't have to worry."

"Really?" I said, surprised. "What?"

Darragh leaned in, his warm breath brushed my ear. "Do you really want me to get into it now?" I shivered. There was only one thing I wanted him to get into. Darragh let out a low moan—he pressed himself against me, teasing me.

"I trust you—"

Darragh's lips crashed against mine as he pushed into me. I closed my eyes, savoring the moment. "Nell," Darragh growled, "look at me." I forced my eyes open, meeting Darragh's gaze as he pushed into me again. I moaned and Darragh's arm tightened around my back. I felt each corded muscle as he pulled me against his chest. The pleasure built as Darragh pushed deeper. My fingers gripped the hair on the back of his neck, pulling him close. I kissed him, begging his lips to let me in. I lured his tongue out with mine and bit it.

A guttural noise resonated in Darragh's throat, and he thrust harder. He wound my hair around his hand and gripped it like a rope. Wrenching my head back, Darragh kissed my throat. Goosebumps prickled my skin as Darragh thrust harder and deeper and—

I couldn't take it any longer. I let go. All the tension and restraint exploded into pleasure, and joy, and happiness. I arched my back as my climax coursed through me. "Yes!" I screamed. "Yes, yes!"

My cries undid him. Darragh moaned and thrust faster. Holding me so tight my ribs hurt, Darragh didn't slow down. Trembling and panting, his hand found the back of my neck. He pulled me in for one, final, hungry kiss and—

He stilled.

Darragh's entire body tensed, and he groaned against my lips.

For one precious moment, we were one. There was nothing but euphoria and bliss and our arms wrapped around one another. And as our chests heaved and sweat poured down our feverish bodies, I smiled. Darragh quivered and smiled back, a wondrous, excited thing that lit up his face. I knew how he felt…because I felt it too.

I'm fucked, I thought.

I'm in love.

Darragh eased beside me, wrapping an arm possessively over my belly. We lay naked, admiring one another. An intoxicating glow shimmered on Darragh's skin. I traced his cheek, brushing dark curls aside. Darragh caught my hand and kissed it, his gaze never leaving mine. As our breathing calmed, the pitter patter of rain echoed against the glass.

"I didn't know it was possible to feel this way," Darragh whispered.

"How?"

As if the fervor in his eyes wasn't answer enough.

"Every day, I feel the kiss of fire…it's an ember compared to the way my skin burns when I'm with you. You leave me witless, and I hardly trust myself to speak. It's humiliating and exhilarating all at once." He swallowed hard. "Though, it frightens me."

"Why?"

"I fear all of this will be taken away." Darragh spoke so quietly, I could barely hear him. "I fear I'll lose you, and that fear consumes me." He traced a finger along my lips. His brows knitted, and a cold seriousness came over him. "I would give my life for you."

A tense chuckle sputtered out of me. "I already had sex with you. You don't have to say that."

Darragh didn't laugh. His hand found my chin, and he held my gaze. "I'm serious, Nell. If anything happened to you…"

"Hey—I'm fine. I'm right here. I'm not going anywhere," I reassured.

The glow faded from Darragh's complexion. His eyes wandered to the middle distance and the creases between his brows deepened. I watched helplessly as the worry crept back, silencing him. "What's wrong?" I nudged his face back to mine.

"Nothing." Darragh's cheeks tugged into a smile, but his eyes were empty. As if someone sought to tear me away, Darragh's body tightened around me. "We have tonight. Just…sleep in my arms for one night, okay?"

I nodded, enjoying Darragh's warmth.

Even if a cold unease settled in my belly.

Sleep did not come easy. I hadn't slept next to someone in a long time, and Darragh emitted an unbearable heat. Once his breathing slowed, I did my best to scooch away—Darragh's arm flexed around my waist. Without waking, he dragged me back and buried his face in my hair.

I didn't try to escape again, even if I was a little hot.

Chapter Thirty-Two

Forest of the Unforgotten

Sunlight trickled through the conservatory windows. I reached for Darragh and found empty sheets.

"He's gone," Alyth said. She sat with her eyes closed, sunbathing on a chair. I bolted upright.

"He's what?!"

Fear stilled me.

The sweet, wafting stench of decay hit my nose and I covered my mouth. A knot of dread rooted in my stomach, and I scrambled out of bed. Wilted, brown leaves hung lifeless over the side of every pot in the conservatory. I took a step forward—*crunch*! The magnificent plumes of leaves that grew from planters now lay flat on the floor. Darragh's words echoed in my head. '*When I'm away, the house cares for them, like an extension of me.*'

The stink of rot filled my nostrils, suffocating me.

Where's Darragh?

Warm tears welled along my lashes.

Without opening her eyes, Alyth said, "He left you something."

"What?"

Alyth squinted against the sun and pointed at Darragh's pillow. Sure enough, a small scrap of thin bark lay beside me. Written in ash, the note read:

Nell,

No one else will die for me. Not you, not Bowyn, not even Marlowe.

If I'm unsuccessful and I don't come back, break the orb. Go home.

Live a happy life for me.

I love you.

I'm sorry I couldn't say it out loud.

- Darragh

Betrayal blossomed in my chest as I focused on those three words, scribbled in Darragh's childlike handwriting:

I love you.

The note burst into flame, and I dropped it with a hiss. The frail bark burned to nothing before it hit the mattress. The orb sat on Darragh's pillow.

"He took the necklace too," Alyth pointed out. My hand shot to my neck, where the necklace *used* to be. Examining her fingernails, Alyth said, "Don't worry, he didn't take the *right* necklace."

"What?"

"I swapped them." Alyth scrunched her face. "Well...*you* swapped them." I stared at Alyth incredulously. She rolled her eyes and said, "Check your sock." I ripped my sock off. Sure enough, the necklace tumbled out.

"I don't understand."

Alyth's head fell back in dismay. "I encouraged you to do some sleepwalking last night. You replaced the Queen's necklace with a fake." Alyth's expression clouded. "And let me tell you, it was a real pain. He had quite the hold on you."

"But why?!"

"I didn't trust him." Alyth shrugged. "Apparently, you shouldn't either."

Darragh had gone to the Queen with a fake necklace.

What had she done to him?

I stared into the middle distance, at the vines that dangled from hanging baskets. Without leaves, the vines swung like brittle nooses from the ceiling.

Dead.

Everything was dead.

I rubbed my chest, hoping to ease the tightness—

"Oh!" I ran to a shelf and shoved several withered plants aside. There, inside a tiny terracotta pot, was a thriving sprout. A speck of green amongst all the death. I dragged the pot out and cradled it.

Hope.

I set the pot down and stomped past Alyth, out of the conservatory. "Where are you going?" she shouted.

"I don't know!" I ripped open the cottage door and made to storm out.

"Agh!" My face smushed against an invisible wall. My arms flailed as I bounced back and landed on my ass.

Alyth examined the door and muttered, "Clever boy." I touched my nose tenderly; I'd been headed pretty hard out that door. "He's enchanted it. We're trapped." Alyth turned to me. "Can you put some pants on?"

I scrambled up and ripped open a kitchen window. Instead of air, my palm pressed against something flat, like the window was still closed. Suddenly feeling very claustrophobic, my mind raced. How could I be trapped? What if something happened, and I needed to get out? What if there was a fire?

What *if* there was a fire?

I ran back into the conservatory. My pants and one of Darragh's sweaters lay discarded on the ground, I yanked them on. I grabbed the orb and sprinted back to the den. A satchel lay discarded by the fireplace. I tossed the orb inside and strung it over my shoulder. "If I know Darragh, he'll have put a fire safety clause in this trap." I jumped on a chair and grabbed a bunch of dried herbs from a beam. Leaping from the chair, I tossed the herbs on the floor. The fragile leaves cracked into pieces.

Nice and dry.

I focused all my energy on the kindling.

Nothing happened.

Hurry!

Darragh could be hurt—or worse.

"Ugh! I can't concentrate!" I took a deep breath. "Can you do fire?"

Alyth held her hands up apologetically. "I only do shadows." I scoured the cottage, ripping open cupboards and drawers. Nothing to make fire. No surprise. Why would Darragh own anything to start a fire? Alyth stood in the den, arms crossed. Pursing her lips, she asked, "Now what?"

I flailed my arms. "You think of something!"

"I mean, if you didn't rely on *him* to make you fire, maybe we'd be out of here already."

"That's rich coming from you!" I snapped. "If *I'm* trapped in here, then *you're* trapped in here with me. Help!" Alyth crossed her arms tighter and sat on the sofa. I picked at my lip. "I have an idea." I grabbed the string that held the dried flowers, and a few bits of wood from the blackened frame of the bay window. I sat down and fiddled with the string and wood. Alyth abandoned the sofa and sat across from me.

"What are you doing?"

"Something I saw on TV."

"What's TV?" Alyth asked, her tone laced with dismay.

"Nothing. Don't worry about." I admired my handiwork. "Ah-ha!"

Looking glum, Alyth said, "It's a pile of sticks."

"It's a bow-drill," I snapped. My foot on the fireboard, I held the spindle down and dragged the bow. The spindle flew out from under me. "Damnit!" I cradled my hand.

"The Queen will kill your boy and come for us if we don't hurry."

"That's not helping!" I repositioned myself and tried again. The skin on my palms blistered and ripped. My arms ached, begging me to stop. Still, I couldn't form a coal. "I'm not strong enough." I threw the bloody bow and hung my head.

"I have an idea," Alyth whispered and pointed to the shadows. "Use them." I calmed myself and concentrated. Twirling my fingers, I pulled the shadows to me. I repositioned again, but this time, the shadows dragged the bow back and forth. My hands might get sore, but the shadows wouldn't tire.

After ten minutes, a small trickle of smoke wafted from the fireboard.

"Ah-ha!" Kneeling with my dried petals and twigs, I delicately placed the small coal in the tinder. It caught and the flame spread.

"Yes!" Alyth punched the air. Smoke puffed to the ceiling. I headed to the door, fire first. Sure enough, I walked right through it.

Alyth breathed in the fresh air. "Seems he isn't as clever as you." She smiled proudly. "What's next?"

I'd focused so much on getting out, I hadn't really thought about what came next. "I guess we…go rescue Darragh? And Bowyn, if we happen to see him?"

"You're going to take on the Queen, and an entire mountain of guardians meant to protect her? All by yourself?"

"Well, I've got you."

Shaking her head in disbelief, Alyth exhaled. Her eyes bugged, and she covered her mouth.

"You're forgetting who else we have," I said.

"Who?"

I smiled.

"No." Alyth crossed her arms. "Absolutely not."

Alyth stood between me, and the garden shed. "Do *not* let him out."

"Is someone there?" Marlowe's muffled voice called. A clattering noise rang out as he tumbled over gardening equipment. Marlowe's eye appeared in a gap between the slatted boards. I looked at the ground. "Oh, Nell! My dear. Come. Release me."

I lowered my voice so only Alyth could hear. "We need all the help we can get." I went around her and stood by the shed. "Darragh's gone. He took the Queen's necklace... I think he meant to trade it for Bowyn."

"Oh, stupendous!" Marlowe said. "Oh, I'm so relieved!"

"The thing is, I still have the real necklace." I pulled my shirt back so Marlowe could see.

Marlowe's eye widened. "Oh, my."

"Yeah, and I have a feeling the Queen wasn't happy when Darragh showed up with a fake." The wilted, dead plants nagged at my mind. "Darragh and Bowyn need us. I'll let you out if you help me free them."

"So, the Queen might cage, mutilate, or kill me? No, I don't think I will."

"You swore you'd help rescue Bowyn! You gave me and Darragh your word!"

"Yes! I promised Darragh *and* you. Not *just* you. I'm not conceited enough to think we have a chance in that mountain."

"You escaped before!"

"Escaping by my onesies is one thing, sneaking both of us in, and four of us out, is another thing entirely!"

"Please! Darragh said your persuasion is unmatched; if anyone can do it, it's you!"

"My dearest Eleanor, why can't you see this for what it is? An opportunity to flee this wretched place." Marlowe's voice was irritatingly calm when he said, "I will not set foot in that mountain ever again."

"Fine!" I shouted. "I'll go alone! Darragh will die, Bowyn will die, I'll die." I shrugged. "And there won't be anyone left to get you out of this shed, so, I guess you'll die too."

The shed was silent.

"See you never." I started to leave. Alyth's shoulders sagged with relief.

"Well…I've changed my mind," Marlowe's voice floated after me.

"Mhm." I halted. Alyth's head slumped forward.

"If you spring me from this shed, I swear on pain of death, I will help you rescue Bowyn."

"Please," Alyth begged, "do not release him."

I lowered my voice. "I'm hoping he won't betray me until *after* he has Bowyn."

"He abandoned his son many times before. What makes you think this is any different? He's an opportunistic parasite."

"That's a bit harsh."

"It's not. Do *not* trust him. Please."

"We don't have a choice." I approached the shed. "We need all the help we can get."

I opened the door.

The walk into Wilbur was longer than I remembered. Perhaps because I was worried about Darragh. But more likely because of Marlowe's constant chatter. Made worse by Alyth, who answered every one of

Marlowe's statements with a scoff, and some disparaging remark like, "That didn't happen." Between the two, there was little silence and, often, they spoke over one another. By the time I saw the tall, crooked buildings of Wilbur, I was ready to tear my ears off.

Though, I noticed Alyth quieted when she saw the buildings.

As we passed the inns and shops, a window filled with bright gowns and robes caught my eye. "I'll return in a moment," Marlowe muttered and hurried toward the shop.

"Wait! What—" Marlowe opened the door, but I slammed it shut before he could slip inside. "We're in a hurry!" I cried.

"No. *You're* in a hurry," Marlowe responded. "I'm in no rush to enter that tomb again." Removing my hand from the door, he said, "I'll be five minutes, I promise."

Marlowe disappeared inside the shop.

"Unbelievable," I muttered and turned to Alyth.

She was gone.

"Alyth!" I whisper-shouted, looking around. Panic sent my pulse racing as I spun in a full circle, searching for her. I ran down the street, peeking around houses and buildings. When I came to an intersection, I didn't see Alyth anywhere. Heading to the left, I muttered, "Damnit, damnit, damnit." I searched frantically down the alleys.

"You!" I pointed at Alyth, who stood in front of a rundown building. Window boxes that once held flowers lay empty, the wood rotted and falling away. Above the door hung an old sign, faded from the sun. It had an image of…a boar? As I approached, I noticed the doors and windows were boarded. The building looked like it hadn't been occupied in half a century.

Alyth's hand slipped from the boards over the door. She remained silent when I stopped beside her. Her gaze was lost, as if she could see through the boards—see through time itself to what this place used to be.

"Did you know the people that used to live here?" I asked.

"I did."

"What happened to them?"

Silence.

I opened my mouth to speak again—

"It doesn't matter," Alyth said.

Though, when she turned away, her tear-stained cheeks glistened.

We headed back to find Marlowe. He was waiting outside the shop when we returned. His boots were shinier, and his black leather coat, less worn.

"Was that really necessary?" I asked.

Marlowe flourished a hand down his body. "If the Queen captures us, I couldn't look like a pauper, now could I?" I shook my head, and then continued on the road out of town.

With the buildings of Wilbur behind us, we trod onward. Shadow Peak loomed in the distance. While Alyth remained silent, Marlowe continued to chatter.

"How'd you like the show?" Marlowe asked.

"Hm?" I tilted my head.

"*Alexander Hamilton.*"

"Oh, right." That seemed an eternity ago. I hadn't really stopped to take it in. "I knew it was going to be better than I expected, but I didn't know how much better." I smiled, recalling the last song. I blinked quickly, thinking it a silly time to be emotional.

Marlowe watched me closely and said, "You were the first one to your feet at the end. You know, I always look."

I chuckled. That was probably true.

Marlowe nodded to himself and said, "I got you something." He withdrew a large bundle from beneath his coat. Where he'd been keeping it, I didn't know.

"How'd you pay for this?"

"I asked *nicely*, and they gave it to me. Go on. Open it." I unfolded the merlot-coloured bundle, revealing a burgundy leather jacket. A matching set of pants fell out; accents of gold thread caught the light and shimmered. I ran my finger along the meticulous stitching. It tingled with magic.

"What's the deal with them?"

"Dunno." Marlowe shrugged.

Is he lying?

I'd scarcely turned to Alyth before she spat, "Of course he is!" I winced, cradling the clothes against my chest.

Alyth perked up, like she'd heard her name. She squinted down the path, and before I could ask, she took off. Up ahead, the path split, and a small sign with the image of a tree pointed to the right. Marlowe's head swivelled to watch Alyth as she followed the side path.

"Ugh! Quick detour!" I shouted and sprinted after Alyth. She ran into a heavily treed area, heading toward an ornate wrought-iron gate. Alyth shimmered and ran through the bars. How would I ever get them open?

Creaaaaaak.

The gate swung open, beckoning me inside. My footsteps echoed along a well-kept cobbled path. Massive, wondrous trees jutted from either side of the cobbled stones. I brushed a willow branch aside as I walked cautiously after Alyth. An elaborate wooden bench sat under a tree with delicate pink buds. The farther I walked, the more benches I spotted beneath the branches. The trees here demanded silence and respect. Not even the birds dared to sing. Marlowe caught up with me, and I whispered, "What is this place?"

"The Forest of the Unforgotten," Marlowe spoke in a hushed tone.

"Our bodies remain here, while our spirits pass on."

"It's a graveyard?"

"Of sorts." Marlowe glanced over his shoulder.

Alyth stopped at a tree and laid her palm on the bark. Shaking her head, she moved to the next one. She walked from tree to tree until a withered and dying sapling caught her eye. Her breath hitched, and she rushed to the tree. The moment her skin touched the bark, she let out an agonized wail.

Alyth fell to her knees.

Marlowe and I approached quietly. Alyth knelt with her head in her hands, her body trembling. I reached out and touched the bark, and a vision of a handsome man with a sharp grey beard floated through my mind.

"Who's that?"

A puzzled expression crossed Marlowe's face when he touched the tree. "Erabus, the king. Well, the late king, I suppose." He crossed his arms. "I didn't know he'd passed."

The sound of Alyth's wails rocked the forest. "Could you give me a second?" I asked Marlowe. He tucked his hands behind his back and wandered away.

I knelt beside Alyth, who's entire body convulsed with sobs. Her hands fell from her blotchy, tear-stained face, and she tried to speak, "I—I—"

"Sh, sh, it's okay." I scooched closer.

"I loved him more than anything," Alyth choked.

"Alyth…how long were you trapped in the burrow with Jorgen?"

She dragged a hand beneath her nose; it came away shiny with snot. "Forty years," she whimpered.

Alyth looked no more than sixteen.

I didn't say anything more, I waited for Alyth to catch her breath. Gradually, her sobs lessened. She ripped a blade of grass from the ground and shredded it. An apathetic look settled on her face. "I met Erabus when I was helping my mother with the smoker one night. He came in—I'd never met someone so charming." Alyth blushed. "He snuck down from the mountain every night for a month to meet me." A tear slid down her cheek. "When he told me he had to wed, we wept. I could hardly breathe when he left that night. I sat outside in the dark, looking at the stars. I thought, if only I was better, stronger, we could be together. I thought of the stories I'd heard of a creature—"

"Jorgen?"

Alyth nodded. "I thought, perhaps if I could take Jorgen's ring, I could be with Erabus. And if I died…well, I thought I might die anyway." She laughed a sad laugh that ended in a sniffle. Her shoulders sagged. "I ripped myself in two. I put half in there." She pointed to the necklace dangling around my throat. "When Jorgen offered me tea, I let him see it. He was so fond of jewelry. When he touched it, I called to the shadows and plunged us into darkness. The necklaced released a *'decoy'*… me." Alyth tapped her chest for emphasis. "Jorgen went after me." She sighed. "The other Alyth snuck the ring from his finger. He whirled on her and she didn't have time to grab the necklace." Her breath hitched. "She left me. She took the ring and ran." Alyth paused, recalling a memory she didn't want to. "I still remember Jorgen's smile as she fled. He told me I'd lose everything I cared for." Alyth grabbed another bit of grass, mangling it between her fingers. "In the beginning, I had a strong bond with the Queen. Jorgen's ring made her powerful, and she got what we wanted. She married Erabus…" Alyth trailed off, as something occurred to her. "Is it true I have a daughter?"

"Yes." I nodded. "She's beautiful and, I assume, powerful."

Alyth beamed. "Is she happy?"

I frowned. "I don't know."

Alyth's smile faded. "Anyway…we thought we tricked the creature, but it was him who'd tricked us. He found a way to get out of that cave. He sent a piece of himself, his evil, with her, as much as she left me with him." Alyth sighed. "Over the years, the Queen became less me, less Alyth. Jorgen's power poisoned her. Occasionally, I'd get a snippet, a feeling or a vision." She sniffled. Her voice dropped so low I could barely hear it. "Deep down, I knew Erabus was dead," she choked. "I *felt* him die." A tear streaked down her face. Alyth looked at the canopy. "I gave up everything because I loved him. I gave up myself, my name, my love… I became nothing but bitterness. Jorgen was right. I lost everything."

Alyth tossed the torn bits of grass and screamed, "I'm not the Queen! I'm not that monster!" She reached for the shadows all around and they swam toward the tree. "Agh!" Alyth shrieked as the shadows tore the pathetic little tree in half. She flung her arms outward, and the two halves fell sideways. "I'm—I'm just a stupid girl who gave up everything!"

The silence in the forest was broken by Alyth's laboured breathing.

"Why didn't you tell me?"

Alyth hiccupped and laughed. "Would you have helped me?"

My silence was a sufficient answer.

"You would have been right not to trust me." Alyth shook her head. "I considered staying in your body, you know, taking it for my own. If Erabus was still alive, I don't know if I could resist. It's evil of me… Perhaps I deserve this."

"No one deserves this." I'd grown close to Alyth, figuratively and literally. While her intentions might have been misguided, she didn't feel malicious. "I think you would have made the right choice when it came to it."

"You're too sweet, and too kind. Don't let this world spoil you." A softness overcame Alyth; she caressed my cheek and my skin tingled. "I felt for Erebus how you feel about that boy. Don't love him so completely you forget to do what's best for you."

My heart tugged. I'd been so caught up with Alyth, I'd forgotten about Darragh.

"I have to go after him."

Alyth exhaled, possessing the same worn-out exhaustion of a parent witnessing a child making the same mistakes they had. "Do what you must, but I beg you…bury me here. Promise me you won't let the Queen have the necklace—have me." Alyth's pleading eyes met mine. "I have suffered a lifetime already. Please, just let me rest with my beloved."

"But I need your help—"

"You don't need me. You have your own power. I know you can do this."

I wish I knew I could too.

Alyth lay down in the soil at the base of the tree. Curling into a ball, she closed her eyes. "I'm ready now." Kneeling beside Alyth, I scraped dirt aside and placed the necklace in the ground.

"May our light meet in the next life," Alyth whispered. As I brushed dirt over the necklace, Alyth faded. The ground rumbled beneath my knees. I scrambled up and backed away. A sprout snaked its way through the dirt. It grew, spiraling into the air. Branches and leaves shot out like spokes on a wheel. I stepped away as the trunk grew, propelling the tree high into the canopy. Beautiful lavender buds formed and blossomed all at once. A wind swept through the forest and shook the tree. Petals swirled around. The tree settled, magnificent and massive amongst the others.

Marlowe rejoined me and breathed, "Remarkable." The tree blossomed, full of life. A beacon in the forest. I touched the bark and an image of two lovers crept into my mind. Alyth, and a handsome young man. They looked at each other, and my heart ached.

I wiped a tear from my cheek.

I had to help Darragh.

"There, there." Marlowe pulled me into a hug. Comfort and warmth coursed through me.

Suspicious warmth.

I arched away from Marlowe's embrace. His shimmering, charming eyes met mine. As easily as one might slip into a warm bath, my control slipped away. Behind Marlowe, Sateen stepped from the shadows. Had they been there this whole time? In their stillness, I'd mistaken them for a trunk. Marlowe released me, and I watched on, giddy as he unburied the necklace.

"Let's go turn ourselves in, shall we?" Sateen slunk closer and Marlowe said, "Be ready when I need you." He handed Sateen the clothes he'd given me. "Help me get these on her." Marlowe snapped his fingers. I happily undressed and struggled into the well-fitted leather. Marlowe admired me, and I thought my heart might burst with pride. "Enchanting, my dear." He picked up my satchel and shoved my clothes inside. Withdrawing the orb, he said, "Do you see this?"

I nodded without looking, distracted by the honey-coloured flecks in Marlowe's eyes.

"This is your way out." Marlowe locked eyes with me as he placed the orb back inside. "Do not forget it's here. Do you understand?"

I did—but I wasn't going anywhere.

Marlowe tucked the satchel over my head and offered an arm.

"Oh!" I took it and snuggled him.

Together, we walked to the mountain.

Chapter Thirty-Three

until my dying day

Content to bask in Marlowe's light, I shuffled through the mountain in a lovesick haze. A guardian pulled me away from him. I swung, punching her in the face. "Why, you!" she cried and grabbed for me. Several guardians separated us and dragged me away. They took my bag and tossed me in a dark room. Only then did the lovesickness ebb.

"Oh!" I remarked. A dirty, naked man lay in the corner.

"I'd recognize that startled surprise anywhere," the man said, sitting up.

"That makes one of us," I whispered. Bowyn's beautiful mane of black hair was gone, shorn roughly at the scalp. A strip of cloth covered his eyes. He looked smaller, malnourished, and sick. "Does the Cage have us?" I asked, hopeful Brana had survived.

"The Cage disappeared. They built this place just for me." Bowyn sighed. "I am both happy and devastated that you're here. What happened?"

"We were coming to save you, Darragh and I. Believe it or not, your father joined us as well."

"Hm." Bowyn grunted in disbelief.

"Anyway, Darragh snuck out and left me trapped in the cottage. After I figured a way out, I followed with Marlowe. He turned me in, unfortunately." I stewed. "What a bastard."

Bowyn relaxed against the wall and chuckled. "That's daddy."

"Speaking of bastards," I started. Bowyn's shoulders hunched, readying for an attack. "Why'd you bring me to the light ball?" I slapped Bowyn's foot. He hadn't seen the hit coming. He dragged his leg back. "I trusted you!" I slapped his other foot. "You betrayed me, and you betrayed Darragh!"

Bowyn shook his head and raised his hands to protect himself. "I knew you could get her silly little trinket! Just like I *know* you can defeat her and free Darragh!"

"Bullshit! You wanted me gone," I snapped. "You sent me to die!"

Bowyn, unused to being called on his bullshit, smiled behind his hands. "Okay, okay, okay, okay. Will you stop hitting me?"

"Maybe," I hissed.

"At first, I wanted you gone. I was jealous." His brows furrowed against the cloth. "And you didn't belong here! I thought, if you went back to Earth, that would be the end of it. We'd live our lives as if you never came to Hiraeth. But that day you fell through my mirror, and I saw how quickly Darragh followed you...well, I knew if you went back to Earth, he'd follow you there too." Bowyn's feet fidgeted against the rock. "So, I thought, perhaps with the Queen overthrown, or gone, there might be a chance you could both stay here. Then I wouldn't lose Darragh entirely."

I crossed my arms. "You sent me to the wolves."

"Listen, it was a calculated risk, but I knew you could do it," Bowyn repeated. I let out a frustrated hiss. Bowyn counted reasons on his fingers.

"One! You display an incredible resilience against our power." He leaned forward. "Two! Despite your constant self-deprecation, you possess kindness and compassion and softness in a world that would have you dead. That is truly magical. You're stronger and cleverer than you think—"

"You'd write wonderful job applications," I interrupted.

Bowyn spoke louder and with particular emphasis. "And *three*, I know love when I see it." He relaxed against the rock, resting his case. "You will not fail him."

His last comment caught me off-guard. "Well…" I started, flustered. "Well, we're all imprisoned, so you were wrong. We're all going to die."

Bowyn grinned. "The night is young, and I believe in you still." Bowyn moved his foot blindly across the stones, nudging mine. "I'm sorry for what I did. I hope you can forgive me one day."

I frowned and bit my tongue. I didn't know if that day would ever come. Stewing in my furious silence, I couldn't help but pity Bowyn. His proud stature was gone. He leaned against the wall, weary and beaten. Through gritted teeth, I asked, "How'd you get caught?"

"I believe Elwyn pointed a finger in my direction." Bowyn sighed. "Lewy was at my home when they came. They took him, and the Truth got to him." His voice caught and he bowed his head. "I think he's dead." He covered his face. "I didn't love him but, I keep picturing him being tortured. His sweet face." Bowyn's breath hitched, and he cried.

I was still mad at Bowyn.

If we lived through this, I'd still be mad at Bowyn.

I crawled across the floor and sat beside him. He leaned on my shoulder. I reached for his hand but drew back when I noticed they both sat in his naked lap.

His hand found mine anyway.

"Would you like my jacket to cover yourself?" I asked.

"No. It wouldn't be big enough anyway."

My face dead panned while Bowyn chuckled to himself. The chuckles slowly faded. We sat quietly while he sobbed.

In the dark cell, hopelessness came easy. Refusing to give up, I thought of my future. I couldn't go back to my apartment. Something inside me cried out for change—to start a new chapter. Once I freed Darragh, we could plan on our next steps, together.

Could Watney survive the trip to Hiraeth? Darragh said I was the only *human* ever to make the journey, but what about cats? Could I still visit Sasha every once and awhile?

Though Hiraeth frightened me, I would continue to sharpen my magic. I would get better, stronger. I would do it for Darragh. Because, wherever Darragh was, I wanted to be.

Wherever Darragh was, was home.

"Wakey wakey!" a singsong voice reverberated through our cell and Bowyn tensed. The Truth pried open the door. "Let's go, girl!" Bowyn's arm snaked around me. "Oh, stop that," the Truth snapped. "You're next." Invisible hands yanked me up.

"Be brave, just a few moments longer," Bowyn whispered.

"See you…" I trailed off. I wasn't sure *when* I'd see Bowyn again. My hand slipped from his. Following the Truth, I asked, "Where's the Cage?"

"Dead!" The Truth beamed. We approached the imposing doors of the great hall. The Truth winked and said, "Brace yourself, dear."

The Queen sat on her throne, with Elwyn standing behind her. Darragh stood farther back, against the wall. His left eye was puffy, and his lip swollen. Beaten, but alive. The Truth and I walked through the hall, passing gathered guardians.

Darragh saw me. His lips parted, and icy dread clouded his face. When I looked at him, I'd hoped to see safety and comfort, but I *felt* his horror. Vomit swelled in my throat. Darragh mouthed, *'Why?'* I didn't have any clever answer for why I'd come. It hadn't really felt like a choice. I just…had to. I half-smiled and shrugged. Darragh's head fell forward; he held his face in his hands.

Marlowe stood before the Queen. "I've given you the girl…" He shuffled in his pocket. "And I've brought you this." A whisper travelled through those gathered.

The necklace.

"In exchange, I beg you pardon my crimes, and free my son."

Silence filled the hall.

"I could take it, if I wanted," the Queen purred.

"Of course—of course you could, my Queen." Marlowe bowed low, flourishing a hand behind him. "I hope you might reward my loyalty and unwavering devotion." The Queen's nails dragged along the arm of her throne, splintering the silence. The longer she stared at Marlowe, the harder she scowled.

Everyone gathered watched the Queen closely. How would she treat those most loyal to her? Would it be punishment, or…

The Queen's eye twitched and she hissed, "Very well." She snapped her fingers. "I have no use for the boy as he is anyway." Two guardians brought a still-blindfolded Bowyn in. They stopped beside Marlowe.

"Don't say I never did anything for you," Marlowe whispered.

Perking up, Bowyn snarled, "You!" and grabbed at the empty air. "I'll rip your eyes out!"

Marlowe dodged with little effort. "You'll thank me later, child."

"Speaking of loyal, devoted members of this community." The Queen turned her horrible, unblinking stare on me. "Allow me to remind everyone what we do to those who are not so devoted."

A curtain of thick shadows fell from the wall beside the throne. The torchlight revealed a corpse, its skin stretched and splayed like a frog in an anatomy lesson. Thousands of delicate nails pinned the skin to the wall. Vibrant red muscles and white tendons popped against the dark rock. Without skin, the corpse was indistinguishable.

I swayed, dizzy on my feet.

It was Brana.

"Come!" the Queen beckoned me forward. "Look!" Bouncing her feet, she giggled. No magic held me still, yet I couldn't move. "Darragh, please!" The Queen swept her arm across the hall. "Help Eleanor take a closer look."

Darragh fought the command at first, walking with strained resistance. With every step he took closer to me, the rigid defiance melted away. When he approached me, it was with ease. Darragh's fingers intertwined with mine. He grunted as his hand ripped up and grabbed my bicep. His chest heaved furiously, but he would not look at the Queen.

"She'll make me drag you if you don't go on your own," Darragh grumbled. To spare Darragh the pain, I forced myself to move. The smell of copper and ammonia hit my throat and I gagged. I doubled over. Darragh yanked me back up and shoved me closer.

Just pretend it's not Brana.

That wasn't so difficult. The thing nailed to the wall barely looked like a person, let alone my friend. Though, the eyes were difficult. Brana's eyes. The same eyes that, only days before, had shone so proudly when she showed me her son. Pip's sweet face danced in my mind. Afraid someone might see him, I pushed the thought away.

A muscle in Brana's throat contracted.

She was still alive.

"Ugh!" I recoiled but Darragh's grip held. He forced me back.

"I kept her alive. Just for you." The Queen stifled a giggle. "With Darragh's help, of course." A choked noise echoed in Darragh's throat. "Look closely. *Feeeel* her suffering." I didn't move. The Queen screamed, "Darragh!" His hand found the back of my head and shoved me against Brana's skinned face. Looking anywhere but her eyes, I focused on the skin beside her face, nailed to the wall. An earring hung from her ear…

My breath caught.

Brana hadn't worn earrings.

They were gaudy, awful, red things. I peeked back at the Queen, to the Truth standing behind her. She wore her iconic jewelry as usual, clanking bracelets, a big, horrible necklace…but no earrings.

I made eye contact.

The Truth winked.

So subtly, I might have imagined it.

Marlowe chimed in. "As much as I am enjoying this"—the Queen's lip curled into a snarl—"and I am," Marlowe quickly reassured, "might I ask that we take leave?"

"Go!" The Queen sneered and waved impatiently. The Truth descended the stairs, and Marlowe bowed low, before handing her the necklace.

Sateen slunk from the side of the hall and took Bowyn's arm. "Hello, old friend." Bowyn protested but they both vanished. Sateen reappeared for Marlowe, who bowed low once more before they, too, vanished.

The Queen took the necklace from the Truth and cradled it. It was a strange, almost maternal gesture that earned glances from the crowd. The Queen snapped her fingers, and Darragh released me. He returned to his spot behind the throne. "Get out!" the Queen shouted. Guardians trickled past me, one-by-one. Many of them met my eyes, not unkindly. With the hall empty, the Queen spoke to the Truth. "Follow the criminal. Kill his son. Kill his friend. Then kill him." The Truth bobbed her head in agreement. She gave me a worried look over the Queen's shoulder before she left.

The Queen stared at me.

When she finally spoke, her voice trembled with glee. "Darragh…"— the corners of her lips turned up—"kill her." Elwyn's mouth fell open; she shot the Queen an incredulous stare. Darragh's eyes closed. He couldn't fight a command…but how long could he resist? His jaw clenched. Cords of muscle rippled down his neck as he tried to control the body that ached to betray him.

"You heard me," the Queen repeated. She clapped and pointed at me. "Kill her now."

For a moment, I thought he'd beaten her.

Only a moment.

Like a candle fluttering to life, flame travelled around Darragh's body. Even across the room, I cowered against the heat. He took a step—

"No magic."

Darragh's fire extinguished and he stumbled. He turned a horrified face on the Queen. "Use your hands," she commanded, raising her own in demonstration. Beside the Queen, Elwyn swallowed, seemingly trying to keep food down.

Darragh faced me, his eyes glistening.

I tried to summon the shadow magic I'd become accustomed to. I called to the shadows lurking around the hall, begging them to help me.

They did not obey.

Darragh stalked forward and I backed away. He walked in a predatory way, his eyes taking in the space around me, should I try to run.

Darragh threw a punch. I dodged and lost my footing. He lunged and grabbed the collar of my jacket. I yanked the knife from his thigh and swung at his midsection. He sidestepped and dodged the blade.

This was pointless. Even if I landed a blow, he could heal himself.

I couldn't.

We circled each other. I'd love to tell you a story about growth and strength. How I pulled out some badass moves and won. The truth is, Darragh spent his entire life surviving in the wild. The most physically taxing thing I'd ever done was wrestle Watney into his crate. The heaviest things I lifted were books and coffee mugs. So, when Darragh feinted and brought his elbow down on my hand, I dropped that knife like it was on fire. Darragh threw a knock-out punch. My head snapped back, and tiny explosions of light speckled my vision.

I collapsed.

Hands, which had only ever shown me tenderness, circled my throat. Darragh's hair splayed around his face in messy tangles, but it did little to obscure the terror in his wide eyes. I tried to summon the same anger I'd had toward Turner.

There wasn't any to summon. I didn't resist. My arms fell to my sides.

Just get through it, I told myself, *one last thing*. The edges of my vision darkened. *I wish he'd use magic, make it quick.* In my last moments, my mind wandered to Sasha and Watney. If I had to leave Watney with anyone, I was glad it was Sasha. I thought of the way the firelight had danced on Darragh's skin last night. Remorse for a life unlived tugged at me. All the places I wouldn't see, all the things I wouldn't experience. I'd never grow old with someone, never see Darragh or myself any older than I saw us now. This was it.

The end.

As the darkness took over, my last fleeting thought was, *I don't want to die.*

"Agh!" Darragh tore himself off me.

I sucked in fresh air so quickly, I coughed. Darragh scrabbled on the ground for something, but my puffy and swollen eyes wouldn't focus. He clutched it, and the light gleamed off its surface—his knife. Darragh flipped the knife around, catching it at an angle, just below his rib cage.

My heart stopped.

"Wait—" I blurted, and warm blood spilled from my split lip.

"I won't have your death weighing on my conscience forever," Darragh said, echoing a phrase I'd said a lifetime ago. Darragh beamed, the crow's feet around his eyes crinkled, and tears spilled down his cheeks.

He plunged the knife into his midsection.

Across the hall, Elwyn shrieked.

Darragh twisted the handle, thrusting it deeper. Blood blossomed around the knife, a horrible, crimson flower unfurling its petals. Darragh fell. Blood dripped from the wound and pooled on the floor. From far away, Elwyn screamed, "Stop this!"

Stop the bleeding.

"No-no-no!" I dragged myself to Darragh. He coughed and blood poured from the corners of his mouth. His head lulled sideways, and I held it in my lap. "Darragh!"

Eyes half-open and sightless, Darragh didn't respond. The hilt of his knife protruded beneath his ribs.

What do I do?!

Do I pull it out?!

Will that kill him quicker?!

A hand pierced my tunnel vision—Elwyn tore the knife free. She threw it aside and it clattered against the stone floor. Blood spilled from the incision in Darragh's skin. I slammed my hand over the wound, and slippery, warm blood coated my fingers. The room spun and I swayed on my knees. Elwyn reached for Darragh but, like a dog on a leash, she was yanked backward.

"He made his choice," the Queen called. "Leave him to bleed." Beckoning Elwyn, the Queen rose from her throne. Elwyn's arms trembled as she resisted. Slowly, she climbed to her feet. With jerky footsteps, she followed the Queen.

"No!" With great effort, Elwyn's footsteps halted. The Queen turned, puzzled. Elwyn ran and leapt on Darragh, her palms covering mine.

"Elwyn." The Queen snapped her fingers and headed toward the doors. "I won't tell you again." The Queen passed a guardian posted at the entrance. "Let the girl watch. Kill her once he's dead." As the Queen vanished through the doors, invisible bonds tugged Elwyn. I swore I saw the hooks stretching her skin. Elwyn fell back, tearing at her finger. Trying to pull off…a ring? It was hard to tell through all the blood. Elwyn stiffened as if electrified and collapsed.

Twisting and writhing, Elwyn shrieked, "The knife!"

In a haze, I blinked stupidly. Darragh's knife lay discarded on the floor. I kicked it and Elwyn scrabbled for the blade. Flipping onto her knees, Elwyn wretched. She raised the knife high above her head. In one quick motion, she slammed the blade across her finger. Inhuman screams escaped her mouth as she drew the knife back and forth, sawing through tendon and bone.

The finger severed from Elwyn's hand, and the pressure tugging her to follow the Queen released. Elwyn lurched forward. Looking at her hands, Elwyn's grimace gave way to a wide-eyed look of wonder. I knew that look. I wore it myself the first time Alyth helped me channel my power.

Elwyn crawled forward and growled, "Move your hand."

Reluctantly, I did.

Elwyn laid her hands on Darragh's wound. After a moment, she pulled a palm back to peek; the bleeding had slowed. We both stared at her hand, astonished. Holding the wound once more, Elwyn closed her eyes.

"Elwyn!" the Queen's shrieking voice called through the halls.

An eerie calm lay behind Elwyn's eyes when she opened them. Kissing Darragh's forehead, she whispered, "I won't let her kill you too." Elwyn climbed to her feet and called, "I'm coming my Queen!" A coy, playful smile tugged Elwyn's lips as she headed to the door. Pausing at the guardian, she said, "If you and the others desire deniability, I suggest none of you come when the screams start."

"What if you require aid?"

"I won't."

Glancing over her shoulder, Elwyn caught my eye. To the guardian she said, "Kill her if she moves." The guardian nodded and Elwyn left.

My grip on Darragh tightened.

We needed to get out.

Now.

Chapter Thirty-Four

against all odds, I will stay alive

Elwyn

It pained me to leave Darragh lying on the ground, unprotected and with *that* girl. Power coursed through me; it would have been easy to kill her…but I needed every ounce of energy for what was to come.

The Queen walked ahead.

My fingertips crackled with energy that had nowhere else to go. A voice inside me whispered, *let it out*. My determined footsteps alerted the Queen. She rounded and eighteen years of rage exploded from my palms. Fire and shadows and hatred, I hurled everything I had at her. Unprepared, the Queen did nothing to stop the assault and it hit her straight on. With a sickening crunch, she struck the stone. In a wisp of shadows, she vanished before she hit the ground.

"It'll take more than that to kill a queen," she whispered over my shoulder. I whirled but found nothing. "Ha, ha, ha!" The Queen's haunting cackles echoed down the hall.

Unable to control the fire that spewed from my palms, I cast it wildly, illuminating the darkness. "Show yourself, you coward!"

My fire extinguished and shadows poured from my palms like puss. "If you insist." A decrepit arm erupted from the murk in my hands. A second followed; like a demon, the Queen pulled herself forth. "Here I am," she teased, pulling herself close.

A force struck the Queen from behind.

A guardian stood at the end of the hall, the one I'd left watching Darragh and the girl. The same guardian who stood outside my bedroom for as long as I could remember. She'd cast a spell and struck the Queen. Without turning, the Queen melted into shadows and pooled on the floor. They slithered across the rock like a massive snake. The shadows reared before the guardian, then a fang lined mouth devoured her head. With a scream and a spattering of blood, the guardian fell to her knees. The shadowy snake spit out her head and transformed back into the Queen. The guardian's blood flowed down the rock, breaking against my feet.

I didn't even know her name.

The Queen rounded on me.

I ran.

Where can I go?! Where can I hide?!

The Queen appeared from the air before me. Stalking forward, she giggled and said, "There's nowhere to go." A force gripped my throat and cast me into the wall. I smashed against it and tumbled to the floor. I tried to move, but the Queen held me on the ground. Excruciating pain radiated from my side. Just below my left breast, blood and bone tented my dress. The room spun and I saw double; two Queen's prowled forward.

"All I wanted was a powerful heir." The Queen pressed one boot on my broken ribs and pushed.

Crack!

Shards of broken bone dug into my lungs. The air left my body and I wheezed. Sharp pain exploded in my side, and I curled around it.

"But the problem with a powerful heir is they're practically impossible to control." The Queen knelt beside me. "Sure, I contained your magic as a child, but I couldn't contain it forever, could I? Not unless…I controlled you with necromancy."

"If you can control death, you don't need me!" I tasted copper and fought the urge to vomit. "Live forever and let me go!"

The Queen shook her head. "No, no. The people would never go for that. Who would trust a queen who lives forever? It *must* be you." One wrinkled palm caressed my cheek. "If I killed you now, I'm sure Ophyr would lend a hand. Puppet you long enough until I figure out how to take his gift and control you myself."

The Queen fell backward, as if torn away by an invisible force. "AGH!" The Queen cradled her head. She fell, and when she looked at me, her face was changed. No longer old and withered, she looked like the mother I'd known long ago.

"I won't let you hurt her anymore!" my mother shrieked. Her body jerked back and forth, as if two forces fought to control her. She collapsed, writhing on the stone. Arching her back, she screamed, "Kill me!"

Shock paralyzed me.

"Please!" my mother begged. "Do it before the creature comes back!"

I climbed to my knees and a broken rib poked my flesh. "Hhh!" With what little power I had left, I called to the shadows. They snaked their way along the floor, wrapping around the Queen's limbs. I crawled over and sat on her chest. My hands surrounded her throat, and a line of blood dribbled from the gnarled stump of my finger.

My mother whispered, "Hurry, please!" Tears lined her terrified eyes. Her gaze focused over my shoulder. She mouthed, "*Stay with her,*" to someone behind me. I glanced back; the hall was empty.

THE FOREST WHERE THE PHOENIX SLEEPS

My mother choked and a chilling laugh seeped from her lips. Hatred pooled in her eyes like dark, murky ink. The Queen's mouth grew wider and wider as the creature clawed its way back, fighting to control her. I tightened my grip around her throat. As the monster inside her screamed, I fulfilled my promise.

I saw the moment the life left the creature's eyes.

It wasn't relief that filled me as I stood and looked over the corpse, just a strange, shocked, numb feeling. I should grieve, but it had been such a long time since I'd loved her...

"Elwyn," a voice whispered. I looked around and saw no one. "Elwyn!" It came from the Queen... A leather strap lay on the rocky ground, spilling from her pocket. I stooped and yanked the strap out.

The necklace.

The necklace she'd fought so hard to retrieve. A trembling, excited energy radiated through my fingers. I ignored it and tossed the necklace back on the Queen's body.

I wanted nothing from her.

Leaving the Queen's remains on the ground, I turned and left. The haunting, desperate voice called my name again, but I had one thing on my mind.

Darragh.

As I walked, I held my side, pushing the bone back in. A cooling sensation lessened the pain. The doors to the great hall greeted me. I shuffled through, wincing with each step.

Darragh and the girl were gone.

Fury heated my cheeks and tunneled my vision. A trail of blood led up the stairs and out of the hall. My heart pounded as I knelt and touched the blood, a memory swept through me.

The girl was broken, her face swollen and ugly. Barely alive, she dragged an unconscious Darragh up the stairs and through the doors.

Anger ripped me from the memory.

The girl could have left, could have saved herself. Instead, she *chose* to bring Darragh with her. Even if it slowed her down, even if it jeopardized her own life, she'd refused to abandon him.

The implications of that action infuriated me more than anything else she'd ever done.

The moment I found that girl, she was dead.

Nell

"Far be it from me to body shame—I mean, I enjoy a good carb myself…" I dragged Darragh's unconscious body a foot farther. "But if you weighed just a *little* less, we might be out by now." Digging in my heels, I heaved Darragh another foot.

I collapsed against the rocky wall and sucked in air.

This is taking forever.

There was a door beside me; I took my chances and peered inside. Empty bedroom. If I hid Darragh, I could go find the orb and come back for him. I grabbed Darragh's wrists and dragged him inside.

"I'll be right back."

Closing the door behind me, I wandered down the hallway. Where would they have put my bag? It probably wouldn't be far from the room they'd thrown me and Bowyn in. I'd been in a daze when they'd led me there. I did my best to make sense of the paths, but they all looked the same. Panic set in the longer I crept around; I needed to get back to Darragh. I rounded a corner.

"Oh!"

Fear rooted me to the spot as I locked eyes with the Truth. Smoke swept up from the floor and cocooned her. The smoke was only half vanished when she shouted, "Thank goodness for that!" The smoke fell away, and I'm not sure who looked more relieved to see the other—me or Brana.

Brana sobbed. "I went back to look for you and there was blood everywhere. I thought I was too late." She embraced me in a crushing hug. "Oh!" Brana tensed like she'd received a shock. Letting go, she glanced at the merlot leather outfit Marlowe had put me in. "That outfit has quite the protection on it." I furrowed my brows over two purple, swollen eyes. It hadn't helped me so far. "Against magic," Brana clarified.

"Ah, right."

Figures.

Brana withdrew a vial from her robes. "Drink this, it'll help." I did, and slowly, the throbbing in my head ebbed.

A far-off shriek pierced the stones around us.

"It's time for you to go home." Brana waved and Darragh's satchel appeared beside her. She gave it to me, and I found the orb tucked inside. Brana saw one of Darragh's sweaters, yanked it out, and forced it over my head. "It's freezing in this place."

Wriggling away, I pointed down the hall. "I left Darragh this way." As we walked, I whispered, "How'd you do it? How'd you become the Truth?"

"I've always been able to transform into whatever—or *whomever*—I wanted. The Cage is just one form." Brana prodded my swollen cheekbone and I winced. "After I was captured, the Truth lurked in my mind, doing her *thing*. Well, I noticed she left her own mind open for the world to see. I snuck in while she wasn't looking, and I transformed her body into mine." Brana smiled sweetly. "A body is just another cage, isn't it?" Brana nudged my chin, examining my neck. "From there, it was simple. I transformed into the Truth."

"It was the Truth nailed to the wall?"

Brana nodded. "I was there when the Queen tortured her." Brana grinned, uncharacteristically sinister. "Her screams of innocence were... quite convincing."

"And Bowyn?"

"Up here." Brana tapped her temple. "Once I'm out, I can release him. Along with the others."

"This is it." I pointed to the door and slipped inside.

My heart stopped.

Wisps of smoke floated over my shoulders as they cocooned Brana. It was the Truth that pushed me into the room. Although, the Truth seemed like a silly thing to call her at this point. She was, after all, a lie.

Elwyn knelt, cradling Darragh. She looked up at us, cream hair hanging in tangles over her wild eyes. Elwyn flicked her wrist and the door slammed shut behind us.

"The Queen is dead," Elwyn muttered.

A glimmer of hope rose within me.

Darragh was free of the Queen!

Elwyn returned her blood-soaked hand to Darragh's eviscerated midsection. Elwyn whispered, "Come back to me." Darragh's eyes lulled and he woke. Elwyn eased him into a sitting position. When he caught sight of me, Darragh's eyes grew wide, and he struggled against Elwyn. She held him back, but he kept struggling. Elwyn's fierce gaze settled on me.

"Shall I remove her?" the Lie said.

Elwyn wrapped her arms around Darragh and glared at me. Her lip curled like a spoiled child clutching a toy they didn't want to share. Elwyn's eyes travelled back to Darragh, and she said, "Are you ready to say goodbye to your friend?" My stomach knotted. This didn't seem like a goodbye between friends. Elwyn's tone suggested this was more of a *goodbye to life.*

While Elwyn was focused on Darragh, Brana briefly let go of her disguise. She mouthed, '*Help me,*' to Darragh.

Darragh swallowed. His stomach convulsed, and he coughed. Struggling to raise his arm, Darragh held Elwyn's chin. "Elwyn, you—you don't have to kill her. You don't have to be like the Queen. Let her go and, and we can be together." Darragh smiled. Elwyn's shoulders relaxed, and her gaze fell to Darragh's lips. Fighting the urge to tear Darragh out of Elwyn's arms, I clenched my fists and looked away.

"Please," Darragh urged.

Agonizing seconds ticked by.

"Take her and leave," Elwyn spat. She kissed Darragh's forehead and stroked his hair. "Relax. You need rest." Darragh's eyes closed. Elwyn waved a hand over Darragh's eyes, making sure he was unconscious.

"Put *her* in a cell to rot," Elwyn commanded.

"What?" the Lie sputtered, earning a curious look from Elwyn. The Lie composed herself. "Yes, of course."

Elwyn's eyes set on me, and she smiled. "He asked me not to kill you. He did not ask that I free you." I'd never noticed the resemblance between Elwyn and the Queen, but I saw it now, in that smile. "You will never see the sun, or Darragh again. You will die in this mountain, while he lives on with me." Elwyn rubbed a finger against Darragh's cheek. "And he'll never know."

The Lie snapped her fingers and hooks tugged my skin.

"Pretend to resist me," the Lie whispered. As she dragged me away from Darragh, I didn't have to pretend.

Safely away from Elwyn, Brana transformed back into herself. "That's it, young lady." She shuffled around in my satchel, looking for the orb. "You're getting out of here right now!"

"Brana, no!" I swatted her hand and backed away. "I'm not leaving without Darragh!"

Brana inhaled, reigning in her temper. "Nell, sweetie…" She gritted her teeth and said, "That's suicide."

"Do you remember when I asked you if you thought I was stupid to risk my life for him? You told me just because he knew who his *melaethien* was, didn't mean I knew mine? Well, I know. It's him. I've chosen." I took a deep breath. "The Queen is dead; Darragh is free of her. All I have to do is get him out, and we can be together."

We can live a happy life, *together*.

"The Queen may be dead, but Elwyn is just as dangerous. Maybe even more so… She's convinced she loves that boy." Brana rubbed my arms, and her eyes pled with mine. "She will kill you if she catches you."

"I better not get caught then."

"Nell…" Brana's eyes darted to my determined shoulders and crossed arms. She sighed and said, "It's your decision. I just wish it were different." Brana's mouth tightened into a line and the corners turned down. "I can't go with you."

Pip's face flashed through my mind. "I know."

Brana's lip trembled, and her eyes shone as she hugged me. The bones in my spine popped as she curled around me. "Be careful."

I nodded, not trusting myself to speak. When Brana released me, I inhaled. "Well, I'm off to die," I joked half-heartedly. "Just like old times, eh?"

Brana didn't laugh. "You stay alive, you hear me?"

"I will."

THE FOREST WHERE THE PHOENIX SLEEPS

We broke our embrace, and I started down the darkened hallway. When I reached the end, I turned and waved. Brana waved with one hand, the other covering her mouth. Thankfully, I couldn't see her crying from where I stood. I continued on alone. Repeating my mantra as I did.

I *will* stay alive.

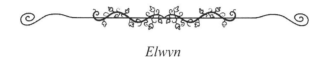

Elwyn

Once I moved Darragh to a more comfortable room, I left to clean myself up. When I returned, he still lay peacefully in bed.

Ophyr loomed over him.

Fear knotted my gut, but a tingle of power flooded my veins. The dread ebbed, and a strange, twisted glee took its place. "Get away from him," I commanded. Ophyr grazed Darragh's cheek and made an, *or what?* face. I approached the bed. "Have you heard the rumours spreading through the mountain? They've found the Queen in the east wing…" I savored the next word as it rolled from my tongue. "Dead."

Ophyr straightened. "If that's true, then the throne is ripe for the taking." He rounded the bed and dragged his fingers along my arm. Behind my back, I palmed Darragh's knife.

"The Queen is dead…" I grinned. "Because I killed her."

I slashed Ophyr's face.

Blood oozed from the line across Ophyr's eye and he stumbled. He dabbed the cut and stared at his bloody fingers. Face contorted in rage, he advanced on me. "I'll kill you—"

I ripped the shadows from the floor, as I'd so often seen the Queen do. Darkness circled the room, furious and alive.

Ophyr froze.

"Come, what's the matter?" I stalked forward. "You won't touch me now?" Ophyr scanned the room. There were two ways out. The window behind him, or the door behind me.

Both led to death.

Ophyr scrabbled at the rock around the window. A tentacle of shadow snatched him. More and more shadows ensnared Ophyr, immobilizing him in a cocoon of darkness. I twirled my hand, turning Ophyr to face me. He kept his eye shut as blood poured over it.

"Look at me!" I wrenched his eye open. "Are you afraid?" Ophyr needn't respond, his wild eyes darted around the room. I leaned against his chest. Euphoric goosebumps prickled my skin as his terrified heart pounded my eardrums. "I've waited a long time for this—"

The door swung open behind us, and a guardian peeked in. "Is everything okay in here?"

My concentration faltered and I rounded on the guardian. "Out!"

The knife slid from my hand.

The shadows tightened around Ophyr, but it was too late. The blade struck the guardian in the forehead. Momentum snapped her head back and she slammed against the door before her body crumpled to the floor.

"Agh!" I threw all of my power at Ophyr. The shadows slammed him into the rock. He laughed, and blood filled the cracks between his teeth.

A low growl rose behind me.

Slowly, I peered over my shoulder. The guardian's bones *click-clacked* as it reanimated. Spit stretched across its mouth as it hissed at my back.

It lunged.

I yanked half the shadows from Ophyr and flung them at the corpse. The shadows stopped it, but barely. Teeth gnashed inches from my throat. Behind me, Ophyr struggled to wriggle free. He climbed closer to the window, and I yanked him back. The corpse pushed the shadows, inching closer. Ophyr tried again to get out the window, and again, I yanked him down.

"The bed!" Ophyr commanded his monster. The corpse's weight lifted. It vaulted over the end of the bed and climbed toward Darragh.

"No!" I sent every shadow in the room flying at the corpse. The shadows dragged it off the end of the bed. The corpse held onto the wood frame, and I pulled with all my might. Sinew and skin stretched as I tore the corpse's arms from its body. Darragh's knife was still imbedded in the thing's skull. I ripped it free, and shadows swarmed the corpse, holding it to the floor. I screamed as I plunged the knife down, again and again.

The corpse's head fell away.

On shaking legs, I stood and turned to the window. Bloody handprints smeared the shutters. I leaned out, searching for Ophyr.

The fall would have been lethal.

Perhaps not to one who controlled death so easily.

Chapter Thirty-Five

a fond farewell

Darragh was gone.

Elwyn must have moved him.

I left the room, feeling disheartened. Where would Elwyn have put him? I leaned against the wall and rubbed my temples.

Crunch-crunch-crunch.

What was that?! Something wriggled at my side.

"Ah!" I tossed my squirming satchel away. A furry, brown critter crawled half out, a piece of dried fruit dangling from his mouth. "Hey, get out of here!" I dumped him out. Standing on hind legs, he pawed at the satchel. He pointed at his mouth, clearly wanting more fruit. I softened. The little dude was pretty cute. "Oh, fine." I snuck him another bit and he devoured it. "What's your name, little guy?" He rubbed his cheek against my shin, and I scratched his ear. "You look kinda… stoaty." Giving him another piece of fruit, I asked, "You wouldn't happen to know where Darragh is, do you?" Stoat caught the sleeve of

Darragh's sweater in his paws. Sniffing it, he paused. He sniffed it again, confirming a suspicion. Stoat bounced away on all fours, like a weasel.

"Bye, I guess?"

Stoat reappeared, standing on hind legs. He tugged my pants and grabbed for my hand. I obliged, and he led me down the hall. It hurt my back to walk hunched over, but his claws dug into my flesh every time I pulled away. Footsteps sounded from somewhere in the mountain. Stoat climbed my leg, squirreled around my midsection, and landed on my shoulder.

I scratched his chin, and he batted me away, as if to say, *'There's no time for that!'* He pointed ahead. *'Onward!'* When we came to a fork in the passage, Stoat pointed one way and squeaked. As we walked, he'd occasionally tug my hair. I quickly learned this meant, *'Stop!'* Once stopped, Stoat leaned forward, paw backing his ear, and listened. When he decided it was safe, he pointed and squeaked, "*Go go go!"* We continued that way until we came to a wooden door, high in the mountain. Stoat squirreled down my leg and jumped up and down, pointing at the door.

"Okay, yes, I got it." I cracked the door and peered in. Darragh lay in a bed, unconscious. "Oh, shit!" I snuck inside. Stoat scrambled in and shut the door behind us. A grim red-black puddle stained the floor, and a coppery, sick smell filled the room. The hair on the back of my neck tingled. I crept around the bed to Darragh. A mess of bloody handprints surrounded the windowsill. I didn't want to know what happened in this room. I just wanted to get Darragh out. "Darragh," I whispered.

Nothing.

I listened to his chest. It rose and fell as he breathed. "Darragh?"

Nothing.

"*Squeak!*" Stoat leapt up and down by the door.

Footsteps.

"Frig." I scurried around the bed, slipping only slightly on the stain, and dove into a wardrobe just as the door clicked open. A wide strip of light ran the height of the wardrobe, where the doors didn't quite meet. I peered through.

"I'm back." Elwyn skirted the bed and knelt beside Darragh. She withdrew a small bottle from her pocket, unstoppered it, and swirled it beneath his nose. As Darragh roused, Elwyn looked like she might explode with glee.

"She's dead!" Elwyn shouted.

"Who's dead?!" Darragh grabbed the neck of Elwyn's dress.

"The Queen's dead!" Elwyn spoke quickly, trembling with excitement. "I killed her!"

Darragh sighed and released Elwyn. "Best wishes on the promotion."

I cringed at the disdain in his words. Elwyn didn't notice. "We can finally be together, just like you said." Elwyn placed her hand in Darragh's lap. Darragh swatted it away. He tossed the blankets aside and swung his legs over the edge of the bed.

"You're on your way to being the next queen," Darragh said. "We can't be together." He snatched his clothing from a chair. "Did Nell make it out?"

"What's it matter if I become the queen?" Elwyn demanded. "I'll convince the people to have you as king. We'll rule together."

"Not if I have anything to say about," Darragh muttered. He may as well have slapped Elwyn across the cheek.

"But you said!"

"I lied!" Darragh's face twisted into an ugly snarl. "I'm a liar!"

"I don't—I don't understand," Elwyn stuttered as Darragh yanked on his pants. "Please," she whimpered.

"My answer is no." Darragh's voice muffled as he pulled his shirt on. He repeated, "Did Nell make it out?"

"But why?" Elwyn begged. "Why can't you love me?" She plodded after Darragh as he headed for the door, toward me and the wardrobe. "What's that girl have that I don't?"

Darragh whirled on Elwyn. "It doesn't matter what she has that you don't! What matters is that I loved her and now she's gone!" Darragh's breath caught, surprised by his own words. He ran his hands through his hair. "She's gone," he repeated.

Elwyn's sobs broke the silence.

"I'm sorry, Elwyn." Darragh softened. Tentatively, he reached out and rubbed Elwyn's shoulder. He smiled and said, "The Queen is dead. You're free. You're free to choose someone to rule with you…but it isn't me." With a weary voice he whispered, "I'm going home."

Elwyn looked pitifully up at Darragh. Blinking back tears, she looked past him—straight at me. We made eye contact through the split in the doors. *Oh, fuck.*

Elwyn's eyes widened. She threw her arm to the side and Darragh flew across the room. The doors to the wardrobe blew open and invisible hands dragged me out.

"Nell!" Darragh jumped up. Elwyn threw her hand out and Darragh's arms snapped to his sides. He crashed to his knees, where he struggled against the binds of her magic. I scrambled to my feet, arms raised to protect myself.

"If you don't have to uphold your end of the bargain," Elwyn said, smiling wickedly, "then neither shall I." Dark streaks veined from Elwyn's wide, burning eyes. I backed toward the door. With each step Elwyn took, she grew taller, more menacing.

"Elwyn, please!" Darragh begged. "She's not the reason we can't be together. Please look at me!" Elwyn stalked forward. A blue flame enveloped her hands. Just like—

"You're my daughter."

Darragh.

The fire in Elwyn's hands sputtered and died. The shadows around her grew weak and faded. Mouths agape, we both stared at Darragh. There couldn't be more than ten years between them. Darragh was ten when the Queen…

"I've suspected for a while now, but…" Darragh stared at Elwyn's hands, as if he could still see the flames. He told me he'd only ever been with two people Bowyn and—

"The Queen gagged me," Darragh said. "I couldn't tell you."

Elwyn's face froze as she processed what he'd said. She recoiled and snarled, "You're lying!"

"Take my hand. I'll show you!"

"Liar!" Elwyn screamed. "You're lying to protect her!" Elwyn rounded on me, her chest heaving furiously.

"Look at me!" Darragh bellowed. His biceps bulged as he fought Elwyn's magic, but it was no use.

Elwyn pointed at me, and my legs stiffened. She swept her hand toward the ceiling, and I lifted. Flames erupted beneath me and the heat licked my calves. The clothes from Marlowe helped a bit—they kept me from burning alive, at least.

"What's she have that I don't?!" Elwyn shrieked. "Is she powerful? She certainly doesn't look it!"

Beads of sweat dripped down my temples, the room turned hazy from the flames…

"Look at me!" Darragh pleaded. "You're mad at me! Not her!" Elwyn released her hold and I plummeted. Rolling from the fire, I clambered up. I called to the shadows on the floor.

Nothing.

I didn't understand.

Had Elwyn bound me? My eyes darted to Darragh, bound on the floor. No...Elwyn hadn't bound me, she'd bound Darragh.

It hit me.

I couldn't use magic, because Darragh couldn't use magic.

I'd never had any to use.

Elwyn laughed. Hysterical, hateful laughter. "Well, she's perfectly basic, isn't she?" Darragh made eye contact with me, as if by some miracle I hadn't heard. Elwyn looked at me piteously. "Perfectly powerless."

Darragh tried to explain. "Nell, I—"

"Shut up," Elwyn snapped.

Anytime I'd used magic, it was Darragh.

Or Bowyn.

Or Alyth.

This whole time, I'd only been a conduit. I was just an ordinary human. They'd used me as a puppet.

I don't belong here.

"What? You didn't know?" Elwyn brought her hands up and slammed them down. A crushing blow hammered me. My legs buckled. Airy pops echoed from my knees, and I fell. "Look at you." Elwyn laughed, kicking me sideways. My head bounced against the rock, and I blinked as the room blurred. "You're pathetic." Flames kindled around me in a wide circle. Elwyn knelt and brushed sweat-soaked hair from my face. "If he really loved you, he wouldn't have lied to you." She stood, calling to the shadows. They swirled around her, gaining strength. "You really should have stayed on Earth, where you belong." She raised the shadows above her head.

As Elwyn prepared one final blow, two things happened at once.

Darragh bellowed, "No!" just as Stoat bounced from under the bed. He stood on his hind legs in front of me, his arms up against Elwyn. Elwyn's lips parted when she saw him. She couldn't stop her attack; she redirected the shadows at the wardrobe. It exploded and bits of wood shot through the room like shrapnel. Shards and splinters struck Elwyn. Blood trickled down her forearms and her face clouded with fury.

"I'm going to destroy you!" Elwyn shrieked. She took one step, and some force sent her flying back.

Smack!

Elwyn's skull hit the rock and she crumpled to the floor.

Darragh turned from Elwyn and crawled over to me. "I've got you." He slid an arm behind my back and the other beneath my legs. I shoved him away.

"I'm not magic?!" I pounded against his chest. "All this time, you lied to me!"

"I know. I know." Darragh strained to keep a hold of me. "I know you're mad. Let me get you out of here. Then I'll take whatever you have to give me." I shook my head, pushing him away. Darragh grabbed my wrist. "Nell." Darragh's irises danced back and forth as he searched my eyes. "Please."

I exhaled one long, furious breath.

Reluctantly, I wrapped my arms around Darragh's neck. He held me tight and struggled to his feet. "How'd you get in here?" he asked breathlessly.

I pointed at Stoat, who pawed at Elwyn's chest. "Ratatouille," I choked. Darragh looked confused. "It doesn't matter. Is she…?"

"She's alive. She'll be okay." Darragh kicked the door open and carried me out. He craned his neck, looking down the hallways. "Let's just get out of here—"

Darragh fell and I smashed against the rocky floor. "Hhh!" My elbows screamed and I cradled them. Darragh's palms scraped the rock as an invisible force dragged him back into the room.

"You're not leaving!" Elwyn cried. Darragh threw his arm up and a flash of fire forced Elwyn back. She cowered against the flame, giving Darragh time to regain his footing. Hands raised, they circled one another.

This will end in death, for all of us, if I don't do something.

The satchel I'd brought lay discarded on the floor. Moving slowly, I withdrew the orb tucked within.

I don't belong here.

I clutched the orb in my hand. What had Senan said?

'If the relic breaks, it will send the user back to their home location. If you drop this and it shatters, you will go back to Earth.'

'What about Darragh?' I'd asked.

'He will remain here.'

"Stop!" I raised the orb above my head. Darragh's eyes locked on it—the bridge between our worlds—with deadly focus. "I may not be magic, but I'm not powerless." I hurled the orb at the rocky floor. Before it shattered, Darragh thrust out his arm.

Time froze.

In a blink, we stood in an empty, moonlit plain.

"Where are we?"

Darragh tapped his temple. In a soft voice, he said, "Up here."

"How long can you hold this?"

"Moments."

"So, it's true? I'm not magic at all, am I?" Darragh's face crumpled, but he shook his head, no. "All this time, you lied to me."

Darragh nodded. "But—"

"I don't belong here," I interrupted. "Bowyn, Elwyn—they're both right."

"You belong with me." Darragh crossed the space between us and took my hands. "I want you here with me, now and always." He stooped, meeting my eyes. "I'm free now."

I pulled away. "You lied to me, from the start."

"I did it to protect you," Darragh said, his voice rising. "I'd do it again if I had to!"

I backed away. "Lying to someone isn't protecting them!"

"I wanted to tell you; I did!" Darragh said. "But every day I loved you more and more, and I was afraid." Rage distorted Darragh's features. "I knew this would happen! As soon as you discovered the truth, you'd go!" Covering his face, Darragh turned away. He ran a hand through his hair, and after a brief silence, his shoulders sagged. "I thought... I thought if you believed you were magic, you'd stay here. With me."

Every moment with Darragh replayed in my mind. A tiny bowl rocking back and forth, a fire sparking to life, all magic that I thought I'd done myself—it was all him. My gut roiled as I remembered the very first time I thought I'd used magic...

"You let me believe I killed a man!" I pointed an accusing finger at Darragh. "You killed Turner! And every day, you watched the guilt eat away at me!" Darragh winced but remained silent. "You were selfish, and you manipulated me!"

Darragh stood, helpless before me.

"People without magic don't belong here!" I cried. "You jeopardized my safety every single day! That was a decision I should have made for myself!" I thudded my chest. "I deserve someone who tells me the truth!"

The words hung in the air.

I *deserve* honesty.

I knew what I had to do.

Darragh stepped in front of me, stooping so our eyes met. "You said you wouldn't leave me." I refused to look at him. Darragh took my face in his hands, drawing my gaze back. "Nell, I want to wake up every morning with you. I want to grow old with you. We can have a lifetime together." His eyes searched mine. "I will give you *everything.*" He tapped his chest, his heart. "Everything I have, and everything I might have—it's yours." His voice dropped to a whisper. "You don't have to do this." I looked at Darragh, at the face I wanted to see more than any other face in the world. I could forgive him, forget all the lies that crossed his lips… But another face came to mind. My own. Staring back at me in the mirror. Could I forgive myself for settling for this—this false life? I *deserve* better than a life of pretty lies. I *deserve* honesty.

If I was on my own, it might have been harder to make the decision. But all the courage, all the strength and bravery I'd learned on my journey was not gained for nothing. All this time I'd strived for happiness, and I thought I'd found it in Darragh. No, I would not allow his lies to break me. I would find happiness, and I would find it *myself.*

A tear fell from my cheek as I met Darragh's eyes.

My beloved, I love you. But I love myself too.

And I am leaving you.

"Before I go…" Darragh hung his head, but I continued despite it. "I want my memories."

Darragh sniffed, still looking at the ground. "Which memories?"

"You know which memories." In my mind, a blank space still existed. The moment Turner died, to the moment I woke up on Hiraeth.

"Are you sure you want them?"

"No." I shook my head. "I'll have them anyway."

Darragh withdrew a scrap of paper from his pocket. As he unfurled it, I recognized my handwriting. He brushed his fingers along the paper, reluctant to let it go.

Darragh's eyes met mine.

I stood on my toes and kissed him. My fingers found the back of Darragh's neck and drew him close. A satisfied, guttural noise rumbled through his chest.

Remember this. Remember his arms holding you so tight you ache. This is the last time.

A tear tumbled down Darragh's cheek as I pulled away. He whispered, so quietly I might not have heard if I didn't already know what he meant to say. "Don't go."

"It's time."

Darragh grimaced. His calloused fingers rubbed the paper, reluctant to release it. Slowly, he did. The paper crackled with energy and, willing or not, I plunged into a memory.

Darragh's memory.

Brick walls and garbage bins appeared. The alley behind my apartment. The night Kristina got hurt. The night Turner died.

Behind a dumpster, Darragh lurked in the dark. At the end of the alley, police officers helped Kristina into their cruiser. She'd told them what she remembered: A man had assaulted her. A woman stepped in to help, but both were gone when she regained consciousness. The officers hadn't found anything suspicious. If they'd bothered to look, they might have discovered a curious amount of ash dusting the concrete.

But they hadn't. No blood, no remains.

No body, no crime.

Darragh waited for the red and blue lights to fade. He crept from the shadows and climbed the steps to my apartment. The door was unlocked but offered resistance when Darragh tried to open it. He wedged the door open and peered inside.

His world came to a crashing halt.

My still body lay on the ground. Blood seeped along the dirty grout lines between tiles.

I remembered it now; how easy it was to slip away. I'd wanted it all to stop. The pain, the loneliness, the stress.

I'd given up.

Darragh sucked in his stomach and slid through the small opening. "No-no-no," he uttered. There wasn't room to kneel beside me, with one swift kick Darragh sent the kitchen table flying. It smashed into a side table and knocked over a lamp. The bulb shattered; glass shards spilled over the carpet. Darragh knelt, taking my head in his hands.

"Why didn't you tell me?" he whispered. "Why didn't you let me help you?" Sadness and fury coursed through Darragh—fury for my unwillingness to fight to survive, and heartache for the same reason. "I've just found you!" Darragh pressed shaky fingers to my throat, searching for a pulse. "You can't leave me!" He leaned in, resting his ear against my chest.

Silence.

A guttural whimper left Darragh's throat. He stood and backed away. Covering his face, he knelt into a fetal position. For several heartbreaking moments, he sat there, unmoving. Every loss—every failure—roiled and rose within Darragh. They cried, "Give up!" and he fought. He fought to hear his own thoughts over the screams.

Through the barrage, he found me. In his memory, I met him with a smile. And he found hope. This was not the end.

He would not allow it.

Darragh ran his hands through his hair and stood, eyes hard as stone. He approached my body, placed his hands on my wound, and closed his eyes. "If you don't start breathing, you'll have killed us both tonight." Darragh focused on his heart, on his pulse. He forced it from himself, willing it to me. Eyes scrunched tight, Darragh listened for a second heart beating with his.

"Don't give up," he whispered. "Come back to me." Darragh blocked out all the noises, the gentle hum of the refrigerator, his own laboured breathing...

I coughed.

Darragh's eyes snapped open. He stilled, not daring to hope. My eyes lulled and I coughed again. A laugh sputtered out of Darragh, and tears spilled down his cheeks. Jumping behind me, he pulled me into a sitting position against his chest. We rocked back and forth while Darragh clutched my throat, savouring the feeling of my pulse against his fingertips. He buried his head in my hair and whispered, "I've got you." His rough hand rubbed my chest, searching for a heartbeat, confirming he hadn't made anything up.

I was alive.

Darragh sagged against the wall. His gaze travelled to the ceiling, and fresh tears welled along his lashes. His Adam's apple bobbed as he tried to regain control of his breathing. A scrap of paper crinkled beneath him as he shifted. He picked it up. In my writing, the note said:

Sasha,

Turner did it.

I killed him.

I'm sorry. I can't do this anymore.

P.S. Please take care of Watney. He's gotten a little chunky so there's diet food in the pantry.

Darragh laughed, dislodging tears from his chin. He curled tighter around me. "I can fix this. I can make you forget." Darragh slipped from behind me and pressed a hand to my cheek. Slowly, a dull glow passed between us. "I'll protect you from now on," Darragh promised.

THE FOREST WHERE THE PHOENIX SLEEPS

He crammed the note in his pocket and snatched my phone from mine. Gentle taps thudded as his shaky fingers messaged Sasha, warning him I'd be out of town, and asking if he'd look in on Watney. Congealed blood still marred the floor, spread farther by Darragh's boots. He waved at the blood; it pulled back and disappeared completely.

Darragh slipped an arm beneath my legs and picked me up. I wrapped around him and let my head rest between his shoulder and jaw.

Holding me in his arms, Darragh walked into the night.

Darragh's memory faded. I felt the familiar whirling sensation of travelling back to Earth. As I fell between worlds, I heard a distant whisper.

May our light meet in the next life.

I gasped as I ripped through the surface of the lake. The November cold nearly killed me as I stumbled home. When I walked in, I found Sasha, wearing a scarf around his hair, scooping Watney's litter.

"Hey, sis—" Sasha looked me over. Lake water dripped from my hair, and I shivered violently. Somehow, those things bothered me the least. "Are you okay?"

I nodded, though my lip trembled.

"Where's your boy?"

The first of the tears came.

"Oh—oh honey," Sasha ran to the sink and washed his hands. He hugged me. "Oh, sh, sh, sh, it's okay."

Once Sasha had calmed me down, I showered. I picked up the clothes on my bedroom floor. I watered my plant. I went to bed.

And I slept.

Chapter Thirty-Six

ever after

Elwyn

A lavender bud floated from the tree above. It landed on the soil before me, where I sat in front of my father's tree. My hands in my lap, I fidgeted with my knuckle. I'd refused to heal it, refused to bring my finger back.

No one would own me again.

I pulled the Queen's crimson ring from my pocket, examining myself in the reflection. The ring sparkled and screams echoed in my skull. "This thing tore you apart," I whispered. Even now, it pulsed with energy. I wanted to slide it on—what would it look like on my delicate finger?

What would it *feel* like?

I flipped the ring in my palm. A low, blue flame erupted around it. It burned brighter and hotter until the band bubbled and melted. The liquid metal dripped on the grass, but the stone remained. No matter how hard I tried, it would not burn. I stood and pulled my arm back. I hurled the stone as hard as I could. It arced through the trees and landed in a small pond with a *plunk*. I withdrew the Queen's necklace from my pocket. I traced my fingers along the flower petals.

"We're so proud of you." I tensed, nearly dropping the necklace. Standing in front of the tree, which now blossomed with life, stood my father, and a young woman I only recognized from memories.

My mother.

She released my father and cupped her hands beneath mine. "My mother gave this to me." A fond smile tugged her cheek. "I want you to have it."

"Are you certain?"

My mother nodded vigorously and closed my hands around the pendant. "I've never been more certain of anything in my life."

I slipped the necklace over my head. It felt warm. Not like the heat from a flame, but of two arms wrapped around me. My mother's eyes softened, and she turned back to my father.

"Take care of her," he whispered.

"I'll return when I'm finished." My mother and father drew each other close, a long-awaited embrace. Their eyes met, and I saw the love I'd always seen in my father's memories. My mother broke the embrace. Father held her hand as she slipped away.

As we walked back to the mountain together, there was a lightness to the girl beside me. She grinned and twirled a lock of hair between her fingers, the way a young lover might. It brought me peace to walk beside her, she wore serenity like perfume. She hugged herself, mimicking the way my father held her.

"Do you have someone?" she asked.

I scrunched my face, forbidding myself from crying. "No."

My mother paused, reading my posture. "Good." Taken aback, I said nothing. "You're not going to settle for anything less than you deserve." A tingle passed through me as she reached out and squeezed my arm.

"When you're ready, someone will set your world on fire."

I glanced at her.

"I promise."

A figure approached us along the path. A familiar, gravelled voice said, "I need to show you something." Disgust and shame quelled the familiar rush of excitement that coursed through me when I heard Darragh's voice. He wouldn't look at me, and I knew a similar shame flowed through him.

My mother's eyes moved between us. She gave me a sympathetic smile. As I followed Darragh, she faded away.

Darragh brought me to a room in the mountain, where he pulled back a deep blue curtain. A foul stench hit my nose. I shoved my sleeve against it.

In the middle of the room, on an iron pike, was Jorgen's head.

"Keep an eye on this," Darragh said. Though dead for days, Jorgen's head remained unchanged. Stepping closer, I examined the hateful scowl.

"Agh!" I leapt away. Darragh's footsteps echoed on the stone as he left. "I think it moved," I called after him.

"Like I said, keep an eye on it."

I followed Darragh and fell in step beside him. With great difficulty, I spoke, "I-I know you cared for that girl."

"Nell."

"Nell." Though I meant to apologize, her name still tasted foul. A thousand words swirled in my mind. Finally, I settled on just two.

"I'm sorry."

For the first time since we'd fought, Darragh's eyes met mine. "I'm sorry too."

We walked in silence until I asked, "What will you do now?"

"I have to find something."

"What?"

"Forgiveness."

One Year Later

Queenstown sits on the southernmost tip of New Zealand's South Island. I still remember the first time I left the airport, how the towering mountains took my breath away. Downtown boasts a lively scene, filled with restaurants and spas. Nestled amongst the other shops and tourist spots is *Bramble & Bee*. A lovely café, *Bramble & Bee* resides on the second story of a building in the heart of Queenstown. The *Bramble* hosts an atmosphere that is slow and warm.

Comfortable and relaxed.

Cozy.

A single brick wall lines the back, behind the counter. Windows comprise every other wall, offering a stunning view of the Southern Alps. I often found myself staring at the snow-capped mountains. I'd heard locals referring to them as the Remarkables, and truly, they were. To gaze at them was to look upon a painting every morning. But more than that, there was a comforting familiarity in those mountains, they reminded me of some place far away—a place that I would hold in my heart, always.

A modern fireplace cast a warm glow over the *Bramble*. It was a lovely, safe space.

Perhaps I was biased because I owned it.

Well, co-owned.

I smiled and sipped my coffee.

"What are you thinking?" my business partner, Anahera, asked. Ana was a vibrant woman with dark-hair, and a moko kauae, a traditional tattoo on her lips and chin. Ana described herself as Maori, an activist, mother, and caffeine addict. Infectiously charismatic and bubbly, when Ana approached me with the idea of going into business, I agreed before I even had a chance to think about it.

"Just happy to be here."

Ana leaned on the counter and gazed out at the mountains with me. I met Ana at the library, giving a presentation about a book she'd authored. I hadn't come to see her, and I had no idea what her book was about, but to see such a passionate woman talking to an empty audience, I felt obligated to sit and listen. Ana had some good points. For a place that celebrates the Maori culture, there sure seemed to be a lot of institutionalized discrimination. After the talk, I stopped to get coffee at this very shop. Back then, it was called *Roast*. I bumped into Ana, and she thanked me for coming. I expressed my wish that the audience were bigger. She brushed it off and asked if I'd like to have a coffee with her. Of course, I'd said yes.

We often came to *Roast* to talk about books and enjoy each other's company. When the owner mentioned he was selling the café, Ana approached me with a—what had she called it? *A bat-shit crazy idea*. Despite having little to offer in start-up capital, and despite trying to convince Ana I wasn't cut out for it, she insisted we could do it. She told me that, believe it or not, her outspokenness wasn't always agreeable. She needed someone compassionate and friendly to be her front of house partner. I took out what loans I could, and we purchased *Roast*. We renamed it *Bramble & Bee*, redecorated, and here we were.

As I looked out at the mountains, pride stung my eyes.

I'd done this.

That evening, I stayed late, enjoying a drink and chatting with Ana as I often did. She asked if I wanted to go out once we closed, an offer I politely declined. "I'm looking forward to some down time at home," I said.

It was nearly 9 p.m. before I strolled up the stairs and into my apartment. I gave Watney a scratch.

"Shut the *fuck* up!" A scream rang out in the backyard. I cracked the door and peered out. I recognized the woman, though I didn't know her name. She yelled at my downstairs neighbour, who's name I also didn't know. He'd introduced himself once. I'd promptly forgotten his name, and was too ashamed to ask again.

Theo? Leo? I think it was Leo.

They were both dressed up, like they'd gone out and just come home. The woman waved her arms in slow, drunken gestures. Across the backyard, another neighbour stood on their porch.

"You're drunk, Amber," Leo whispered. Amber pushed him. Hard. Leo stumbled but stayed upright.

The neighbour ran inside and shouted, "Call the police!"

"Hey!" I started down the steps.

Amber wound up, ready to punch. Leo cringed, but Amber's fist stopped mid-air with a sickening *thwack!*

She'd hit something.

And it wasn't Leo.

Memories from a lifetime ago halted my steps.

"Ow!" Amber screeched, cradling her fist.

The same way Turner had cradled his hand.

Leo approached her. "I'm so sorry! I-I didn't mean to!"

The same words Kristina had uttered.

"Get 'way from me!" Amber slurred, swinging at Leo again. This time, when she struck him, an unseen force sent her sprawling across the lawn. She skidded to a halt on the cement. Red and blue lights permeated the cracks between the houses.

Amber wailed, just as two officers stormed the gate into the yard. One went to Amber, helping her up. "He pushed me!" She pointed at Leo. Leo put his hands up and shook his head as the second officer approached him. Amber couldn't stand on her own; she leaned on the officer. She drunkenly slurred her thanks, and muttered, "I think I peed my pants." The first officer gave the second a look before escorting Amber out front.

"Why don't you come on down?" The second officer called to me. "I'd like to speak with you."

Ugh.

I headed down while the officer addressed Leo. "I'm officer Singh. What's your name?"

Leo blinked like he'd forgotten. "Uh, Levi. Levi Robinson"

Levi! Not Leo.

Officer Singh jotted it down. "You live here?" She pointed to our house.

"Yes."

"Alright. How about you tell me what happened."

Levi crossed his arms and hugged himself. "We were, uh, we were out with some friends. Amber—"

"That was the woman on the ground?"

THE FOREST WHERE THE PHOENIX SLEEPS

"What? Oh, yeah," Levi continued. "Anyway, she uh, she had a lot to drink. I brought her back. She went out to have a smoke. She started yelling and I came to check on her. She started hitting me."

"Is that when you struck her?"

What?

A flicker of fury leapt within me. "He didn't touch her," I blurted.

Officer Singh gave me a stern gaze. "Sorry," I backtracked. "I just—I was here the whole time. He didn't touch her."

Officer Singh pointed at my balcony. "Why don't you wait up there after all? I'll talk to you once I finish with Mr. Robinson."

"Uh, okay."

Levi gave me a grateful smile as I trudged up the stairs. Once finished with Levi, Officer Singh came and talked to me. I told her the truth.

Mostly.

Amber pushed Levi. She tried to hit him, but she fell. Officer Singh jotted down my information and thanked me. She went and talked to the neighbour who'd called in the complaint before she left.

Levi sat in the backyard, on a cheap patio set we shared. On her way out, Officer Singh told Levi that Amber's sister had picked her up. I snuck down and pointed at the chair beside him.

"Mind if I sit?"

"Be my guest," he muttered.

The red and blue lights faded.

"Has this happened before?" I asked. "If you don't mind me asking— it's none of my business."

"She's yelled, but she's never hit me." Levi was talking about the domestic abuse. Of course, he was talking about the domestic abuse.

"I'm sorry."

Levi's lips compressed, but he didn't say anything.

I looked around to make sure all the nosy neighbours had gone inside. "What about the, uh, the other thing?"

Levi's eyes darted toward me. "What other thing?"

I lowered my voice. "I saw what happened."

Levi brought his elbows to rest on the table. He buried his head in his hands.

"Hey, I won't say anything. I promise."

Levi dragged his hands down his face and let them fall onto the table.

"I just," I started. "I might have some answers for you." Levi stared me down, assessing whether he could trust me. "What's your number?"

Levi gave it to me.

After I added it to my phone, I sent him a message. "There. When you want to vent, you can come upstairs. Okay?"

Levi nodded.

"I won't tell anyone, I promise."

"I appreciate it."

To say the day had gotten away from me was an understatement. I plowed back a Tom Yum soup I'd made the night before. After I'd tidied the kitchen and watered the small array of plants on my balcony, I wandered into the bathroom and spun the faucet in the tub. I poured a generous dollop of bubble bath into the running water and lit several candles. Once undressed, I hit play on my phone. Enya's calming, breathy voice filled the bathroom.

The hot water welcomed me as I slid into the tub. I rested my head on the rim and closed my eyes. Deep breath in through the nose. Deep breath out through the mouth. Let the day slip from my shoulders. Far away, Enya sang of shadows, and our journey to find the sun.

I allowed myself a moment to think about *him*. The warmth of the water wrapping around my body reminded me of *him*. The flickering candles danced through my eyelids. I could almost pretend—pretend I was back on Hiraeth.

Back at the fire with *him*.

Like one might go through a box of old photos, I summoned memories of Darragh. Those memories were all I had, and I cherished each one of them. Fragments of Darragh's keen, quick-moving eyes and lopsided smile teased my mind. If I tried, I could still remember the way his heart pounded when he held me. He'd offered me everything. That face, that smile—offered that very heart to me and I left it.

Enough.

Deep breath in.

Deep breath out.

I lifted my foot to rest on the tap. The candles danced to-and-fro across the white tiles. I focused on the flickering lights; they calmed me. All at once, a flame shot from the nearest candle and licked my foot.

"Ay-ya!" I yanked my foot down. Bubbly water splooshed up and out of the tub as I scooted into a sitting position. Arms poised on the sides, my chest heaved as I drew panicked breaths. Water *drip-dripped* from my drenched hair, echoing against the tiles. I scanned the room, focusing on any shadow the candlelight didn't penetrate. A strong odour overtook the subtle scent of my caramel pumpkin bubble bath. A familiar, smoky smell that somersaulted my stomach and sent my pulse racing.

I didn't dare to breathe.

I didn't want to lose the feeling that suddenly…I wasn't alone.

Acknowledgements

For everyone who had to tolerate me during this trying—I mean—terrific time, I thank you.

Matthew, who held me through the writing process. Who read my book not seven, not eight, but *nine* times, and still wants to read it again. Casey, who made sure I laughed every day. Trisha and Rebecca, who kept me sane, or insane, depending on what I needed at the time. Charity and Jan, who call me Potato Jones. Kerry, who showed me that one episode of *Doctor Who*, and I wanted to hurt. Seanie, who provided jokes I occasionally borrowed. Sharon, who looks out for me. Aunt Cathie, who provided a lifetime of English advice. And Callie, who is just as nitpicky as I am.

I'd also like to thank Michelle Hazen at Sanctuary Editorial, who gave me the cold hard facts, even if I didn't want to hear them, but did it kindly, so I could. Kate Studer, who stopped me looking like a damn fool, and made this whole writing thing look effortless. Rae Davennor of Stardust Book Services, who put it all together. And Eeva Nikunen, the artist who translated my dreams, and turned my imagination into a painting.

And finally, for Mrs. RK, who told me I *was* magic, just when I needed it most.